LEAVE OF ABSENCE

TANYA J. PETERSON

INKWATER PRESS

PORTLAND • OREGON
INKWATERPRESS.COM

Peterson, Tanya J.
    Leave of absence / Tanya J. Peterson. -- Portland, Ore. : Inkwater Press, c2013.

    p. ; cm.

    ISBN: 978-1-59299-883-8 (pbk) ; 978-1-59299-884-5 (Kindle) ; 978-1-59299-885-2 (ebk.)

    Summary: A novel portraying human beings stripped to their core and made to redefine reality and themselves. It reveals the emotional latticework of those suffering from mental illness, as well as the lives they touch. Aimed at readers seeking a stirring depiction of grief, loss, and schizophrenia, it will also reach anyone who has ever experienced human suffering and healing.--Publisher.

    1. Mental illness--Fiction. 2. Mentally ill--Fiction. 3. Mentally ill--Family relationships--Fiction. 4. Post-traumatic stress disorder--Fiction. 5. Grief--Fiction. 6. Bereavement--Psychological aspects--Fiction. 7. Loss (Psychology)--Fiction. 8. Depression, Mental--Fiction. 9. Schizophrenia--Fiction. I. Title.

PS3616.E8478 L43 2013   2013902802
813.6--dc23   1304

Publisher: Inkwater Press

Library of Congress Control Number: 2013902802

Paperback
ISBN-13 978-1-59299-883-8 | ISBN-10 1-59299-883-6

Kindle
ISBN-13 978-1-59299-884-5 | ISBN-10 1-59299-884-4

ePub
ISBN-13 978-1-59299-885-2 | ISBN-10 1-59299-885-2

Printed in the U.S.A.
All paper is acid free and meets all ANSI standards for archival quality paper.

5 7 9 10 8 6 4 2

For Eric, Hailey, and Avery. Thank you for believing in me, for supporting me, and for understanding me. And for Mom and Dad. Thank you for your encouragement throughout my life.

CHAPTER 1

OFFICER GREGORY JACOBI EASED HIMSELF SLOWLY INTO A SITTING POSITION ON the ledge of the roof of the eighteen-story building. He planted one foot firmly on the floor of the roof and allowed one leg to dangle over the edge so that he straddled the low wall in a seemingly relaxed, casual position. Far below him, a crowd gathered on the Chicago street. He noticed a distinct lack of fire trucks and ambulances. Knowing they were on their way, he silently implored them to hurry. He was worried about the man teetering on the edge a few yards away from him. As a police officer working in downtown Chicago for over a decade, Gregory had assisted in more than one suicide rescue, and in his experienced opinion, this man was ready to jump. Immediately.

"My name is Gregory," he said gently. *Come on, man,* he thought. *Look over here. Make eye contact with me.*

The man didn't look over, but stared straight ahead, and then closed his eyes.

"What's your name?" Again, no answer.

The man's eyes remained closed.

Where are you with the landing pad, rescue squad? Gregory continued to talk to the man in a calm, soothing voice. "What's

"

going on? Things must be pretty rough right now to get you all the way up here. I'm a pretty good listener, and I'm great at keeping secrets. Tell me about it." If he could get the man to talk, he would buy some time. People often desperately needed someone to listen, to provide a human connection, and he could build on that connection to talk them down. Gregory felt confident that he could form enough of a connection to keep the man in place, if only he would make eye contact. The avoidance of eye contact, though, meant he had already checked out. More than likely, he didn't have it in him to make connections anymore. Gregory's brow furrowed in concern. He wanted to distract the guy, get him to look over. Random questions often threw people off enough to break them out of their current thinking. "So what's your favorite thing to eat?"

Nothing from the man on the ledge. Not a sound. Not a twitch. Just deep breaths, which meant he was preparing for the plunge.

With relief, Gregory saw the rescue squad approach. Quickly, with efficient, almost super-human movements, the responders were out of their vehicles and inflating the landing pad. The jumper didn't react to the bustling scene below. Perhaps he didn't notice; his eyes were still closed, as though he were blocking out the entire world and the pain it had evidently caused him.

The pad was ready below and help was standing by, so Gregory slowly moved his leg back over the ledge and rose to his feet. "I can't imagine how awful you feel right now. Believe it or not, I care, and I want you to stick around so you can be okay again." His voice was low as he crept toward the jumper. "I'm going to come a little closer to you, okay?" In a slightly bent position, he inched toward the man, who gave no indication that he noticed or even cared. Upon reaching him, Gregory stepped up onto the ledge. "I'm right beside you. I'm going to put my hands on your arms, and I'm going to help you step back off the ledge so we can talk for a little while, okay?" Touching a suicidal person was contrary to all Gregory's training and regulations, but he sensed the desperation in the man. He would most definitely jump if Gregory did not physically remove him from the ledge.

Carefully, tentatively, Gregory grasped the man's arms. Ideally, they would have made eye contact, and Gregory would have pulled him back gently so he stepped off the ledge and onto the flat surface of the roof. Instead, the man jerked as though thoroughly startled. He looked at Gregory, briefly, just long enough to reveal the depths of pain in his eyes. And then he lunged forward.

It happened so quickly, Gregory didn't let go. Together, the two men—hopeless jumper and hopeful would-be rescuer—plummeted downward toward the chaos below.

Gregory heard the gasps and screams of the crowd. The noise grew louder until he hit the landing pad with a thud and a jolt. Before either man had a chance to move, other police officers and emergency medical technicians descended upon them in a flash of movement. Someone grabbed Gregory and helped him up.

"What the hell, Jacobi? What'd you grab onto the guy for? No jumper is worth risking your life like that. You okay?"

Slightly out of breath and more than a little shaken, Gregory replied, "Yeah. Fine. Pad broke my fall." He turned to see how the jumper was. Another officer had already pulled him to his feet and was now cuffing his hands behind his back. "Hey! Whoa. What are you doing to him?"

"Restraining him for his own protection. He's obviously impulsive and dangerous to himself. You know the regulations."

"Yeah, but it just seems a bit much." Gregory stepped closer to the man with whom he had just taken an eighteen-story plunge.

The jumper's shoulders sagged, and he didn't struggle against the restraints. Beneath scraggly whiskers, his chin quivered slightly. Speaking to no one in particular, he muttered, "No. Why?" His voice was a barely audible whisper.

In another attempt to connect with the distraught jumper, Gregory answered, "Maybe you are supposed to live."

In response, the man's face contorted and he squeezed his eyes closed. Gregory was compelled to fully observe the man for the first time. He was tall, a good two inches taller than Gregory's own six foot two. He looked about the same age, in his late thirties. He was utterly disheveled. His clothes were wrinkled, faded, torn, and stained, although, oddly enough, they appeared to be recently laundered. His brown hair was unruly and reached well below the frayed collar of his plaid shirt. It would have been a nice shirt had it been treated better, but the man didn't look like he'd been treating much about himself very well, other than the fact that, despite being completely unkempt, he was clean.

Gregory tried again. "Can you tell me your name, buddy?"

"It's Oliver Graham." The response came, not from the jumper, but from a woman who had approached Gregory and stood just behind him.

Startled, Gregory spun toward her. "You know him?"

"Sort of. He's been frequenting my shelter." She gestured across the street. A group of people, many of whom looked similar to Oliver, stood outside under the awning of a brick building. Painted on the awning were the words "SafeSpace Shelter." The woman continued speaking. "My name is Lilly Brown. I'll tell you the little I know, but maybe we should get him out of here and away from this crowd. This is pretty intense, and it's definitely not helping him right now."

They both glanced at Oliver. He had dropped to his knees, but the officer continued restraining him so he couldn't bolt should he experience a sudden burst of adrenaline. He hung his head and looked down, maybe to avoid eye contact with anyone in the large crowd still gathered nearby, and he breathed heavily.

"I know you'll be transporting him to Airhaven," Lilly continued. "Why don't I come along? I don't know a lot about him, but I can give you a few details."

"That would be helpful. Thanks. I'm Gregory Jacobi, by the way."

He stepped closer to Oliver and took the officer's place. Gregory helped Oliver to his feet and walked him toward the car. "Hey, Oliver. I hear you know Lilly here. We're going to get you some help. Okay?"

No response from Oliver.

"I'm going to put you in my police car, but you're not under arrest. Lilly and I are taking you to Airhaven Behavioral Health Center. It's a place where you can get better." Gregory gently eased Oliver into the backseat of his squad car.

Oliver made not a sound. He simply closed his eyes and leaned his head against the window when Gregory closed the door.

Oliver knew deep in his heart that he would never, ever be better.

CHAPTER 2

OLIVER FELT THE CAR ROLL FORWARD. HIS HEART STILL POUNDED FROM HIS leap and the shock of knowing he was alive, but he was exhausted and the motion of the car nearly lulled him to sleep. Instantly she was there, filling not only his mind, but his entire being, with her presence.

She stood with her back to him, her wavy, brown hair falling loosely over her shoulders and blowing in the wind. Her summer dress, too, billowed as the warm air swirled about. Everything about her was carefree and relaxed, and Oliver smiled to himself as he leaned casually against the doorframe, taking her in. Her back muscles contracted and relaxed as her arms pushed forward and dropped, pushed forward and dropped. The rhythmic squeaks and creaks he heard seemed to be caused by the pumping of her arms; she was pushing something.

Laughter lifted into the air, its lilt making Oliver smile. For now, he remained where he was. He enjoyed just watching the scene. Her arms continued their work, and the object of their efforts could soon be seen over the top of her head. She was pushing a swing. A toddler strapped securely inside was clearly enjoying the ride. Giggles that seemed to originate from deep within the little belly erupted and mingled with the laughter that already danced in the air. Oliver couldn't tell who was having more fun, the beautiful woman or the adorable toddler. Actually, he was pretty sure he was the one taking the most delight in the moment. Her happiness, her love of life, were so contagious. The child clearly enjoyed her. Oliver did, too. How lucky they both were to be in this yard with her, to experience this beautiful day in her presence. Part of him wanted nothing more than to stand in the doorway forever, watching her push the child in the swing and listening to the sound of her gentle laughter.

But that wasn't enough. He suddenly ached to approach her, to take her in his arms. And he wanted to be near the child, too, to share in the delight of pushing him higher and higher in the swing. Oliver started to move toward her. He wanted to sneak up behind her to surprise her, but he couldn't seem to get close. He tried to move quickly, but something worked against him, making it difficult to move. Despite his tremendous effort, the distance between them wouldn't narrow.

Nevertheless, she must have sensed him because she spoke to him. "Oliver," she called out. "Oliver, where were you?"

Beeeeep! A car horn blasted somewhere outside the car, jolting Oliver back to the present. He bolted upright and looked around wildly, uncertain, at first, where he was. His pulse raced. Beads of sweat popped onto his forehead. He tried to move his arms, but they were stuck. Alarmed, he jerked them in an attempt to free them. Pain shot through his wrists and up to his shoulders, and he cried out.

"Oliver!" Lilly turned around. "Calm down! It's okay. We're taking you to get help."

"Let me go!" Oliver cried, anguished. He continued to fight against his restraints.

"Gregory, pull over! We need to calm him down."

"The traffic is too heavy. But we're almost there." Gregory glanced into the rearview mirror. "Hold on, Oliver. The ride's almost over. Hang in there."

Lilly continued to talk to Oliver in a soothing voice through the metal cage that separated the backseat from the front. "Stop moving. You're wearing handcuffs for your own protection, but when you move, you make them tighter."

Oliver didn't seem to hear her. "I...need...to...get...to...them. I...need...to...get...to...them!" He was panicking, and his breathing was deep and rapid.

"Gregory, he's hyperventilating. We need to do something."

"We're here. I'm pulling up and stopping the car." Gregory eased into a parking space in the section reserved for police vehicles. Patients often arrived at Airhaven via squad car, and the upfront parking made it easier for officers to escort them into the building.

Nearly simultaneously, Gregory and Lilly jumped out of the car. Instructing Lilly to wait before opening Oliver's door, Gregory rushed to the trunk and returned with a first-aid kit and paper bag. Oliver continued to thrash against the restraints and struggled to breathe.

"Lilly, I need to unbuckle the seat belt so he's not so constrained, but he might try to take off. Stand back for a moment while I settle him down. Then we'll get him inside."

Gregory opened the door, bent over, and put one knee on the bottom of the doorframe so his face was level with Oliver's. Swiftly but quietly, he unfastened the seat belt and eased it off Oliver. Shaking open the bag, Gregory gently put it over Oliver's mouth and nose. Oliver jerked away, scared by the motion. Gregory moved in closer. "Oliver, I need you to calm down. You have to breathe more slowly and you can't do it on your own right now. I have a bag, and I'm going to put it over your mouth. Breathing into it will help."

"I...need...to...get...to...them...I...need..."

"Who, Oliver? Who do you need to get to?" Lilly had slipped into the backseat while Gregory was occupied with getting Oliver to breathe into the brown bag. When Oliver would not answer the question, she kept talking quietly. "You're going to get help, Oliver. You're at a place now with lots of people who can make you feel better. They're all right inside, and we're going to take you to them as soon as you're breathing right. Officer Gregory has a paper bag to help you, and he's going to put it over your mouth and nose again right now. There. Now breathe into it."

Gregory held the bag in place for fifteen breaths and then pulled it away. "Good job. Now take deep breaths from your belly. Slower. Okay, you need the bag again. I'm putting it on your mouth, and I want you to breathe into it like you just did." Once again, he placed the bag over Oliver's mouth for fifteen breaths. "More deep belly breaths. Okay, now the bag is coming back again." He repeated this several times, and Oliver's respiration returned to normal. "That's it, Oliver. Good job."

Oliver's brow furrowed, and his eyes shifted from Lilly to Gregory and back again.

"You look a little confused. Do you recognize me? I'm Lilly from SafeSpace Shelter, where you've been hanging out. And this is Officer Gregory with the Chicago Police Department. You and he had quite an adventure together this afternoon. We just brought you to a place called Airhaven Behavioral Health Center. We're going to take you inside to meet some people who will help you sort things out."

The woman's words sounded as though they were coming from far away. Oliver felt dizzy and sick. Why was he still here? He didn't want to go somewhere to get better. He just wanted to die. Why were they punishing him like this? Instantly, he knew the answer to his question. Of course he was being punished. After all, that's what he deserved.

He felt defeated and drained. He slumped back against the seat. He didn't want to move, but he cooperated when the officer placed a hand on his shoulder and gently tugged on his arm. After all, what else could he do?

"Let's go inside, Oliver." Oliver wondered why Gregory's voice sounded so kind.

CR

The silence engulfed Oliver the moment the heavy glass door shut behind him. He hadn't experienced silence for quite some time, and it was disconcerting. He stiffened, causing the two people escorting him to ask if he was okay. He didn't answer them because answering them would be pointless. No, he wasn't okay, but there was nothing they could do about it, so why bother answering?

Feeling apprehensive, he glanced around to make sense of his surroundings. He stood in a waiting room filled with clusters of chairs that were separated by square tables. The tables each held small stacks of magazines and clear plastic trays filled with pamphlets. Along a side wall was a large aquarium in which half a dozen fish swam back and forth, up and down. One darted through the open door of a castle and out the other side. The multicolored gravel in the tank looked out of place in the waiting room. Everything else in the room was muted beige or pink—even the abstract artwork on the walls boasted shades of pink in varying degrees of paleness—but the tiny rocks at the bottom of the tank were brightly dyed in every color of the rainbow. Oliver didn't really feel like watching the lively fish darting above the rainbow rocks, so he turned away and continued examining his surroundings. Large windows were cut into the outside wall, but they were covered with mauve mini-blinds that were open only enough to let in a small amount of light from the outside. The light that filtered in made a striped pattern on some of the furniture and accentuated the layer of dust that had accumulated. A water cooler stood in a back corner of the room, and it reminded him that he was thirsty. He wanted to fill one of the white paper cups and quench his thirst, but to walk over there seemed like too much of an effort. Besides, his hands were still cuffed behind his back and he wouldn't have been able to get a drink anyway.

He was led to a chair, and he sat down facing a woman who sat behind a clear plastic window. The police officer who had brought him here—was his name Gregory?—approached the window and spoke to her. They both glanced in Oliver's direction, and he dropped his gaze to the floor. Like the rest of the room, the flat carpet was beige, and it even had little pink flecks in it. The room's blandness matched the way he felt inside most of the time these days: sad and lifeless.

He kept his gaze fixed on the floor. After a while—he really didn't know how much time had passed because, for him, time was always agonizingly slow—the officer sat beside him, on his right. Lilly, from the shelter, was on his left. He should say something to them, but he couldn't talk. He still felt ill and, as usual, his mind raced, but he felt numb. It was too hard to summon his voice. Plus he didn't know what he could possibly say. He was relieved when Gregory spoke.

"Oliver, the receptionist is calling an intake counselor. She said that someone will come down here shortly. I'm really sorry about this, but I have to keep you handcuffed until we're told we can take them off. Hopefully it won't be too much longer."

Oliver nodded slightly. The metal shackles chafed his wrists, and his arms and shoulders ached miserably. He accepted this, though, as part of his punishment.

Gregory looked toward Lilly and directed his next comments to her. "Whenever I bring people in, I'm expected to provide information during the check-in process. Your input will be helpful too. Are you okay to stay? It could be around an hour, depending on how things go."

"Of course. I sent a text to my coworkers at the shelter to let them know what's going on. It's completely fine for me to be here right now. The others will hold down the fort until I get back. We're still a couple hours away from dinnertime anyway. That's when it gets really busy, right, Oliver?"

To be polite, Oliver nodded again. His head throbbed, though, so the motion was brief. Over the past couple months, he had come to know the patterns of SafeSpace well, and Lilly wasn't exaggerating. Dinnertime was wild. But then, so were breakfast and lunch. And right before bedtime. The rest of the time wasn't quite so hectic, although there were always people in the shelter.

Hundreds of men, women, and children used SafeSpace on a daily basis. That's why it was always noisy, especially at mealtimes, when throngs of people crowded into the cavernous old warehouse. There were rules in place to keep things orderly, and Lilly and the others who worked there did a great job of keeping things under control. Still, being with such a large number of people in one building was difficult. Add to that the fact that Chicago summers were hot and windy, and the shelter could be unpleasant.

That didn't mean that Oliver was ungrateful, though. He didn't have any place else to go, and he needed the services. Day after day, three times per day, he stood in long lines with all the others to get food. Some of the patrons were angry and mean and would push and shove him out of the way to get their plates first. Once, when he didn't back up fast enough, he received a hard, sharp blow to his gut from someone's elbow. Oliver had doubled over in pain and was promptly thrust out of the way. The two men who had attacked him probably would have continued if it weren't for the three shelter workers who instantly descended upon them to break it up. There were strict rules against violence at SafeSpace, and any problems were typically stopped before they escalated. The men were escorted outside—the zero-tolerance policy meant they wouldn't be allowed to return until the next day—and Oliver was told to take his place back in line. Having lost his appetite though, he had instead sat at a table and watched people.

Over many weeks of observing, Oliver had learned that the majority of people using SafeSpace weren't violent. On the contrary, most were kind and considerate of one another. They all understood that everyone was doing everything they could to survive. They had all found a place where they could get help: food to eat, a bed to sleep in, showers and hygiene supplies to keep clean; laundry facilities to wash clothes, computer stations to search for jobs and build résumés, and caring people to assist them. Yes, Oliver appreciated having a place to go where he could get his physical needs met, but he still felt as though he were withering away inside. And a homeless shelter isn't exactly a haven of restful calm, so in addition to the languishing feeling, he was constantly agitated. He didn't understand how he could experience both these feelings at once, but he was too tired to question it. Plus, he didn't have the right to hope for anything better.

"You must be Oliver."

The voice shocked him out of his musing, and his body jerked in surprise. The sudden motion shot fiery pain through his wrists, up his arms, and into his shoulders. He grimaced.

"I'm sorry. I didn't mean to startle you. I'm Brian, one of the intake counselors here at Airhaven. I'm going to take all of you back with me into one of the intake rooms so I can find out a little more about you and see what we can do to help you."

Brian motioned for them to follow. Gregory and Lilly walked with him toward a metal door beside the check-in window. Oliver, however, remained seated. Lilly and Gregory exchanged glances.

"Oliver? We need to go with Brian now." Lilly spoke softly but firmly.

When Oliver still didn't move, Gregory walked back over to him and squatted down so they were face to face and, without waiting for Oliver to look him in the eye, reassured him. "This is going to be a good thing. You'll see."

Oliver closed his eyes and heaved a sigh. How could this possibly be a good thing? He didn't want to cause trouble though, so he slowly rose to his feet. Gregory gave him a quick pat on the back before they followed Brian through the door and down the hallway toward the intake room.

Brian led them into a cubicle equipped with a small desk upon which sat a laptop computer. Florescent lights bathed everything in an artificial glow. Across from the desk were two chairs identical to those in the waiting room. He offered the chair closest to the wall to Lilly and gestured to Oliver to sit in the other. He then disappeared briefly and reappeared with a gray plastic chair for Gregory, which he placed against the wall to the left of the desk. He sat down behind the desk and logged into his computer, beginning the process of admitting Oliver to Airhaven.

"Let's get some simple stuff out of the way first. I know that you're Oliver Graham. What's your date of birth, Oliver?"

Oliver opened his mouth slightly as if to answer, but no sound came out.

Brian repeated the question but didn't succeed in learning the information. "Oliver, this process doesn't have to be difficult. I just need your basic background information."

Lilly interjected. "I don't think he's trying to be difficult. I work at a homeless shelter called SafeSpace. He arrived there about two months ago, maybe a little more than that, now that I think about it. He's extremely quiet and keeps to himself. I've never seen him talk to anyone, actually. He's withdrawn, not oppositional. And he's very compliant with our rules and procedures. We require that our clients register and at least provide their names, and to do that he showed us his driver's license. Could he do that here?"

Brian studied Oliver. To Gregory, he said, "The cuffs will have to be removed in order for him to show his license. He really doesn't seem to be hostile or resistant. And if he were to try something, he's seriously outnumbered."

I'm sitting right here, thought Oliver, but he kept his own counsel.

Brian turned to Oliver. "If I ask Gregory to take your handcuffs off, will you show me your driver's license? And an insurance card too, if you have one?"

The room was quiet for several seconds as Oliver considered the question. Finally, he nodded. Gregory leaned across the empty space between his chair and Oliver's and unlocked the metal shackles. Oliver reached into his back pocket and extracted a small leather wallet. His fingers were numb, and it was difficult to grasp the thin pieces of plastic inside. After fumbling, he grabbed ahold of first the license and then the insurance card, and, with trembling hands, he passed them to Brian. He returned the wallet to his pocket and absentmindedly massaged his sore wrists. He was glad the cuffs were off.

The keyboard clicked as Brian entered Oliver's information into the system. Then Lilly discussed his time at the shelter. She told Brian how Oliver kept to himself, and that he showered and brushed his teeth every day but only shaved when the volunteer barbers stopped by and did it for him. She didn't know, and thus didn't mention, it was because he couldn't bear to look at himself in the mirror for the length of time a shave required.

She told Brian how Oliver wore the same clothes night and day, every day, except for once a week when he laundered them, and how he was repeatedly offered new clothes by the shelter but always declined. Again, she didn't know, and thus didn't mention, that it was because his outfit had been a special gift and he didn't want to wear anything else.

She told Brian how the night workers reported that Oliver had horrible nightmares every night, and how he was encouraged to leave the shelter during the day but rarely did. Once again, she didn't know, and thus didn't mention, that he didn't like being outside anymore. She told Brian lots of things, but there was much she didn't know.

Then Gregory described the afternoon's events. When he told of the plunge off the building, Oliver blanched. His heart beat wildly in his chest again. He turned his head sharply to look at Gregory, and spoke directly to him for the first time. "What?" he croaked.

Gregory looked at him quizzically. "What do you mean, 'what,' Oliver?"

"S...say th...that again." Oliver's breathing had become rapid.

"I grabbed your arms to pull you back, but before I could move you, you dove off the ledge, and you and I hurled all the way down to the landing pad."

"I...I t...t...took you with m...me?"

"Well, I startled you when I grabbed you. I didn't let go soon enough, and we fell together."

Oliver began to sweat. He had difficulty breathing. "Y...you c...could h...have d...died! I...I'm s...so s...sorry." His head spun, and the room seemed to tilt. The nausea he had fought all afternoon suddenly overpowered him. He spotted the trash can beside the desk, snatched it up, and vomited.

Brian grabbed the phone and summoned the nursing staff. Turning to the others, he said, "We need to get him out of this small room. There's a conference room down the hallway; let's take him there."

"Oliver, are you done?" Lilly asked.

Oliver paused before answering. His body trembled, his head pounded, and his stomach roiled, and he wasn't completely sure he wouldn't get sick again. Nothing more happened though, so he nodded. Someone removed the trash can from his shaking hands and asked him to get up. As much as he wanted to get out of that room, he couldn't move. His entire body was leaden. He remained seated, with his forearms on his thighs and his head drooped. He breathed heavily.

Suddenly, someone grasped him under his arms and lifted him to his feet. He willed himself to move, but his legs were too unsteady, and he stumbled. Instantly, Gregory and Brian were on either side of him. He allowed them to lead him down the hallway, first to the restroom to rinse his mouth and splash cold water on his face, and then to a different room, where they helped him into one of the chairs positioned around a large table.

His mind reeled. He chastised himself. He didn't deserve to be there. He almost killed that police officer. The man would have died, and it would have been all his fault. He would have been responsible for another death. One of the memories that haunted him, one that was never too far from his consciousness, flooded back.

He paced frantically in the sterile, brightly lit emergency room. He was panic-stricken and, though he paid attention to nothing around him, his senses were heightened, and aspects of his surroundings registered somewhere in his brain. Shoes click-clacked on the hard tile floor as doctors, nurses, and various other hospital staff members rushed in and out. Other patients and their friends or families were in the room too. Some were agitated, others, listless. Phones rang incessantly at the nurses' station. Voices called over the PA system.

When a female voice announced a code blue in ER, Oliver became hysterical. He rushed to the nurses' station so quickly that he collided with it, sending a pencil cup and its contents scattering across the desk. "Who is that code blue for? Has someone responded to it? What's going on? I need to know if they're okay! Please, tell me—"

"Sir, I need to you calm down and go back over to the waiting area. Someone will be with you when information is available."

"Please—"

"Sir, please wait over there." The nurse nodded at a security guard, who gently escorted Oliver away from the nurses' station.

The noises in the room echoed in his head. The smells nauseated him. But he pushed the sensations aside. All his thoughts were focused on what was going on in the operating room. "Please, God. Let them be okay," he begged over and over and over as he paced.

Suddenly, two figures burst through the door from outside. Mick and Nancy. They paused long enough to scan the room. As soon as they spotted Oliver, they dashed toward him.

Mick spoke immediately. "Oliver! My God. So this is real? My friend Tim was there, and he called me. But it doesn't make sense. What—"

Just then, an ER doctor approached. Oliver turned away from Mick without a word. All the sounds of the ER seemed to suddenly cease. He gave his full attention to the doctor. The doctor's mask hung loosely around his neck. His clothes were smeared with crimson stains. Worry lines were etched into his forehead. His expression was blank, but the corners of his mouth, tight and turned slightly downward, gave away the news before he even spoke. Oliver's blood ran cold.

"Mr. Graham, I am so sorry. There was nothing we could do for either of them."

Tears sprang to Oliver's eyes, making the doctor appear blurry. "No! That's not true. Go try again!"

"They couldn't be saved. I'm sorry."

Oliver tried again to implore the doctor to go back to the operating room, but the only sound that came out was a sob.

Nancy's venomous shriek pierced the air. "You bastard," she screamed at Oliver. "You selfish son of a bitch! You should have been with them. You could have saved them. But you weren't there. You weren't there! This is your fault. Their blood is on your hands. You son of a bitch!" Nancy pummeled Oliver's chest with her fists.

The memory was so keen, it felt real, as though he were in that emergency room again, right now. When Nancy pounded his chest in his memory, he jerked forcefully, causing his arms to smack against the table and the memory to stop.

As Oliver's eyes focused on his surroundings, he gradually remembered where he was and what was happening. He gasped for breath, and his heart pounded against the inside of his chest as painfully as Nancy's fists had pounded the outside. He closed his eyes for a long moment. When he opened them, he looked for Gregory and held his gaze. "I am so, so sorry, officer. I..." His voice cracked with emotion, and he couldn't continue.

"Hey. No need to apologize. My fall was my own fault. I'm just glad that we lived."

Before Oliver could comment, a nurse entered the room pushing an empty wheelchair. Brian filled her in and informed her, "Because he's a suicide risk, I'm admitting him to Side A. Dr. Willis is the psychiatrist on call this evening, and I'll send her my report so she can see him later tonight. I'll send the admittance documents up.

He needs to get upstairs now so his belongings can be checked in and he can get a room."

Brian helped the nurse settle Oliver into the wheelchair. Lilly touched Oliver's shoulder. "Hang in there, okay, Oliver? These people will take good care of you. You'll probably like it here a lot better than the shelter."

Gregory extended his arm for a handshake. Oliver hesitated, and then weakly placed his clammy, shaky hand in Gregory's. Gregory clasped it with his other hand and gave a firm shake before letting go. "Things will get better. And truly, you have nothing to be sorry about."

If he only knew... Oliver couldn't find his voice. He sighed and dropped his gaze. Then the nurse rolled him out of the room toward the elevator that would take him upstairs to the inpatient ward of Airhaven Behavioral Health Center.

CHAPTER 3

IN THE ELEVATOR, THE NURSE INTRODUCED HERSELF AS JENNIFER. IN A CHEER-ful, almost singsong voice, she told him what to expect, but Oliver wasn't really listening. He couldn't get his mind off what he had done to the police officer who had tried to help him. He tried to be angry at him—after all, Oliver had gone to the top of the building to die; who was the cop to try to play hero? That didn't even work for an instant, however, so he went back to hating himself. He was used to that. It felt natural. It was the only thing that made sense.

As usual, Oliver was completely lost in his thoughts, yet, on an instinctive level, he was aware of his surroundings. The elevator's ding was sudden and seemed unnecessarily loud. With a start, he sat up straight, his eyes darting wildly back and forth to assess his surroundings.

He felt Jennifer's hand rest on his shoulder. "It's okay. It's just the elevator. Here we are."

Slightly embarrassed, Oliver slumped back down.

He looked around as Jennifer wheeled him off the elevator and down a hallway. The same person who had decorated the waiting room must have done this floor too, for the muted pinks and beiges were repeated here. Generic prints depicted fields containing various pink flowers. The prints hung between doorframes and were reminiscent of a hotel. Clearly, though, this was no hotel. The first door Oliver rolled past was closed. Jennifer paused at the next door, which was open. "Hey, Barry!" she called to the man who sat on a chair in the dim room. "How are you feeling?" Her voice remained cheery and singsongy. She spoke loudly, as though the man were hard-of-hearing. Perhaps he was; he looked to be in his seventies.

"Oh, I'm pretty tired right now, Jennifer. Don't you worry, though. It's just that ECT. But the doc says it's making me better."

"Do you think it's making you better?"

"You know, I think it is. I sure hope it's not wishful thinking. Say, who's that?" Barry pointed at Oliver.

"Just a new face coming to stay with us for a while. But I don't think you'll have a chance to get to know him. I hear you're being transferred downstairs. There's room for you on the senior floor now, Barry."

Oliver's mind raced as the two continued their conversation. Was this his fate? Would he be here when he was seventy, sitting alone in a gloomy hospital room wondering if he was feeling better? No. He didn't want to do this. He didn't want to be here at all. Why had there been a landing pad on the ground? He didn't even know it was there. He should have jumped sooner, before it was too late. He needed to leave this place immediately, to go back and do it right. This time he wouldn't hesitate at all.

Oliver jumped out of the wheelchair and headed back toward the elevator. His legs were like rubber, but he forged ahead. It wasn't far. It wasn't far for Jennifer, either, who had followed him when he bolted. He jabbed frantically at the button, trying to make the door open before she reached him. Someone else who worked at Airhaven hurried to help. Oliver ignored them and kept pressing the button. When the door opened, all three stepped inside and took a ride downstairs.

"So where are you going, Oliver?" Jennifer asked nicely.

Oliver wasn't going to answer, but the other person on the elevator pushed a button and the elevator came to a stop. He introduced himself. "I'm Matt. I'm a behavior health technician. Most people just refer to us as techs. We help take care of the people who stay here. I stopped the elevator because this is as good a place as any to chat. I'm wondering the same thing as Jennifer. Where are you heading off to, man?"

Oliver knew he wouldn't get anywhere unless he told them, and he suddenly wondered that if he asked them to let him go, perhaps they would oblige. He had known a lawyer, and he had loved to listen to her discuss the law. He was pretty sure he had the right to leave.

"I decided that I would like to leave. Thanks anyway, but I would rather not be here. May I please go?"

Matt responded first. "Oh. Okay. That's fine, of course."

Yes!

"I'm curious, though. Where would you rather be?"

The way Matt worded the question threw him off guard. He would never, ever be where he would rather be. They were gone forever. The thought zapped the bit of energy he had summoned to escape. A wave of pain washed over him, leaving him even weaker than before. He leaned against the wall for support and squeezed his eyes shut. He just wanted to complete what he had failed at earlier today.

"You seem to be struggling with that question. Why? What's going on?" Matt continued to press him.

"Just let me go. Please. I was supposed to die today, not come here. Please, just let me go," Oliver mumbled.

Jennifer chimed in. "Maybe you weren't supposed to die today. Maybe you were supposed to live."

"Why do people keep saying that? You have no idea! You don't understand..." Oliver's voice cracked. Unable to support himself any longer, he slid down the wall until he sat on the floor. He pulled his legs up, wrapped his arms around them, and laid his forehead on his knees.

Matt and Jennifer sat down beside him. Matt spoke. "You're absolutely right. We don't understand. But that's what we're here for. We want to listen. We want to understand. And, most importantly, we want to help *you* understand. Why don't you stay with us for a while? Just give it a little try."

Oliver had no energy left to argue. Without looking up, he simply shrugged in defeat.

"We're going to take that as a 'yes.'" Matt reached up and pushed a button. The elevator ascended.

As before, when they reached their floor, the elevator's ding startled Oliver. Jennifer and Matt stood, and then helped him to his feet. "Do you want me to get the wheelchair again?" Jennifer asked.

Oliver shook his head. He let them lead him once again past Barry's room, past more rooms. They turned a corner into a spacious room and came to a stop at a large, oval nurses' station.

The majority of the counter was at about an average adult's chest height. The middle of one side, though, was low and appeared to be used as a desk. A single chair, upholstered in dusty pink, sat in front of the desk on the patients' side. A matching chair was across from it on the other side. Beside the low portion, an open space allowed staff to pass in and out. The desk held a blood pressure machine and a computer for staff use. The high counter was mostly bare, but a few piles of paper were neatly stacked and placed near the desk.

The shelter had had a large counter too, Oliver remembered. But that one was long and straight and cluttered with trays, papers, pens and pencils, games, and other objects. That counter looked and felt busy. People constantly approached it to talk to the volunteers and employees, to find information, or to grab games to play at the various tables that were scattered about. The hospital's counter was different. It was orderly, and there was a hush about it that permeated the entire room.

There were several tables placed about the quiet room, some round, others square. All were surrounded by at least four chairs. Beyond the chairs, a long couch, a few recliners, and some plastic chairs faced a television. Past the television area, two rooms were separated from the main area by glass windows and doors. The purpose of those rooms was unclear to Oliver. Lining the walls along both sides of the long room were doorways that presumably led to rooms similar to Barry's room. About ten people sat in silence in various areas of the room. Three staff members worked behind the counter.

Oliver settled into the chair and waited for the next round of this horrible day to begin. Jennifer asked him if he was thirsty. He nodded. He had forgotten how parched he was. She disappeared briefly and returned with a white plastic mug with a lid and straw. His first name was written on it in black permanent marker. He accepted it gratefully and drank. As he did so, a woman stormed to the counter. "Hey!" She slapped her hands on the surface. "I told you fifteen minutes ago that I was hungry, and you told me I had to wait for dinner. Why does he get something?" She spat out the word *he* as if it were evil.

At this, Oliver leaped to his feet so quickly, he dropped his cup. He bent down, grabbed it, and shoved it back to Jennifer. "Here, take it. Give it to her. I don't want to cause trouble. I'm sorry."

"Shut up, chatterbox. I don't want your stupid cup. That's disgusting. I want something to eat, like I asked for."

Matt stepped in. "Kate, you know the rules. We don't talk to each other like that. And dinner will be here in about an hour. No snacks after four o'clock, remember?"

"That guy gets something." Kate glared angrily at Oliver.

"He's following the rules too. Now why don't you go work on your puzzle some more, before we come get you for supper?"

"Humph." Kate grunted and stomped back to a table in the open room.

Oliver watched Kate go. He didn't know what to do. Everywhere he went, disaster happened, and he seemed to be unwanted. His heart pounded in his chest. He was dizzy, too, but he remained frozen to his spot, standing rigidly and avoiding eye contact with the staff at the counter.

"Don't mind Kate, Oliver," Jennifer said. "We can't discuss patients, of course, because everything here is confidential. Just know that what she says and does isn't personal. It doesn't have anything to do with you."

"I think it would be better if I just left."

"You look like you're about to pass out. You need to have a seat." Jennifer helped him sit back down. She handed him his water and told him to drink.

He complied. He was physically and emotionally exhausted, so the arousal he had just experienced quickly faded.

"After our talk in the elevator, you decided to stay. So let's get you ready for a room."

He said nothing but simply endured the rest of the check-in process with Jennifer. First, she recorded his blood pressure and temperature readings on the computer. Next, she walked him down a hallway he hadn't noticed before and through a wooden door. He stood on a scale so she could record his weight. Then he stood with his feet shoulder-width apart and his arms outstretched as she moved a wand over him. She explained that it was a metal detector. The staff confiscated anything dangerous to patients and stored them in a locker. After swiping him, she asked him to remove the laces from his shoes. "You'll be able to keep your shoes," she said, "but the laces have to be removed. We can't let you have anything in your room that you could use to hurt yourself."

So Oliver removed his shoes and attempted to extract the laces, but his fingers shook.

"Here. Let me help." Jennifer took his shoes and swiftly removed the laces. She asked for his wallet next, and then she let him watch as she locked it up with the shoelaces in a locker that she labeled with his name.

She reached into a cupboard and pulled out a pair of faded blue cotton pants, a large gown—also blue, but with little white squares scattered all over it—and an equally faded robe. From a drawer, she pulled out a package of terrycloth socks. "Here are some new duds for you." She placed them in his hands. "I'll step out so you can put them on. The gown ties in the back. A handy trick is to put it on with the ties in the front. Leave your arms out, tie it, turn it around so the ties are in the back, and then stick your arms in. Some people think it's chilly here, so you can wear the robe if you want to feel warmer. As soon as you're dressed, open the door a crack and I'll step back in." She turned to leave.

"Wait! I don't need these." He handed them back to her and shoved his hands into his pockets. "I like the clothes I have."

Jennifer smiled. "I'm sure you do. You'll be more comfortable in the clothes I've just given you. All of our patients wear these."

His stomach knotted. Give up his clothes! How could he convince her that he needed to keep them on? He shifted fretfully as he tried to craft an argument for his case. "Actually, these are special. I feel better when I'm wearing them. I'm here to get better, so doesn't it make sense for me to wear something I feel better in?"

Jennifer set the items down on a chair. "You have to wear these, Oliver. Please put them on and open the door when you're ready. Put your own clothes on this chair. You'll be able to take them with you to your room and keep them in your closet. We're not taking them away from you." As if to make it clear that there was nothing to discuss, she turned and left the room.

Oliver stood there, unmoving. He was dismayed. He had worn these same shirts and pair of jeans for a long time, taking them off only once weekly to wash them. As a result, they were frayed and stained—some spills didn't come out in the poor-quality washing machines of the homeless shelter. And once, before he found SafeSpace, he had gotten into a fight when he unknowingly sat in someone's space under a bridge. His plaid shirt suffered a tear, but it wasn't ruined. His jeans, too, were tattered from months of homelessness. But he loved them with all his heart. He would always remember the day he got them. It was this past February...

After many failed attempts, Maggie's friend Lisa had finally talked her into going on a Saturday shopping spree to the city. Early that morning, Maggie left reluctantly, telling Oliver that she would much prefer to spend the day with "her men." Oliver, though, had convinced her to go. It would be fun for her, he insisted. She deserved to enjoy herself and to pick up some new things for her wardrobe. While she was gone, they missed each other, and they texted each other throughout the day. When she finally arrived home that night, Henry was sound asleep in his little fire truck bed, and Oliver had the dining table set with wine and homemade raspberry cheesecake. By candlelight, they ate, sipped the wine, and shared the stories of their days. His heart soared when Maggie told him she had thought about him all day. While she had done some shopping for herself, she had shopped for him and for Henry too. With glee, she retreated to the foyer and returned with a bag from Nordstrom and presented it to him.

He reached inside and pulled out the outfit. She knew him so well! It was perfect: a long-sleeved plaid shirt in white, greens, and purples; a green t-shirt to wear underneath; and a pair of jeans. She seemed pleased by his happy reaction. Then she told him to check the bag again. He was delighted to pull out a miniature version of the same outfit. He couldn't wait to see Henry in it, and he wanted to go wake him up and put it on. Maggie convinced him to wait until morning though, as she blew out the candles, took his hand, and led him toward their bedroom.

Now he was being asked to take this special outfit off. He wanted to keep it on forever, like Henry. Taking it off would be like removing a piece of Maggie and Henry. With trembling fingers, he reached into the pocket of his t-shirt and pulled out their picture. Like his clothes, it was wrinkled and faded from overuse, but he could usually see their faces distinctly as they smiled broadly at him. Right now, though, they looked blurry. He wiped at his eyes. He wanted to see Maggie and Henry clearly.

There was a soft knock and the door opened partially. "Oliver?" Jennifer called. "Are you ready for me to come in?"

He was going to have to change. He had no choice. "Umm.... Not yet. I just need another minute or so." When the door shut again, he whispered to the picture, "Forgive me. I'm so sorry." He knew, though, that forgiveness was too much to ask. He tucked the picture back into his pocket and, with quivering fingers that felt awkward and heavy, unbuttoned his shirt. Item by item, he changed clothes. When he was done, he sat on the chair, scooped up his beloved outfit from Maggie, buried his head in the bundle, and wept. He tried to stop, but he couldn't. It was all too hard to take, and he just couldn't control himself any longer.

He didn't know how much time had passed when he felt a hand on his shoulder. Jennifer handed him a cool, damp towel and instructed him to put it on his face. Hugging his clothes to his chest with one hand, he took the proffered towel in the other and did as he was told. He continued to cry hard into that, but the coolness felt good and helped him calm down a bit. With effort, he eventually stopped the tears. He kept his face buried in the towel until Jennifer gently tugged at it, pulling it away.

"Would you like to talk about it?" She spoke very softly.

He shook his head slowly.

After pausing and letting the room fill with silence for several long seconds, she offered him aspirin. Although his head throbbed and his throat burned, he again shook his head. He had absolutely no right to take something to make him feel better.

"Okay. If you change your mind, all you have to do is come find me or one of the other nurses. We're often with patients, but there's always a nurse available to help at the front desk. There's always at least one tech stationed there too. Whenever you need anything, even just a listening ear, don't hesitate to come get one of us. Now let's go find Matt. He'll get you settled in your room."

Unsteadily, Oliver stood and shuffled behind her. Matt was waiting for them near the desk. He took Jennifer's place and led Oliver through the large seating area beyond the station—he said it was called the day area—and to his room. Matt entered first and turned on the lights.

The room was plain and bland. Nothing adorned the beige walls. Matt explained, "We allow people to customize their rooms. You'll be creating things that you can hang up."

Oliver continued to take in his new surroundings without comment. At the far end of the room, under a window covered by a pink shade, were a desk and a wooden chair. A single bed was pushed up against the wall to his right. A closet with a door was to his left, and beside that was a sink with a small bar of soap and a hand towel, and a closed door.

"I'll unlock your closet for you so you can put your shoes and clothes down."

Reluctantly, Oliver placed his belongings on one of the closet shelves.

"While I'm at it, would you like me to unlock your bathroom so you can use it?" Matt gestured toward the door beside the sink. Oliver nodded.

When Oliver emerged from the bathroom, Matt relocked it. As Oliver washed his hands, Matt told him more about Airhaven. "Side A is a high-security area," he explained. "You tried to end your life today. We don't want that to happen again, so we take steps to protect you. Your bathroom has to stay locked, but whenever you need to use it, we will gladly let you in. You probably saw the shower in there. You can shower each day in the morning or in the evening. At those times, you'll find a supply cart near the front desk with toothbrushes, toothpaste, soap, lotion, shampoo, towels, and electric razors. After you use the items, you'll return them to your personal container on the cart. Do you have any questions?"

Why am I still here? Not wanting to be told, once again, that he was supposed to be here, Oliver kept the question to himself and just shook his head.

"Dinner will be here in about fifteen minutes, and I need to help with preparations. You can either wait here in your room or out in the day area. We encourage people to be out in the main room, but it's understandable if you'd like to lie down. Either way, I'll come find you when it's time to eat." Matt turned to leave but paused at the door and looked back. "We're glad you're here, Oliver. Hang in there." He walked out, leaving Oliver alone for the first time since the police officer had joined him on the ledge.

He wanted to see Maggie and Henry, and he longed for the security of his own clothes. He pulled the closet handle, but the door wouldn't open. Matt had locked that, too! Why the closet? How could he possibly harm himself with the closet? Maybe the door was just stuck. He shook it, and then shook it again, harder. It still wouldn't budge. No! Distraught, he collapsed onto the bed. He curled into a tight ball on his side and closed his eyes. Hot tears seeped out and streamed down his face. Exhaustion overtook him, and within a few short minutes, he was asleep. The nightmare came quickly.

He was running. Far in the distance he saw red-and-blue flashing lights. Fear gripped him, and he ran faster. He moved his legs harder and harder until they ached. He pumped his arms vigorously. Despite the exertion, he couldn't move. He was running against a strong force, a violent wind, and he got nowhere. He pushed harder. Nothing. His limbs felt like cinder blocks, and his lungs burned. Sweat dripped from every pore. He ran harder. Finally, he began to move, but it was like running through gelatin. Somehow, he knew that he was nearly out of time.

His heart threatened to burst through his chest. He choked on his fear. On and on he ran. Finally, the lights grew brighter and he heard noises. Someone screamed, but he couldn't make out the words. Curse the force that held him back! With a surge of adrena-

line, he burst through the invisible force and lurched forward, into the chaos. Ambulances, fire trucks, and police cars were everywhere.

Now he could make out the shouts. "Oliver! Help us! Where were you?" Frantic, he ran like wild, looking for the source.

He shouted, "Maggie! Henry! Where are you?"

Suddenly, everything went silent. The only response was the wind. His feet slipped on something, and he fell to the ground with a thud. He looked down. The sidewalk turned into a river of blood that threatened to drown him. He yelled. "No! No! No!"

He sat up on his bed, screaming. He was drenched in sweat and out of breath. Tears poured down his cheeks. Someone had sat down beside him on the bed and was saying something to him, but he didn't know who it was or what he was saying.

He looked around the room in a panic. They were nowhere to be found.

What was this place? Confused, he tried to focus on the person beside him. He was still talking. Oliver started to make out the words.

"It's okay. You're safe now. You had a nightmare. It's okay." The man repeated these phrases rhythmically. Someone else entered the room and placed a warm blanket around his shoulders. It was heavy, and the pressure, combined with the warmth, helped settle him down.

He began to register where he was. The behavioral health center. The man beside him was Matt. The person who had given him the blanket was Jennifer, a nurse. She stood over him now. He closed his eyes against it all. His heart still raced and his breath came in pants, but he was calming down.

Matt repeated the same phrases a few more times, and then was silent for a moment. "I was walking down the hallway rounding up everyone for dinner when I heard you scream."

"I'm sorry."

"Don't be sorry, Oliver. It's time to eat, but let's take our time. I'm going to sit here with you until your breathing returns to normal. We won't wait too long—I don't want your food to get cold—but let's just take it easy here for a little bit longer. Let me help you breathe." Matt told Jennifer that he had things under control, and she quietly left the room.

Oliver clutched the ends of the blanket that was still draped over his shoulders as he followed Matt's instructions to breathe deeply, in and out. It helped. After a few minutes, Matt stood and pulled Oliver to his feet. Oliver sat back down. He didn't want to go anywhere, and he certainly didn't want to eat.

Matt insisted that he come with him though, so Oliver rose to his feet. Matt removed the blanket and set it on the bed. Without his own clothes and now without the blanket, Oliver felt vulnerable and exposed. He started to shake. Without hesitation, Matt snatched the blanket back up and draped it around Oliver's shoulders. "Better?" Oliver nodded. Matt told him he could keep it around him and led him down to the dining area.

The dining area was behind the front desk. Matt showed him where to stand to receive his tray. He explained that normally, there would be a crowd near the door to the kitchen. Tonight, though, because Oliver was late, he was able to go right up to the door.

An older gentleman with a long, gray ponytail worked in the kitchen and called out cheerfully when he saw Oliver in the doorway. "Well, hello! I've got one tray left here with the name 'Oliver' on it. By any chance, would that happen to be you?"

Oliver nodded.

"Welcome to Airhaven. My name is Ted. I'm one of the techs." Ted extended his arm for a handshake. Oliver, still wrapped in the heavy blanket, slid his hand out only slightly. That was enough for Ted. He grasped it firmly and gave it a shake. Ted dropped Oliver's hand, grabbed the tray, and handed it over. "Here you go! Tonight you get one of the extra trays. After this, you'll get to choose your daily meals. Every night after dinner, you get a menu from the front desk and circle your meal choices for the next day. There are two or three things to choose from for every meal. Like I said, this is just an extra one. Enjoy!" He turned back to his tasks in the kitchen.

Now what? Matt had gone off somewhere, so Oliver stood alone with his tray, staring into a room filled with people he didn't know. Some talked to each other as they ate; others silently watched TV. All the tables in the room were taken, and many people stared in his direction. He suddenly felt very discomfited. He had been alone at SafeSpace, but it was so busy and loud, it was easy to be invisible. Here, though, he couldn't hide. He wanted to hide, to disappear. To die. Weak, and desperately needing to sit down, he shuffled through the dining room and out the door, toward his room. A staff member told him no trays were allowed in the rooms but that he could eat in the day area.

He noticed then that there were some patients scattered about the day area eating dinner, mostly in groups of three or four. He sat at the nearest empty table and stared at his tray, which held a glass of water, a napkin, a plastic spoon, and a round plate with a metal cover. With a sigh, he lifted the lid and revealed a small pile of moss-like limp broccoli, some rice in the shape of an ice cream scoop, and a soggy grilled-cheese sandwich. He gagged at the strong smell of overcooked broccoli and quickly replaced the lid. He returned the tray to a tech in the kitchen who checked the contents and made a note in a chart. Clutching the blanket tightly around him, he went back to his room.

He was physically and emotionally drained, but as much as he wanted to sleep, he dreaded the idea. He was haunted enough when he was awake; when he was asleep, his demons overpowered him. He sat on the edge of his bed and stared at the closet, forlorn. A sharp rap on his door started his heart racing again and sent little shocks through every fiber of his being. He jumped up too fast and became lightheaded and dizzy. He wavered. Matt walked through the door just in time to catch him and help him back down onto the bed.

Accompanying Matt was Dr. Willis, the psychiatrist Brian had mentioned earlier. She took one look at Oliver and declared, "My plan was to meet with you tonight, but I don't think that's the best thing for you." She studied his chart before continuing. "I want to talk to you before prescribing anything else, but I'm starting you on prazosin immediately. It will help with your nightmares and sleep problems. It won't do much right off the bat—don't expect a peaceful night tonight— but we need to get that working in you. A nurse will bring some in to you soon. For now, park yourself on that bed and stay there. I'll see you tomorrow." She abruptly left the room.

Matt sat with Oliver until Jennifer brought the medication, which he accepted reluctantly. Then they left him alone. He curled himself into a ball and steeled himself for yet another long night ahead of him, a night he wished with all his heart he didn't have to face.

CHAPTER 4

Penelope Baker sat alone at a table in a quiet corner of the day area of Side B, coloring. Many different coloring pages were scattered about. They were various mandalas—pictures and geometric shapes, some simple, some elaborate—that she had gathered from the art therapy group that met each morning, each in a different state of completion, but none fully colored. The sheet currently in front of her was an elaborate flower with petals that grew progressively smaller as they spiraled inward toward the center. She bent forward over the picture, her face close to the paper, and her long hair spilled down over portions of the image. She moved a gray crayon swiftly back and forth over one of the larger petals and talked out loud to herself. "No...This...is...very...wrong. Shapes... and...colors are...important. No. ...This is...very...very...wrong." She didn't look up when Dr. Daniels, her psychiatrist, approached.

"Well, good morning, Penelope. It looks like you're hard at work today."

Penelope continued to color the single petal without looking up.

Seemingly unfazed by Penelope's lack of response, he pulled up a chair and continued. "Did you start all these this morning?"

Penelope stopped coloring and looked up. Eventually, she answered, pausing as she spoke, as though she were thinking about her responses. "Yes. I started them all this morning. ...Yes. Did I start them all just now?...Yes, I did. I had...great ideas for them...but she took the ideas...out of...my...head. They just... disappeared...when I was working. ...They went completely out of my head, and...my mind went blank. ...That's why I had to... start new ones. I started...all...of these...this morning...I wish she...wouldn't...have taken...the ideas out of my...head when I was...coloring. She doesn't...understand...the...meaning...of the... shapes...and...colors...like...I...do. The...Kerffies...only told... me...and...I...needed to...use...their meanings...but she...just... took...them...right out...of...my head and...she...won't...give... them...back."

"That must be frustrating. Who took the ideas out of your head?"

Again, Penelope took her time before answering. Finally, she said, impatiently, "Eleanor...Roosevelt. You should...know that... by now. ...She...always...does that to...me." Penelope's voice became softer, kinder. "She just...zapped...them away...right while I was...working. So...I had to start...a new one...every time. And she...wanted me...to use a different color each...time too...She... doesn't...understand...the...meanings of...the colors. ...She took my ideas and...then told me her own ideas. ...This time she told me...to use gray. Mrs....Roosevelt told me...she would do...her magic and...turn it into a beautiful color."

"Did you want to use gray?"

"No," she mumbled after a long pause. "Did I...want to use gray?...Of course I didn't...want to use...gray." Her eyes suddenly grew wide, and she glanced about, frightened. She dropped her voice to a whisper. "Please...don't tell...her...that. I...didn't mean... to say that. Please don't...tell her."

"You're afraid of what would happen if I told her?"

Penelope had resumed coloring the single petal. Frantically, she rubbed the crayon back and forth across the single petal. She made a small tear in the paper, but still she continued.

"Penelope? What do you think would happen?"

"I don't...want to talk...about it...anymore....You need to...go away now."

"How about this: I'd like to stay, but we'll change the subject." He waited patiently while Penelope scribbled her crayon up and down, back and forth, with hard, swift strokes. The tear widened, and she colored on the surface of the table. Dr. Daniels gently placed his hand on the paper. "Penelope. Look at what you're doing. You're coloring on the table. Slide your crayon over."

Penelope didn't look up. At first, she didn't even seem to have heard Dr. Daniels at all. Slowly, though, she moved her hand over, away from the gaping hole she had made. As she did this, the speed of her strokes slowed down and eventually stopped. She continued to stare at her paper. "It...isn't changing to a pretty...color....I've... angered her."

"Is she telling you that she's angry?"

She cocked her head as though she were listening. She concentrated for almost a full minute before responding. "No....She isn't... talking to me...right...now. I...think she is too...busy."

"Doing what?"

"I don't...know." Penelope stared at Dr. Daniels. Her face was nearly expressionless, but the corners of her mouth drooped into a slight frown. "She will...be back."

"Has she been coming around as much since you started your medication again?"

Penelope fidgeted in her chair. She snatched up her crayon and resumed her activity.

"You've become agitated," Dr. Daniels observed. "What is your body saying right now?"

"I...I..."

"Penelope?"

"Your...glasses...are...circles....Circles...mean...caring...but... they are...silver and...I...haven't...learned...the meaning...of... that...so...you...need to...go...now. I have to...color. Just...go now."

Dr. Daniels jotted notes down on his notepad. He clicked his pen closed, tucked it into its holder, and closed his leather padfolio. "These medications take time to work, and you've only been on them again for six days. They will help, though. Tonight we'll be increasing your dosages, and that may help you feel a difference. We'll talk more about it later." He watched Penelope.

Her fingers squeezed the crayon tightly, and her entire forearm moved furiously. Again, her head was bent forward and her hair hid her face from view. She uttered not a sound. Clearly, she was done talking. When he said goodbye, she gave no acknowledgement that she heard him.

She colored and colored in an attempt to placate Mrs. Roosevelt. Sometimes Mrs. Roosevelt talked about things that didn't make any sense. When she did that, it sounded like a loudspeaker in Penelope's head, like she was a spectator at a bizarre event she didn't fully understand. Other times, Mrs. Roosevelt told Penelope things she should do. This morning, it was coloring. But Mrs. Roosevelt was being mean and critical. *That looks dumb. Why would you do it that way? Your idea of art is pathetic, so I'm not letting you think about art at all.* And then she just deleted Penelope's thoughts.

Mrs. Roosevelt didn't understand that Penelope's work wasn't based on human ideas of art. Penelope followed the Kerffie language, a complex system of shapes and colors even she didn't fully understand. Mrs. Roosevelt didn't comprehend this, so she had emptied Penelope's mind. Penelope's mind just went blank, and she didn't know what to do next. Then Mrs. Roosevelt had shouted at her, *What the hell are you just sitting there for? Don't be so goddamn lazy! Pick up the crayon and color. No, not that crayon. Use gray. You're not creative enough to choose your own color. I'll work my special magic and turn it into a beautiful color when you're done. You don't have the right to choose a beautiful color. Don't just sit there. Work! No. Not that picture. A different one. And remember—if you don't do what I want, I will hurt you.*

Penelope didn't want to be hurt; therefore, she did what she was told. Plus, she wanted to please Mrs. Roosevelt. Eleanor Roosevelt had been Penelope's heroine for years and years, and it hurt her feelings when her beloved idol disapproved of her, especially since she had always thought that Mrs. Roosevelt was a kind, compassionate woman. What was so bad about Penelope that she brought out this wonderful woman's wrath?

Thankfully, though, it seemed that Mrs. Roosevelt had gone away for a while. She did that from time to time. Penelope didn't know where Mrs. Roosevelt went, but, despite the fact that she admired the great woman, she was always glad when she was gone. Actually, "glad" was perhaps the wrong word. She was never glad anymore. When Mrs. Roosevelt was around, Penelope was anxious and tense and afraid. When she was gone, there was room for different feelings. When Mrs. Roosevelt took her occasional breaks, Penelope was desolate and hollow and depressed. Always, always—whether the woman was hanging around harassing her or off doing who knows what—Penelope felt "off."

Simply put, Penelope knew she wasn't normal. And this knowledge wasn't just from the conversation with Dr. Daniels when she was first diagnosed. "Penelope has schizophrenia," he'd said so matter-of-factly, as though he were telling them she had a cold. Without waiting for a response from either her or her fiancé William, he had continued his delivery of her diagnosis. "It's a very individual disorder; it looks a bit different in each person who has it. Penelope, in your case it's called *undifferentiated schizophrenia*. It's different from the paranoid version we so often see stereotyped by Hollywood."

Disgusted, Penelope pushed the memory of the rest of that conversation out of her mind.

No, it was not just from that conversation that she knew she wasn't normal. It was more than knowing the label. She was aware that she was different. She wasn't like everyone else, and she hated that. She hated knowing it too, because knowing it made it all even worse. Dr. Daniels didn't hate it. He thought it was wonderful that she was so aware of herself. When they first talked about her feelings about being different, he had been thrilled. He had called her awareness "insight." About half of all people with schizophrenia lacked insight into their condition, he had explained. Of course, that meant the other half were aware that the hallucinations, delusions, and everything else associated with the illness were not things most people experienced. According to Dr. Daniels, having this insight meant the person had a better chance of managing schizophrenia.

Penelope didn't feel that her insight helped her one bit. She wondered if she would actually be able to feel happiness if she didn't know how different she was. Sure, Mrs. Roosevelt would continue to lurk and beleaguer her, and the Kerffies would keep teaching her about their language and ideas. They would keep taking Penelope's thoughts away and leave her mind frighteningly empty, and then invade her by forcing their own thoughts and ideas into her mind. She would probably continue to physically feel the source of the Kerffies, too, as they tickled her or poked her to make sure she knew they were right there beside her.

But what if she didn't *know* this was abnormal? Would ignorance be bliss? Would she just be able to live life thinking that she was okay? Certainly that would be better than the way she experienced it now. How was she supposed to feel happiness, or even slight contentment, when she knew she was mentally ill? She was only thirty years old, and the life she had known and loved for twenty-eight of those years was over.

Penelope looked down at her coloring pages. They were all incomplete, just like she was. She stared at the hole she had made in one of the papers. How fitting. The picture was broken, just like Penelope. Tape wouldn't work. Nothing could fix that hole, and nothing could fix her.

You think you're broken? Mrs. Roosevelt was back. *I'm here with you. I'm not good enough for you? You ungrateful bitch! You want to* be *"fixed?" I'll fix you. Eat the crayons. All of them. Chew them up and swallow them.*

Penelope stared, wide-eyed, at the pile of crayons on the table. Mrs. Roosevelt must have sensed her apprehension, because she lowered her voice to a whisper and crooned, *It's okay. Please trust me. You know I'm magic. Eat the crayons, and they'll plug up the hole that's inside you, and I'll make them glow brightly in all their dazzling colors. You'll be dazzling then, Penelope. The whole world will be in awe of your alluring radiance. They'll admire you again. They'll admire you as much as they admire me. You'll see. Try it. Eat the crayons, now.*

Penelope wanted to be better, to be complete, to be attractive again, and, if eating the crayons would transform her, then eat them she would. One by one, she cracked them into pieces. Snap! Snap! Snap! She split the wax, slashed through the wrappers, slid her fingers into the stack, and shoveled smidgens of color into her mouth.

A tech chose that moment to check up on her. "Penelope! Stop!" She grabbed one of the coloring sheets from her table and held it under Penelope's face. "Spit it out."

Penelope grabbed for more crayon pieces and continued to chew vigorously. The tech quickly pushed the pile across the table, sending broken bits rolling and scattering onto the floor. Penelope cried out and tried to swallow. The crayons wouldn't go down, and she gagged. Involuntarily, she spit them out onto the paper that was still held under her face.

"No! Claire, why did you do that? I have to have those!" Penelope shouted and grabbed at the paper.

Claire crumpled it up and shoved it into the pocket of her smock, so Penelope dove onto the floor to snatch up more pieces. Claire intervened. She knelt down by Penelope and gently covered her hands with her own. "Stop, Penelope," Claire said gently. "Eating crayons is bad for you. I need you to stop."

Just forget about it, you worthless loser, Mrs. Roosevelt sneered. *I was going to "fix" you. You only had to do one little thing, but you screwed it up, just like you screw up everything. You ruin everything. William knows what I mean, doesn't he, Penelope? You don't deserve to eat those crayons anymore. I won't help you.*

Angry and hurt, Penelope jerked her hands away from Claire's. She sprang to her feet. "Mrs. Roosevelt was going to fix me, but you ruined it!"

"Let's talk about it. Would you like to sit here, or should we walk and talk? We can do laps around the day area."

Mrs. Roosevelt shouted at Penelope. She summoned others, people Penelope didn't even know. And from nowhere and everywhere, the Kerffies joined in too. There were so many of them, and they all spoke at once. Penelope couldn't understand what they were saying. This wouldn't happen to her anymore if she had only been able to eat the crayons. Mrs. Roosevelt had been right; she screwed up everything. Maybe she could have eaten them, though, if Claire hadn't come along.

"Where do you want to talk, Penelope?"

Between the shouting and Claire's chatter, Penelope couldn't think. She grabbed her head. "I..." What did she want to say? If everyone would go away, she could think again. She had to make herself heard above all the noise. "Leave...me alone!" She yelled at Claire. Even her heart was upset. It pounded angrily in her chest as though it were trying to bruise her on the inside. Her head felt her hands tremble, and it felt their sweatiness too.

"What would help you right now?" Claire remained calm.

Even though Penelope wanted her to leave, she appreciated Claire's soothing voice. "I...need...a...cigarette." It took a long time to form the words because of all of the roaring voices.

Claire glanced at the clock at the wall. "Well, you're in luck, my dear, because the morning break is going on right now. The others went down already, but I'll take you down so you can join them outside."

Gratefully, Penelope followed Claire to her locker for a cigarette and then to the elevator.

CHAPTER 5

When Penelope returned from her smoke break, she felt better. Not better, exactly, but different. Calmer, at least. The mellow essence of the smoke relaxed first her chest, and then spread throughout her being and soothed even Mrs. Roosevelt and the Kerffies, even though the Kerffies weren't really part of her. She knew better than to hope they had vanished completely. Unfortunately, they were still there and she knew it.

That was the complete and total hell of it all. She knew that Kerffies existed, but no one else did. That confused her. Maybe she was wrong, but it didn't feel like it. They were so real. So was Mrs. Roosevelt and all of her emotions. When Mrs. Roosevelt was loud and angry, Penelope was so terrified, she would do whatever Mrs. Roosevelt said just to be left alone. But as bad as that was, it was even worse when Mrs. Roosevelt, indeed, left her alone. Then the terror gave way to despair, for Penelope was acutely aware that Mrs. Roosevelt was never really absent.

Penelope glanced up at the large wall clock that hung near the workstation. It was ten after nine. Music group would start soon. People were heading in that direction already, but she didn't feel like going quite yet; sitting around a conference table for twenty minutes making small talk with other patients didn't sound appealing. Instead, she went to her room to retrieve the insulated plastic mug she had been given when she checked in, and then went to the dining area for coffee.

At the moment, the room was vacant. There was no evidence that breakfast, or any other meal, had ever been served. The tabletops were shiny, clean, and devoid of objects, and all the wooden chairs were pushed tightly against the tables. The door that led to the room where the techs distributed trays at mealtime was shut and locked. The television was turned off, and the counter below it was spotless. The motor of the large, silver ice-and-water dispenser droned loudly, disrupting the silence of the rest of the room. Two industrial coffee machines like the ones commonly found at gas station convenience stores stood next to the dispenser. Penelope bypassed the one with the orange spout. She didn't want decaf. Because of her medication, she wasn't supposed to have caffeine, but what did it really matter, anyway? The steam rose and swirled before her as she filled her mug.

Look at that. It looks like a dancing ghost. Look how fast it moves. Caffeine even makes ghosts hyper. Let's remember that next Halloween. We'll send caffeinated ghosts out trick-or-treating and really raise some money for UNICEF. Penelope laughed. Mrs. Roosevelt wasn't always mean. Sometimes she was funny.

"Hi, Penelope. It's good to hear you laugh. What's so funny?"

Penelope turned in the direction of the sound and flushed with embarrassment. Two people had entered the room. One was her favorite tech, Matt. She didn't want him to know she had laughed out loud because of something Mrs. Roosevelt had said. "Oh! Um, nothing, really. I was…" Damn it. Her words had left her.

Mrs. Roosevelt roared. She was angry with Penelope for being ashamed of her, so she took her thoughts away again. Penelope could say nothing more, and simply looked at Matt and the other man with a blank expression.

Matt didn't seem to mind. "Well, it doesn't matter what was funny. I just liked your laughter. Don't mind us. I'm just giving a little tour of Side B before music group starts." He gestured to the man beside him. "Penelope, meet Oliver. Oliver, this is Penelope."

Penelope remained expressionless as she stared at Oliver. He clutched a bundle of clothing, and he had a caramel-colored blanket draped around his shoulders. Penelope recognized it as one of the weighted blankets she sometimes saw around here. Caramel was a shade of brown and, in Kerffie, brown meant desire. Penelope assumed the staff used brown because of their desire for people to get better. She returned to studying Oliver rather than lingering on the blanket. His shoulders sagged, but it didn't seem like it was from the weight of the blanket; rather, it seemed like something much heavier pressed down upon him. When Matt introduced him to Penelope, Oliver's eyes met hers briefly in acknowledgement before he turned his gaze back to the floor. His eyes were the saddest she had ever seen.

She wanted to say something to him, but the only words that came to her were those of Mrs. Roosevelt. *Stupid bitch. You think you're too good for me? You're wrong. You're not good enough for anyone. You can't talk to them right now, Penelope. Go ahead and try. But you can't.* Mrs. Roosevelt was right. Penelope had not a single thing to say. She wished Mrs. Roosevelt would stop grabbing ahold of Penelope's words and thoughts and playing tug-of-war. Wrestling for them was tiring. Mrs. Roosevelt kept all of Penelope's words in a box, and if Penelope wanted them, she had to struggle to get them. She remained silent and expressionless as she stared at Matt and Oliver.

"Penelope, would you excuse us, please? You can head down to the group room if you'd like. It's open. Oliver's room isn't ready yet, and I need to have a private chat with him. Is that okay?"

Penelope said nothing in response, but simply walked out of the room. She hoped her action was enough to show Matt that yes, it was okay with her that they use the room privately.

ᘒ

Oliver studied Penelope as Matt spoke to her. He knew that he should greet her, but he didn't know what to say. He hadn't really talked to anyone in months. She didn't appear eager to talk, though, so maybe it was okay that he was too empty to converse.

When Penelope had gone, Matt shut the door and pulled out a chair for Oliver. "So you can see that Side B looks pretty much the same as Side A, but like we told you, it's a bit different. Notice how we walked right into the dining area without my having to unlock it, and how Penelope was helping herself to coffee? You'll have more freedoms over here. You can get water or coffee without having to ask someone. There are snacks in the cupboard, too, that you can help yourself to whenever you'd like. Granola bars, crackers, fruit, things like that. Do you have any questions about the dining area over here?"

Oliver shook his head. "No, not about the dining area."

"Do you have questions about something else?" Matt prompted him to continue.

"Will my bathroom and closet be locked over here?"

"Yes, they will."

"Why?" It was more of a plea than an affront to Matt's answer.

Matt looked at him earnestly. "Your doctor feels that you're still not safe for yourself."

"But you're moving me out of Side A, the higher security side."

"I know. We all think you're going to do better over here. Side A isn't helping you much. Over here, there are more groups. There are two different art groups, rather than just one. There's a music group and a group where you get to play board games or card games. You even get to leave this floor for one of the groups. There are more opportunities to go outside." He paused before delivering the next piece of information. "Dr. Willis has written orders that you have to participate in everything over here."

Oliver's brow creased, and he tightened his grip on his bundle of clothes.

Matt continued quietly, "You don't want to."

Oliver shook his head slowly.

When he said nothing, Matt spoke again. "I bet these past few days have been pretty long. You've done nothing but sit in your room or in the day area. That won't help you get better." His tone was gentle rather than accusatory.

Oliver stared at his lap. Still gripping his clothes in the crook of one arm, he moved his other hand down to pick at a loose thread on the pocket of his robe as he responded in a small voice, "I don't want to get better. I just want to die."

Matt put his hand on top of Oliver's. "That's precisely why we still need to keep your stuff locked. And that's why your doctor wants you doing all the activities over here. The programs are designed to help you heal, but you have to participate in them for them to work." Matt glanced up at the clock. "And speaking of that, music group is about to start. Come on. I'll walk you down there."

"Matt?"

"Yes?"

"Um...Are you ever going to be over here on Side B?" Oliver liked Matt. He was nice. He talked kindly to him, and he didn't try to force him to talk. Oliver didn't mind any of the techs, actually, but he especially liked Matt. And Jennifer was his favorite nurse. He hoped he would still see them.

Matt grinned. "Of course! Sorry to give you bad news, but you're not getting rid of me. We all work on both sides. You're stuck with all of us."

Oliver looked at Matt and nodded. He would have smiled back at him, but he couldn't. His heart was simply too heavy, and it pulled every part of him down with it.

Matt didn't seem to be offended. "Come on," he said cheerfully. "Let's get you down to the group room for music."

He escorted Oliver out of the dining room, past the oval work-station, through the day area, where he paused and announced to those sitting at various tables, "Hey everybody, last call for music group," around the television, and into a large room. Matt approached a man who stood at the head of the table, fiddling with a CD player and an MP3 player, hooking them together in a bizarre way. The man wasn't a patient; he was dressed in normal clothes.

Oliver envied him. He didn't approach him alongside Matt; instead, he remained frozen in the doorway and glanced around the room, feeling extremely awkward. The room was full. Every chair around the large rectangular table was taken by patients, both male and female. Packets of papers were spread around the table. Note-books and pens sat in front of each person, but no one was using them. In general, the patients behaved here the way they behaved in the day area: some conversed quietly with each other, some sat alone in silence.

Penelope sat in the first chair to the left of the man with the music players. She made a small gesture with her hand when Oliver looked at her; he thought that maybe she waved at him, but he wasn't quite sure. He was still clutching his bundle of clothing because, apparently, his room wasn't ready, so he just nodded in response. His nod was as small as her wave had been.

Relief washed over him as he realized that because the chairs were all taken, the group was full, and he wouldn't be able to stay. He ducked out of the room and back into the day area, and sat at an empty table with his back to the group room. Barely a minute had passed before Matt slid into the seat beside him. To avoid startling him, Matt had circled to the side of the table opposite Oliver, so Oliver could see him before he just popped unexpectedly into the seat, and he didn't start talking until Oliver registered that he was there.

"It's going to be a little hard to hear the music from out here, you know."

Oliver nodded.

"Remember what I told you about Dr. Willis's orders? You need to go. Dr. Powell leads the group. He's really nice, and it's a great group. People typically love going."

"I know. But the room is full."

As he usually did in response to Oliver, Matt smiled. "Nice try! Impressive way to try to get out of this, but unfortunately it's not going to work. Did you happen to notice the stack of chairs in the corner? And the spaciousness of the room? We use those chairs all the time. Dr. Powell already set up a chair for you. C'mon."

As he usually did in response to Matt, Oliver sighed. It wasn't an angry sigh but, rather, a sigh of sad resignation.

This time, when Oliver entered the room, the man approached him and shook his hand. "I'm really glad you came back. I'm Dr. Powell, but please call me Frank like everyone else does. 'Dr. Powell' is far too formal. We've just begun, and we're going around the table taking turns stating one thing that's good about today. Please, have a seat." Frank gestured in the direction of the empty chair. The other patients had spread out, away from the table, so his chair wasn't an isolated island separate from the group.

An anxious knot formed in Oliver's gut as other patients took turns stating something good about the day.

A slightly overweight woman with blonde hair that was pulled back into a braid declared, "I'm looking forward to my husband and kids coming to visit this evening. I can't wait to hear stories about how they're doing."

A frail-looking woman with frizzy, red hair and a mass of freckles meekly stated, "The sun is shining on me through the window, and it feels good on my arms."

A bald man with a tattoo of a dragon on his neck said, "I'm glad the night is over and it's a new day. This is the third day in a row that I've seen the new day as a fresh start, and it feels good."

Oliver tuned out after listening to a few. The knot in his gut expanded into his chest and exploded up into his head. He had nothing to say. There was absolutely nothing good about today, nothing at all. He closed his eyes and searched his mind for a small bit of good, but only painful images came to mind. And once a few images came to mind, others followed in a rush. He bit his lip, hard, to give himself something else to focus on. It hurt. Concentrating on one physical sensation caused him to focus on others, like his pounding heart and rapid breathing.

"Your turn, Oliver. What's something good for you today?"

As he struggled for control, Oliver was vaguely aware that Frank had addressed him, but he didn't know how to respond.

Frank didn't let him off the hook. "I know this isn't easy. But there's always something good in our day if we train ourselves to look for it. Just think of a single, little thing for today."

Oliver couldn't. He looked at Frank and shook his head.

Frank helped him out. Speaking softly, he said, "It's definitely not always easy. I noticed that you left the group earlier. You didn't want to be here, did you?"

Oliver shook his head.

Frank continued, "But you came back. And this is difficult, but you're sitting here. You're doing this. It takes a strong person to do what you're doing. I'd say that's a really good thing for today, wouldn't you?"

Clearly, Frank didn't understand. In an unsteady and tightly controlled voice, Oliver informed him, "But I'm not supposed to be here at all. This is not what I wanted."

"I know that. I've read your file. Believe me, I know this isn't what you wanted. But I'm telling you that you *are* here, you *are* doing this, and you might not want to believe it right now, but it's a very good thing." Frank paused for effect. "So there you have it. Your good thing for today is that you're here and you're doing this. Well, hey! That's actually *two* things, isn't it? Go figure! And you thought you didn't have any."

Frank moved on to the next person, leaving Oliver a bit confused. He wasn't quite sure what to make of the declaration that his being here was a good thing. And that it took a strong person to do this.

Strong? Strong? Hardly. Frank might have read Oliver's file, but there was a lot of information that was not in that file. "Strong" was not a word Oliver would have chosen to describe himself. A strong person would have been there. A strong person would have prevented what had happened. The knot was still growing inside Oliver, threatening to burst.

Suddenly, music blasted from Frank's CD/MP3 contraption, sending Oliver's pulse racing for a different reason. He hadn't expected that, and, like every other sudden noise or movement, it freaked him out. Frank must have seen him start, for he strolled over to him, bent down, and talked to him quietly while the others listened to the song.

"Sorry about the sudden blast of music. I didn't realize you didn't hear us talk about starting the songs." Frank adjusted the weighted blanket that was still draped over Oliver's shoulders. The shift in weight helped Oliver refocus. "This is what music group is all about," Frank continued. "People take turns selecting songs from a long list that I have. Copies of the list are on the table for everyone to look at. I've got more than three thousand songs from different genres. Music can be inspiring, soothing, energizing, and many different other things. Some people want to request songs; others just want to listen to the music selected by others. Don't worry about selecting a song today. Just sit back and listen. There is absolutely nothing else you have to do right now."

When the song ended, Frank took a song request from someone else, selected it, and let that one play. They listened to six songs, and then Frank chose a classical piece to play. Quietly, he instructed the participants to take out their journals. He then turned, reached into the cupboard behind him, and extracted a composition book and pen. He approached Oliver and gently placed the items in his lap. "This is for you," Frank whispered. "It's your own personal journal to write in or draw in or both. These often become friends that people can tell their secrets to." He returned to the front of the room.

Oliver watched the others work in their journals. He stared down at the one in his lap. He let it lie there. He was still clutching his clothes to his chest. Knowing that he would soon be forced to put them down, he didn't want to let go of them now. Besides, he didn't know what he could possibly put in the journal anyway.

He recognized the music as Tchaikovsky. He closed his eyes and listened. Instantly, they were there.

It was the middle of the night, and he and Maggie attempted to soothe their unhappy baby. It was something they were used to, because when Henry was an infant, the poor little guy suffered from colic. Oliver and Maggie took turns with him through the long nights. They tried everything to soothe him—car rides, bouncy seats, pacifiers, his baby swing, infant massage. Some worked better than others. On this particular night, Oliver and Maggie were up with Henry together. Maggie had Henry over her shoulder and rubbed his back as he cried. Oliver put on Tchaikovsky, their favorite composer, and then took Maggie in his arms, Henry and all. The three swayed to the music together. They didn't know if it was the music or their slow dance, but whatever it was, it worked. Henry quieted and fell sound asleep. They continued to dance until they thought they would fall asleep on their feet. Oliver took Henry from Maggie's arms and tiptoed to his nursery. Gently, he placed him in his crib and, miraculously, he stayed asleep. Oliver returned to the living room in search of Maggie. She was waiting for him. "Let's go make our own music," she whispered in his ear as she turned off the CD player.

Oliver became aware that the music had stopped. He felt a presence beside him. He opened his eyes and tried to register his surroundings. His heart sank when he realized that he wasn't at home, dancing with Maggie and Henry. He looked at the person sitting beside him. It was the woman he had met briefly in the dining area, Penelope.

"Here. Have…a Kleenex." She held a box of tissues out to Oliver.

"No thanks." He wasn't sure why she was offering them to him.

"You…should take…one. For…your face."

Instinctively, his hand went to his face. It was wet. "Oh." With one hand, he grabbed some tissues and wiped his face. He wadded them into a ball and pressed them into his eyes to stop the flow. Mortification became his overriding emotion, and soon, he no longer needed the tissues. He removed his hand and gazed around the room. He and Penelope were the only ones left.

"The group...ended a few...minutes...ago," Penelope explained. Her speech was slow and halting. "Everyone else is...gone. It's... okay that we're...here. Sometimes...people...stay in...here afterward to...talk or...whatever. Frank leaves us...alone...to do that.... Tears are...colorless...white...is...colorless....You're...sad." The last statement was a matter-of-fact observation that Oliver didn't quite know how to respond to.

"Yeah."

"Me too."

"I'm sorry." Oliver didn't know what else to say, but he thought he should say more. He didn't want to seem rude or uncaring. Even though he hated it, he decided to use the line that, since the tragedy, everyone kept using on him: "Do you want to talk about it?" He shifted uncomfortably in his seat. To his tremendous relief, Penelope shook her head.

Neither spoke, but neither stood to leave the room. Penelope broke the silence. "I'm too...ashamed...to talk about it."

Oliver's gaze met Penelope's. He wanted to say something else, but, again, he didn't know what. It was tempting to reassure her by telling her that he understood, but he knew firsthand how irritating it was when people said that. He couldn't possibly know what it was like for Penelope, any more than people could truly know what it was like to be him. He wanted to tell her that things would be okay, but he couldn't promise that, because he knew it wasn't true. He simply repeated what he said before. "I'm sorry."

"Stop...saying that....It's...not...your fault."

What happened to Maggie and Henry was very much his fault. Oliver squeezed his eyes shut.

"Penelope? Oliver?" Their still silence was interrupted by Matt's voice.

Oliver's eyes flew open in surprise, and he sprang to his feet.

"Oh, jeez. Oliver, I'm so sorry. I wasn't trying to sneak up on you. Look around you. You're in a safe place." He waited for Oliver to look around and then look back at him before continuing. "I was just coming to tell you two that the fifteen-minute break is over. It's almost ten forty-five, and time to move down to the other group room for art."

After a long pause, Penelope spoke. "Time for the...art...group....Time is strange. It...is time for...something...new....Oliver, why did...you...jump...when...Matt spoke? Time...for...art...now.... Mrs....Roosevelt says...I...have...to go. Oliver, answer...me."

Oliver looked at Penelope. He had to retrace her words to figure out what he was supposed to answer. He flushed slightly in embarrassment when he realized that she had asked him why he had jumped when Matt spoke. He thought about avoiding a direct answer, but there was something earnest and trustworthy about her that made him want to tell her the reason. That, combined with the repeated advice from Dr. Willis, the psychiatrist he was seeing here, that he needed to talk and stop bottling everything up, made him willing to at least answer her question honestly. "I feel really jumpy and startle easily. They tell me it's part of post-traumatic stress disorder."

"Why...do...you have...that?"

Why? His throat constricted around the lump that had formed. That was a question he was not ready to answer. He shifted nervously and looked at Matt, who stepped in.

"Penelope, that's a pretty personal question. Remember, we need to respect others' privacy. Come on. Let's get you two over to art."

"It wasn't...me....Eleanor Roosevelt...made...me...say...it. She...always gets me...in...trouble." Penelope stomped past Matt and stormed down the hall into the other group room.

"That's just Penelope being Penelope. Don't mind her." Matt paused before asking, "You okay?"

Oliver just shrugged.

Matt gave him a small smile. "Stupid question, huh? Hey, you've still got your stuff," he said. "Your room is ready; you'll be in room eight. Let me take your things for you, and I'll put them in your room while you're at art." He bent to pick up the journal that had fallen to the floor when Oliver had jumped up, and then reached for the bundle of clothes in Oliver's hands.

Oliver clutched them tighter for a second. Only reluctantly did he let go.

"Nice! Good job. I know it's hard. They'll be in your closet, I promise. Why don't I take the blanket, too, and put it on your bed. It might be hard to be all artsy with this draped around you." Matt lifted it off Oliver's shoulders.

Oliver shuddered but didn't protest. He forced himself to follow Matt to the other group room.

The group was just beginning when Matt escorted him in. The leader introduced herself as Camille and invited Oliver to sit. Oliver gazed around this room. It was exactly the same as the other one. For this group, though, there were fewer participants. Some were from the music group; others were different.

Penelope sat at the far end of the table beside an empty chair. "I...saved...this seat for...you, Oliver."

Oliver felt extreme uneasiness as he stood in the doorway of yet another group room full of people, and he welcomed the chance to slip into a chair. He made his way toward the end of the long table and sat down beside Penelope. Neither had a chance to speak, for Camille immediately resumed where she had left off.

"Spread out in front of you is an assortment of clay in every color of the rainbow. To begin, I'd like each of you to choose three or four colors."

None of the colors looked appealing. Green had been Maggie's favorite color, so he grabbed a lump of green clay. It was cold and heavy. He squeezed it. It smooshed a little, but not as much as the Play-Doh Henry used to play with. The thought hurt. He stared down at the clay in his hands and absentmindedly worked it with his fingers. The clay changed shape and began to warm up in his palms. He worked it some more. He developed a rhythm: squeeze, smoosh, twist, squeeze, smoosh, twist. Over and over again. It was soothing, and he became lost in the repetition and the tactile sensation of the clay.

A man's voice beside him broke him out of the trancelike state he had fallen into. "The poem you read to us reminded me of what I want to become, and I made this chameleon to symbolize it. All the colors on it show how it doesn't fight what's going on around it. It just goes with the flow and blends in, you know? That's what I wish I could do."

What? Camille read a poem? I was supposed to make something? Oliver looked around the table. Everyone had created some sort of sculpture. They were all different, though, and he could not fathom what he was supposed to have done.

"Oliver?" Camille addressed him next. "Do you want to share?"

"I…uh…" Oliver stammered. He looked at the green clay in his hands. It was still a lump. A softer lump, but a lump nonetheless. He looked at the clock on the wall. Eleven twenty-five. *I spaced out for more than half an hour? Now what? What do I say?*

Camille spoke. "I always invite participants to share the things they make in art group, but everyone's journey is personal, and sharing is never required. Just say that you'd like to pass, and we'll move on, no questions asked."

"I'd like to pass, please," Oliver mumbled.

"Of course." She smiled at him before continuing around the table. "Penelope, what about you? Would you like to share?"

Penelope sat frozen in her seat, staring at the bizarre clay formation in front of her. She had blended every color into a huge, amorphous figure, with spiky clay rods protruding in all directions. Without emotion or expression, she began to talk, presumably about her creation but, despite her slow and deliberate speech, Oliver couldn't follow her illogical words. Others around the table turned their attention away from her, exchanging looks that showed they thought she was bizarre.

When she stopped talking, Camille thanked her for sharing, just as she had thanked the man on the other side of Oliver.

Camille continued around the table. Two more people shared, and then they were invited to either keep their creations, or leave them on the table. As the other patients left, Oliver approached Camille and asked, "Do you have something I can put this in? I kind of like the feel of it and would like to take it with me."

Camille opened a manila folder in front of her and studied something inside. "Oh, Oliver, I wish you could, but I'm afraid you're not allowed to take things from groups yet."

"Because of the suicide watch?"

"Yes. I'm sorry."

"But Frank gave me a notebook. Matt put it in my room."

"The composition books don't have spirals that you could use to hurt yourself. And the pens and pencils are kept in the group rooms and at the front desk, rather than in patient rooms."

"How could I possibly hurt myself with clay?"

"You'd be surprised at what patients have tried. You can't take the clay with you, but I have something else you might like. Hold on a sec." Camille turned to the large cabinet behind her and rummaged through containers. A few seconds later, she turned back and handed Oliver an object. "It's even green," she said.

Tentatively, Oliver reached out and took it from her. It was a ball-like thing covered in smooth rubber, and filled with something that felt like sand, giving it a weighty quality. He worked it in his hands. It wasn't as malleable as the clay, but he could poke his finger into it or squeeze it and change its shape slightly. He closed his fist around it and it shifted. When he pressed his fingers into it, they made small indentations. Like the clay, it was soothing. "Is this something I can take with me?"

"Of course."

"Thanks."

"You're welcome. Are you coming back to my next art group? In a few minutes, people will be going downstairs for a short outside break before lunchtime. Right after lunch, at one o'clock, I'll start another art group. The activity involves painting. It'll be fun. You should come."

A burst of laughter from the back of the room interrupted them. Penelope sat by herself, laughing. Calmly, Camille approached her.

"What's up, Miss Penelope?"

Penelope continued to laugh, and then abruptly stopped. Her expression now blank, she stared at Camille. "Mrs....Roosevelt... can be...very...funny...sometimes. We...need a...cigarette...now. Oliver...will you...come...too?"

Panic gripped Oliver's chest. He tightened his hold on his new stress ball, grateful for its presence. He hated being outside and didn't want to go, but he liked Penelope and didn't want to be rude. He had seen the way the other patients reacted to her when she shared her clay creation, and he didn't want to be mean to her, too, by rejecting her. "I, uh, I don't want to go outside. But maybe we could eat lunch together when you come back in?" Oliver surprised himself with this suggestion. He had eaten alone for months because he couldn't bring himself to share the company of others. No one could replace Maggie. And even if they could, which they most certainly could not, he didn't deserve the company of others. Loneliness was part of his self-inflicted punishment. *This isn't about me, though. It's just for Penelope's feelings.*

Penelope said, "Okay," and left the room.

Oliver felt weak and sick. He muttered a quick good-bye to Camille and beelined for his room before Matt could spot him and reroute him outside. He crawled into the bed and covered himself completely with the weighted blanket Matt had left for him. Soon, it was difficult to breathe, and he was glad. Who was he to frolic around when Maggie and Henry could not do anything, would not ever again? He clenched the stress ball until his fingers turned white and his muscles cramped in pain. His head was sweating, and the lack of oxygen made him light-headed, but he didn't want to do anything about it. He heard a tech calling people to lunch. His stomach churned at the thought of food, and his heart pulled and pounded at the thought of betraying Maggie by eating lunch with Penelope. He heard Matt's voice in his room. "Hiding from the world, are you?"

Oliver ignored him.

Matt, however, refused to be ignored. He reached down and gently pulled the blanket away from Oliver's head but left the rest of him covered. Oliver took deep breaths of cool air but otherwise didn't react to Matt's presence.

"Penelope is looking for you. Says you told her you'd eat lunch with her. That was incredibly nice of you. I think she'll enjoy not eating alone for a change."

Oliver sighed and rolled onto his back. He opened his eyes and stared at the ceiling. "Matt?"

"Yeah?"

Oliver wanted to ask him how he should handle this situation, how he could get out of eating with Penelope without hurting her feelings. He was afraid to talk about it though, because that might require explaining, and that would somehow give it all a final reality. Also, in talking to Matt, he would have to disclose what he had done. So once again, he kept it inside. "Will you unlock my bathroom for me before I go to lunch?"

Matt hesitated before answering. "Is that really what you wanted to say?"

"Yes."

Matt unlocked the door. "There you go. I'll wait for you and lock it back up when you're done. And Oliver?" He paused and waited for Oliver to look in his direction. "If you change your mind and want to talk about whatever it was you were going to say, come find me, okay?"

Oliver could only nod.

CHAPTER 6

OLIVER FOUND PENELOPE SITTING IN THE MIDDLE OF THE DAY AREA, STARING straight ahead. His eyes followed the direction of her gaze. She appeared to be staring at nothing in particular, just the blank television screen at the end of the room.

"Thanks for waiting for me. Are you hungry?"

"Shhh!" Penelope shushed him. "Just a minute. This is the best part of the documentary."

Oliver was puzzled. "What documentary?"

Penelope didn't answer but remained focused on the blank TV screen. Without warning, she started to cry. Oliver had no idea what to do. Should he comfort her? Get Matt or another tech? Stand there and wait it out? Before he had a chance to decide upon a plan of action, though, Penelope stopped crying as abruptly as she had started.

"I'm...starving....Let's go...eat."

"Are you okay?"

"I'm...starving," she repeated, as if that explained the quick emotional outburst. Oliver wished he could turn his emotions off like that.

They walked into the dining area in silence, received their trays, and walked back out to the roomier day area. Penelope tore the paper wrapper off her turkey sandwich and began to eat. Oliver poked at his with his plastic spoon. At breakfast, Jennifer had approached him about his food intake, explaining that they monitored how much patients ate and that he wasn't eating enough. He was supposed to eat his lunch, but his stomach was already protesting and he hadn't even unwrapped the sandwich.

Penelope ate her sandwich, carrot sticks, side salad, and pudding without chatting. When she finished her last bite, she wiped her mouth and looked at Oliver. "Can...I ask you...something?"

"Sure."

"You...didn't see...it...did you?"

"See what?"

"The...documentary. It was...a...story about the first seal in space."

Oliver wasn't sure if he should humor her by saying that he did see it, or if he should tell the truth. Always one to believe in the virtue of honesty, he decided to tell her the truth. "No, I didn't. To me, it looked like the TV was off."

Penelope looked down at her plate. When she looked up, her eyes were watery. "That's...because it probably...was off. I...see... things that others...don't, and...it's...scary. It...also makes...me... very sad...because sometimes...I don't...know...what's...real...and what's...in...my mind....It's...depressing...to be like this."

"That must be awful," he said sincerely.

"I...miss my...old...life....William...says he...wants to...marry... me anyway, but...I...don't...understand why...because I'm...not... loveable...anymore." With this last statement, tears spilled down her cheeks and splashed onto her plate.

"William is your boyfriend?"

"My...fiancé...at least...for...now."

As Oliver searched for something to say, Jennifer approached their table and sat down. "Hi, you two. Oliver, how's your day going?"

He shrugged in response.

"Hang in there." She held his gaze briefly and smiled at him before turning to Penelope. "Penelope, I'm sorry you're down right now. I brought something from Dr. Daniels. Can I talk to you alone for a minute?"

Oliver stood to leave, but Penelope protested. "No...he's my... new...friend....I want...him to...stay."

"Penelope, if this is private, I should leave."

She looked at him imploringly. "Please...stay."

Oliver sat back down, and Jennifer continued. "The doc said you were pretty anxious again this morning, so he increased your clonazepam to three times per day. He increased your dose of paliperidone, too, but you're still only taking it once a day at bedtime. It'll just be stronger."

"I...don't...want...medication."

"I know you don't." Jennifer's tone was patient, gentle. "But it will help you. It will help your thoughts, your speech, your feelings. After tonight's dose, you'll see a difference in your speech right away, and soon the other things, like the delusions and hallucinations, will get noticeably better too."

"It's...pathetic...to need...medication to...control...who I am....I shouldn't...need...pills...to be...a...normal...human being."

"Oh, Penelope. These pills aren't meant to control who you are. These pills let you be you by settling down the things in your brain that are playing tricks on you."

"Easy...for...you to say,...Jennifer."

Oliver wanted to help, to reassure her. "You were just saying that you miss your old life and that things are scary sometimes. If there's medication to help you, you should take it. There's nothing wrong with taking medication to help you."

"Do...you...take...anything?"

Oliver hesitated, deciding what he wanted to admit. Perhaps if Penelope realized she wasn't the only one who took medication, it might make her more willing to help herself. "Dr. Willis prescribed stuff for depression, anxiety, nightmares, and sleep."

"Do...you...take...them?"

"While I'm here, I don't have a choice."

"Do...you want...to?"

After a pause, he answered, "No. But it's different with me, Penelope. It sounds like you have something going on in your brain that medication can help. I can tell already that you're a good person who deserves to be well. For me it's different. I—" He stopped. When he spoke again, he talked very quietly and looked down at his untouched food. "I don't deserve to feel good ever again. And I don't want to. It's impossible. That's why I don't want to take my stuff."

"What? Oliver! I had no idea you felt this way," Jennifer said. "What you said to Penelope was absolutely right. Medication can help people, there is nothing wrong with taking it, and she does deserve to feel good. And the same goes for you too. It might not feel this way right now, but you do deserve to feel good again. We're here to help you believe it."

Oliver didn't trust himself to speak or look up.

When he said nothing, Penelope said, "You...said I'm a... good...person. I...think...you...are too....Everyone...here...avoids me. Well, the...staff doesn't...because...they get...paid...to be... nice....But...you...don't...have to...be...nice. No, you...don't... have to...be...nice. The...others aren't...nice...to...me. You...sat... by me...and...you...talk to me...and you...willingly...had...lunch... with...me....Yes, you are a...nice...person,...Oliver...I...still...don't really...want to, but...I...will...take the...pills, Jennifer."

"I'm glad to hear it, Penelope." Jennifer handed her the little white cup with the medication in it, and waited until she took the pills before speaking again. "I think you're both very nice people, and I truly want you to get better. Penelope, you're right that we get paid, but we all choose to be here. We could've had different careers or worked for different places, but this is where we all want to be, and it's because of people like you two. Now it's about time for the next art group, so why don't you take your trays to the dining room and then head to the group room." She gave Penelope's arm a light, reassuring squeeze and rubbed Oliver's shoulder briefly before standing up to leave. She didn't mention that Oliver hadn't eaten a single bite.

This time, the art project involved painting. Oliver sat next to Penelope and watched her create her picture. She stopped and started, and stopped again. Sometimes she stopped mid-stroke and then just sat there. Throughout the process, she mumbled to herself, but Oliver couldn't make out much of what she was saying. He wondered if she was talking to him, but she wasn't looking at him and didn't seem to be addressing any of her comments to him. So then he wondered if she was talking to herself, or to someone only she could see.

The leader of the group, Camille, had instructed the group to paint freely anything that came to mind. He had never thought of himself as overly artistic, and he didn't know what to paint. After holding a dry brush and staring at a blank page, he gave up and put his brush down. The empty paper was a perfect representation of the emptiness he felt inside. He took the stress ball from the pocket of his robe and absentmindedly moved it in his hands for the duration of the session. He passed again when it was his turn to share, helped with the cleanup, and left the room with Penelope.

"What's next?" he asked when they entered the day area.

"We...get to...go...outside again....Mrs. Roosevelt and I... want...a cigarette. Are you...going to...come?"

"I, uh, I'd rather not."

"Why...don't...you...want...to go...outside? You...don't have to...smoke. I...smoke...because it...relaxes...us...Mrs. Roosevelt... gets...agitated when...I don't...smoke. Yes,...very agitated....It isn't...pretty. We...need...to...go...have a...cigarette. Why don't... you...want...to?"

"I don't smoke." Oliver hoped that that would be enough of an explanation. It wasn't.

"I...told...him...that already,...Mrs....Roosevelt....Didn't I, Oliver? I...told you...that...you...don't have to...smoke...outside."

"You did tell me that. It's not that. I just don't like to be outside."

"Why...not?"

Oliver looked at Penelope. Clearly, she wasn't going to let it drop. But he sensed she wasn't trying to pry or bother him. She seemed genuinely baffled as to why he didn't want to go outside. He decided to offer her a short explanation. "Being outside brings back painful memories, and it's too hard to deal with. So I'd really rather stay in."

Penelope stared at him with a blank expression. "Oh. That's... too bad...I'm sorry." She went to wait with the group of patients gathered by the desk waiting for a trip downstairs to the courtyard.

He thought about retreating to his room, but he didn't want to seem like he was avoiding Penelope. Looking around the day area, he spotted a table off to the side with a single chair pulled up to it. He strode over to it and sat down. He massaged the stress ball and thought of Penelope's earlier comment that she wasn't love-able anymore, and he wondered what her fiancé William thought. He wondered if William loved Penelope as much as Oliver loved Maggie. *Maggie. I miss you so much.* He folded his arms in front of him on the table and laid his head down.

"We...are...back. Are you...ready for...the...next...group? We... need...to go...to the...desk...and a couple of...techs will take...us... downstairs."

Oliver jumped to his feet, alarmed at the sudden sound of Penelope's voice.

Penelope didn't seem to notice his reaction. "Let's...go...they... are...waiting...for us...we...need to...go....Let's...go."

Oliver stood there, breathing heavily. He was too focused on his pounding head and racing heart to fully comprehend what Penelope had said. When she turned and walked toward the desk, he just followed. He walked with the group toward the elevator. He was beginning to recover from the shock when the elevator dinged, sending his heart racing, yet again. This time, though, it was just a little jolt and, by the time they reached the room at the end of the hallway, he was able to fully register that he had left side B, ridden in an elevator, and had arrived in a place he had never before seen.

Matt and Claire were the techs that brought the group down. Claire unlocked the door, and the group filed in. Oliver stopped short when he entered the room. It was an exercise room. Four treadmills and two elliptical machines lined the back wall. In front of these sat three exercise bikes and a weight system. There were three colorful exercise balls, an assortment of exercise bands, and a variety of free weights off to one side of the room. Fans blew cool air across the room. In one corner, a TV mounted from the ceiling sat waiting to be turned on. The room smelled slightly of sweat mixed with cleaning fluids.

Oliver felt as though someone had punched him in the stomach. His chest constricted instantly, and he couldn't breathe. Images flashed across his mind: himself lifting weights, riding an exercise bike, running frantically in a panic, flashing lights, chaos, a crowd of people in his way, pushing through, but not getting there fast enough, blood...Maggie! Henry! What was happening? He needed to get through! "Help! Please! No!" The room spun. His heart hammered painfully in his chest. His breath came in deep, rapid gasps. Sweat stung his eyes. It ran down his face and mingled with the tears. Where were they? Why weren't they answering his calls? "Oh, please, no!"

Arms wrapped around him, restraining him from getting to Maggie and Henry. He thrashed against them and cried out. He was vaguely aware that he was being led away. No! He needed to stay, to get to them. Please! He should have been with them in the first place, but he wasn't. They needed him. He needed them. "Oh, God! No!"

Suddenly, something heavy was placed on his shoulders. It felt good, but it didn't register that it was the therapy blanket he had been given the evening he had arrived at Airhaven. He didn't have time to linger in the feeling of it. He had to get to them. He thrashed and tried to throw it off. Hands pressed down on his shoulders. He felt them through the heavy thing. A soothing voice said, "It's okay. You're safe. It's not happening now. It's over. It's okay. You're safe. Breathe with me, Oliver. Slowly."

"No! You're helping the wrong person! Go find them. Help them!" He struggled against the force that held him down.

"Oliver. You're here at Airhaven. Whatever it is, it's just a memory. It's not happening now. You're safe. You're safe. Now breathe with me."

The hands continued to press down on his shoulders, and the voice continued to soothe him. Gradually, he came back to the present. Everything hurt: his head, his chest, his whole body. He ached with sorrow. He had failed. He hadn't been there for them. They needed him, and he wasn't there like he was supposed to have been. He groaned.

Someone sat beside him. He opened his eyes and looked around. He didn't recognize the room he was in. He was sitting on a floor that was carpeted with a rough, somewhat bumpy rug. Chairs were stacked up high along the wall across from him. Some boxes were along a different wall. He was confused. The person beside him slipped an arm around him and rubbed his hand along his arm. Oliver looked at him. Matt. That's right; he was at Airhaven. He closed his eyes and groaned again.

"Take it easy and just breathe. In and out, slowly. That's it." Matt continued to rhythmically rub Oliver's arm, but Oliver's ragged panting continued.

"Here. I need you to take this."

Oliver opened his eyes again to see who was speaking to him now. It took a few seconds to register that Jennifer crouched in front of him, holding a small, white paper cup.

"What is it?" he asked, his voice hoarse.

"Lorazepam. It's a fast-acting anxiety medication to help calm you down."

Oliver shook his head.

"That was a hell of a flashback," Matt said quietly, his arm still around Oliver. "You've got to be feeling pretty miserable. The lorazepam will help."

"I don't deserve it." He choked on the words and hyperventilated again. His heart revved up, and he thought he was having a heart attack. He was scared, and the emotion only fueled the panic.

"Oliver, listen to me. I'm putting this in your hand, and you are going to put it in your mouth. All you have to do is hold it under your tongue; it will dissolve on its own. Do you understand me?" Jennifer spoke in a tone that commanded attention. Oliver complied.

Within minutes, his body responded to the lorazepam. His heart rate slowed, and so did his breathing. Exhaustion hit. He closed his eyes and leaned his head back against the wall.

"Hey. Don't go to sleep on us yet," Matt gently shook Oliver's shoulders. "We're sitting in a storage room in the basement, which is no place to snooze. Come on. Let's go back upstairs to your room where you'll be comfortable. The last group of the day will be starting up there in a while, but I think Dr. Willis will understand if you miss it today. You need to sleep this off. Let's go."

Matt stood, and he and Jennifer helped Oliver to his feet. The trio rode the elevator back upstairs, and Matt and Jennifer helped him to his room and into his bed. Matt looked at him and, his voice filled with concern, said, "You need to talk, buddy. We need to know what's going on inside of you in order to help you."

Oliver didn't respond. He couldn't. He was already asleep.

CR

He awoke with a start. His heart thumped against the wall of his chest. He was disconcerted. Clearly, he'd had a nightmare, but it wasn't as intense as usual. Was the dream different, or was his physical reaction just milder? The prazosin must have started to work. For a moment, he felt relief. But then, a guilty pain stabbed at his heart and sliced through his very being. He didn't deserve for the nightmares to lessen in intensity. He felt the pressure of tears but blinked them back. It felt as though the walls were closing in on him. He needed to get out of this room.

He bolted out the door but came to a halt when he entered the day area. It was more crowded than usual. Groups of people sat in clusters all around the room. Many of the people were not dressed in hospital clothes. What was going on? Wasn't it the middle of the night? He glanced at the clock on the wall. Seven thirty-five. Visiting hours. He was confused. Why had he been sleeping? It came back to him: the exercise room, the flashback. He closed his eyes and sighed.

Not up to seeing the other patients interacting with their families and friends, he turned to go back into his room. A voice called out to him loudly before he stepped back through his door, though. "Oliver! Are you...okay? Come...meet...William...Yes...come... over here...Where have...you been?...Mrs. Roosevelt wants...me... to introduce you...to William...So...come...here. You...missed... dinner...Are...you...coming...over...here...to   meet...William?" Penelope called from across the room. People turned to look. They stared at him, but avoided looking at Penelope.

Oliver was appalled that people so blatantly avoided even making eye contact with her. He would not be one of those people. His desire to be kind to her overrode his desire to retreat into his room, and he strode to where Penelope sat with William.

"So this is the new friend you told me about?" William asked Penelope when Oliver reached their table.

"Yes." She offered nothing further.

William stood up and extended his hand. He gave Oliver a firm handshake, despite the fact that Oliver barely gripped his in return.

Oliver managed to say, "Hi. I'm Oliver Graham."

"Nice to meet you. William Vaile, Penelope's fiancé." He emphasized the word "fiancé" and gave Oliver a pointed look. "Please, have a seat and join us." As William sat back down, he put his arm around Penelope. She continued to sit stiffly in her chair with her hands on her lap. William rubbed her shoulder. "You okay, sweetie?"

"Mrs. Roosevelt...took...my...words...away."

That's enough, Penelope. I told you to shut up. You are nothing but an embarrassment. Didn't you see how people scorned you when you opened your mouth? You disappoint me, and you disappoint William. Cover your face with your robe. We don't want to look at you. Penelope removed her robe and put it over her head. She sat stiffly and didn't react when William put his arm around her once again.

"That's okay, Penelope. You can just listen while Oliver and I chat." He leaned over and kissed her head.

The gesture heightened Oliver's grief. It had been months since he had placed his arm around Maggie, or since he'd given her a simple kiss. He reached into his shirt pocket to pull out their picture, but his fingers only brushed against the fabric of his hospital attire. Tears threatened, and he pressed his palms hard against his eyes to stop them.

"Are you okay?" William asked.

Oliver nodded.

"Penelope told me you came in today. This isn't a place that people typically want to be. I'm sorry."

Oliver swallowed hard and forced himself to focus on the content of William's words, rather than his presence with Penelope. He looked up and began to converse with him. "I've been here for a few days, actually, but I've been over on the other side. They moved me over here today. What about Penelope? Has she been here long?" He wanted to shift the focus away from himself.

"She's been here about a week so far, this time."

"This time?"

William looked at Penelope and spoke to her as if she could actually see him through the robe covering her head. "Sweetheart, are you comfortable sharing with Oliver?" When she continued to sit rigidly without speaking, he took her hand and continued, "Squeeze my hand once if it's okay for me to share some things with Oliver."

Penelope sat unmoving. Then, she gripped his hand and held it tightly in hers. William tenderly placed his other hand around hers, brought it to his lips, and kissed it. Oliver bit down on the insides of his cheeks and looked down at his lap until William began to talk again.

"Penelope was diagnosed with schizophrenia almost two years ago, a few months after she turned twenty-eight. Symptoms came on gradually, but steadily worsened until she came here. She spent a few weeks here and was given medication. She was on it for over eight months, and it worked well, but had a lot of unpleasant side effects. Plus, she hated having to take it. As it worked well enough to minimize her hallucinations and delusions, she decided she no longer needed it. She stopped taking everything, and, well..." William trailed off. It was his turn to look away.

"This must be really difficult for both of you. I'm sorry," said Oliver.

Without warning, Penelope leapt to her feet. "Ouch! Stop... hurting...me! Why...stop...why...are you...poking...me? Ouch!... Stop!" Abruptly, she fell to the floor. She lay in a heap, doubled over in apparent pain. William knelt to help her, but before he could do anything, she broke into laughter. "No! Stop! I...don't...want... to be tickled...Stop!"

William rubbed her back in a circular motion. "You feel the Kerffies again, and I know you hate it. This is my hand on your back. Concentrate on the circles I'm making." He began to count the times his hand moved clockwise around her back. Eventually, Penelope sat up. She threw her arms around him in a fierce hug and buried her face in his shoulder. William pulled her close and rocked her, seemingly unbothered by their position on the floor of the day area of Airhaven's Side B.

Oliver wasn't sure if he should stay or go. Seeing Penelope and William made him yearn for Maggie and Henry so much it hurt. It was almost too much to bear, and he wanted to retreat under the covers of his bed in his lonely room. But he was worried that leaving might be rude; he didn't want to appear that he was spurning them or the situation. He also wanted to say something supportive, but he had no idea what he could possibly say. He shifted uneasily in his seat as he struggled with the emotions roiling inside of him.

Before he decided what to do, one of the night-shift techs, a portly, grandmotherly type woman named Bertie, approached their table and set down a tray of food. She slid a chair over from a nearby table between Oliver and William and Penelope, and eased herself into it. She surveyed the three of them and declared, "Well, I'd ask you all how you're doing this evening, but it seems like the answer is pretty obvious. Anyone want to talk?" When no one spoke, she continued, "Didn't think so. That's okay. Everyone around here always wants to do the talkie-talkie thing, don't they? That's because we know it's helpful. But we also know that sometimes it's hard. So no talkie-talkie tonight. Penelope, would you like to come back up and sit on your chair? I brought some snacks."

Penelope loosened herself from William's embrace long enough to look up at Bertie, who smiled down at her warmly. With the same blank expression with which Oliver had already become familiar, Penelope looked at Bertie, then at Oliver, and then at William. Without comment, she rose to her feet. William stood too, and helped

Penelope settle back into her chair. Penelope selected an apple and a granola bar and began to eat.

Bertie turned to Oliver. "Okay, sir, your turn. I understand you've eaten absolutely nothing today, and that's not good for you. What'll it be?" She gestured toward the assortment on the tray that, in addition to apples and granola bars, included crackers, cheese, yogurt, and grapes.

"I'm not hungry, but thanks anyway."

"I understand that you don't feel hungry, but your body still needs nourishment. You have to eat something."

Oliver sighed. Reluctantly, he plucked a single grape from the cluster. He rolled it in his fingers and studied it. His stomach churned at the mere thought of eating it. Nonetheless, he put it in his mouth and, with great effort, chewed it. It felt like he was chewing a mouthful of wet sawdust. He tried to swallow but gagged on the lump that lingered in his throat. He spit it out into a tissue from the box on the table. He looked at Bertie and shook his head. "I can't. I'm sorry."

In a compassionate tone, Bertie responded, "Sometimes when we're dealing with a lot of hard stuff, our emotions take over and fill us up. They can make even simple tasks like eating seem almost impossible. But feeling filled up with other stuff doesn't mean you don't need food. I know it doesn't feel like it, but trust me, there's room in the pit of your stomach. Let's try something you don't have to chew." She selected a yogurt, peeled back the lid, and handed it to Oliver with a spoon.

He wanted to run far away, but he was locked up here, and there was nowhere for him to go. He didn't want to make a scene in front of Penelope, William, and everyone else in the room, so he took the yogurt and spooned a tiny bite into his mouth. He gagged again but managed to swallow it. Slowly, laboriously, he ate it, look-ing down at the container the entire time. He was glad that Bertie took the focus off of him by chatting on with William about the White Sox.

When he had emptied the container, he looked up. Penelope was leaning into William as he talked with Bertie. Oliver simply couldn't bear to stay any longer. He excused himself and stood to leave.

"Don't forget to stop at the window by the front desk for your medication," Bertie reminded him.

Damn it. Despite the fact that he didn't want to, he complied with the orders; he knew that if he didn't go to the window, someone would barge into his room later and make him take the medication anyway. As he stood in line to receive his pills, he looked around the room. The visitors were beginning to say their good-byes. Bertie had left William and Penelope's table, and the two of them now stood and embraced each other. Thankfully, it was Oliver's turn at the window. With difficulty, he swallowed the pills and then hurried to his room. He barely made it before the dam broke. Diving under the covers, he cried himself to sleep once again.

CHAPTER 7

THE EARLY MORNING SUN STREAMED THROUGH THE WINDOW AND RESTED ON William's face, waking him before he wanted to be awake. He lay on his back, arms and legs stretched out, hogging the entire bed. Lying like that was lonely. He didn't want the whole bed to himself; he much preferred to share it with the woman he loved. It was usually Penelope who was the bed hog, gravitating past the center of the bed over to his side and using his chest as a pillow. She kept him warm both inside and out when she did that. He was suddenly cold despite the sun shining on him. He didn't want to be in that empty bed any longer. He scooted to the edge, swung his legs over the side, and sat up.

He sat, unmoving, for a few moments. Slowly, he reached for the picture frame on the nightstand near the bed. It was a cute frame, colorful and hand-painted with images of frisky dolphins jumping above ocean waves. Penelope had picked it out in the open-air market of the little Jamaican village. It looked happy and playful, and it was a perfect match for the image inside. The picture was taken two summers ago. Penelope had just turned twenty-eight. William was thirty. They had been together for two years, and, to celebrate, they had taken a Caribbean cruise. In the picture, he and Penelope were decked out in snorkel gear and tangled in a tight embrace—flippers, masks, breathing tubes, and all. He had just proposed to her, and she had accepted without hesitation and thrown her arms around him. He returned the hug fiercely. One of the ship's photographers, who followed the passengers around like paparazzi, had noticed the scene and snapped the photo. Of course they had purchased it. It was their favorite moment of the entire vacation.

Now, with the tip of his finger, he gently traced the image. They were supposed to be husband and wife by now. They had planned to be married on a cruise the next summer, exactly one year later. But that fall, a few months after their engagement, Penelope's symptoms began. It started with headaches and confusion. Then vague voices began to plague her. Thought disruptions and speech difficulties followed. The hallucinations worsened, and the delusions began. Her once enthusiastic and joyful demeanor gradually waned, and she became almost flat. Depression struck. It was hard for both of them. But William loved her. It was a deep, all-encompassing love that didn't just stop when things became difficult. When he looked at her, not just at her happy images in photographs, but at *her*, no matter how she was in the moment, he saw Penelope. He didn't see a mental illness. He saw the whole picture—the woman he loved who happened to be experiencing something awful. He wished Penelope would see it that way.

Something warm and furry brushed against his ankle and wove itself between his legs. He placed the picture on the nightstand and reached down to scratch the cat between its ears. "Let me guess; you're hungry, aren't you?" The white cat looked up at him and then jumped onto his lap. "If it had been up to me, you'd be living with a different family, you know." The cat purred and rubbed its head against William's stomach. "You're only here because I couldn't say no to Penelope." William picked up the cat with the intention of plopping it onto the floor, but changed his mind and hugged it to him instead. "I'm actually glad you're here, though." Apparently not appreciating the confinement, the cat squirmed away and jumped to the floor. "Well, at least you're not letting it go to your head. Come on, Johixilan, let's go get breakfast." *Johixilan.* William smiled and shook his head. Penelope had made up the name. He had no idea where it came from, but he didn't care. It was funny. He remembered how they had laughed when she thought of it. The little white kitten had reacted to their laughter, bouncing around on top of them as they played with him on the floor. Since he seemed to like the name, they kept it.

After feeding Johixilan, William made coffee and then grabbed the morning paper from outside his apartment. He sat at the table sipping his coffee but couldn't concentrate on the paper. His thoughts kept drifting to last night's visit to Airhaven. He'd been really happy for Penelope when she had told him that she made a friend. So many people had turned away from her, and she'd certainly had difficulty meeting new people in the last couple of years. He knew from his conversations with Dr. Daniels that connections to others were essential in improving her prognosis, so learning that she had a new friend delighted him. But she hadn't told William anything about this new friend, and he was a bit taken aback when he discovered that her friend was a man. He was ashamed of himself for that, though. Their relationship had never been based on jealousy; they trusted each other and had never been suspicious of each other's interactions with the opposite sex. Yet, for some reason, William had felt a twinge of possessiveness when she introduced him to Oliver. After all, Penelope had become increasingly resistant to marrying William, and now here she was hanging out all day with another man. He had actually briefly wondered about the man's intentions. Penelope had such a sweet, gentle, and kind personality. It felt good to be around her. And even in her hospital garb, she radiated a pure, natural beauty. Is that what that guy saw, too? People usually shied away from her these days, but not him. What exactly was his aim in hanging around her?

Thankfully, though, the ugly thoughts were short-lived. They were two patients in a behavioral health center, for Christ's sake. Penelope needed a friend. The way she held William's hand and hugged him close last night reassured him that she still had feelings for him. Clearly, this other guy was just a fellow patient who happened to be nice to her. And truly, William was glad that there was actually someone who didn't recoil from her in discomfort or fear. She deserved to have people treat her like a human being. Maybe this would help her see that not everyone was repulsed by or afraid of schizophrenia. It was refreshing for him, too, to meet someone who didn't seem to judge, someone who didn't know them in the past and thus keep mentioning how tragic this all was.

Plus Oliver's behavior didn't indicate that he had any interest in Penelope beyond a shared hospital experience. The guy seemed to be withdrawn into himself; he was extremely quiet. Throughout the time Oliver was at the table, William had the impression that he would burst into tears at any moment. It seemed that he had to work pretty hard to keep from doing just that. William wondered what his story was. Whatever it was, it was bad enough to land him at Airhaven. Maybe he would learn more about him tonight when he returned to visit Penelope.

He glanced at the clock. It would be ten hours before he could see her. He hated this. He wanted her home. Her medication was being increased. Maybe she could come home soon. But to do that, and to stay home, she would have to stay on the medication. Getting her to agree to that would be difficult. They had to take things one step at a time, though. He drank the last swig of coffee and walked out of the kitchen to get ready for work.

❦

Less than an hour later, William headed toward the elevator. One of his neighbors joined him. "Good morning!" she called cheerfully as she matched his stride.

"Hi." William didn't recognize her.

"My name's Mariska." She extended her hand toward William's and shook his in a confident handshake. "I'm in the process of moving in, as you can probably tell." She gestured toward herself, indicating hair pulled back into a messy ponytail, sweats, and a t-shirt. "I need to be comfortable when I unpack boxes, but of course this is the time I had to run into a new neighbor."

"Not a problem. My name is William. Nice to meet you." He wasn't quite sure what else to say, so he merely stood in awkward silence as they waited for the elevator.

Mariska broke the silence. "I can't believe I'm finally moving into this apartment building. I've been on the waiting list for over a year. I work downtown, so it'll be nice to live close by. No more long subway rides for me. Plus, I absolutely love downtown Chicago. Living here is going to be amazing. What about you? Do you like it here?"

"Yeah. It's nice." He was about to add that he and Penelope both liked it, but the elevator swooshed open before he had a chance. He was spared from having to continue the conversation by the other passengers. Chatting incessantly on a crowded elevator was poor etiquette, so everyone rode down to the lobby in silence. Thankfully, it made no stops on the way down, so it was a short ride. When the door opened, William stepped out, turned to Mariska and said, "Welcome to the building. Have fun settling in. Sorry to be in such a rush, but I don't want to be late for work." With that, he disappeared down the busy Chicago sidewalk.

He smiled at Mariska's enthusiasm at living downtown. Penelope had been excited, too. So had he, actually. The pulse of the city was energizing, and they loved being at the center of it. They used to love it, anyway. Lately, though, things were different. His smile faded. Schizophrenia had affected them so much. Noises and crowds overwhelmed Penelope now, and she was constantly worried that she would do something embarrassing and shameful, so they hardly went out anymore. William didn't mind for himself, but he hurt for Penelope. Early in their relationship, she had shared with him how throughout her adolescent years in rural Kentucky, she had dreamed of moving to Chicago and of life in a big city. She had moved here for college and stayed after graduation. She thrived here. Then mental illness took over and changed everything. Almost, everything, anyway. He still loved her, and they were still engaged to be married. Unless, of course, she refused to go through with it.

He was glad when he reached his destination; he could push his thoughts aside and throw himself into his work. He fished for the key, unlocked the door, stepped inside, and locked it again behind him. As usual, he was the first one there. His smile returned as he flipped on the lights and began to prepare the kitchen of Gustav's on Michigan. He donned his toque and apron and whistled as he bustled around making minor preparations at various stations for the line chefs who would soon arrive.

"Greetings, Monsieur Sous-Chef! You definitely fit the part, William. Congratulations on the promotion, man."

William turned to his friend and coworker. "Hey, Rod! Thanks."

"Sous-chef for the lunch shift of a five-star restaurant and catering service. How does it feel?"

"Pretty damn good."

"Paula and I celebrated on your behalf last night. We went to Navy Pier. It wasn't the same without you and Penelope. Paula misses her. How's she doing?"

"She's doing okay. They're working on new medication to help control her symptoms."

When William said nothing further, Rod continued, "I know I've said this before, but it really sucks that this happened to her. You guys don't deserve this. I hope they can help her. She hasn't been the same for nearly two years, and that's a shame. She used to be such a great person."

Used to be a great person? For a moment, William was speechless. He knew Rod didn't mean to be hurtful, but his comments stung. When he spoke, his voice was tinged with hurt and anger. "What the hell does that mean?"

"Hey, no need to get pissed. I didn't mean anything by it. She's still Penelope and all, but just, well, you know…" Rod trailed off and made a vague gesture.

"No. I don't know."

"Come on. Schizophrenia…" Rod trailed off again, as if that single word said it all.

"I don't know what you're getting at. Why don't you enlighten me?" William challenged.

"It's gotta freak you out, man. It would freak anyone out. Doesn't she think that aliens are going to abduct her, or that the CIA is out to get her or something like that? Aren't you scared? People with schizophrenia are unpredictable and violent. What if voices tell her to kill you, William? You go to sleep one night, and she sneaks into the kitchen, grabs a knife, and stabs you or something."

"You've got to be fucking kidding me, Rod," William practically shouted. "Why don't you stop watching so much TV and start living in the real world? Not everyone with schizophrenia is paranoid, and most people suffering from it aren't even remotely violent. You don't have a fucking clue. How could you even think something like that, let alone say it?" The memory of Penelope rocking in his arms last night, scared and sad, flashed through his mind, and the anger he felt toward Rod was joined by sorrow. One thing Rod had said was right: Penelope didn't deserve this, not the illness, and not the stereotyped opinions of both strangers and people they thought were their friends. He lowered his voice and said, "She's still a great person."

"Hey, I'm sorry. I really didn't mean anything by it. Are you going to see her tonight?"

"Of course."

"Tell her we said hi and that we're thinking about her."

"Will do." William paused before adding, "She really still is a great person, Rod."

"Yeah, of course she is." Rod slapped William on the shoulder, and then turned and walked off.

William returned to his duties. He didn't whistle this time.

CHAPTER 8

THAT EVENING, WILLIAM RETURNED TO AIRHAVEN CARRYING A SMALL COOLER. Inside was a pot of one of Penelope's favorite summer soups, a cold cucumber-yogurt-mint soup, the precise recipe for which he himself had created. He was glad that Airhaven policy allowed visitors to bring in food to the patients; he thought it would be a nice treat for Penelope. He also remembered Oliver's difficulty with food the previous night as well as Bertie's comment that he wasn't eating meals. Perhaps it would be easier for him to eat something that wasn't heavy and pasty like the normal hospital fare. After his conversation with Rod, William had a renewed appreciation for Oliver. Both William and Penelope needed someone new in their lives, someone who might not be so harshly judgmental. He wanted to do whatever it took to keep Penelope engaged to him and to make a new connection with Oliver, so he had called ahead and received special permission to arrive at dinnertime, before visiting hours began. He left work a bit early, rushed home and prepared the soup, and arrived at Airhaven just as the patients were being summoned to eat. He glanced around the day area and spotted Penelope and Oliver at a table at the far end of the room.

Oliver saw him coming, but Penelope's back was to him. William put a finger to his lips, indicating that he didn't want her to know he was coming. When he reached Penelope's chair, he place the cooler quietly on the floor and covered her eyes with his hands. Leaning into her, he kissed the back of her neck lightly and whispered, "Guess who?"

Penelope pulled away and turned to look. She stood and threw her arms around him in a bear hug. "William! You came early!"

Even though she hadn't said much, William noticed immediately that her speech had improved. The hesitation and the pauses were gone, and there was just a hint of emotion in her voice. He didn't want to ruin the moment by pointing it out and reminding her of her difficulties, though, so he didn't mention it. Instead, he hugged her fiercely in return. "I didn't want to wait until visiting hours."

Oliver watched them. He and Maggie had often approached each other the very same way. He vividly remembered a particular time...

That cold, blustery, winter evening, Oliver had arrived home before Maggie. He turned on the stereo and busied himself starting a fire to make the house warm and cozy. Because of the music and his clanking around at the fireplace, he hadn't heard her enter the house. He was crouched down and bent over the fire, poking at the wood to help it along, when suddenly a pair of hands covered his eyes, startling him enough to drop the iron poker. He heard the logs shift just before he heard a better sound spoken into his ear: "Guess who?"

Without fully standing, he pivoted around and grabbed Maggie in a bear hug. The awkward position caused both of them to lose their balance and tip over onto the floor. They laughed.

"Maggie! You scared me!"

"I'm sorry. How can I make it up to you?" They were still tangled together on the floor, and she ran her fingers through his hair. He closed his eyes and kissed her.

"Stay right here with me, forever."

"As wonderful as that would be, I think it might make it hard to take care of the baby."

His eyes flew open, and he looked deep into her dark, twinkling eyes.

"I just came from the doctor's office. Oliver, I'm finally pregnant again!"

"Oh, Maggie! That's fantastic! How are you feeling? Here, let me help you up. The floor is no place for you to be. Oh my God! Maggie! I can't believe it! How far along are you? Are you feeling okay? Why are you still on the floor? This is fantastic! What did the doctor say?"

Oliver talked in a rush of joy, and Maggie laughed. She made no move to get up, but instead embraced him tightly and buried her face in his neck. Their mood became solemn as they lay on the floor, the fire crackling behind them. Several minutes passed in silence. Oliver's neck and shirt dampened with Maggie's tears. Eventually she pulled back and looked at him, tears still streaming down her face. He, too, was crying silently.

"It has taken so long," she whispered.

"It's okay, Maggie."

"Oh, Oliver. What if I miscarry again? Please, not again," she begged as if he had the power to prevent a miscarriage. "I can't handle yet another one, and I don't want to do that to you, either. You've hurt as much as I have every time we've gone through this. As much as we both want a child, I'm scared at the thought of having to go through this again. And if it doesn't work this time, it might never happen. We're in our mid-thirties. Soon it's going to be too late. Honey, I'm afraid."

He stroked her hair with one hand and rubbed her back with the other. "We'll take it day by day and hope for the best. I love you, Maggie. We have each other, and that won't change, no matter what happens."

"Oliver, I love you so much."

They remained where they were, neither one wanting to let go of the other.

"Oliver?"

"Hmm?"

Her voice filled with sorrow. "We needed you. Where were you?"

In his mind, they were no longer snuggling by the fireplace in their home. The scene abruptly changed: they were outside, and although he heard her clearly, she was gone. His heart caught in his throat. "Oh, God, I'm sorry. I'm so, so sorry."

"What? What are you sorry about?" The voice didn't belong to Maggie.

He looked around, but everything was watery and blurry. He wiped his eyes and blinked the present back into focus.

Penelope asked again, "Oliver, what's wrong? Why are you sorry?" She and William sat with him at the table and looked at him with bewildered expressions.

"Uh, I'm sorry that I'm in your way," he muttered as he stood up. "I'll go so you two can be alone together."

"No. Wait." William rose and stepped in front of Oliver, blocking his path away from the table. "Please, stay. You're not in our way. I came to see both of you, actually. I brought you guys something."

Oliver stared at William, speechless. It was difficult to breathe. He clenched his jaw and worked the muscles as he tried hard not to cry. William placed a hand on Oliver's arm and pulled him gently back to his chair. "I think you should sit down. I'd really like you to stay, and I bet Penelope would too."

"Yes, I would. Please stay."

Oliver was torn. He wanted to retreat to his room, but at the same time, he dreaded the thought. The walls would inevitably close in on him, and there would be no escape from the horrific images and memories that danced around in his mind. If he stayed here, he could keep them at bay, at least for a while. But who was he to think he had the right to a reprieve? He needed to go, to let his monsters have at him.

Yet, Penelope and William had asked him to stay. Leaving now would be impolite. But watching them together intensified his sense of loss and his aching loneliness and his unrelenting guilt. Their love was obvious, and William was here helping Penelope. If it had been Penelope there that day, William would have been there for her. Unlike Oliver. No, he had been selfish. He wasn't there when they needed him. And now they were gone. If only he had a second chance. He'd be there this time. Really, he would.

He couldn't decide whether to stay or to go. He didn't want to do either. For the umpteenth time in the last several days, he cursed the landing pad that had broken his fall. He sighed a deep, ragged sigh.

Something was placed in his hand—the stress ball Camille had given him yesterday after the first art group he attended. Penelope squeezed it into his palm, and her hand lingered on his for a brief moment. When she slid her hand away, he looked at her. Her expression was blank, but her eyes were kind. "When you lent this to me today after music group, it helped. Now you need it back. Squeeze it and say something that is going well."

Oliver squeezed but said nothing.

"One thing, Oliver."

"You've been listening to Matt too much around me, Penelope. Which means you should know that I'm not going to say anything."

William looked from Penelope to Oliver. To break the silence that had fallen over their table, he said, "We want you to stay here with us, and I brought you two something so you don't have to eat hospital food tonight. Does that count as something good?"

Oliver looked at William. He fiddled with the stress ball and, although he remained silent, he nodded.

"Will you stay with us?"

Again, Oliver nodded in response.

"Good." William turned to Penelope and took her hand. "I have wonderful things in my day; I'm here with you, and you seem better, sweetie. I can hear it in the way you're talking. How're you feeling?"

"I don't know. Stupid. Worried about what the side effects of this new stuff will be."

"Worrying about the side effects makes sense, but why do you feel stupid? That doesn't make sense to me. You're the farthest thing from stupid I know."

"I'm only doing better because of medication, William." Despite the fact that she still lacked emotion, Penelope's voice was forlorn. "I need pills to help me be a regular person. A lot of pills: paliperidone, sertraline, clonazepam, and a bunch of others, too. That's stupid and pathetic. I shouldn't need antipsychotics, antidepressants, anti-anxiety medication, sleeping pills. It's embarrassing to need all this stuff.

"And even with these pills, Mrs. Roosevelt is still here. I mean, she's not at our table because she went to our room to rest, but she was with me all day." Penelope tucked her hair behind her ear and looked down at the table. "In music group, she made me sing to the music. She said I had to practice using my voice or she would stop the medication from working. She told me she would give me all of the bad side effects of it but take away the helpful things. You know I can't sing, but she made me do it anyway, and she wouldn't let me stop, even when the others looked at me funny, and even when Frank told me to stop. She made me keep singing, and made me do it louder. Even when Frank went to the phone to call a tech to take me out, she wouldn't let me stop. I was escorted out of the group. I'm stupid and pathetic."

William inched his chair close to Penelope and put his arm around her. "Sweetheart." He kissed her head. "You are not stupid and pathetic. I promise. You are going through something really difficult, but that doesn't make you stupid."

"Yes, it does."

"No. It doesn't."

"There's something wrong with my brain. That makes me stupid," Penelope argued.

William looked at her imploringly. "You are so smart and delightful and wonderful. Awful things are happening to you with this, but they're just things that are happening to you, they aren't who you are. All this medication will let you be yourself, the true Penelope."

"The true Penelope is psychotic, William. I'm nothing but a worthless embarrassment. Look at this. It's Friday night, and where are you? Out having fun? No. You're in a mental hospital, coddling me. It's bad enough that my life is ruined. I shouldn't be ruining yours too. I need to be out of your life so you can be happy and free."

"That's not true, Penelope!" The frustration was apparent William's voice.

Oliver came to William's aid. "There's more to you than schizophrenia, Penelope. Even I see that, and I just met you."

"You're lying. You saw me today, making an ass of myself, getting removed from group. I was an embarrassment."

"If I had thought you were an embarrassment, I wouldn't have left with you when Matt came. So you sang out loud. Big deal. At least you can participate. I sit around like a lump in those groups." He paused and swallowed. "And I can't even go downstairs to..." He couldn't even say the word exercise. To avoid becoming overcome with sorrow, he rushed on. "Again today, just like yesterday, I passed all day whenever it was my turn to talk or to do something. Other people get emotional. They yell or cry. You have a right to express yourself too. Singing isn't a bad thing."

"It is when it's inappropriate and makes you make an ass of yourself. I'm pathetic."

William's response was emphatic. "It hurts when you talk about yourself like that. I love you, and I don't think you're pathetic."

"I love you, too, William. And you know what they say. If you love someone, set them free."

"Penelope, no. You're so wrong. I don't want to be set free. I want to marry you."

"You'd be marrying pills, William, not me." Penelope looked down at her lap and said nothing further. Oliver watched the two of them. Creases of concern were etched deeply into William's brow. Tears pooled in his eyes but did not spill over, perhaps because his clenched muscles held them in place. Penelope's face was flat and expressionless. She didn't move away from William though; she allowed him to keep his arm wrapped around her shoulders, and she still held his other hand.

Oliver's own emotions threatened to get the better of him again. To stop that from happening, he changed the subject. "Hey, can you smell that? It's the hospital food. Disgusting. I'm never hungry as it is, and the food here makes it even worse."

William perked up. "How could I forget? I brought dinner, remember?"

"William is a chef," Penelope explained to Oliver. "And he's absolutely amazing. What did you bring us?"

"One of your favorites." William pulled out the pot and uncovered it to reveal a smooth, light-green soup with a sprig of mint and curls of cucumber decorating the top. It was thick and looked almost like a blended ice cream drink. "I even brought your favorite set of bowls." He reached back into the cooler and produced spoons and three colorful soup bowls with bright summer vegetables painted on the insides.

Penelope threw her arms around him briefly and then began to fill a bowl to the brim with William's treat. "I'm starving, and this will be so much better than the meatloaf I ordered. How fitting that this is green. To the Kerffies, green means acceptance. I accept your soup, William. Thank you."

"Yeah, this is definitely better than meatloaf. Thanks." Oliver sounded sincere, but his bowl remained empty in front of him. William filled it for him as he filled his own, and then watched Oliver lower his spoon into it and slowly swirl it around.

"It's a chilled summer soup made with cucumber, yogurt, mint, and other spices. I chose this one because it's Penelope's favorite and because I thought this would be easier for you to eat since you don't have to chew it. I didn't want you to have to wrestle with dinner the way you struggled with the grapes last night. But if you don't like it, you don't have to eat it."

Oliver flushed slightly at the mention of his attempt to eat last night. He was quick to reassure William. "No. It looks fantastic. I love stuff like this. I just don't have much of an appetite these days, but I know the staff is going to hound me to eat. Trust me, I'd much rather have something decent. And this looks beyond decent. Really, thank you for bringing this. I appreciate it." He spooned a small bite into his mouth. His gut protested instantly, but it tasted good. It had been months since he'd had a palatable meal. He ate a second spoonful. And a third. Before he realized what he was doing, he had eaten the entire bowl. Instantly, he was full of self-hatred. His stomach churned and threatened to expel what he had just fed it. What was he doing? How could he sit here and take pleasure in food and company? He pushed the bowl away from him in disgust. He snatched up the stress ball, closed his hand around it, and pressed his fists into his forehead.

William had been telling Penelope about the picnic he was helping cater tomorrow afternoon, but when Oliver did this, he stopped talking and, with Penelope, turned his attention to the distraught man. "Oh, damn. I didn't mean for this to upset you. I'm really sorry."

Oliver remembered his manners and looked up. "No. You didn't. This was really delicious. I just...Well..." Oliver took a deep breath and tried again. "I..." He squeezed his hands around the stress ball as he squirmed slightly. He looked down. Penelope walked around to his side of the table and stood by him, one hand on his shoulder. She didn't speak, but simply kept her hand there for a moment before returning to her seat by William. Oliver gave her a weak smile. He looked at both of them and simply said, "Thanks."

"No thanks necessary."

As they wrapped up dinner, William suggested, "How about a Friday night card game?" He slapped the deck he'd brought on the table. He looked at Oliver and asked, "Or do you have visitors coming?"

Oliver shook his head. "No. No visitors." His voice was hollow.

"Why not?" Penelope asked.

Oliver had already grown accustomed to Penelope's bluntness and figured that her mental illness affected her interactions with the world. He wasn't offended. He studied his new companions as he decided how to answer. After a long pause, he answered so quietly that Penelope and William had to strain to hear. "I lost the people who meant the most to me in the whole world. My wife and son died four months ago." His voice trembled and he couldn't go on. He bit his lip to keep from crying.

"God. I'm sorry," William exclaimed.

Penelope simply reached forward and touched Oliver's arm. "Isn't there anyone to come see you, to help you through this?"

Oliver shook his head. "I doubt anyone knows where I am or that they even care."

"Are you serious?" William sounded completely puzzled by this.

Oliver sighed. He took a breath and looked like he was going to speak but remained quiet. Finally, he managed a meek request. "Um, how about that card game?"

"Absolutely." William paused and made eye contact with Oliver before continuing, "What'll it be? Hearts? Round the World? Bullshit? Rummy?"

Penelope voted for Rummy. Oliver consented, and William dealt the cards. William stayed for hours, until he was ushered out at the end of visiting hours. They ended up playing all four games during the course of the evening, and while no laughter rang out from their table, they conversed as they played.

The experience was bittersweet for Oliver. On one hand, the casual company of people he was growing to like filled his aching need for human connection. On the other, his loneliness was intensified by the harsh knowledge that he was living life without Maggie and Henry. As he sat in the relaxation group beside Penelope that night, he couldn't relax at all. And, alone in his hospital room, he drifted off into a restless sleep with a troubled heart, an awake sort of sleep that was punctuated by the ubiquitous sound of the clock's loud cadence of despair, by bad dreams, and by a shameful feeling of envy for the love William and Penelope shared.

CHAPTER 9

OLIVER WASN'T THE ONLY ONE WHO SLEPT FITFULLY THAT NIGHT. WILLIAM tossed and turned until he finally gave up and rose from his bed at four-thirty in the morning. He stood, stretched, yawned, and looked unsuccessfully for Johixilan before shuffling toward the kitchen. He opened the fridge and stood and stared into it, long after his eyes adjusted to the bright light that assaulted them. Specifically, he stared at the pot that held a small amount of left-over soup from the dinner he had shared with Penelope and Oliver less than twelve hours ago. It had been a nice evening, except for the fact that Penelope had said she wanted to set him free. She had told him that twice, once before dinner and again as she hugged him before he left. How could he convince her that he didn't want to be set free? He felt cold and almost empty, like the pot that sat dumbly on the shelf. He slammed the fridge shut. Frustrated and discouraged and needing to rid himself of this negative energy, he stomped back to his bedroom and changed clothes. He threw extra clothes into a gym bag and headed for the indoor pool of his apartment building. He didn't even wait for the elevator, preferring instead to expend some of his energy on the ten flights of stairs that led down to the pool.

He was relieved to have the pool to himself. If this had been a weekday, he surely would have had to share the pool with a few people, even this early in the morning. Because it was a Saturday, though, William was blessed with rare solitude. He tossed his bag and shirt onto a chair and, only slightly out of breath from his ten-flight descent, dove into the water without hesitation. The cool, refreshing water energized him. He swam vigorously up and down the length of the pool, over and over again. At first, he counted his laps, but stopped after only a few and simply felt the power of his strokes and the movement of his body through the water. The rhythmic motion and the feel of the water calmed him. He cut through the water, back and forth, back and forth, until his muscles felt like rubber, and then he pushed some more. After sustaining that for over an hour, he stopped on one end of the pool, held onto the edge, and simply hung limply, his body resting on the side of the wall. He allowed the minutes to pass like that, and then he hoisted himself up and out of the water. He was fatigued, and the muscles of his arms trembled as he did so. He smiled wryly to himself as he wondered how heavy his tools would feel as he worked the grill at the picnic Gustav's was catering this afternoon. The price of sore muscles was worth it though. He felt much better—calmer, more centered—after his swim. The water dripped off him as he picked up his bag and walked into the locker room. He toweled off, changed into the dry clothes he had brought along, and returned to his apartment. He took the elevator this time.

It wasn't even seven o'clock yet when he closed the door, engulfing himself in the little world he shared with Penelope. The swim had cleared his mind and renewed his resolve. He would do whatever it took to hold onto the love of his life. There was not a thing he could do about it now, however, as patients could neither have visitors nor take phone calls at this time of day. He had a few hours before he needed to head to work so, with heavy legs, he trudged to the bedroom and collapsed into bed.

Thankfully, he had set his alarm the night before. He fell into such a deep slumber, he would have slept through the afternoon if not for the alarm's annoying buzz. Thankfully, too, it was only the alarm clock and not the smoke detector that shouted at him, for when he looked at the time he realized that it had been buzzing for almost ten minutes before he responded. The swim had tired him out physically, and worrying about Penelope drained him emotionally. Still, the early-morning power sleep had refreshed him, and, as he as he prepared for the day, he looked forward to both the catering event in Lincoln Park as well as his evening visit to Airhaven. One way to convince Penelope that he wanted to spend his life with her was to be there for her every single day. Before he headed out the door, he threw a change of clothes into his duffel bag so he could go directly to Airhaven without having to waste time returning home to change. As he headed to Lincoln Park to cater the company picnic, he whistled.

☙

The crew of Gustav's on Michigan was already setting up the chefs' work stations by the time William arrived. Gustav's was one of the few catering services that actually owned mobile equipment, and two grills and various portable counter stations were placed in an open area, slightly away from, but in sight of, the main picnic area. Portable refrigerators, specially designed for catering services, held the various ingredients for the dishes some of the top chefs in Chicago would soon prepare. In the actual kitchen of Gustav's, William acted as sous-chef; for catering events, though, he was a line chef. Today he would be grillardin so, after donning his apron and toque, he headed toward one of the refrigerators and grabbed chicken, pork, and steak as well as various sauces and spices. Arms full, he moved to the counter that had been placed near the grills for him and began to prepare the main dishes that would be served to the picnickers.

He spotted Rod at the other end of the outdoor cooking area, working with the cold dishes and thus located strategically away from the heat and smoke of the grills. William waved at him and then made himself look incredibly busy, too busy to be interrupted. He didn't feel like talking to Rod, for he was certain he would ask him about his visit with Penelope last night. He had nothing to hide, of course, but Rod's interest would undoubtedly extend beyond mere details about the food and the card games. He would ask about Penelope's condition, and William did not want a repeat of yesterday's conversation. So he avoided contact with him. Avoidance seemed to be a pattern for Penelope and him lately. Well-meaning people who had been part of their once-active social circle had, in these last two years, begun to act uncomfortable around them or had begun to make comments similar to Rod's. True, up until yesterday no one had been as blatantly insensitive as Rod had, but there was a prevailing implication by friends and acquaintances that Penelope would never be the same again. It was wearing, and William preferred avoiding such conversation whenever he could.

Once he began to work, he had no time to ruminate about Rod or his own changing social life. He had fun as he worked. In one hand he held his turner and moved it swiftly across the grill, sliding it under the slices of meat and flipping them over. As he did this, he frequently reached beside him with his other hand and grabbed a shaker of seasoning. From time to time, when he sprinkled the meat with the special blend of spices he had personally developed, he flipped the shaker in the air and caught it before placing it back on the tray beside him. Occasionally, he glazed a dark sauce over the top of every piece of meat with a small, circular motion. He was so intent on his work that he didn't notice when someone approached.

"William?"

He turned toward the sound of the woman's voice.

"It is you!" she exclaimed.

William recognized her as his new neighbor. He searched his brain for her name but came up blank. "Uh, hi. How's your moving in going?"

"It's going very well, thanks. In fact, I now have all of my unpacked boxes confined to the spare bedroom. And, by the way, my name is Mariska." She smiled broadly in response to the recognition that flashed across William's face. "Don't worry. I'm typically horrible at remembering names. I have a brother named William. He goes by Will, but it made it easy for me to remember your name. You probably don't have a sister named Mariska, do you?"

William returned her smile. "No. I don't have a sister at all, actually. I'm an only child. And you're the first Mariska I've met."

"Well, then you have a good excuse for forgetting my name. You recognized me as your new neighbor, though, so I'll give you kudos for that."

"I'm much better with faces than I am with names."

"Me, too, actually. I typically don't forget a face. That's why I came over here. I was sure that I recognized you; I wanted to come over here to prove to myself that I was right. I spotted you on my way back to my station. I've been face painting kids." She held her hands up and wiggled her paint-smeared fingers. "But I just took a quick break. I couldn't help but stop and watch as I was walking back to the children's area. I've never actually seen professional chefs in action, and I must say, it's neat to watch." She glanced briefly at the two other chefs working their stations, but then her eyes settled back on William. She took in his white toque with his blond hair peeking out from under the brim, his chef's coat, his black pants, and the bowl and brush in his hands. "I think it's a combination of the uniform and the way you work. You look like an artist in motion, William."

He felt himself flush with a mix of pride and discomfort. "Thanks. I do think of this as an art, and I love what I do." He set the bowl down and picked up a turner. The meat didn't need flipping, but he wanted to tend to the grill as a way to put something between himself and Mariska.

"I can tell. Everything sure smells delicious. I can't wait to eat. Right now, though, I'd better get back to the kids. There are a ton of them here, and they all seem to want pictures on their faces. Have fun at the grill!" She turned and walked away but, after only a few steps, she looked back and gave William a smile and a little wave before continuing on her way.

Mariska hadn't even been gone for two minutes when Rod appeared at William's grill. He got William's attention by elbowing him. "So who was that?" he asked.

"No one." William was still irritated with Rod over yesterday's conversation, and he was not in the mood for this.

"Really? Because it looked to me like someone was standing here talking to you. I know I wasn't hallucinating." He took a sharp breath. "Oh, God. That was insensitive. I mean, because Penelope hallucinates and stuff. I didn't mean—"

"Go away, Rod."

"Hey, don't be like that. I really am sorry about yesterday. And the comment I just made. Are we cool?"

"Yeah, sure."

"Good. Now who was the chick?"

"I told you. No one. She's just someone who moved into my apartment building this week, but I don't know her."

"No way! Why didn't you tell me you have a hot new neighbor?" A look of surprise suddenly lit up Rod's face. "Did you bring her along today?"

"No. Of course not."

"Then why is she here?"

"I have no idea."

"Is she single?"

"I don't know." William couldn't keep the irritation out of his voice. "But I'm not, and neither are you."

"That doesn't mean we can't appreciate all the beauty in the world."

"You're an ass. Don't you have work to do? They want to serve soon."

"Yeah, I'm going. You didn't disagree with me about her being hot, by the way."

"That's because it didn't deserve a response. Quit being an ass."

Rod only laughed.

"My friend is an ass," William grumbled to himself as he removed the meat from the grills. He took his irritation out on the food in front of him, shredding the meat more vigorously than was necessary. The result, though, was good: an improved mood and meat that was perfectly prepared for sandwiches. He delivered it to the serving crew and returned to the grills to begin the cleanup process. He wanted to get it done quickly so he could get to Airhaven.

"William, this meal is amazing! Thank you."

He turned from his task to find Mariska standing behind him. "I'm glad you like it, Mariska. I didn't do the whole thing myself, though. I can't take much of the credit."

She grinned. "You remembered my name this time. And given that you prepared the main part of the meal, I'd say you deserve the majority of the credit."

Suddenly unnerved, William resumed scraping the grill surfaces. "Not really. I'm just part of Gustav's." He didn't want to comment on the fact that he remembered her name.

He was relieved when she let the name thing go and simply kept the conversation business related.

"I was so excited when I discovered that Gustav's on Michigan was catering our company picnic this year. I feel like I'm living the dream—living in downtown Chicago and working for a company large enough to hire a five-star restaurant to cater our picnic."

"So you work for Prairie Winds Insurance?" William had a strong desire to keep this conversation as neutral as possible. He thought it better to comment on the obvious facts than to get into the more personal aspects, like her dreams.

"Yeah. I'm a human resources assistant. And you're a chef."

"Not just a chef. William here was just promoted to sous-chef, just a step under the head chef." Rod had approached. He threw his arm around William's shoulders as he enthusiastically joined the conversation.

"Wow! That's impressive. Congratulations. Given the way the sandwiches tasted, I'm not at all surprised."

"Hear that, William? What a nice compliment." Rod tightened his grip and shook William's shoulder. William glared at him and pulled away. Unfazed, Rod kept talking. "So, are you going to introduce me to your new friend?"

Reluctantly, William responded, "Rod, this is Mariska. She works at Prairie Winds. Mariska, this is Rod. He works at Gustav's."

"Wow, William, don't gush so much. You make me blush." He turned to Mariska and extended his hand. "Nice to meet you."

"Likewise."

"So William tells me that you moved into his building."

"He did?" Mariska smiled and blushed slightly, evidently pleased by this revelation.

William was less than pleased. "Rod asked me how I knew you, and I told him I saw you yesterday as you were moving in." He tried to make it sound as unimportant as possible, because it really was unimportant. His irritation at Rod turned into outright anger, and he wondered how much of a friend he really was.

William was spared from further comment as another person approached. He sighed. Why were people suddenly so interested in him and who he was talking to? He wanted them all to go away so he could wrap up and go see Penelope. And Oliver. He doubted that Oliver would act like Rod. He was happy that the person who approached them was the catering manager ordering them back to work.

"Well, the boss has spoken. Back to my cleanup duties. It was nice to meet you, Mariska. Catch you in a bit, William."

After Rod had left, William excused himself, too. "I'm glad you liked our meal. I guess I'd better get back to work."

"Of course. And I suppose I'd better get back to my coworkers." She paused but didn't turn to leave. After a moment's hesitation, she asked, "Hey, do you happen to have plans tonight? My kitchen is settled, which means I've got coffee or beer available, as well as mugs to drink out of, if you'd like to stop by later."

William absolutely did not want to stop by later. "Uh, thanks for the offer, but I'm not going to be home. My fiancée is in the hospital, and I'm going to see her right after I'm done here. Visiting hours are extended on Saturdays, so I'll be there for a long time." William was a bit disgusted with himself for not disclosing that it was a behavior health center, but he really wanted to keep the conversation short. He didn't want to explain Penelope's personal history at length.

When Mariska answered, William heard the disappointment in her voice. "Oh. I'm sorry your fiancée is in the hospital. It's nice that you'll be able to spend time with her today though."

William nodded. He didn't feel like talking, and he wanted the conversation to end. He waited for Mariska to leave, but she didn't. Instead, she continued, "I don't want to pry, so I'll just say I hope she's going to be okay. And I'd like to get to know my new neighbors, so my offer still stands. You're welcome to come over any time. That goes for your fiancée too, if she's up to it when she comes home."

"Thanks. That would be nice."

"Yes, it would. Now I'll let you get back to work. Have a nice time with your fiancée tonight. I hope she's feeling well."

"Me too. Enjoy the rest of your picnic."

As William returned to work, he thought about Mariska's invitation for Penelope and him to come to her apartment. Would Penelope be willing to do that? She used to be so social and outgoing, and in the past, she would have loved making a new friend right down the hall. Since she had been diagnosed with schizophrenia, though, she had become increasingly isolated. It had a little to do with the fact that her medications had harsh side effects and she sometimes didn't feel well, but there was more to it than that. Part of it was that group interactions were often overwhelming, and part of it, too, was that she was embarrassed. She also thought she was an embarrassment to William, and he was having difficulty convincing her that this was untrue. Occasionally, he admitted to himself that sometimes he was troubled when she talked to Eleanor Roosevelt aloud in public or became lost in her delusions, but he hated himself for that because he still loved her fiercely. He wondered if he could convince her to meet Mariska. Having supportive friends was crucial to her well-being. But these days, who knew who could be counted on to be supportive? Take Rod and Paula, for example. They had all been so close once, but now, the two of them didn't seem to understand at all. If past friends found it difficult to continue this friendship, how would somebody new react? Oliver seemed to be supportive. But what would Mariska be like? Would she be appalled and shy away, or would she be accepting and willing to befriend them? It was so hard to know.

He tried to push the thoughts aside and instead clung to what he did know. He knew he loved Penelope and that he looked forward to seeing her today. He needed to hear her voice. He pulled his cell phone from his pocket and dialed Airhaven. When the receptionist answered, he asked for Penelope. "Tell her that William is calling." He waited for more than five minutes. When Penelope finally came on the line, his heart skipped a beat in response.

"Hi, William."

"Hi, sweetie! I miss you, and I needed to hear your voice. I can't wait to see you. I'll be there in about an hour. How's your day going?"

There was a long pause before she answered. "It's awful. I hate today."

"What happened? What's wrong?"

"I don't want to talk about it. In fact, I don't even want you to come tonight."

William felt as though the wind had been knocked out of him. "Penelope, I want to see you. I can listen and help you through whatever it is."

"I can't be helped. Why don't you understand that?"

"Yes, you can be helped. Listen to you. You're already speaking better. I want to be there for you no matter what. We can talk about it tonight."

"No, William, we can't. I don't want you to come tonight. Just stay away. Please."

William's heart caught in his throat. "Penelope, let me come see you." He heard himself begging like a child, but he didn't care. He didn't want to be pushed away. "I want to spend the rest of today with you. Not just that. I want to spend the rest of my life with you. I'm going to come."

"I don't want you to. Do us both a favor and leave me alone."

The click as she hung up the phone echoed in William's ears. It was loud, and it hurt. It hurt his ears, but it hurt his heart more. He slammed his phone onto the worktable in exasperation. Furiously, he returned to his cleanup tasks, shoving ingredients into containers, slamming lids. She didn't want to see him! Why did she insist on pushing him away, right when she needed someone the most?

Wait. He stopped working for a moment. Had she found a better replacement? What exactly went on all day with that Oliver? The tips of his ears burned at the thought. He slammed cooking utensils into a carrying case. One fell to the ground, and he kicked it, sending it skidding. Promptly, he stomped after it, snatched it from the ground, and stuffed it into the case. He picked the case up to pack it away with the containers and bottles of spices; unfortunately, however, he had forgotten to zip it shut and the contents clattered to the ground. "Goddamn it!"

Heads turned in the direction of the racket, and he remembered where he was. He took a deep breath to calm himself and bent to pick everything up. He was more careful and deliberate this time as he placed everything gently into the case. As he breathed, his anger cooled, and his jealousy faded. He dismissed those thoughts, but he couldn't dismiss the hurt. She didn't want to see him? Fine. He wouldn't go. Maybe it would make her regret her request and realize they should be together after all.

"So, I'd say that this is a successful catering job, wouldn't you? I saw some people come through the line for thirds, and everything is practically gone. What…" Rod had packed up his station and come over to lend William a hand. He was talking as he approached, but he stopped short when he actually looked at William. "Hey. What's up? You look upset."

"Nothing. I'm fine."

"Sure?"

"Yup."

"I noticed Mariska hanging around after I went back to my area. Anything happen with that?"

William grabbed his phone and left the other stuff for Rod and the others to haul to the trucks. Before he stormed away, he looked Rod in the eye and told him to fuck off.

CHAPTER 10

OLIVER WAS ALREADY AWAKE AT SIX FORTY-FIVE ON SATURDAY MORNING, SO HE heard the tech in the day area as she progressed from door to door, waking the patients. Every morning it was the same: The sound of knuckles rapping on a wooden door. Knock, knock, knock. Three times in quick succession. Oliver wondered about that. Why three quick taps? Was it part of some handbook for dealing with people with mental health issues? Maybe it was for patients with obsessive compulsive disorder. Or maybe the techs, the night techs who did this as the last part of their shift, had OCD themselves. Or was three a magic number that would summon a magic genie, who would come poofing out of something and cure everyone? If that were the case, it wasn't working. At any rate, it was knock, knock, knock. Then a short pause as the tech pushed the patient's door open slightly. Next came the call, lilting, almost like a song, in a voice slightly raised in pitch, like a mother crooning to a young child. "Good morning! Time to get up!" A longer pause as the tech waited for the patient to stir and acknowledge that he or she was awake. A few steps by the tech to the next door and once again, knock, knock, knock. "Good morning! Time to get up!"

When she arrived at Oliver's door this Saturday morning, he didn't stir in acknowledgement. He remained curled in a ball, buried in his blankets, because he simply did not want to get up and face another day. He keenly felt his loss, and it was all-encompassing. He pretended to be asleep. "It's morning. Time to get up," she repeated. He didn't know her name because he didn't have much to do with the night staff, seeing them in the middle of the night only occasionally when he needed his bathroom unlocked. He breathed deeply to feign slumber. She flipped the lights on and took a few steps into the room. "Oliver, you need to get up. It's almost seven o'clock. Breakfast will be here soon."

Still, he ignored her.

She took a few more steps, placed a hand on his shoulder, and shook gently. "Oliver?" Nothing. "Oliver," she repeated more loudly and firmly. Clearly, she was not going to go away.

"I feel ill. I need to stay in bed." It wasn't a total lie.

"Okay. You just lie there and rest." She left him alone.

Really? He should have tried this days ago. No sooner had he settled back into his misery, though, than a new voice interrupted him. "Hey, Oliver. I'm glad I get to start my day with you, but it's too bad it's because you're not feeling well. What's going on?" Jennifer sat down on the edge of his bed.

Oliver sighed. He said nothing.

"Can you roll onto your back for me? I need to see you so I can figure out what's wrong."

"Everything's wrong." He stayed on his side.

"I'm sorry." She paused. "I need you to roll over."

With another sigh, he complied. She took his temperature, listened to his heart and lungs, took his pulse, and looked in his throat. She did a quick visual assessment too, and when she studied his face, Oliver wondered if she could see that he didn't feel well the way Maggie always could. Maggie. He never used to have to tell her when he was sick. He could just stand there in front of her and she could see it. Maggie always told him that he radiated misery when he was sick, and that his eyes, dull, red-rimmed, and underscored with dark circles, were what gave him away the most. Maggie always took such good care of him. She had always been there for him. But he hadn't been there for her. He moaned and covered his face with his arms.

For a moment, he had forgotten that Jennifer was there, and he startled slightly when she spoke. "By looking at you, I can tell that you aren't feeling in top shape. But it's not because of a physical illness, which means you need to get up. Getting ready for the day and having some breakfast will be good for you."

Good for him? How could those things possibly be good for him when he dreaded them with all his might? Who was Jennifer to know what was good for him? And he didn't deserve something good for him, anyway. He rolled back over onto his side to face the wall and drew his knees up against his torso.

"I'm glad that you moved, but that's the wrong direction."

"I don't want to get up."

"Do you feel that you can't do it, or you won't do it?" Jennifer's tone wasn't challenging. She was merely asking kindly.

"Both," he whispered.

"Okay. I'm going to let you stay here for a little while. I'll be back with your morning medication in a minute though."

When she returned, Oliver barely sat up. He remained on his side, facing the wall, but propped himself up slightly on his elbow. Jennifer handed him the little white paper cup, and he looked at its contents: a group of colorful little pills, some round, some oval, that included an antidepressant, an anti-anxiety medication, the nightmare-fixer, and something they called an atypical antipsychotic that was supposed to help the other ones do their jobs. This little concoction that he took several times each day was supposed to make everything better?

"Staring at them isn't going to make them work for you, Oliver. You actually have to swallow them."

He couldn't summon his voice to state what he was thinking, that unless these pills could change the past and bring Maggie and Henry back, they weren't going to do a damn thing to help him. He sighed and dumped the contents of the cup into his mouth. Jennifer handed him a cup of water. He took a drink and swallowed, but only the water went down. The pills stayed in his mouth. Their bitterness was repulsive. It took three attempts before they washed down. Even then, though, they didn't go all the way down but stuck in his throat. He cleared his throat and swallowed the rest of his water to dislodge them. It didn't work. They seemed to swell and burn in his throat, but when Jennifer offered him more water, he shook his head and plopped back down onto his pillow. He'd just deal with it, and maybe, just maybe, the pills would expand and choke him to death. He could only hope.

"I'm going to let you be for now, but you'll have to get up pretty soon. You can't spend your whole Saturday morning in bed." She left the lights on and the door open when she exited.

Saturday morning in bed. He and Maggie used to love their weekend mornings in bed. Sometimes they were up early, but when they didn't have to be, they would lounge in bed, reading the paper together and discussing its contents. After Henry was born, he became part of their relaxed weekend mornings. They'd scoop him up out of his crib and bring him into their bedroom. Instead of reading the paper, they read children's books aloud to him. As he grew, he held some himself. He'd chew on the corners, and they'd joke that he was thoroughly digesting the story. By the time he was three, he had parts of some of the stories memorized, and he'd fill in the words when his parents paused. Oliver used to love weekend mornings.

This Saturday morning, like all of the mornings since that tragic day just over four months ago, was not like those other ones at all. Now his mornings were desolate and torturous. He squeezed his eyes shut, curled himself up even tighter, grabbed a fistful of the weighted blanket, and pressed his fists hard into his eyes. He remained like that for a long time as the clock on his wall loudly ticked away the seconds, each click shrieking at him that he would never again hear the sounds of weekend morning togetherness with his family.

His muscles eventually cramped, but he didn't care. He remained like he was, feeling all the agony. After thousands of ticks of the clock, two chairs scraped across the floor of his room. He wasn't expecting it, and the sudden noise scared him. He jerked into a sitting position and inched himself back against the wall at the head of his bed, pulling his blanket up and hugging it against him as he did so. He panted heavily and looked around the room wildly. Doctor Willis and Matt sat beside his bed in the chairs that they had dragged across his floor, one from the desk under the window, and one from the day area. Matt held a tray of food on his lap.

Dr. Willis spoke first. "Still jumpy, I see. Is it always this bad, or has it improved?" As always, she was businesslike.

Oliver hadn't yet recovered. He sat wordless and winded.

Matt spoke on his behalf. "I've noticed that he's a little less jumpy. It takes more to alarm him than when he first arrived, but he still startles fairly easily."

Dr. Willis addressed Oliver. "What about your nightmares? Are they any better?"

Still a little breathless, Oliver managed to answer. "The images are less vivid. But I still feel just as awful when I wake up from them."

"Still the same nightmare?"

Oliver nodded. "I think so. The feeling is the same."

"How many times each night does it recur?"

Oliver shrugged. "I don't know. I lose count. I'm sorry."

Dr. Willis gave him a small smile. "That's okay. That answer tells me what I need to know. These medications do take time to fully work, and you've been on them for less than a week. Still, I think you need stronger doses of prazosin and propanolol." She scribbled notes on the legal pad she carried. "How's your mood?"

"Peachy. I feel like I'm on an extended vacation in the South of France."

She ignored his comment and read his annotated file instead. "I'm increasing your nortriptyline, your antidepressant, too. Aside from the nightmares, how's your sleep? Can you get to sleep and stay asleep between nightmares?"

"I don't know. Kind of, I guess."

Dr. Willis thought for a minute. "I think I'm going to leave your sleep medication alone for the time being. I don't want to increase everything at once." The room stayed silent as she studied his chart. "I still want you to have the lorazepam during panic attacks or flashbacks. It looks like the dose I've prescribed works fairly well, so I'm going to leave that alone, too."

"I don't want any of it, Dr. Willis. Please don't make me take it." His voice was almost a whine.

"I want to hear about that. As we talk, I want you to have breakfast."

At that cue, Matt handed Oliver a tray containing lumpy oatmeal, a little cup of brown sugar to stir into it, some toast that by now was surely cold and soggy, and a glass of apple juice. Oliver shook his head. "I don't want that, either. I'm not hungry."

Dr. Willis remained clinical. "A lack of appetite often accompanies major depressive disorder, but that doesn't change the fact that your body needs the nutrition and energy. Start with a single bite of toast or cereal, your choice."

Oliver sighed and made no move to pick up anything on his tray.

"This is important, man. Seriously. Take a bite of something." Matt's voice sounded almost pleading, so Oliver tried to do as he was told. He picked up the spoon and poked it through the thick oatmeal. He collected a small amount and, hand trembling, shoveled it into his mouth. Despite his best efforts, it wouldn't go down. He gagged. With great difficulty, he held the pasty goo in his mouth as he watched the doctor and the tech watch him. Matt urged, "Swallow it. It's okay. You can do it."

Oliver wondered if this was how Henry had felt when he stubbornly sat in his high chair while his parents tried to get him to eat something he didn't like. That thought wasn't helpful at all. Forcing the oatmeal past the sad memories that welled up and settled in his chest and throat was no easy task, but he did it.

"There. I ate breakfast." He clunked the spoon back down on the tray, leaned back against the wall, and closed his eyes.

"Is eating always this difficult?" Dr. Willis asked.

Oliver nodded. "Like I said, I'm not hungry. I always feel too full."

Dr. Willis let the subject drop. "I see you're not actively participating in any of the groups."

Oliver shrugged. He was despondent.

"The services we offer here might not be able to help you. I'm considering transferring you to a hospital."

"Isn't that where I am?"

"No. People tend to use that word for us, but this is technically a behavioral health center."

"So? What's the difference?"

Matt spoke. "We're structured differently. You have more freedom here, and while you have individual sessions with a psychiatrist in both places, here we're centered on group therapy and other activities. A psychiatric ward in a traditional hospital is more sterile. Given your history, they'll hook you up to an IV for nutrition and medication, and you'll be pretty much confined to a hospital room other than for, perhaps, a couple of groups that are far different from ours. You'll probably have a roommate separated from you only by a curtain. It's not a place you want to be."

"Whatever. Nothing even matters anymore anyway. This is all part of my punishment. I'll just endure the torture until I can finally die." His voice faltered.

Dr. Willis said, "We're not threatening you or trying to punish you. You might need to be transferred, but I don't want to jump the gun."

Oliver reacted involuntarily. Instantly, he paled and inhaled sharply.

Dr. Willis observed him and scrawled something in her notes before addressing him. "There was something that I said that you didn't like. Tell me about that reaction."

"Uh, well...I don't know."

"You didn't react before when I mentioned the possibility of a transfer. Was it my phrase about jumping the gun?"

Oliver bit his cheeks.

"I think you reacted to that phrase for a reason."

He bit his lip.

"We can't help you unless we know about what happened," said Dr. Willis.

Oliver remained silent.

"I don't think I want to transfer you quite yet after all. We have more to learn about you. And also, as I think about it, you might not be participating in the groups, but at least you're attending. What is it that's getting you there?"

"You ordered me to go to them."

"There's more to it than that. You were told to get up this morning but you didn't. Something other than my orders is getting you to the groups. Why are you going?"

Oliver thought before answering, but not for long. "Because I've seen how people shun Penelope, and I don't think that's very nice. She's a good person who deserves to be treated better. I don't want to go to the groups, but I also don't want her to think I'm avoiding her. She needs a friend."

"That's very compassionate of you. And it tells me there's a part of you that is still connected to this world." She paused and appeared to be thinking. "Today, I have a specific assignment for you. As you sit with Penelope in the groups, you need to pick one thing to do in the group of your choice. You can be an observer in the other groups, but in one group you have to participate. Okay?"

Silence hung heavy in the room. Oliver felt as though he were being crushed. Finally, he mumbled, "I really don't want to."

"Go on," Dr. Willis prompted.

He sighed deeply. "Do you have any idea how it feels to be doing things without my wife and son? And knowing that they can never, ever do anything again?" His voice had risen in pitch in response to his increasing emotional distress. He swallowed hard and kept himself in check.

Dr. Willis leaned forward and quietly responded, "I can't even begin to guess what that would be like. Can you tell me?"

He looked at her with a pained expression. "It's...it's awful. I..." His eyes welled with tears, and he looked away. He knew if he tried to say anything further, he would cry in earnest. He just shook his head.

"I'm still giving you that assignment," Dr. Willis spoke softly. "Why don't you do something in one of the art groups? Perhaps make something to honor your wife and son, something to put up here in your room as a tribute to them."

Slowly, Oliver nodded.

"Nice. Very good." She stopped again to give him the opportunity to speak. When he said nothing, she informed him gently, "Now it's time to get up and moving. Tell me one thing you can do to feel better right now."

"Feeling better is impossible, and I don't want to anyway."

"You know what? For the moment, that's okay. So tell me, instead, one thing that's going to get you up and out of this room."

Oliver was quiet as he thought. Both Dr. Willis and Matt gave him space. Finally, he answered, "I'd like to check on Penelope. I don't want her to think that I'm hiding from her."

"That works. Connection to others is important for her and for you, too. But Oliver," Dr. Willis cautioned, "you can't hide behind Penelope to avoid your own healing. It's great that you want to be kind to her, but first and foremost, you're here to help your-self." She paused to let that sink in before continuing. "After you've showered and otherwise prepared for the day and you go out into the day area, Matt will bring you some Ensure. Let's at least get that into you and we'll gradually work on real food."

She stood, and Matt did the same.

"We're going to leave you to get ready for the day. I trust in your compassion for Penelope, so I know you're going to get up. I'll see you again on Monday, and I'm looking forward to seeing what you create in the art group today."

Matt remained after Dr. Willis left. "I'm glad you're sticking around."

Oliver looked him in the eyes. He wanted to respond, but he couldn't. He gave a small sigh and tried a weak smile.

Matt smiled back. He then unlocked Oliver's bathroom and left him alone to get ready to face another day.

CHAPTER 11

Oliver stepped out of his room and found Penelope at their usual table off to one side of the day area. She sat with her elbows on the table and her forehead resting in her hands. Her hair was pulled back into a ponytail this morning, and he could see her profile. She appeared to be talking. Oliver reached the table, greeted her, and pulled out the chair across from her.

"No! Don't sit in that one or you'll crush Mrs. Roosevelt!"

He moved to a chair beside Penelope and sat down. She gave him no further acknowledgement; instead, she continued her conversation with Eleanor Roosevelt. Oliver could hear Penelope's portion of the conversation, and he listened with interest.

"But you *are* my heroine, Mrs. Roosevelt. I have always admired you. You know that."

How do you know what I know?

"You're right. I don't know what you know. I'm sorry. I hope you know that I admire you."

How would I know that I'm your heroine? You're trying to make me go away.

"No! It's not that. It's just—"

It's just what? If you aren't trying to make me disappear, why are you sitting here at Airhaven, lounging around all day like a schmuck, taking pills to kill me?

"I just want to have a normal life with William."

So now you're not normal because of me? You think I'm a freak!

"Please don't shout at me!" Penelope hands flew to cover her ears. "I'm sorry. I didn't mean that. Of course I don't think you're a freak."

That's because I'm not a freak. Am I, Penelope? I am not the freak here. Who's a freak Penelope? Who?

"I am. I'm the one who's a freak, Mrs. Roosevelt. I'm nothing but an abomination."

Don't you ever forget that. You're lucky that I chose you. I should have chosen someone else. But I chose you because I liked you. And now you don't like me anymore. You want me to go away. That hurts my feelings, Penelope. I'm so sad.

"Oh, please don't cry, Mrs. Roosevelt! I'm sorry. I'm really not trying to kill you."

Yes you are. That's why you're taking all those pills. You know it, too. You think you're so great, so intelligent because you're speaking on your own now. But that doesn't make you special, Penelope. You were special because I controlled your thoughts and helped you speak. I let you channel me. You and I were going to be a team together. My greatness would be in the world again, and I was doing it as part of you. But you don't want that. You just want to kill me. You said I was your heroine but, in reality, you're embarrassed by me and want me dead."

"No! I don't want you dead! I do want your greatness in the world again. But I hate losing myself. And William. I love him, Mrs. Roosevelt, and I'm sad that he can't have a good life now."

I'm sad, too, Penelope. Sad because you're so ungrateful and mean to me. You can feel my sadness. I know you can. You can feel how miserable I feel. Those pills are poisoning me.

"They make me sick, too, Mrs. Roosevelt."

That's because they're toxic.

"I don't feel good when I take them."

Good. I hope they kill you.

"I would rather be dead than live like this."

You mean, ungrateful, bitch! I'll show you. I'm not letting you kill me. Get rid of the pills you took at breakfast. Now!

"What?"

You heard me! Get rid of them. I don't want to die.

"I'll get in trouble. I'm supposed to have them."

Expel them now! They're making you nauseous anyway. Throwing up will fix that. You'd be doing us both a favor.

"What will William think? He'll think I don't want to get better for him."

You'll be doing him a favor, too. You said it yourself: he can't have a good life now. You're no good with or without the pills. When you're on your medication, you feel sick and unmotivated. And don't forget how fat they're making you, too. Don't do that to him. Or to me. Throw up those pills!

Penelope crammed her fingers down her throat and began to gag.

"Penelope! Stop! What are you doing?" Oliver lurched forward and grabbed her arm. Quickly, but gently, he pulled her arm away. She resisted and tried to put her hand back to her mouth. "No. Don't. Just relax." With his other arm, Oliver rubbed her shoulder, causing her muscles to loosen. Soon, he could place her arm down on the table, but he held his hand lightly over hers and continued rubbing her shoulder. They sat this way in silence, Penelope's head bowed, and Oliver watching her in concern. Minutes passed before Matt arrived at their table with Oliver's Ensure.

Matt sat down in the same chair that Oliver had originally chosen; the one Penelope had told him belonged to Mrs. Roosevelt, but Penelope didn't stop him. Oliver asked, "Is it okay for Matt to sit there?"

Penelope nodded. "Yes. She's gone now. She's been disappearing more and more since Dr. Daniels made my medication stronger."

"Are you talking about Mrs. Roosevelt?" Matt asked.

"Yes."

"It's good that she's starting to leave you alone. She'll be around less and less as your meds really kick in, but it takes time."

"We just had a fight about it."

"And it looks like you survived."

"I don't know about that."

"You don't have to. Don't judge. Just listen to the words I said and let them be with you."

"Okay."

"Atta girl."

"I'm a freak," Penelope declared without looking up.

"Hmm. I don't think so. And it looks like Oliver doesn't think so."

"No, Penelope. I don't think you're a freak."

Penelope looked up at Matt and Oliver. A corner of her mouth turned up in a small, crooked smile. "What's that for?" she asked Matt when she noticed the bottle in his hand.

"Oh. This is for Oliver." Matt twisted the cap, and it came off with a crack, seemingly warning Oliver's stomach that something was on the way. His stomach twisted in protest. Matt slid the bottle over to him.

Oliver removed his arm from Penelope's shoulder and held the bottle with both hands. He toyed with it, but made no move to drink it.

"Oliver, you really have to drink this."

Slowly, he brought the bottle to his lips. He took a small sip and put the bottle back down on the table.

"Keep that up and you'll have it gone just in time for lunch," Matt teased.

"I'm sorry. I can't guzzle it down."

"No need to be sorry. I was joking with you."

"Sorry."

"You sure apologize a lot. It's okay to drink this slowly. Take it with you to music group and work on it as you listen."

"Don't you need to watch me to make sure I drink it?"

"Your friend will help with that, won't you Penelope?" Matt looked at her. "It's really important for Oliver to drink all of this. Can you make sure he does?"

"Yes, of course. I'd like to do something helpful. Matt's right, Oliver. You're positively gaunt. You need this."

"Thanks. I knew I could count on you. Now you two should head to the group room and settle in before it starts."

When they entered the group room, someone other than Frank was at the head of the table preparing the music. Penelope knew him. "Good morning, Balan."

"Good morning, Penelope, and happy day to you! Who is this with you?"

"This is my new friend, Oliver. He arrived this week. Oliver, this is Balan. He's really talented. He leads the music group and both art groups on the weekends. He's from India, and I love his accent."

"Accent? What accent? It is you who has the accent." Balan laughed. Turning his attention to Oliver, he shook his hand and gave him a hearty welcome before resuming his preparations for the group. Oliver and Penelope sat down, and Penelope made him drink his breakfast.

Balan signaled that the group would begin. To Oliver's relief, he began the group with a different ritual than did Frank. However, his opener still involved sharing, but rather than asking the participants to share one good thing, he tossed a beach ball to someone. Many questions were written on it, and the person who caught it answered the question closest to their right thumb and then tossed the ball to someone else. While Oliver was glad to have a break from Frank's opener, he certainly didn't enjoy this activity, either. He worried about what question he would get, rather than paying full attention to the activity. He didn't see the ball come at him diagonally. From his perspective, it came out of nowhere, bonking him on the head and thoroughly shocking him. He turned and retrieved the ball from the floor behind him and held onto it with sweaty, shaky hands. His heart pounded and his head throbbed. He was supposed to read his question aloud and then respond, but he couldn't speak. He merely sat, holding the ball and breathing heavily.

Balan was at his side. "Why don't you hand it to Penelope? She can take her turn and then give it back to you." Oliver nodded and followed the suggestion.

Penelope took the ball but ignored it. She watched as Balan spoke quietly to Oliver. When she continued to sit there, staring, Balan instructed her to read her question. "But I want to help," Penelope replied.

"Keeping the focus on the activity will be helpful."

"Okay." She read her question aloud, "What are you most proud of?" After pausing to reflect, she answered, "I used to be proud of myself. I graduated from the University of Chicago and worked as an advertising executive at Anderson Fletcher." She paused and hugged the beach ball against her chest. When she resumed, she spoke quietly. "But then I changed, and I'm not the same anymore. I had to take quit the job I loved. At first, I thought I could take a leave of absence, just a little break to get well and then go back. But I never got better enough to go back. I had to quit completely, and now I'm just a loser." Tears rolled down her cheeks and splashed onto the ball. "Here you go, Oliver. It's your turn, if you're ready." She held the ball out to him.

He was still dizzy from the surprise of being hit with the ball, but listening to Penelope had helped him calm down and reconnect to the world outside himself. He touched the ball but did not remove it from her hands. "Penelope, you're a great person. It sucks that you had to quit your job, but that doesn't make you a loser."

"Thank you for telling her that, Oliver. Let's let her think about that as you read your question," Balan prodded him to keep the group moving forward.

Oliver looked at his hands and read the question near his thumb, "If you could invent one thing that could make the world a better place, what would it be?" He didn't have to give that one a second thought. He instantly knew the answer. "I would make something that would bring back my family." He shoved the ball across the table, letting it roll toward no one in particular, and pressed the heels of his hands hard into his eyes. He remained that way for the rest of the group, letting the music wash over him. Penelope spent the duration of the group with her arms folded in front of her and her head on the table.

At the conclusion of the last song, Balan spoke. "This seemed to be an emotional session for almost all of you today. What a good, shared, group experience. Yes, many of you seem to feel sad right now, but vocalizing your thoughts and honoring your feelings are actually important aspects of the healing process. Let us end today with a peppy song that will hopefully be an inspiration. It is about taking charge of your life. As you listen, I would ask you to reflect on what will happen when, like it says in the song, you open your window even just a small crack. What will be different? I invite you to write in your journals about this." He let the group listen to Natasha Bedingfield's *Unwritten*. Oliver didn't have his journal with him, but he did listen to the lyrics. His only thought as he listened was that he didn't want to do as the lyrics said. He didn't want to open up his dirty window, because there was nothing left for the sun to illuminate. He didn't want a different life without Maggie and Henry.

☙

As they waited in the other group room for Balan to arrive and begin the first art group, Oliver and Penelope sat together, away from the other participants, and conversed quietly. Oliver had positioned himself so he could see the door and the movement of others and thus keep watch to avoid being startled. They were discussing *Unwritten*. "Anyway, I don't think that song is very realistic," Penelope informed Oliver matter-of-factly. "I mean, it's not that easy just to write your future. I was writing mine, but then my brain went haywire. I am a schizophrenic. Period. End of story."

"Why does it have to be the end of your story, Penelope? Your story is different now, but it's not over."

"But I'm not in charge of it anymore, so it feels like it's over."

"Well, the characters are still the same, right?"

"Eleanor Roosevelt didn't used to be in my story, Oliver."

"But William was, and he still is."

"I don't think he should be. This is a stupid 'book.'" She made air quotes with her fingers. "It's bad enough that I have to deal with this. I love William, and I don't want to make him have a life of suffering because of me. Like I said, my story is over." She wiped tears from her face.

"It doesn't have to be over."

"You're a good one to talk. What about your story?"

What about his story? His was different. His was very much over, or at least it would have been if that landing pad hadn't been there. Penelope still had love in her life; her main character was very much alive. But his own beloved characters would never, ever be in his story again, no matter how he tried to "write" it. He couldn't answer her. He squeezed his eyes shut and hung his head.

"Oh, Oliver, I'm sorry. I didn't mean to make you feel bad." Penelope tugged on his sleeve until he looked at her, and she whispered, "I don't know how to act around people anymore. I say and do such stupid things. I hate myself, and I'm really, really sorry that I made you hate me, too. I didn't hurt you on purpose." The tears rolled freely down her face, and she didn't even try to wipe them off.

Oliver stuffed his emotions down and focused on Penelope. "You didn't do anything wrong. I don't hate you. Far from it, in fact. I think you're a great friend."

Balan entered the room in a rush of joyful energy, thus sparing Oliver from continuing the conversation. "Look at all of these wonderful faces, ready for art! Today, we will be making sock puppets." He plopped a large container onto the table and pulled off the lid. "Let us begin with a story..."

Oliver tuned out immediately. "Penelope," Oliver whispered in a panicky voice, "Dr. Willis said I had to do something in art today, but I can't make a sock puppet. My son, uh, he..." His voice cracked, and he paused. "What am I going to do?"

Penelope sat stiff and unmoving. Without warning, at the top of her voice she screamed. "Not sock puppets! Not sock puppets! Not sock puppets! No, Mrs. Roosevelt, calm down!" Then she grabbed a handful of materials from the tub and threw them at the wall. She grabbed a second handful and threw it at a different wall. "No! Stop that, Mrs. Roosevelt. I know you're scared of puppets, but you can't do that! Oh, yeah? Watch me!" And Penelope threw some more materials, straight up in the air this time so that they rained down on some of the people in the room.

Balan tried to stop her. "Penelope! Please stop this. Do you need to leave the room?"

"Mrs. Roosevelt is upset. We need to leave. Now!"

Oliver sprang into action. "I'll take her out so you can have the group, Balan."

He took Penelope's hand and led her out of the room as she continued to scream, "Not sock puppets! Not sock puppets! Not sock puppets!"

People were still sitting around the day area, and, given that Penelope was still shouting, he didn't want to subject her to continued stares and scorn. He led her all the way across the day area and into the dining room, where they could sit down behind a closed door. Yes, there was glass that people could see through, but at least they would have semi-privacy. He helped her into a seat then sat down beside her. "It's okay, Penelope, we're out of there. No more sock puppets. It's okay now, see? Look around you."

She quieted down and declared, "There, that did the trick, didn't it?"

"What?"

"Pretending that Mrs. Roosevelt was afraid. It got us out of there so you don't have to make a sock puppet."

"Penelope!"

"Why are you surprised? I thought you knew I was faking it."

"I didn't." His brow furrowed as he studied her. "Thank you. I really didn't want to be there. That was a very brave thing to do. I'm sorry that you had to do that. Did it bother you?"

"Don't be sorry. It actually didn't bother me. I was in control of it, and I did it to help you get out of there, so I actually feel good about it." She smiled. It was the first time Oliver had seen her fully smile. "It was kind of funny, really."

He gave a small smile in return. "Yeah, it was. Especially when socks, ribbons, and buttons landed on people."

"I did that on purpose."

"Penelope?"

"What?"

"Thank you. I really appreciate it."

CHAPTER 12

OLIVER WAS FILLED WITH DREAD AS HE AND PENELOPE HEADED TO THE GROUP room after lunch for a second attempt at an art group. Penelope had saved him from the last one, but there was no escaping this one. Dr. Willis had ordered him to make something in an art group today, and this was now his only chance. As much as he didn't want to do it, he also didn't want to be sent away from Airhaven. Not now. Not when Penelope needed a friend.

When they entered the room, some participants stared and others blatantly averted their gaze. As usual, Oliver and Penelope sat in the back of the room. Other people came in, but not a single person sat next to them, and the chairs on either side of them remained empty. Penelope leaned toward Oliver and whispered, "I wonder if people just hate me or if they're afraid they might catch what I have. It's been like this for almost two years. Do you see why I can't do this to William? I don't want him to be shunned by the world because of me. It feels really awful, and I can't do that to him." She looked down at her hands and picked at her nails.

Oliver had never been a violent person, but at that moment, he wanted to strangle the people who were being so insensitive. These people were also in a behavioral health hospital. Shouldn't they, of all people, have a little empathetic understanding? If people here reacted to her this way, what must others, who had no experience with mental health struggles, be like?

"I realize I don't know William very well, but from what I've seen, he isn't like these others. It seems to me he cares about you, not about them."

"And I care about him. I can't subject him to this any longer. It hurts so much, Oliver."

"What hurts? The idea of 'subjecting him to this,' or the idea of leaving him?"

"Both!"

Oliver reached for one of the ever-present boxes of tissues and handed it to her. He hated the world, and he didn't want to be sitting here in this stupid group room. How in the hell was art therapy supposed to change a damn thing?

As if that thought were his cue, Balan started the group. He got right to the point. "We cannot change the past. We can, however, find beauty in life. We can also shape our lives by what we choose to focus on. What is beautiful to you? What is your focus? With these questions in mind, I would like each of you to create a collage. Take charge of it." He offered a bit more commentary and direction as he spread dozens of magazines around the table, passed around a pile of large construction paper, and distributed scissors and glue. He put in a jazz CD and instructed the group to begin.

Oliver sighed and reached for the magazine closest to him. He didn't care what it was. He considered cutting out random images and gluing them down just to make it look like he was participating. But he remembered Dr. Willis's comment that he should make something to honor Maggie and Henry, and that she wanted to see it on Monday. He had to make somewhat of an effort to appear like he had taken this seriously. He studied the magazine in his hand. It was a *Newsweek* issue about the European economic crisis. That surely wouldn't contain anything useful. He tossed it back. He leaned forward and sifted through the pile. None looked right. With another sigh, he grabbed a couple more, opened one up, and began to page through it. He saw words and shiny, glossy pictures. All meaningless. He kept turning pages. How, exactly, was he supposed to "honor" Maggie and Henry? Here was an ad for lotion. Stupid. He turned the page. How about fertilizer? Nope. An article about technology? Pointless. Oh, gee, cookies. How profound. Really, a Nestlé Toll House ad? He started to turn the page, but then he paused and stared at it. Henry had loved chocolate chip cookies. God, he made a mess with them, but it was fun. He would sit on the counter while his parents made the cookies. Oliver would help him sit still—no easy task—and Maggie would let him pour the ingredients into the bowl. The first time Henry "helped," he kept picking up the mixing bowl and dumping out the contents, but once he figured out that the end result was a yummy treat, he kicked the habit. Every time they baked, Henry would pour and help stir, and then he'd sit on a little stool in front of the oven and watch the cookies bake. Then he'd sit in his high chair willingly and take absolute delight in squishing them, smashing them, squeezing them, and shoveling them into his mouth.

Oliver rubbed his finger thoughtfully over the image, tracing the outline of the cookies and moving from chocolate chip to chocolate chip as if completing a connect-the-dots picture. The image blurred. He blinked hard. No. He would not break down. Unexpectedly, the idea of having the picture of a plate of chocolate chip cookies felt extremely important, and he reached for a pair of scissors and slowly, meticulously, cut around the edges. He took extreme care to cut perfectly, and then he carefully ran a glue stick along the back and gingerly pressed it down onto the paper in front of him. The paper looked empty. He needed more pictures. He resumed his search through the magazine. He flipped only three pages before finding a picture of a wildflower meadow. Maggie had created a beautiful flower garden in their backyard. Approaching this picture as tenderly as he had the one of the cookies, he added this one to his paper, right beside the first one. He resumed his search through the magazine. He discovered music notes. He and Maggie loved music, and Henry was crazy about the parent-toddler music and movement class they had been part of. The music notes went beside the wildflowers.

He added a construction site to his neat row of images because he and Maggie would take Henry for stroller rides, and any time they passed construction in progress, they stopped and watched, sometimes for nearly an hour, because Henry was fascinated by the big machines in motion. He found a picture of a courthouse. Maggie had been a lawyer, a passionate one, and a damn good one, too. He removed it from the magazine but cut around the images of the people in the picture because those people weren't Maggie. He had time to add one more image, an umbrella that reminded him of long walks in the rain with Maggie, before Balan stopped the group.

Oliver studied his paper. Six images marched neatly and orderly across the page. They tugged at his heart. He fought the urge to rip it to shreds. Maggie and Henry were so much more than the six, two-dimensional images glued onto white construction paper! He couldn't bring himself to do it though. How could he destroy something that represented, even in a small way, his cherished little family? He picked it up and hugged it to his chest. Balan asked him if he wanted to share. Oliver tried to look neutral and nonchalant, but his chin trembled and belied what he was trying to portray. He shook his head, and Balan moved on.

Oliver needed to focus on something else. He turned to Penelope to see what she had created, but he found an empty seat. She was gone! When had she left? He had become so engrossed in his project that he hadn't noticed her leave. He felt horrible, and he jumped up and headed for the door, only to be stopped by Balan. "Hold on there. Nobody is allowed to leave while others are sharing. It is when we have finished and everyone has helped with the cleanup that you may leave."

"I'm sorry." Oliver sat back down. Seven full minutes passed before the group was dismissed, and he was completely agitated by the time he could finally leave. He brushed past people and was the first out of the room, even though he had sat at the back. He spotted her immediately; she was at their table with her head down. He approached her and asked, "Hey, what's the matter? Can I sit beside you?"

"You can, but I don't see why you want to."

"Because I like you and I'm concerned about you," he answered after he sat down. "I'm so sorry I didn't come out here with you. I guess I got lost in what I was doing and spaced out. When I noticed you had left, I tried to leave, too, but Balan wouldn't let me because it was sharing time, and then I had to help clean up. I'm really sorry, Penelope. Why did you leave?"

She kept her head down but turned her face so she could see him. "Because I couldn't do it, Oliver. Mrs. Roosevelt wasn't even there bothering me, and I still couldn't do it. She's disappearing a little bit, but..."

"But what? You can tell me. It's okay."

Her eyes filled with tears. "But there's nothing back in her place. Schizophrenia has destroyed me." She let out a cry and put her face back down into her arms.

Not knowing what to say to make her feel better, Oliver simply rubbed her back. Her body shook in despair.

She sat up and looked at him. "My life is ruined. I don't even know who I am anymore. I used to be so creative, but now I can't even make a stupid collage. I used to think that if only she would go away, then I could be myself again. But now when she's not there, nothing is. Nothing but a sick person."

"You are not a sick person."

"I am! My head hurts so much from that stupid medication. It makes me tired and dizzy and nauseous and I hate it. These pills aren't making my life better. And it's bad enough that my life is over, but knowing that I'm ruining William's life makes it all a million times worse." She sniffed and reached for a tissue. "William's life will be terrible if he stays with me. Either he will have to deal with a crazy, mentally ill person, or a sick, empty, lifeless shell. I'm worthless and unlovable." She plopped her head back down and said nothing further. She only cried.

Claire, the tech who had stopped Penelope from eating crayons the other day, approached them. "Hi there. Looks pretty intense over here. I'd like to join you, but first you have a phone call, Penelope. It's William."

"I don't want to talk to him."

Oliver urged, "Penelope, it's clear that he cares for you a great deal. You should talk to him."

"I don't want to. I care for him too, so I need to get him out of my life. He can't possibly want a life with someone like me."

Claire said, "Wow. I didn't know you had the power to read his mind." Her tone was neutral and non-accusatory.

"I'm not reading his mind. It's just common sense. You heard Mrs. Roosevelt this morning, Oliver. I'm nothing but a freak."

"I didn't hear that."

"God! See? Of course you didn't hear that! It's all me and my craziness. I don't want to be around anyone anymore! I'm not going to ruin William's life!" She stomped off to the set of phones located on the other side of the workstation near the dining room. She stared at the phone for several minutes and then picked it up and made it clear to William that she did not want him to come see her tonight. She banged the receiver down, marched straight into her room, and slammed the door. Seconds later, someone knocked. She ignored the knock until it stopped.

Hospital rules didn't allow patients to enter one another's rooms. So when Penelope refused to answer her door, there was nothing Oliver could do about it. With his collage in his hand, he crossed the day area and entered his own room. He pulled the shade shut and crawled into bed. He slid the collage under his pillow and listened to the agonizing sound of the ticking clock.

CHAPTER 13

As William stormed to his car, his conscience told him to turn around and finish his share of the catering cleanup. He ignored the thought. He would rather face a reprimand on Monday than deal with Rod now. He unlocked his car as soon as he was in range, and when he reached it, he jumped in, slammed the door, started the engine, and lurched into traffic.

His mind reeled. What was wrong with everybody? Rod, a long-term friend of both his and Penelope's, seemed hell-bent on being a jerk. And Penelope didn't want to see him; she had actually told him to stay away. Penelope was his fiancée. He had asked her to marry him for a reason. He loved her, plain and simple. She was a sweet, caring, intelligent, beautiful woman with a zest for life. Yes, he had proposed before she was struck with mental illness. But her struggle with schizophrenia didn't change the core of who she was. Some behaviors had changed; she did things and had beliefs that were "bizarre"—the doctor's term, not William's—and her outward demeanor was different, more "flat" and less enthusiastic. But those things didn't change who she was. Deep down, Penelope was still Penelope. Was he the only one who understood this? Why didn't Penelope realize this? Just last night, they had had a good time, enjoying themselves playing cards with a new friend. Why was she so stubborn?

He had been lost in thought and driving without purpose. Without realizing it, he had driven to the hospital. He parked and sat in his car, debating whether to go inside. After a few minutes, he got out and headed for the building. Her words echoed in his head as he walked toward the door: "Stay away. I don't want you to come tonight." He turned around and went back to his car, but he couldn't bring himself to get in. He didn't want to be pushed away. He loved her, and he needed to see her. He turned and walked back toward the building. In his mind, he heard her say, "Leave me alone." The hurt of the rejection made him stop. He looked up at the hospital and squinted his eyes against the blinding sun. What was she doing up there? What had happened today? She wanted to be left alone? Fine. He spun around and marched back to his car. This time he got in. He started it up, slammed it into reverse, and roared away.

He didn't care where he was going; he was just compelled to drive away. He ended up on the Dan Ryan Expressway. Welcoming the flat stretch of freeway, he maneuvered into the fast lane and accelerated, not caring where he was going. He roared along, accelerating when he could, until he saw the red flashing lights in his rearview mirror. "Son of a bitch." As the officer scribbled out a ticket, William offered neither argument nor explanation; he couldn't argue because he knew he had been driving too fast, and what could he say for an explanation? That he was trying to outrun his feelings? He collected his ticket and headed for home. To add insult to injury, the traffic had increased by then, and the drive home was agonizingly slow and only served to increase his agitation.

He arrived home feeling worse than when he had left the park. He threw his keys on the table by the door and went straight to the kitchen to make himself a gin and tonic. He studied the glass. It was from a set that Penelope had bought for him when they had gone to a Renaissance festival. He downed the contents and made another one. After quickly finishing that one, he went to the bedroom. As he changed his clothes, his eyes fell on the snorkeling picture. He hurried out of the room. In the living room, he found photos, objects—more reminders of Penelope. Everything seemed to accentuate the fact that he was alone, spending the evening without her. He couldn't stand it. He left his apartment. He stood in the hallway, not knowing what to do or where to go. He walked toward the elevator but stopped at a door and knocked. Mariska opened the door and smiled when she saw him. "William! I thought you were going to the hospital."

"Um, yeah, Penelope isn't feeling well and wasn't up to a long visit."

"I'm sorry to hear that. Want to come in?"

"Oh. Uh, sure, I guess. But I can't stay long." He stepped inside, and she shut the door. What the hell was he doing? He stood awkwardly at the door.

Mariska broke the silence. "Welcome to my place." She moved her arm in a sweeping gesture. "I have a lot to do yet to make this into a home; it's pretty bare bones right now. At least I've got some places to sit though, and I'm hoping that hanging some things will jazz it up a bit." She held up a hammer and wiggled it in the air. The motion seemed to break William from his stupefied trance.

"It looks great. I can't believe you're not tripping over boxes and stuff."

"I took the last couple of days off work and have been working in high gear to settle in. Plus, it's not like I have a lot of stuff. I've been waiting for this apartment, so I haven't wanted to accumulate a lot of things that I would have to haul. This way, I can shop for things that will look great here. For now, I'll make do with the prints I have so it doesn't look so sterile and empty."

Sterile and empty. Like a hospital. Guilt twisted at him. Why was he standing here in Mariska's apartment while Penelope was suffering in the hospital? He turned to leave.

"Well, it's looking good already, and I'm sure you'll have fun decorating. Thanks for showing it to me." He grabbed the door handle.

"Wait! You're leaving already?"

"Yeah, I've got a lot to do."

"Okay. But before you go, will you help me hang a couple of things? I really hate to impose, but I've got a couple of big pictures that are difficult for one person to work with. It'll be quick."

He thought for a few seconds. What would be the harm in hanging a couple of pictures? Helping a neighbor wouldn't be betraying Penelope. "Yeah, sure. No problem."

She smiled broadly. "Oh, thanks! They're this way." She talked as they crossed the living room. "So what's it like to be a chef at Gustav's on Michigan?"

"It's pretty incredible. I love what I do."

"It shows. I meant it earlier when I said the meat you grilled was delicious, and I was totally captivated when I watched you today." Her eyes widened. Then she laughed. "Oh, God. That totally made me sound like a stalker! I didn't mean it that way. I was watching your whole crew. I mean, not staring or lurking obsessively in the shadows, or anything, I just noticed when I was walking through, and you, in particular, got my attention..." She groaned and rolled her eyes. "I'm making this worse! Just forget everything I just said." She laughed again.

William couldn't help but laugh in response. "It's okay. I think I know what you mean. My Uncle Jack was a chef. I spent a lot of time with him when I was a kid, and he'd often let me go with him to work. He was good friends with the owner of the restaurant. I'd sit off to the side on a stool they made just for me, and I'd be completely mesmerized by some of the chefs, especially my uncle. He was amazing, a great chef and a great person; he was my hero. From the time I was eight, I knew I wanted to be just like him when I grew up."

"I bet he's honored that you followed in his footsteps. Is he in Chicago? Does he ever get to come see you in action?"

"He was. He did. But he passed away three years ago. He lost a battle with cancer."

"Oh, that's awful. I'm sorry to hear that."

"Yeah, it sucks. He was probably the kindest man on the planet. I'll never understand why good people have to suffer so much." Like Penelope, too. And even Oliver. He stuck his hands into the pockets of his jeans and fell silent.

Mariska said softly, "I really am sorry, William."

He looked at her. "Thanks." He looked away and spotted the pictures on the floor. "You asked me to help you, and I'm just standing here babbling. Let's get these hung so you're a step closer to being settled. Where's the measuring tape?"

"Measuring tape? What for?"

"You want the pictures centered on the wall, don't you? And at the right height? And straight?"

"Oh. Yeah. I usually just eyeball it. It works. See?" She pointed down the hallway to where she had hung a small African mask.

He looked. "Mariska?"

"Pretty good, huh?"

"Let's find the measuring tape. And after we hang these, we'll fix that one, too." He grinned.

She feigned exasperation. "Fine." She walked toward a different room. He followed. "Remember how I said that all of my unpacked boxes were confined to the spare bedroom? Here they are. There's still kind of a lot, I guess, but not too many. I didn't label anything, so I have to open them and dig through them until I find the measuring tape. Do you have time to wait?"

"That's fine. I can help look, unless you've got personal stuff you don't want me digging through."

"No. There are absolutely no shameful secrets or embarrassing things in these boxes. I unpacked those first and hid the stuff." She laughed again. "I'm kidding, of course. You can definitely help look if you want to. I just don't want to make you."

"It's no trouble. I don't mind."

They began to dig through boxes. After about ten minutes, Mariska pulled the measuring tape from a box and held it triumphantly in the air. "Ta-da! Found it."

"I don't suppose I dare ask for a pencil now too?"

"That's easy. I've got some in a drawer in the kitchen. Come on."

When they entered the kitchen, Mariska exclaimed, "Jeez. Where are my manners? Can I get you anything? Beer? Soda? Water?"

William stiffened. He hadn't realized how much he had relaxed, and he was suddenly ashamed of himself. Helping a neighbor hang a couple of things was one thing, but casually socializing was another thing altogether. He needed to get the hell out of there.

"What's wrong?" Mariska asked. "Are you okay?"

"I, uh, I shouldn't be doing this. Let's get those pictures hung, and then I'd better get going."

"Doing what? I merely offered you something to drink. What do you think I'm going to try to do to you?"

He shifted uncomfortably. He felt like an idiot. "Nothing. I'm sorry. I didn't mean anything like that. It's just that..." He paused as he thought of what he wanted to say. He decided to be honest. "It's just that I feel guilty being here when my fiancée is in the hospital. I really care about her, and, well, I just— "

"William," Mariska interrupted, "I'm not trying to seduce you. You're doing me a favor by helping me with the pictures, and giving you something to drink is just a polite thing to do. Nothing more. Would you like something or not?"

His expression betrayed how sheepish he felt. "I'm sorry. If I say that I could really use a beer, would you forgive me for being an ass?"

She smiled at him, and then reached into the fridge and extracted two bottles. "You're not an ass. Far from it, actually." She pulled a bottle opener out of a drawer, popped open the drinks, and handed him one. "Let's take these into the living room and get to work."

Focusing on the tasks at hand helped William lighten up again, as did sipping the beer as he worked. After they hung the two large prints, William said, "Now let me fix that mask. It's interesting. Where'd you get that, anyway?"

"My brother's in the Peace Corps. He gave it to me as a Hanukkah gift last year."

"Wow. That's really cool. Let's do it some justice by hanging it right."

He headed down the hallway. Mariska disappeared into the kitchen and returned with a second beer. She handed him the open bottle and he took it without protest. "Thanks." He moved it in a cheers-like gesture and took a swig. In a matter of minutes, the mask was rehung. They stepped back and admired the work.

"Fine, I admit it, your way is better. From now on, I'll use the measuring tape rather than eyeballing it."

"Or find a handyman. There happens to be one living down the hall from you."

"Now, that's a brilliant idea. I'll remember that."

William's stomach growled loudly. He laughed. "I guess that gives away the fact that I'm famished. I had a quick bowl of cereal before leaving for work this morning, but I haven't eaten since." He took a drink in an attempt to placate his stomach.

"There's irony for you, a professional chef who eats nothing but cereal."

He shrugged. "I was running late this morning and was busy this afternoon."

"Well, what's your excuse now?"

"I'm doing charity work."

"Charity work? Whatever. I don't take charity. And to prove it, I'm buying you dinner. Is ordering a pizza beneath your standards? There's no way I'm attempting to cook for a chef. How about it?"

He considered it as he downed the last of his beer. Maybe it was the two gin and tonics followed by two beers on an empty stomach, or maybe he was simply enjoying casual company, but the idea appealed to him. "Sure. Can we order it now before I die of starvation?"

They plopped down in the living room and conversed while they waited for the pizza. William worked on his third beer and his intense stress melted away. The pizza arrived. They talked and ate. After his hunger disappeared and his fourth beer coursed through his system, he was relaxed enough to talk about Penelope. Once he began, he couldn't stop. He told Mariska of their life together before her diagnosis and their struggles of the last two years. He talked of his concern for her and of the depths of his love. He spoke of the rejection and isolation, what they faced from others as well as how she was starting to reject him. He talked for a long time, and Mariska listened. When he had emptied his heart to her, he stopped talking and sat in silence. He was dizzy. He found his voice again. "Wow. I kind of talked your ear off, didn't I?"

They sat side by side on the couch. She took his hand, and he let her. "I think you really needed to talk."

"Yeah, I guess I did. Thanks for listening."

"Any time. I mean that. And I'd really like to meet Penelope. She sounds like a wonderful person."

"These days, most people only see the schizophrenia."

"That's ignorant. I think you'll find that I'm not like most people."

He studied her. "My uncle would have liked you. He knew Penelope briefly before he died. He liked her too. And I know he would still like her today. I wish he were here."

"He was really important to you, wasn't he?"

"Yeah. He practically raised me. My parents, were, uh, let's just say they were less than stellar. When the abuse got really bad, Uncle Jack let me come stay with him. I was with him more than I was with my parents, and I'm so glad about that. He did so much for me. He was always there for me, even when I was a pain in the ass. I was kind of difficult in middle school and my freshman year of high school, and still he stayed there for me." William's voice quieted. "He only asked one thing in return."

"What did he ask?"

"That I never, ever give up on anyone, the way he didn't give up on me." He was quiet for several minutes. His head spun. So did his heart. When he looked at Mariska, his eyes glistened. "I wish Penelope wouldn't push me away. I don't want to give up on her. I haven't given up on her. I truly love her."

Mariska held his hand tighter. He looked down at their clasped hands. He was confused. To his very core, he believed everything he had just said aloud. But for the first time, he realized that if Penelope cut him out of her life, he would have options. Instantly, he regretted the thought. He was furious with himself for it and dismissed it as only the alcohol talking. He pulled his hand away and stood up, too quickly. His head pounded and he saw stars. Mariska grabbed hold of him to steady him. When his vision recovered, she was very close to him. She felt good. He held onto her and leaned closer. Their lips touched.

He jumped back in horror. "Oh, God. What the hell am I doing? Mariska, I am so sorry. I need to leave. Thanks for a wonderful evening." He practically ran to the door.

"William, wait! Please."

He paused at the door but didn't turn around.

"You didn't do anything wrong. Nothing happened."

He only nodded. "Good night, Mariska."

He stepped out into the hallway and shut the door behind him. He started to walk down the hallway but stopped and leaned against the wall for support. He pressed his back into it and closed his eyes and felt like the scum of the earth. He was standing like that when a door opened and Mariska approached him.

"I was coming to see if you were okay."

"I will be after I go see Penelope tomorrow."

"Do you want to come back inside? Nothing will happen, I promise. We'll just talk, or you can simply crash on my couch."

He shook his head. "I can't. Thanks for the offer though." Saying nothing further, he returned to his own apartment. All the reminders of Penelope were still there. They made him feel worse. Johixilan meowed loudly and bounded at him. "Whoops. I forgot to feed you, didn't I? I even let you down. I'll never let it happen again. I promise. Hear that, Uncle Jack? Penelope? Never, ever. I really do promise." He fed the cat, and then stumbled into bed, cursing himself and aching for Penelope as he fell asleep.

CHAPTER 14

Once again Oliver was awake before the tech began her round of wake-up calls. He had been in bed, sleeping between the bad dreams, since yesterday afternoon, yet he was still exhausted and numb. He wondered how Penelope was. He hadn't seen her since she had stormed into her room after her phone call with William. Oliver had retreated to his room then, too, but Matt eventually dragged him back out for the last group of the day, the group where people were forced to play these strange board games, supposedly to foster interaction that would lead to meaningful discussions. He hated that group. He hated all of the groups. At least he hadn't been forced to go back downstairs to the exercise room, but he wished he could be excused from all of them. Unfortunately, he wasn't. After the last group yesterday, he had knocked on Penelope's door again, but she wouldn't respond. So he had isolated himself in his room. A night tech brought him Ensure and a nurse brought him medication, but other than that he had lain in his bed, acutely aware of his loneliness.

Still lying down, he slid his hand under his pillow and pulled out the collage. The image that caught his attention at this moment was the umbrella. He stared at it for a long time, and then closed his eyes and remembered.

The sky was gray and the air was cool as they walked along the shore of Lake Michigan. Their rain parkas flapped noisily in the wind. For most people, it was not an ideal beach evening. For Oliver and Maggie, though, it was perfect, because the weather almost guaranteed they would have the stretch of shoreline to themselves. They strolled on and on, sometimes talking, sometimes comfortably silent. At one point, they stopped walking and sat on the sand to watch the waves angrily slap the land. A few seagulls played in the wind, calling loudly to each other. Like Oliver and Maggie, the birds decided to park on the beach. He and Maggie watched them prance around at the water's edge, hopping out of the way of the waves. Maggie reached into her backpack and pulled out some crackers. She broke one into pieces and tossed it toward the birds. The wind blew the pieces back to her. She laughed. "Come on," she said "Let's move closer." They approached the birds, who didn't bother to fly away. Maggie tossed the cracker bits again. This time, they made it closer to the seagulls. The birds descended on the crackers in an instant. Maggie tossed more. Other seagulls landed, seemingly out of nowhere. Oliver joined in. A few of the birds began to squabble over some of the bits. Maggie scolded them. "Hey, stop that! There's enough to go around." They scattered more bits, farther apart, causing the birds to spread out too. "Can you believe that, Oliver? Why do living things fight like that?"

"Do you suppose it's a survival thing?"

"I wonder. You'd think they'd figure out that they don't need to attack each other to ensure their own survival."

Oliver absent-mindedly flung another handful at a group of birds and watched as they greedily chased each other away. "Humans don't seem to be able to figure that out. Why should birds?"

Maggie shrugged. "Good point. I'm glad you and I don't treat each other like that. I mean, we have our disagreements, but even then, we don't attack each other."

"I respect you too much to resort to that."

"Ditto." Maggie slipped her arm around him.

The birds complained that they were out of food. Oliver and Maggie resumed their cracker toss. Fat raindrops accompanied the crackers to the ground. Oliver opened the umbrella, but the wind turned it inside out. The rain fell harder, and they ran for shelter. They stood under a lifeguard stand and watched the rain dent the waves. Maggie shivered. Oliver drew her close to keep her warm.

"I'm glad you're here."

"I'm glad you're here, too, Maggie."

"Oliver?"

"Hmm?"

"Where were you when we needed you? You weren't there."

Oliver's eyes flew open, and his heart pounded. He shoved the collage back under his pillow and sat up. He stared at his closet. His clothes from Maggie and his picture were in there. He lurched forward and pulled on the door, hoping that, somehow, it had been unlocked. It moved only slightly because it was still locked. He groaned in despair. He needed to be close to his things, to hold onto what he had of his family. He pulled the blanket off his bed and threw it on the floor in front of his closet, and then threw the pillow on top of it. His gaze fell on the collage that lay exposed on his mattress, and he put it under the pillow. Then, wrapping himself up in his weighted blanket, he lay down and inched himself as close as he could possibly be to what was inside the closet. He was too numb to cry. He just lay there, desolate and hopeless.

After a while came the inevitable knock, knock, knock, "Good morning! Time to get up." The door inched opened. "Oliver, why are you on the floor?"

"Because I didn't want to be on the bed. I'm getting up now." Not that he wanted to get up, but he was absolutely not in the mood to have people poke and prod him to get moving.

"I'm glad." She stepped over him to unlock the bathroom door. "There you go, all ready for you. Do you have everything you need from the supply cart?"

"Yes, thanks."

"Okay. Have a good day. "

He didn't say what was on his mind, that there was no such thing as a good day anymore, that the only thing that would make a day "good" would be the death that would end his suffering and take him to his family. Reluctantly, and with tremendous effort, he pulled himself up off the floor.

He joined Penelope in the day area twenty minutes later. Her mood matched his. Together, they endured the day as it progressed slowly by, coldly marching on with no regard for them whatsoever. Oliver suffered through the music group and the art groups. He was happy that these were the only groups held on Sundays. Penelope had gone out for a smoke break, and he sat alone in the day area when visitors began filtering in. William was the first to arrive. After checking in at the front desk, William scanned the day area. Oliver waved him over.

"Hey, Oliver! Do you know where Penelope is?"

"She went outside for a cigarette. The group should be back soon; they've been out for about ten minutes already."

"Mind if I wait for her here with you?"

Oliver gestured to a chair. William sat. "How was yesterday?"

Oliver shrugged. "Agonizing, like every other day."

"It was for me, too. Penelope told me not to come. I shouldn't have listened. I really missed her. I was looking forward to all of us playing cards again. What happened to her? Do you know why she didn't want me here?"

"She's pretty down on herself. She has it in her head that you'll be better off without her."

"She's wrong!" William was emphatic.

Oliver nodded. "I know. I'm trying to tell her that. I'm sorry."

"It's not your fault."

"They're back." Oliver nodded toward the work station. A small group of patients and two techs rounded the corner from the elevator area and headed toward the day area. Some talked to each other. A few, like Penelope, distanced themselves slightly from the others and walked alone. She looked down as she walked. William didn't wait for her to approach the table. He rushed toward her and threw his arms around her in a tight embrace. Penelope returned the hug, and Oliver lowered his head. His hands were clasped in front of him on the table. To an onlooker, it might have looked like he was praying. He wasn't. He hadn't prayed since he had begged God for their lives in the emergency room that day.

"Oliver, I'm back." Penelope whispered. She didn't move or speak again until he looked up. "I didn't want to scare you," she explained. "Did I do okay?"

"Of course you did." After Penelope and William sat down, Oliver felt uncomfortably out of place. "I'm going to head back to my room so you two can spend the afternoon together."

"Please stay, Oliver," Penelope looked at him imploringly.

"I brought the cards again. I thought it would be fun." Without waiting for a response from Oliver or an objection from Penelope, William began to deal.

"No!" Penelope shoved the cards away before he finished. "This is not a good way for you to spend your Sunday, William! You should be out living a normal life with a normal person."

"Don't tell me how I should be spending my Sunday, Penelope!" The hurt and frustration were apparent in his voice. "I'm doing exactly what I want to do, if you don't mind."

"Actually, I do mind. I mind very much."

"You didn't seem to mind a minute ago when you hugged me."

"That's because I love you. And that's why I want you to go away. Go live a normal life."

"That's a funny way of showing me you love me."

"I'm sorry you don't like it. But it's the only thing I have left to give you. I give you your freedom."

"Goddamn it, Penelope! You're not listening to me."

"How can I listen to you when Eleanor Roosevelt always yaks at me? This isn't what you bargained for when you proposed to me. I don't accept your marriage proposal anymore." She ran to her room and slammed the door.

"Penelope!" William followed her and knocked on her door, but she wouldn't answer.

He stomped back to Oliver. "She wants me to leave! She wants me to leave? Fine. Tell her to have a nice life." He pivoted and hurried toward the elevator.

Believing in his heart that this was not truly what either of them wanted, Oliver caught up with William and grabbed his arm. "Stop. Let's talk. Come into the dining area with me where we can shut the door."

William just looked at him.

"Please," Oliver continued. "I know you care about her."

"Fine," William huffed. He went with Oliver into the dining room where he stormed across the room and stood with his back to Oliver, gazing out the window.

Oliver leaned against a table waiting for William to turn around so he could talk to him. Out of the corner of his eye, he saw Matt enter the room and stop just inside the door. Oliver ignored him and focused on William. Even from behind, it was obvious that his arms were folded tightly against his chest. William's hurt and anger were palpable in the small room. Oliver spoke quietly. "I know this sucks, but let's talk about what to do about it."

William spun around. "How the hell do you know anything about what this is like?" William was still agitated, and his voice was almost a yell.

"Well, I guess I don't know exactly what you're going through, but I do know about love, and I understand what it feels like to lose the person you love more than life itself."

"Your situation isn't anything like this. You've got it easy. You're not being rejected. Yeah, sure, you lost your wife, but not in the same way that I'm losing Penelope. The Penelope I loved is gone but still very much here. She's changed. It's really, really hard, but I love her anyway. But no matter what I do to try to convince her of that, she keeps pushing me away. She doesn't want me in her life anymore." William gestured angrily toward Oliver. "You don't have to deal with anything like this. My fiancée is very much alive, but in a lot of ways, it's like she's gone. Your wife and son are dead. They're just plain gone. You're lucky; you got to bury them, and they can live on perfectly in your memory. So don't pretend to know what this is like."

Oliver felt as though he had been punched hard in the gut, and he thought he might be sick. He felt the blood drain from his face. His heart thumped. Lucky? How was he lucky? At first he couldn't speak, and silence hung heavy in the room. He found his voice. In contrast to William's shouting, Oliver's voice was faint. "I'm sorry, but I don't think I'm very lucky." Water pooled in his eyes. He wiped it away.

"Oh, God, Oliver, I didn't mean—" The anger had disappeared from William's voice.

Oliver interrupted him. "How am I lucky?" Another pool. Another swipe. "Maggie and Henry are dead, and they're never coming back." The tears flowed freely now, and he didn't try to wipe them away. "You can talk to Penelope, hold her, cherish her. I am never, ever, going to see Maggie and Henry again. I'll never be able to hold them and tell them how much I love them. Their lives were cut short; they are gone forever and..." His voice cracked. He tried again. "And it's all my fault! They died a horrible death because of me. Oh, Maggie, I'm...so...sor...ry!" He absolutely couldn't hold it in any longer. A sob escaped, followed by another, and another. His legs gave out, but William stepped forward and grabbed ahold of him. William eased him down, and the two knelt on the floor. Oliver clung to him, squeezing his shirt in his fists, and sobbed uncontrollably. He tried to talk, to tell what had happened, but he was crying so hard, he was incomprehensible. He choked on his words.

Matt rushed to his side. He knelt down, placed his hand on Oliver's back and spoke softly. "Shhh...We want to hear it, okay?

We want to hear all about it. But not right now. Just let the feelings out right now." He rubbed Oliver's back.

William spoke to Oliver, "I'm sorry. I'm so sorry. I didn't mean what I said. I was upset, and I just lashed out, and you happened to be the one there. I didn't mean it. I—"

Matt stopped him. "Don't say anything," he whispered. "I think this has been a long time in coming. He needs to get this out. Just let him be."

William nodded his understanding. He let Oliver hold on to him and cry.

Oliver completely broke down. Images flashed through his mind, images of the scene of the tragedy, the ambulance ride, the hospital, the funeral, the homeless shelter that was a constant reminder that he wasn't home with his family. He keenly felt the fear, the emptiness, the loneliness of the last four months, and the unrelenting guilt, shame, and remorse about his absence. He felt the regret that the landing pad had broken his fall. He experienced everything as if it were all happening again, all at the same time, and he shook as he sobbed. William held him tighter. Oliver squeezed harder in response.

Matt rose to his feet and walked to the door. Opening it slightly, he called out to Claire, who happened to be at the workstation. "Could you come over here for a second?"

"What's going on in there?"

"I think Oliver might finally talk. But he's in no condition to do so right now. I need to stay in here with him, so could you go get Penelope? She went into her room a little bit ago. And will you get the weighted blanket we gave Oliver too?"

"Yeah, of course. I'll be right there."

Matt pulled the miniblinds down over the glass windows. Then he returned to Oliver and rubbed his back again.

A few minutes later, Claire delivered Penelope and the blanket. Claire looked at the scene, and her brow creased in concern. "Do you need any help?"

"Not in here, but will you cover for me out there? And can you put a sign on the door to indicate that the room is closed? The last thing he needs is a parade of people through here."

"Of course." Before she left, she unfolded the blanket and draped it gently over Oliver. The weight of it did not affect him immediately. He was completely inconsolable. He didn't even give any indication that he heard Penelope ask him what was wrong.

Penelope looked at William and at Matt. "What happened?" she asked.

"Oliver's upset," Matt stated the obvious. "I hope you don't mind that I had Claire come get you."

"Of course not."

"Good. Right now he just needs to cry. But in a while, he's going to have some things to talk about, and he could really use the support of a friend."

"I'd like to stay too. Can I stay, Penelope? Please?" William's voice was tight with emotion, and he didn't care that he was begging.

Penelope dropped down to her knees to join the other three. She touched William's cheek. "Yes. I'd like that."

"Thanks," he whispered.

They fell silent. The only sounds in the room were the hum of the icemaker and the racking sound of Oliver's grief.

After ten minutes, Penelope asked, "Matt, how long can he sustain this?"

"I don't know."

After another ten, she asked, "Should we try to get him to stop?"

"No. Let him stop on his own."

It took over thirty minutes for Oliver's tears to decrease in intensity, and another ten before he stopped altogether. Slowly, he peeled himself off of William. He dried his face with his hospital robe. His head felt as though it would explode into bits, and the lump in his throat felt the size of a watermelon. He was dizzy.

Matt spoke first. "Hey, buddy. We're here for you, and we're ready to listen, but first I'm going to have Jennifer bring you something for that headache you undoubtedly have, and we're going to get you some water to drink so you don't feel dehydrated."

Oliver shook his head. "No."

"Why do you always resist things that will help you?" Matt asked.

Oliver closed his eyes and hung his head. "Because I don't deserve to feel better. And as miserable as I feel, I bet I feel better than Maggie and Henry did when…when…when they…" He buried his face in his hands and the sobbing resumed. He doubled over so his torso was bent over his knees and his face was inches from the ground. He rocked slightly as he keened for his wife and son.

He was more aware of his surroundings this time, and felt a hand moving in circles on his back and another squeezing his shoulder. He wanted to pull away; who was he to accept support like this? He didn't move, though, because it was comforting. The minutes passed. He loathed himself for allowing others to console him, and because of this he was able to stop crying. He sat up. "I'm sorry."

"What on Earth for?" Penelope asked him.

He sighed. He tilted his head back and looked up at the ceiling. The images flashed through his mind again. Attached to the images were the feelings. The ceiling blurred. He blinked rapidly and then looked back down. His eyes brimming again, he looked at his three companions. His breathing was uneven.

Matt's hand returned to Oliver's shoulder. "Hey. It's okay. You don't need to fight it anymore. Come on. Let's sit at a table."

"The tables don't make sense," Penelope protested. "They are rectangles, and rectangles mean fairness. What Oliver is going through doesn't seem fair to me. We should stay here on the floor. The floor is a line, which means truthfulness. The truth is that Oliver shouldn't go through this, and if we stay on the floor, maybe he won't have to go through this anymore."

"I think the table is easier to sit at than the floor," Matt told her. "Why don't we ignore the shapes so Oliver can be comfortable." It wasn't a question.

"Shapes can't be ignored, but Kerffies have complicated rules that I don't fully understand. Maybe it would be okay to sit down, even though the table is a rectangle." Penelope pulled out a chair as Matt and William helped Oliver to his feet. William and Penelope sat on either side of him. Matt crossed the dining room and filled a cup with ice water, adding a straw to make it easier for Oliver to drink. He returned and slid the cup across the table. "Here. Sip on this."

Oliver just stared at it.

"It's not a request. I need you to drink this."

Oliver pulled it toward him, leaned forward, and took a sip. He wanted more, but pushed it away.

Matt spoke with a mellow, inviting tone. "Tell us what happened."

CHAPTER 15

OLIVER HAD NO IDEA WHERE TO BEGIN. HE HAD NEVER TALKED ABOUT IT because it was too hard on so many levels. He sighed and began. "Uh, one hundred twenty nine days ago..." He stopped. He tried again. "I..." He stopped again. His eyes filled with tears.

"It's okay. Take your time," Matt told him.

Oliver put his elbows on the table and leaned his head into his hands. His breathing was labored. He closed his eyes.

The morning sun streamed through the kitchen window. It was Saturday. After their morning routine of reading in bed, Oliver, Maggie, and Henry were in the kitchen and had just eaten break-fast. They all sat in a sunny patch on the kitchen floor, surrounded by wooden blocks. The activity was a favorite of Henry's: build and destroy. The blocks would go up into towers of various widths and heights, and the blocks would come crashing back down at the hands of the almost-four-year-old. The dishes sat on the table, waiting to be cleaned up. "The sun feels fantastic," Maggie declared. She rose and strode to the patio door, opened it, and stepped onto the deck.

"Your turn to stack, little man. I'll be right back." Oliver kissed the top of Henry's head and followed his wife outside. She stretched

into the sun, arms high in the air. Oliver stood behind her, slipped his arms around her waist, and pulled her close.

She reached back and wrapped her arms behind his neck. She inhaled deeply. "Smell that, honey. I love the smell of spring."

He breathed in. "I do too." He nuzzled her neck. "But I like the smell of you better."

She wriggled around and embraced him. Inside the house, they heard a loud crash as blocks tumbled to the ground. Henry squealed in delight. Outside, birds chirped. "I love the sounds of spring, too."

The April air was cold, but it promised to be a beautiful day. The forecast was for an unseasonably warm day with the temperature rising to the 60s. "Maggie, let's go on a picnic today."

"That's a great idea!"

"Do you mind going to the store with Henry to get food? I'll go to the gym this morning and get that out of the way, and I'll get my run in by jogging from the gym to Algonquin Park. I'll meet you guys there."

Maggie stood on her tiptoes and kissed her husband. "Do you really need to work out this morning?"

"Yeah. The triathlon is only four weeks away."

"You could do it later, after the picnic."

"If I do it this morning, I'll have it out of the way. This way we can just enjoy the whole day and spend as much time as we want at the park. We could even go to a movie this evening."

"True. I was just thinking it would be fun to all go to the park together, but this works too."

"Maggie, you're the best. Do you know how much your support means to me?"

She stretched up and kissed him again. "Why don't you show me later?"

He returned the kiss. He would have shown her immediately, but a certain someone ran onto the deck.

"Me, too!" Henry yelled as he raised his arms straight up, indicating that he wanted to be picked up.

Oliver swooped him up, lifted him high into the air, and zoomed him around like an airplane before whooshing him down into a hug. He transferred Henry to one arm, put the other around Maggie, and pulled her close. Despite the fact that he had wanted to be included, Henry wiggled loose and struggled to get back to the ground. Oliver let him down and he took off toward his pile of blocks. Oliver and Maggie laughed at him.

"All right. Let's get the kitchen cleaned up, and then I'll get ready for the gym so we can get to our picnic in the park."

"You go ahead. I'll take care of the kitchen."

"You sure?"

"Yeah. That way you'll be done sooner."

He pecked her on the cheek. "Love you, darling."

"I love you too."

Less than twenty minutes later, he popped back into the kitchen. He gave each of them a quick kiss and headed out the door, destined for the gym.

It was the last time he ever saw them alive. A sob escaped as he sat with his head in his hands, remembering that last morning. His fingers entwined themselves into his hair and he pulled on it with a tight grip. This time, William rubbed his shoulder. Minutes ticked by like that. Eventually, Oliver pulled his arms down and tightened them around his middle. He slouched into them. He swallowed hard and tried again.

After giving them the background, he lamented, "It was my idea. I'm the one who suggested the picnic. I'm the one who insisted on going to the gym." He faltered and closed his eyes. "Why was the workout so damn important?" he whispered. "If I wouldn't have suggested the picnic, they wouldn't have been there. Or if I had gone with them right away instead of going to the gym, I would have been able to protect them. But they were there, and I wasn't, and so…" He squeezed his eyes shut tight, but the tears found their way out anyway.

"What happened at the park?" Matt prodded in a low voice.

Oliver shook his head.

Penelope touched his shoulder. "Please tell us."

"I didn't even see it happen because I arrived too late." He paused for a long time before continuing. "I jogged from the gym across town to Algonquin Park. I heard the sirens as I ran, but I didn't think anything of it at the time. When I neared the park, I could see police cars and fire trucks and ambulances." He had to stop again. His breathing became more rapid, and his heart pound in his chest as he remembered. "It was chaotic. I was scared because I didn't know what was going on." He began to sweat.

Matt spoke up. "Oliver, take it easy. Remember where you are; you're safe."

Oliver was becoming lost in the recollection and didn't really hear Matt. "I ran faster. But it wasn't fast enough. Finally, I got there, but there was a crowd. I couldn't get through. I didn't see Maggie and Henry in the crowd. I didn't know where they were." His voice rose in pitch, and he was breathing hard. He could hear his heartbeat in his head. "I called for them, but they didn't answer me. I pushed through the crowd, but when I finally got through, I was stopped by the police." Oliver coughed and struggled to breathe.

"Oliver, stop for a minute. You're panicking. I want to you stop and breathe."

Oliver didn't hear the command. "They didn't want to let me through, but I broke away from them and ran to find Maggie and Henry because they still wouldn't answer me, even though I was shouting for them really loud." He began to hyperventilate, but he was consumed by the memory and kept talking. "Even though… EMTs…were…bent…over…them…I…saw…them…they…were… lying…on…the…ground…and…blood…was…everywhere…" In his mind, it was no longer a memory. It was happening again, right now. He leaped to his feet and looked for his family. "No! Get up! Maggie! Henry! No! Oh God! Help them! What is happening? No!"

"Oliver!" Matt jumped to his feet. He approached but didn't touch him. "Oliver, it's not happening right now." He paused before repeating firmly, "Oliver. Oliver, it's not happening right now."

Oliver stopped searching and looked around the room. He was confused. His chest constricted in pain. Where were Maggie and Henry? He couldn't get enough oxygen because his respiration was too rapid and too deep.

Again, someone said, "Oliver, it's not happening now." The person kept repeating it over and over.

Oliver realized that he wouldn't be able to help Maggie and Henry. He dropped to his knees. He still couldn't breathe.

"Okay, Oliver, you're going to feel something heavy. We're placing a blanket around you. It's going to help ground you. I want you to focus on the way it feels."

Weight settled onto his shoulders. Even though someone had told him it was coming, he jumped. His breathing accelerated even more.

The same person was now instructing him to breathe. "Okay, now William is going to take over and help you breathe. Listen to his instructions and breathe slowly, in and out."

Matt turned to William and Penelope and explained what to do. "William, just tell him to inhale with you as you take a slow, deep breath, and then tell him to exhale with you as you breathe slowly out. He won't fall into your pattern right away, but it's important to be repetitive and keep up the rhythm. Penelope, kneel beside him and place your hand firmly on his shoulder and keep it there. I need to go find Jennifer, but I'll be right back. Stay calm and keep doing what I told you."

Matt returned promptly with Jennifer. He found a paper bag in a cupboard to help Oliver stop hyperventilating. Jennifer knelt down and instructed Oliver to take the lorazepam she had brought for him.

Oliver's heart rate slowed, and with help, his breathing returned to normal.

Matt said, "It was a flashback. It's not happening now."

Oliver nodded. "I know."

Matt kept talking. "I'm going to help you to your feet and get you settled in your chair again. Is that okay?" Oliver nodded, and Matt helped him stand. He couldn't get the bloody images of Maggie and Henry out of his mind. As Matt steadied him, Oliver leaned into him, held on, and once again started to cry.

Matt dropped his arms to his sides and glanced at Jennifer. "You were only helping him up," she whispered. "Technically, you didn't hug him; he hugged you, and you know that hugging helps ground someone after a flashback. You're fine." Matt nodded to her. Given the confirmation that he hadn't broken policy, he wrapped his arms around Oliver in a strong, comforting embrace.

Eventually, Oliver calmed down again. They moved back to the table. Jennifer left. Without being prompted, Oliver resumed his story. The lorazepam in his system helped him remain calm this time. "Later, when it was all over, a police officer told me about it. The park was fairly busy, so there were witnesses." He paused. Matt, William, and Penelope waited. He continued, "There was a young man in the park who was high on meth. Apparently, he was really strung out and he thought that people were after him. Maggie and Henry were in the sandbox. The guy thought it was his secret fort or something and shouted something about intruders invading it, I guess. He charged at them." Oliver had to stop again. He grabbed a handful of tissues and wiped his nose but let the tears cascade freely. "I was told that Maggie stood up and picked up Henry. She tried to walk away, but the man screamed at her. Henry started to cry, I guess. He was probably so scared. I bet they both were." Again, a pause as he struggled for composure. "She tried again to leave, but the guy pulled a gun on her. I guess it happened really quickly. He pointed it at her and pulled the trigger. The bullet passed through Henry and right into Maggie." When he resumed after another long pause, his voice was barely a whisper. "They didn't die right away. I rode in the ambulance with them. They were still alive then, but I couldn't talk to them because they were both unconscious; they had already lost too much blood. They made me ride in the front, out of the way. I tried to see them, but I couldn't. I didn't know it, but Henry died in the ambulance. I was only a few feet away from him. I don't think he knew I was there. Maggie didn't know either. The only thing that she knew was that I was absent when she needed me to protect her. She died in the operating room." He groaned and looked at his companions helplessly. "Why did I suggest a picnic, and why in the hell did I go to the gym? I could have protected them, but I wasn't there. It was all my fault! Oh, God, I'm so sorry!" He folded his arms on the table in front of him and collapsed onto them, wracked with another round of sobs.

The other three exchanged concerned glances. Penelope reached over Oliver and touched William's arm. "I love you, William," she whispered, her own eyes brimming. He took her hand and expressed the same sentiment.

Time seemed to stand still. Oliver eventually sat up.

William was the first to break the silence. "Good God. Oliver, I am so, so sorry."

Spent and shaken, Oliver could only nod.

Matt slid the glass of water to him. When Oliver shook his head, Matt insisted. "You need to sip on this."

"I don't see the point. I don't see the point in anything."

"I know you don't," Matt said. "You don't have to see the point right now. You just need to take a drink."

Oliver took a tiny sip. Matt made him take a few more and then let it go.

Penelope said, "Can I ask you something?"

Oliver looked at her and nodded.

"You mentioned Algonquin Park, but I don't recognize that. It didn't happen here in Chicago, did it?"

"No."

"Is that why you don't have visitors? Because you're not from here?"

Oliver shrugged. "I suppose that's part of it."

"Why are you in Chicago?"

When Oliver didn't answer, Matt stepped in. "Let's give him a break. He's shared a lot, and he might be feeling pretty overwhelmed."

"Oh. I'm sorry. I wasn't trying to be insensitive. I'm really sorry, Oliver. Should I leave now?"

He gave her a small smile. "It's okay. You didn't do anything wrong. I would actually like you to stay, if you don't mind."

"I don't mind." She reached out and took his hand in hers.

Silence passed between them again. No one said a word until Oliver said, "I'm sorry. I know I'm not being very good company right now. I feel kind of dazed, and I keep thinking about..." He swallowed hard. "I'm just sorry, okay?"

"Your reaction right now is exactly what it needs to be. We're just giving you the space to think and the opportunity to talk if you want to. If we're talking, you can't. So please don't worry about us, okay?"

"Okay, Matt." Oliver glanced at William. William reached over and squeezed his shoulder.

Oliver didn't speak again until out of the blue he asked, "Do you guys want to see a picture of them?"

"We would love that. Do you have a picture?" Penelope spoke for all of them.

Slowly, Oliver nodded. "Yes, I do. It's in my shirt pocket in my closet. Every minute of every day I need to see it, but I can't get to it because it's locked away. I need it, but I can't have it." He sounded like a little boy.

"You should have said something! We weren't trying to keep your picture away from you. You're so quiet; I had no idea. Would you like me to go get it?"

Oliver nodded vigorously. "Yes."

"You got it. I'll be right back."

Oliver was looking down at the table when Matt returned with the picture. Matt sat down across from Oliver. "Hey," he whispered. Oliver looked at him. "Here you go, buddy." He slid the picture to Oliver, who let go of Penelope's hand, and with trembling fingers, slowly picked it up and turned it over. There they were, smiling out at him from wrinkled, worn-out photo paper.

Instantly, tears sprang to his eyes once again. His voice was unsteady as he explained the picture to his friends. "I, uh, I snapped this in March, a few weeks before they...before they were killed." He sniffed and swallowed hard. "We were at Henry's music class, and...and Henry and his mommy were banging on a big drum." The tears came hard and fast again. It was difficult to talk, but he kept going. He didn't take his eyes off the image. "See how in the picture—" He paused and sniffed. "—Henry's face is bursting with glee? He...looks like he's having...the time of his little...life." He wiped tears off the picture with his sleeve before continuing. "And look at Maggie. Her expression is...just like Henry's...When I, uh... when I t...took th...this pic.....ture, I didn't know...I didn't know th...that Hen...ry would...nev...er...take another...class...a...gain. Oh, God! Why?" With both hands, he clutched the photo to his chest. By this time, his sobbing was out of control again.

Penelope scooted her chair closer to him, put her arm around him, and pulled him in so he literally had a shoulder to cry on until he was ready to sit back up.

When he did sit up, he looked at her. "I'm sorry about getting your robe wet. But thank you."

She took his hand again and squeezed it gently.

"I guess you guys didn't get to see the picture, did you?" He passed it to Penelope first.

She studied it for a long time. "This is a really great picture. Maggie is beautiful. And Henry is a little version of you, Oliver. He's got your eyes. His hair has big, loose curls and flips like yours." Gently, she reached up and brushed her fingers against his hair.

Oliver's breath caught. Maggie had been fond of playing with his hair, and he ached with the desire to feel her do it again. He exhaled audibly when Penelope dropped her hand and continued talking. "I don't know if he's got your smile, though, because I've never seen you fully smile. Check it out, William." She leaned back and handed the picture to William behind Oliver so he wouldn't have to see it right at the moment. Matt nodded his approval at her.

William agreed with Penelope. "She's right, man. He is the spitting image of his dad. Maggie's really pretty." He paused and looked Oliver in the eyes. "It really, really sucks that this happened."

Oliver teared up but held it together. He didn't trust his voice, so he nodded.

Matt said, "I'd like to see it too, if that's okay."

Oliver nodded again.

William handed the picture to Matt. "Oliver," he said after staring at it, "This is a great picture. They look wonderful."

"They are wonderful. I mean, they were." Oliver had to wipe his eyes. "I'm sorry I keep doing this."

"You need to stop apologizing to us. You have nothing to apologize for."

"Haven't you been listening? I have everything to apologize for!"

"Okay, that's not what I meant. This is important, Oliver, so look at me." When Matt had Oliver's full attention, he continued. "I know you feel that everything that happened is your fault. I'm not going to argue about it with you because that won't be helpful. But you need to hear this: You did not kill your wife and son. A meth user is the only one responsible for their deaths. He pulled the trigger, not you."

"But if I had been there—"

"The outcome might very well have been the same. Speculating is pointless. What you need to know is the truth: you did not kill them, Oliver."

"But—"

"Shhh. Not now. You'll have a lot of opportunities to process this. I just wanted to tell you that single fact, and I don't want you to argue with it. Listen to it, and then file it away for the time being."

Penelope added to the conversation. "He's using his serious voice, Oliver. He does that to me, too, and I've learned that I can't win when he talks like that."

Matt laughed. "Good. I'm glad you figured that out."

Penelope responded matter-of-factly, "Well, Mrs. Roosevelt is the one who figured it out. She told me. Anyway, Oliver, Matt is right. You didn't kill Maggie and Henry. I know that a lot of the time I don't know what I'm talking about, and I don't always know what's real and what isn't, but I am very sure about this. This horrible, horrible thing wasn't your fault."

"I don't agree at all, but I don't feel up to arguing." The intensity of the afternoon was taking a toll on him. His stomach burned and twisted, and he hurt from head to toe, especially right in his heart. The lorazepam had mellowed him to the point of exhaustion. Yet despite this, he still felt the pressure of tears behind his red-rimmed eyes.

"Do you want to talk some more?" Matt asked.

Oliver sighed. "I don't think I can right now."

"That's perfectly okay."

"Is it alright if I go to my room?"

Matt thought for a moment. "Actually, no. I don't want you to be alone right now. You need the support of friends. I'd like the three of you to hang out together in the day area. We've got games, cards, and puzzles. Penelope and Oliver, I'm giving you specific instructions to do just that. William, I have no jurisdiction over you. I can only suggest that you stay if you can, because it would be good for both Oliver and Penelope."

"I'd like nothing more than to stay, but I guess it's up to Penelope." William looked at her expectantly.

Oliver encouraged her. "You two love each other. Please don't waste that." He reached for another tissue. When Penelope stood, stepped to William, and hugged him, Oliver picked up the box.

Matt came over to Oliver's side of the table and sat in Penelope's seat. He put his hand on Oliver's shoulder and squeezed. "I'm so glad you opened up. Hang in there, okay?"

Oliver dropped his gaze. Deep inside, he thought, *I have absolutely nothing to hang in there for.*

CHAPTER 16

WILLIAM SAW THE PIECE OF PAPER ON HIS APARTMENT DOOR AS HE WALKED toward it. He grabbed the note but didn't look at it; he didn't want to linger in the hallway and risk seeing Mariska. He quickly unlocked the door and stepped inside. After he shut the door behind him, he unfolded the paper. As he suspected, it was from Mariska.

Dear William,

I hope you had a nice day with Penelope, and I hope that she is feeling well and doing better.

I'm sorry that you felt the need to rush away last night. To me, we're two neighbors getting to know each other and forming a friendship. Nothing more. I hope that we can continue to build a friendship, and I would like to include your fiancée, too. Please stop by again anytime you'd like to talk. Here's my business card, too. Give me a call or send a text.

Your new neighbor,
Mariska

It was innocent enough. Still, he crumpled it up and tossed it, along with his phone and keys, onto the kitchen table on his way to the bathroom. His head throbbed relentlessly in what was probably the worst headache of his life. After downing three extra-strength aspirin—he started with the recommended maximum of two but then took one more for added oomph—he shuffled to the bedroom, flopped down on his bed, and stared at the ceiling. He massaged his temples and tried to clear his head. He was unsuccessful; too many thoughts vied for his attention.

He still felt like a worm for lashing out at Oliver and telling him that he was lucky. Seriously, what had possessed him to tell a grieving man that he was lucky that his wife and son had died?

When they left the dining area after Oliver was done talking, he had pulled Matt aside to apologize and ask if should apologize to Oliver. Matt had assured him that it was okay and that it had been the catalyst Oliver needed to finally talk, and he advised him to let it go. Accordingly, he hadn't mentioned it to Oliver at all, but he still felt sheepish about it. He clearly hadn't been thinking; he had just been upset over Penelope's rejection.

As he lay on the bed ruminating, he remembered childhood conversations with Uncle Jack and how, when William came to him, upset over a cutting comment from his father, his uncle would reassure him that his father hadn't meant it but was upset about something different and had taken it out on William. That thought made him feel worse. He had promised both himself and Uncle Jack that he would never, ever, be like either of his parents in any way. What he had done to Oliver felt pretty damn abusive.

He groaned. Good Lord, he was breaking promises all over the place; he was also irritated with himself for listening to Penelope and leaving before visiting hours were officially over. Granted, he only left forty-five minutes early, but still, he left early after he had promised himself he wouldn't. As he had listened to Oliver's tragic story, he became overwhelmed by a desperate need to keep his precious love, his darling Penelope, in his life. He was struck with the desire to never, ever let her out of his sight. Knowing that was unrealistic, he had vowed to himself that he would at least be at her side every minute that the hospital allowed him to be. So what had he done? He left almost an hour before he needed to. It wasn't his choice though. As the evening progressed, Penelope had felt increasingly worse, until she asked him to leave so she could go to bed.

He wondered if that had just been an excuse to get rid of him. He continued to stare at the ceiling and ponder that. It had been a decent evening. Despite the fact that they were in a behavioral health center rather than at home, William truly enjoyed being with Penelope. And with Oliver, too. They played rummy and conversed casually about easy, impersonal things like the various events in the news. Understandably, Oliver was pretty quiet, but he threw in an occasional comment or question. After dinner, as they played Scrabble, Penelope began to complain that she felt sick all over from her medication. Oliver kept falling asleep at the table. Apologizing unnecessarily, he had excused himself and went to his room. Alone with Penelope, William had tried to talk about their future. Penelope didn't want to talk though. She went to her room, returned with her hairbrush, and asked him to brush her hair. It felt wonderful to sit in silence and brush her hair. It made him feel intimate and close to her. He thought she liked it too, and he was taken aback when she told him that she felt physically ill and asked him to leave. True, she didn't look very good; she was pale, and her eyes were dull and bloodshot. He was aware that the medications she took were harsh and had nasty side effects. She was likely telling the truth when she said she needed to go to bed.

Should he have insisted on staying until the end anyway? He wanted to show Penelope that he supported her no matter what. He was confused. Did supporting her mean staying with her for that extra forty-five minutes? Would it prove to her that he wanted to be with her no matter what she was like? Or did supporting her mean respecting her wish to be alone because she didn't feel well? He absolutely did not know the answer. He was unable to think and wanted a mindless distraction. He wandered into the living room and flipped on the TV. The White Sox weren't playing, but the Cubs had a night game. He hated the Cubs, but yet a baseball game was a baseball game.

Even as he watched, he couldn't get his mind to stop its obsession with whether or not he had supported Penelope by leaving the hospital. Maybe a second opinion would help.

He grabbed his phone to call Rod, and then abruptly stopped himself before he completed the call. Rod was being a complete ass. More than likely, he would use William's uncertainty as an opportunity to run down Penelope and then start hounding him about Mariska. No thanks. His eyes fell on the crumpled note on the table. She had said last night, and again in the note, that he could talk to her any time. She seemed nonjudgmental, and she had been easy to talk to. Or was that because of the alcohol? Not that he had been drunk, but he had consumed enough to be influenced by it. Either way, she had listened and had not reacted negatively to his discussion of Penelope. Hey, and wasn't she in human resources at her job? She was probably good at dealing with people. Perhaps she could offer some insight into how he could show his support for Penelope.

He made it halfway down the hall before he stopped in his tracks. What the hell was he doing? Wasn't it bad enough that he had betrayed his fiancée last night and violated Mariska when he practically threw himself at her? He spun on his heels and returned to his apartment, but stopped outside the door.

On the other hand, Mariska herself had said that nothing happened. Maybe he was making too much of it. He had experienced a head rush by standing up too fast, she caught him, and he kind of stumbled into her. Maybe by avoiding her, he was acting like he really did have something to feel guilty about. He truly didn't. Nothing had happened, and he was glad about that. And nothing would happen again, because he loved Penelope and had no interest in Mariska. He just needed some input. He turned around.

This time he made it to her door, but he couldn't bring himself to knock. Just what kind of a bastard was he? Not only did he leave the hospital too early, but now he was running to another woman's apartment. No, his interest was not sexual, but to be even building a friendship with a different woman, one who was not mentally ill, seemed like the ultimate betrayal. He again whirled around and marched back toward his apartment.

He had almost reached his door when a door clicked behind him. He stopped short and squeezed his eyes shut. *Please don't let that be Mariska,* he thought.

His heart pounded when he heard a familiar voice call, "Well, hello, William!"

Very slowly, he turned toward her. "Hi, Mariska. How's it going?"

"It's going great. How's Penelope?"

"She's doing okay. I, um, I got your note. Thanks."

"I meant everything I wrote. Were you coming to talk to me about it? I was just on my way out, but not for anything major. Want to come over?"

"No. That's okay. I was just going to thank you for the note, but I wasn't going to stay. My head is killing me and I'm afraid I wouldn't be very good company. I don't want to keep you from what you're doing. Have a good night, and I'll catch you later." He all but ran into his apartment. He almost slammed the door behind him but caught it before it made too much of a noise. *Great. That was rude. William, you're a jerk,* he chastised himself. He opened his door a crack and peeked out. She was gone. With relief, he closed his door again, retreated to the living room, and flopped onto the couch.

His mind continued to mull over the day. Too tired to resist, he let it wander freely without stopping and thinking too hard about anything in particular. One of the thoughts that paraded through his head was that of Penelope asking Oliver about Algonquin Park. At that, he did stop and wonder. Penelope had also asked why Oliver was in Chicago, but he didn't seem to want to answer. Matt had shifted the focus. William sat up straight. He thought back to the other night when he had asked Oliver if he had visitors coming. He said something about no one knowing or caring where he was. What was up with that? He wondered suddenly if he could find out more about where Oliver came from. He had to have someone in his life who cared where he was.... Didn't he?

He rose from the couch and went into the spare bedroom, the room he and Penelope used as an office. He sat at the computer and opened his web browser. Now what? Oliver wasn't from Chicago. He had to be from somewhere. If no one knew where he was, that probably meant he hadn't told anybody where he was going. If someone were concerned about him, would they have filed a missing persons report? He typed "missing persons" into the search box. A bunch of official sites popped up, but they either had to do with wanted criminals or were location-specific. Because he had no idea where Oliver was from, trying to search by location would be like trying to find Johixilan when the cat was in an antisocial mood. He clicked on a random site just to see what it was like. It listed a bunch of information for the various missing people, including police department contacts and case file numbers. William realized there probably weren't any official police reports filed about Oliver. When Penelope had been admitted to Airhaven, her name had been entered into their computer system, and a background check was automatically run. A background check on Oliver would have uncovered police records, including a missing persons report. The police department and, through them, the person who filed the report would have been notified. Given that no one had come for him, it was unlikely that anyone had filed a report.

He didn't really know what else to do. He couldn't just search Oliver's name and have the answer pop onto the screen. Or could he? He didn't have any other ideas, so he figured he could at least give it a shot, as ridiculous as it seemed. Now what was Oliver's last name? He had said it when he introduced himself. William closed his eyes and recalled the conversation. He had been paying close attention, because he was sizing up what he thought might be competition. He flushed in embarrassment at the thought; it seemed ludicrous now. He pictured Oliver approaching him meekly and shaking his hand limply as he introduced himself. Graham! That's right. He typed "Oliver Graham" into the search box. A few random things appeared on his screen. He scrolled down. Nothing. Nothing. Wait. What was this? Underneath the link to a website that included Oliver's name was partial text from the site that read, "This is my brother. His name is Oliver Graham. He disappeared from Fairmont, Wisconsin…" That sounded too close to be a coincidence. Fairmont, Wisconsin was a suburb of Milwaukee and less than an hour-and-a-half away from Chicago. William clicked on the link.

A picture of Oliver dominated the screen. It was him! Granted, in the picture, he looked healthy and happy rather than haggard and hopeless, but it was without a doubt the right Oliver Graham. Underneath the image, the following message was written:

This is my brother. His name is Oliver Graham. He disappeared from Fairmont, Wisconsin on May 21st. He's having a tough time with life right now, and I'm very worried about him. If anyone out there has seen him, or knows anything about him, I'm begging you to please contact me using the contact form on this website. My name is Frannie. And will you tell him to come home? I love him, and so do his two little nieces and his nephew. Please help me locate him if you can.

So Oliver had been right about one thing: no one knew where he was. But he had been wrong in thinking that no one cared. William was excited. He had to contact Oliver's sister so she could stop worrying. He clicked on the tab leading to the contact form and began to write her a message. He couldn't wait to tell Oliver. That thought made him pause. Maybe Oliver didn't want her to know. William had no idea what their relationship was or what reason Oliver might have had for taking off without telling her. Perhaps William should wait and discuss it with Oliver first. After all, he had already hurt Oliver once today. He wanted to do something now to help him rather than make things even worse. He decided to talk to Oliver about it tomorrow night during visiting hours. For now, he closed the website. For Oliver's sake, Frannie would have to wait at least one more day before learning her brother's whereabouts.

CHAPTER 17

OLIVER WAS SITTING WITH PENELOPE, STRUGGLING TO CHOKE DOWN AN Ensure, when Dr. Willis found him on Monday morning. Never one to make small talk, she got right down to business. "Good morning, you two. It sounds like you had an intense day yesterday. Oliver, let's go to your room to chat for a bit. Penelope, Dr. Daniels is on his way to see you, so please wait here." Despite her focused and direct content, her tone was kind.

Oliver followed her to his room. She gestured for him to sit on the edge of his bed, and she pulled his desk chair over to sit, facing him. "I'm glad to see you getting some nutrition into your system," Dr. Willis said as they sat down. "How are you doing with that?" She reached for the bottle and removed it from his hand. "Oliver, this is almost full. You must have been given this an hour ago when breakfast was served."

"I'm sorry. I'm trying. It's just hard." He sighed and tilted his head back. "God, everything is so damn hard."

"Help me understand what you mean by 'everything.'"

"Anything that has to do with being alive."

"Let's try to pull things apart a bit, shall we, so we can step back and look at little pieces instead of one big, overwhelming picture."

"I'm already in pieces, Dr. Willis. My heart, my life, every-thing. It's like Humpty Dumpty in the nursery rhymes that Maggie and I used to read to our little boy." His eyes began to swim. "The moment I saw them sprawled on the sidewalk, bleeding and dying, I fell off the wall and shattered, and nothing can put me back together again." He choked on a sob but steadied himself and continued. "Not sitting here talking about it, not sitting around a table listening to music, not playing with clay or making puppets or gluing pictures on paper. None of that stuff is going to help me because none of that stuff will bring back my wife and son. Tell me how in the hell any of this will do any good at all." His voice was a mix of agony and anger, and to his own ears, it sounded like a strange combination of a lament and a challenge. He bit his cheeks in an effort to calm down. He'd be damned if he'd sit here and break down in front of this doctor.

"You are absolutely right. Nothing we do here will change what happened." This only intensified his struggle for restraint. She asked him to close his eyes and waited patiently for him to comply. When he didn't, she said, "Oliver, I want you to close your eyes. Nothing bad is going to happen."

He closed his eyes, but only because he wasn't up for a power struggle.

"Good. We're going to get your breathing under control. Inhale slowly. That's it. Hold your breath. Now exhale slowly until all the air is out. Good. Breathe in again, slower this time. Hold it. Breathe out." She led him through ten breaths, and then allowed him to open his eyes.

"Why does everyone keep feeling the need to help me breathe?" His voice was steadier but still held an undercurrent of agony and anger.

"Because when you get worked up, your breathing goes haywire. It's very normal for that to happen because our minds and bodies are linked together, and one responds to the other. If one gets worked up, the other usually does, too, but if one is calm, the other copies. Controlling your respiration is an important first step in settling yourself down when you're upset."

"What if I don't want to settle myself down? What if I want to let my body go haywire and die?"

Dr. Willis looked at him thoughtfully.

Oliver became uncomfortable. "I'm sorry," he said, contrite. "I'm not trying to be a jerk."

"You don't need to apologize; I know you're not. We've got to take things one step at a time. Our first step is to work on the basics, like eating and breathing. I'm not asking you to like it right now. You follow our instructions, and I won't insist that you love it. Deal?"

"I guess."

"Good enough; I'll take what I can get." The muscles of her mouth formed a small, thin smile. She held it there only briefly and then fell silent for several seconds before saying, "I heard multiple things going on in what you said a while ago. I'd like to explore some of them. First, how often would you say you get angry?"

He sighed and looked at her with a pained expression. "I'm sorry I got angry. I didn't mean to. I'm just frustrated, but it's my own fault, not yours."

"Oliver, I'm not looking for an apology. There is no reason for you to apologize. Are you aware of how often you apologize?"

He shrugged.

"It tells me that you're struggling with some pretty deep guilt."

The frustration of a few minutes ago hadn't fully disappeared after the doctor-led breathing exercise, and it flared up again. "You think? Did you actually read my file, because I'm pretty sure Matt put everything in there; you all seem intent on writing down every little thing we say or don't say, or do or don't do. If you read it, you'd know that yes, I feel guilty. I killed my family! Maggie and Henry are dead. Their lives are over. And it's because of me. I'm the one who wanted to go to that park, and I'm the one who wasn't there to help them when they needed me the most. It's...all...my...fault!" He paused between the last words for emphasis.

"Stop right now. Inhale deeply."

"No!" He jumped up and paced around by his desk. He put his hands to his head. His fingers worked their way under his hair to grasp his head hard. He squeezed tightly and concentrated on the sensation of his nails digging into his scalp in a desperate attempt to keep from bursting into tears.

Dr. Willis remained still and silent, calmly observing him.

Oliver couldn't stand the silence any longer. He turned to her, and with his hands still on his head, bemoaned, "You asked me how often I get angry. I get angry sometimes." He dropped his hands and folded his arms across his chest. "I try to get angry at the druggie who killed two innocent, beautiful souls. I try to get angry at the situation. I try to get angry at the world for just being the way it is and because Maggie and Henry aren't part of it anymore. Once, I got mad at Maggie for not getting out of the way sooner, but that thought absolutely killed me, and I cried for a long time and begged Maggie for forgiveness for it, but guess what? She wasn't there to forgive me. There's only one person I can truly get angry at and mean it, and that's me. Of course I hate that druggie, but the truth is that if I had been there, he wouldn't have been able to kill them, so I hate myself more. So yeah, I get angry sometimes. But most of the time, I don't have the energy to be angry. I'm too numb and hollow and empty. I feel angry sometimes, but I feel very, very sad all of the time." He paused briefly and took a deep breath. "There. Does that answer your question?" His voice broke. He turned away from her to face the window. Tears of sorrow and frustration escaped against his will, and he wasn't comfortable enough with her to cry in front of her. He tried to control his breathing, like she suggested. It actually worked. Sort of. He still ached inside, but he was able to calm down on the outside. He kept taking deep breaths to make sure he was under control and to avoid facing Dr. Willis.

"Yes, that answers my question." She fell silent briefly, and then told him, "I'm impressed with your breathing. Nice job. I'd like for you to come back and sit down when you're ready. I'd rather talk to you face to face than shout at your back."

He sighed. He didn't want to talk, but he was afraid that if he didn't go back over there, she would just sit there all day. Wanting this to end, he returned to the bed and faced her.

"You've really been through the wringer, Mr. Graham." A pause, and then, "Since you arrived here, I've seen and heard grief and fear and anxiety and guilt and anger and self-loathing and loneliness." She seemed to drag out each of those words for emphasis, and each individual word jabbed at Oliver's very core. "These feelings can be a natural part of every loss, but in your case, the loss was an unexpected and violent trauma, so all of your emotions are heightened and magnified. As a result, you're experiencing complicated mourning, major depressive disorder, and post-traumatic stress disorder. It is nearly impossible for someone to deal with all of these things by himself. That's what we're here for. I know you think the sessions with me and the group activities are pointless."

Oliver flushed and looked down.

"No. Don't feel bad. It is perfectly okay for you to feel that way. I bet it's pretty damn hard to see the point in anything right now. But these things most definitely have a point. Everything we do is designed to help you explore what happened, to fully express your thoughts and feelings safely, and to come to terms with what happened so you can live your life."

"I don't want to live my life! I have nothing to live for. Why can't everyone just accept that and let me go?"

"Because that's the trauma talking, not you."

"That doesn't make any sense."

"What does make sense?"

"Absolutely nothing. Nothing at all makes a bit of goddamn sense."

"Exactly. You need help processing all of this. You participated actively in an art group on Saturday. That played a part in allowing you to open up yesterday."

He remembered the blow he felt when William told him he was lucky. "It wasn't just because of the group."

"Of course it wasn't. But in making that collage and keeping it with you, you were starting to process this mess." She stopped talking. When she resumed, her tone was softer. "It is indeed a mess, isn't it?"

He nodded.

"Hang in there. Let people help you through this very difficult time."

"I don't deserve it." His voice quivered as he whispered.

"I know that you fully believe that you don't deserve help. But you're the only one who feels that way." She tried a new angle. "Think of it this way: What if it had been you and Henry that had been shot and Maggie were sitting here with me now? Would you blame her for what happened? Would you want her to stew in misery?"

"Absolutely not." He still spoke in a whisper.

"Then tell me why it's different for you."

"Because it just is. And it isn't the other way around. She's gone and I'm here and it's my fault and I don't deserve help and I miss them so much and I don't want to betray them by getting better." Try as he might, he couldn't keep his voice steady.

"Oliver." She waited for him to look at her. "Oliver, look at me for just a minute." When he made eye contact, she continued. "When someone is wrestling with something this devastating, it is often extremely difficult and painful to look down the road and even imagine moving on. To try to picture that is overwhelming. So let's back this way up. I'm not asking you to give me a plan for a perfectly cheery future. I actually don't want you to think about that at all right now. I want you to instead think about little things. What can you do each hour to stay afloat? For right now, that means what can you do in each group, or what can you do at mealtime, or during visiting hours, or whenever, to find something good at that moment? Just think hour by hour right now and nothing beyond that." She allowed him some time to digest what she had directed. "On a scale of one to ten, with one being impossible and ten being very easy, how much do you think you can do that?"

He grappled with her question. Why couldn't he make her understand that he didn't want to be here? Why couldn't people accept that he could not and would not recover from this horrific loss? Why did people keep telling him to hang in there? He didn't want to hang in there. He just wished she and everyone else would go away and leave him alone. But at least she wasn't forcing him to think about the future. Perhaps she sensed that he absolutely couldn't handle trying to be optimistic about a future that, in reality, was bleak and hellacious. All she was trying to do, he realized, was help him deal with the moment. If it were up to him, he wouldn't be alive to deal with any more moments. But he had screwed up, his plan went awry, and now he was sitting here. For now, he couldn't do a thing about it, so maybe it would be okay to try her suggestion just to get by temporarily. On the one hand, it sounded like a sinful indulgence he didn't deserve; after all, Maggie and Henry didn't have the luxury of deciding how to live in any given hour. He felt the wetness in his eyes again at that thought, and he closed them so the doctor wouldn't see it. On the other hand, he continued to wrestle with himself, perhaps there wouldn't be too much harm in thinking in terms of getting by hour by hour. He sighed deeply. He just didn't know. Finally, he answered, "I don't know. A two maybe."

"Fantastic. That's a step beyond one already. So, to recap, you are going to think only of what you can do each hour to stay afloat. That involves participating in the groups. You need to be just a little more active in each one, whether that means sharing something or journaling or creating something. What you decide to do is your choice, but you have to do something in each one. And each hour, ask yourself what small thing you can do to make it through to the next hour? Okay?"

He shrugged and muttered, "Okay, I guess."

"Thank you."

"For what?"

"For not saying 'no.' Now go make each hour of today bearable. I will see you tomorrow." Unceremoniously, Dr. Willis left his room without giving him a chance to protest.

"How am I supposed to do that?" He asked the empty room. He pulled his picture of Maggie and Henry out of the pocket of his robe. "My doctor just told me to do something to make each hour bearable," he said to the smiling faces. "But without you here, nothing is bearable." He tipped over sideways onto his pillow and curled up. He ignored the voice calling though the day area to signal the upcoming music group. He remained motionless until he heard a soft knock on his open door.

"Are you going to come with me to the music group? It's starting in a few minutes," Penelope asked in an exaggerated stage whisper. "I'm talking like this so I don't startle you. You haven't moved, so I guess it's working. Are you awake?"

He rolled onto his back. "Yeah, I'm awake. And thanks for not startling me." He swung his legs over the side of his bed and sat up.

She looked at his hands. "You have their picture. Can I see it again?" She looked to her left and to her right and behind her, and then she closed her eyes. "Is it okay to go in?"

Oliver didn't answer because he had a feeling that she wasn't asking him.

"Okay, I'll count with you. One, two three, go!" She tiptoed quickly into his room and plopped down beside him on the bed. She offered no explanation for the conversation but instead looked intently at the picture. Both of Oliver's hands grasped the bottom corners of the photo. Penelope slid her hand into one of his without causing him to let go. She leaned against his shoulder and said simply, "I'm sorry, Oliver."

"Thank you." They sat quietly together, her hand snaked through his, taking in the image. Guilt pricked him. It pierced the hand that Penelope held and the arm where she leaned her head and traveled through his skin, into his bloodstream, and straight to his core. He shouldn't be accepting this comfort. But after months of stark comfortlessness, this just felt good. He wanted to pull away, but he didn't. It was nice in a way, too, to let someone see the beauty of his family. Was this part of doing something to make the moment bearable? It felt good, and because of that it felt lousy. God, he hated himself.

"Last call for music group! Five minutes to Fra-ank!" This time the tech calling was Matt. Oliver looked out the door, and seconds after the call, Matt walked past his room. A second after that, he walked backward to return to Oliver's doorway. "Is there a reason rules are being broken in here?" Matt's tone was light and held no anger or reprimand.

Penelope stayed exactly in the same position. "Oliver seemed down, Matt. When he sat up, I saw that he had his picture and I wanted to see it again, and I wanted him to know that I care."

Oliver spoke. "I'm sorry. Don't be upset at Penelope. It's not her fault. It's mine." He dropped his voice and repeated. "It's mine. It's my fault. It's all my fault."

Matt entered the room and crouched down in front of them. "Take it easy." He placed his hand on Oliver's knee. "We're talking about why one patient is in another patient's room, remember? Only that. And you don't need to apologize for it." He addressed Penelope. "It's great that you're giving him some support. Next time, wait until he comes out into the day area, okay? Patients can't be in each other's rooms. And right now, you two should be in the group room. Come on. I'll walk you there."

Matt and Penelope rose to their feet, but Oliver remained seated. Matt sat beside him. "Hey. What's up? It's not you, that's for sure, because you're still sitting down." He winked at him and grinned.

Oliver didn't feel up to returning Matt's banter. He didn't feel like talking, either. If it had been any other tech, he wouldn't have answered, but because it was Matt, he explained, "I don't want to go. I'm supposed to participate now, but I don't know how to, because I can't bring myself to request a personal song, and I don't want to anyway." He looked at Matt with a pleading expression. "I just want to stay in bed."

"Given what you're going through, that makes a lot of sense. It's very important though that you don't give into it. Would you like a suggestion for how to participate in the music group?"

"Sure," Oliver said with a sigh.

"You don't need to request a song. Participating can mean engaging with yourself. You could use your journal while you listen to the songs requested by others. Draw or doodle or write in it. Put down on paper the things that pop into your mind as you listen. Does that sound doable?"

"I don't know."

"I'll do it too, Oliver," Penelope chimed in, "and then we could share our journals with each other later today. But you have to promise not to talk about what's in my journal with anybody else, because usually the things I put down on paper are private. I know that my mind is very strange to others, and I'm embarrassed to show the things I put in a journal. Or sometimes Mrs. Roosevelt gets really mad if I show a secret she's given me, and that makes me scared. If she comes around today, I'll explain it to her, and I'm sure she'll be okay with my showing you my secret journal. Wow. I'm excited about the idea of showing each other our journals. What do you think? Would you like to do this with me?"

Despite all she had just said, her voice remained as emotionless as usual. Still, Oliver was certain that underneath the surface, Penelope did indeed have feelings. She typically looked and sounded dispassionate, but when he looked beyond that, he saw a person who very much experienced the gamut of human emotions. He sensed it was a big deal for her to offer to share her journal with him, and, as much as he didn't feel like creating one of his own, he absolutely did not want to hurt her. Perhaps he could put something in his so they could share. "Okay. That sounds like a nice idea."

"Well, listen to you two. This is fantastic! If I don't get you in there though, you won't be able to journal. The group has begun, but Frank would rather you come late than not at all. Let's go."

Matt stood, helped Oliver to his feet, and ushered them out the door. He stopped just outside of the room though. "Oliver? Forgetting something?"

Oliver sighed, returned to his room, and came out with his journal. "Fine. Let's go." With effort, he forced himself to follow Matt and Penelope into the group room.

CHAPTER 18

OLIVER SAT NUMBLY BESIDE PENELOPE, LISTENING TO YET ANOTHER SONG. HE glanced at her. Her pen moved furiously on the paper in front of her. She was bent low over her notebook, and her arms encircled it, as though she were guarding it fiercely from the eyes of the world. She probably was. He forced himself to look at his own notebook. It was still completely blank. He was trying to write in it, but the task was too overwhelming. It wasn't that he didn't have thoughts and words; he most definitely did, but there were so many and they were jumbled up in this intense knot inside of him, a knot he had a hard time untangling and sorting out. Whenever it untangled a little bit, everything inside him came completely unraveled. He didn't want that to happen here in this group room. So he sat. And he heard the music.

Someone requested the song *Airplanes,* performed by The Ready Set. Oliver only half listened and didn't know or care what the song was about, but he heard something about a wish. He knew what he would wish for. And he knew it would never come true. He tightened his grip on the pen in his hand and began to scribble on the paper to keep himself in control. The song played on. His ears picked out the phrase, "...like shooting stars..." Stars. He moved his pen in the shape of a star. Up, down, up in a diagonal, across, down in a diagonal, up, down, up in a diagonal, across, down in a diagonal, one, two, three, four, five; he traced his lines over and over again. He stared at the star he drew on his paper. Stars. He and Maggie liked stargazing. He recalled the night they first used their new telescope.

"I can't wait to see Saturn! I wonder if we'll be able to count its rings." Maggie's voice was filled with excitement.

"I bet we will. I've only seen it in pictures. I want to see the real thing." He stared up at the sky, dotted with white lights. "Which one do you think it is?"

"Let's find out." She pulled out her phone.

"What are you doing?"

"Look at the app I found when you were putting the telescope together: Google Sky Map!" She held the phone to the sky, and stars appeared on the screen. They were labeled, and lines appeared to illustrate the various constellations. "It works! There's the moon. See? It says 'moon.'" She laughed. She stood in front of him so he could see the screen, too, and she moved the phone around to various locations. The constellations and labels changed according to the position of the phone. "This is cool!" she exclaimed.

He laughed. He put his arms around her and pulled her against him. "It is. But put it away. I doubt the ancient astronomers consulted a cell phone to show them where the stars and planets were. They didn't need Google Sky Map, and neither do we. I'm going to find Saturn on my own."

"You're such a man. This falls into the category of refusing to stop and ask for directions."

"Damn right!" He thumped his chest. "Me Tarzan. No need help finding way."

"Me Jane. Me wise. Use Google Maps in car and use Google Sky Map outside."

"Tarzan say please? Want to try on own. Tarzan scientist. Can do this."

She laughed and stuck the phone back in her pocket. "Fine, Tarzan! Have at it."

He searched for twenty minutes. Maggie sat cross-legged on the grass watching him in amusement. Finally he said, "Uh, Maggie?"

"Yes, my darling man?"

"Tarzan environmental scientist. Not astrophysicist."

She giggled. "Tarzan very intelligent, very skilled environmental scientist. And a cute one, too." She stood and kissed him on the cheek. "What do you say to get me to use the app?"

"Please."

"No-o."

"Fine. You were right."

"As usual."

"As usual," he repeated.

"Yay! I get to use Google Sky Map," she said with glee as she pointed her phone to the sky. About ten seconds later, she located Saturn.

Ten minutes later, they were still taking turns trying to find it in the telescope.

"Sweetheart, let's try something easier. Why don't we start with the moon?" Maggie suggested.

"What's that phrase? Aim for the stars; even if you miss you'll still hit the moon?"

"Something like that. Let's try to hit the moon."

Fifteen minutes later, they still hadn't zeroed in on the moon.

Oliver stood from his crouched position over the telescope's eyepiece. He let out a sigh of frustration. "Oh my God. This should not be that difficult! What kind of an idiot can't locate the freaking moon? I'm a moron."

"I can't get it, either, and I happen to think I'm pretty smart."

"You are incredibly smart. I, on the other hand..." He peered through the telescope. "Ugh!"

"Relax." She massaged his shoulders. "Turn around." She kissed him gently at first, and then with increasing passion. She pulled back. "There. Did that help you feel better? Let's try again."

"Try what? I forgot what we were doing."

She laughed. "Step aside. We're going to get the damn moon in our telescope if it takes all night."

After nearly a half hour of taking turns tweaking the telescope, Maggie shouted, "Yes! I got it! Check it out. It looks amazingly cool." She stepped aside so Oliver could see.

Eagerly, he peered through the lens. "Wow! That's incredible." He turned to Maggie and bumped the telescope in the process. "Oh no!"

"Oliver!" She collapsed in a fit of laughter. Her laughter was contagious, and he couldn't help but join in. When they had settled down, he said, "That's it. I want to see it again, and I'm going to get it this time."

It was only a few minutes before the moon once again came into sight of the lens. They took turns gazing, more calmly this time.

"Oliver, as I look through this telescope, I can't help but wonder…"

"What do you wonder, my love?"

"Where were you?"

His heart pounded, and the sensation returned him to the present. He felt like crying, and he struggled to contain it. Fervently, in an attempt to change his thoughts, he stared at his paper. Without consciously realizing it, at some point he had slid his pen over, beside the star, and begun scribbling in the shape of a crescent moon. Through watery eyes, he watched his hand as though it belonged to someone else. It swooshed in a downward curve, and then upward. In his head, he put words to the movement: *swoosh down, swoosh up, down, up.* He needed to control his emotions. He pressed his pen down harder. The pool of tears in his eyes deepened, and the image became amorphous. He remembered the breathing exercises, and he took slow, deep breaths and gradually calmed himself down. His hand became still. He blinked several times, and, once again, he saw the star and moon he had drawn in his journal. He became aware that people were leaving. He hadn't even heard Frank end the group.

Penelope said, "You drew a picture. I used my journal too, like I said I would. It's not all my own work, though. We will share at lunch. Let's go to the art group now."

He sat, unmoving. He didn't want to go to the art group. He didn't want to do a damn thing. Penelope touched his arm. He looked at her hand, and then at her face. Her expression was stone-faced, but soft. The memory of the first night he and Maggie had used the telescope to look at the moon was still fresh in his mind, and the grief, the guilt, the shame, the utter misery, beat at him. He tried to focus on the moment like Dr. Willis had instructed. What could he do to make this moment bearable? He didn't want to experience this moment, or any moment, and he didn't deserve for it to be bearable. His desire to be gone didn't change the fact that he was, indeed, sitting here. He was sitting by a kind human being who was also suffering. Her experience was completely different, but equally painful. He didn't deserve to have kindness in his life, but Penelope certainly did. He could make this moment bearable by focusing on her. As he took her in and pondered the situation, he felt himself pull a little bit out of himself. He was a terribly horrible and awful person, but maybe he could do something good. He could be a friend; not just someone trying to be nice, but a real friend.

"What is it, Oliver?" she asked as he continued to look at her.

"Nothing. I was just thinking that I couldn't go to the art group alone. Thank you for going with me."

"You're welcome." She stood and moved toward the door. He followed close behind. A moment later, still remembering Maggie's voice, searching and forlorn, asking him where he had been, he trudged through the door of the art room.

"Good morning! I'm happy to see you; having you come to my group ten whole minutes before it starts is a great way to start my Monday!" Camille greeted them warmly as she dug supplies out of the closet and placed them on the table. Numerous colorful plastic figurines were spread out in the center of the table. There were land animals, sea animals, plants, dinosaurs, and people. Oliver sighed. *What now?*

As they settled into chairs, Penelope poked through the pile. "Oh," she said as she grabbed one, a horse. "Look." She held it up for Oliver to see. She closed her eyes and said nothing more.

"Do you like horses?" Oliver needed to focus on something outside of his own head. Plus, he was genuinely interested; he wanted to get to know more about who she was. Certainly there was more to her than mental illness.

She opened her eyes and studied the horse. Eventually, she told him, "This reminds me of my childhood. I grew up in rural Kentucky, and my family owned horses. I helped care for them every day, as far back as I can remember."

"I've never been on a horse. Are they fun to ride?"

She looked at him. "Yes, they are."

Oliver had to prompt her to continue. "Do you miss them?" When she didn't answer, he said, "I'm sorry. I didn't mean to pry. You don't have to talk about it. I'm sorry if I upset you."

"No. Please stop apologizing. You did not upset me." She took his hand and held it briefly then let it go and continued slowly, "I am trying to find words. This horse is brown. In Kerffie language, brown means desire. Desire can be good or bad. I think it's good right now, because I don't think I'm being greedy. I just want to talk to you, but Mrs. Roosevelt is angry at me. She's telling me that I'm being greedy by wanting to tell you about myself. She's trying to take my words away from me so I can't talk to you. The medication I'm taking makes it harder for her to do that though. I'm trying to get my words back so I can talk to you." She closed her eyes and wrinkled her brow, making her look deep in concentration. As he had the other day, Oliver heard Penelope's part of the conversation.

"Please let me talk to him, Mrs. Roosevelt."

No! You have me to talk to. You don't need other people.

"But I do."

What?! I'm the only one you need. You are privileged that I chose you. It was you I chose. Not William. Not this Oliver guy. They are to be removed from your life. I won't let you talk to them.

"Mrs. Roosevelt, I love William. And I am so happy that I am making a new friend. I like Oliver, and I want to talk to him. Please let me."

The only way to show William and Oliver that you care about them is to be absent from their lives. You know how strange you are. Do you want to embarrass them by being around them? That horse in your hand gives me a good idea. Why don't we go back to Kentucky? We can get a quiet ranch together, and be away from the cruel world. You'll be able to enjoy me, and you won't have to fight who you really are. That means you won't have to take these pills that make us sick. It will be just you, me, and some beautiful horses. Wouldn't that be nice?

"No! I left Kentucky and I don't want to go back!"

Oliver heard the distress in Penelope's voice and was astonished. Normally her voice was utterly dispassionate. The fact that her tone contained emotion accentuated the degree of her angst. He took her hand in both of his. "Hey," he said quietly. When she didn't acknowledge him, he squeezed her hand lightly and repeated, "Hey. Penelope, look at me. Did you say Kentucky? I've never been there. Can you tell me about it?"

She looked confused as she stared at him.

"Tell me about Kentucky. You said your medication makes it harder for Mrs. Roosevelt to take your words. You're strong and you can do this. Just look at me and pull away from her."

Penelope stared at him intensely. Oliver held her gaze. Slowly, she began to speak. "I grew up in Kentucky."

"Did you like it?"

"I...Mrs. Roosevelt, I'm going to talk to Oliver now." She took a deep breath as if summoning her will. She began to speak to Oliver, haltingly at first. "I didn't hate it...I had a nice family and good friends and everything...but from the time I was in junior high, I dreamed of living in a big city, like New York or Atlanta or Chicago...Especially Chicago." As she talked, the words came more easily. "I would check out books and magazines from the library, and every evening after my homework and chores were done, I would take the books and magazines and hop on one of my horses and ride for miles, until I reached my favorite peaceful spot. It was a small pond hidden in a grove of trees on one end of a large, grassy meadow. The land actually belonged to my friend Bonnie's grandfather. When we were in grade school, Bonnie and I used to spend countless summer hours playing in that meadow and swimming in that pond. When I got older, it was the perfect place to escape and daydream. Whenever I went there, I would let my horse graze while I settled into a comfortable position, sometimes with my back against this big old tree, or sometimes sprawled out on my stomach in the bluegrass, and I'd just lose myself in one of the books or magazines." She smiled wistfully. "I never grew tired of gazing at the striking photographs of city skylines with their soaring skyscrapers. It was like the metal and glass of the buildings reflected life and energy right out of the pictures and into my very being. When I read articles about urban life, I pictured myself attending concerts and plays and art shows and museum events. As I read restaurant reviews, I could all but taste the exotic foods. Who knew then that I would meet and fall in love with a chef at one of those very restaurants?" She stopped and looked thoughtfully at Oliver. "I really do love him, you know. That's why this sucks so damn much." Her voice trailed off. Oliver searched his mind for something to say to make it better for her, but words failed him. He simply rubbed her hand.

With a small sigh, she continued, "Anyway, the more I read, the more I knew that city life was the life for me. Of all the cities, it was Chicago that captured my heart and soul, and I knew without a doubt that I wanted to live my life here. Over time, as I loved the city more and more, I liked rural Kentucky less and less. The bluegrass underneath me as I read began to feel itchy and irritating. The meadow became too quiet. The sound of frogs and cicadas that used to be so melodious began to sound lonely and hollow. My family life was fine, but I didn't want the country life my parents and siblings embraced. Throughout high school, I couldn't wait to leave Kentucky and start a life of my own in Chicago."

When she said nothing further, Oliver said, "And you did just that. That's amazing. Some people don't have the courage to pursue their dreams, but you did. Are you glad?"

"I was, until schizophrenia ruined my life. I loved my life, but it's over." She buried her face in her hands.

Oliver touched her shoulder. "Penelope—"

He didn't finish, because Camille signaled the beginning of the group. "Happy Monday, everyone! I see that all of you are interested in the figurines on the table. I like that you are examining them and even talking to each other about them. It shows curiosity, and curiosity is a good thing. It's a way of being involved in life. What I want you to do today is think about yourself in your own life. Look through all of the figurines, and find one that represents the person you are becoming. I'm going to pass around some paper, and as you can see, there are markers, crayons, and watercolor paints on the table. I want you to really think about the person you want to become and how your figurine represents that. Draw or paint the figure on your paper, and then put words to it. Either write a paragraph, or label the features of your figure that you feel symbolize the way you want to be. Then write down what you are doing to become that person." She set the group to the task of reflecting and creating.

Oliver was overwhelmed and didn't know what to do. He still hurt from the music group, and the last thing he wanted to do was find something to symbolize himself. He seriously doubted there was an ugly monster among the plastic figures. And the crap about what he wanted to become? There probably wasn't a coffin on the table, either. Plus, he was hurting for Penelope, too. Screw this exercise; he wanted to talk to her. He leaned close to her and said, "Come on. Let's go into the day area where we can talk."

"Oh, no you don't." Camille had been walking around the table and had overheard Oliver's suggestion. "You two need to be here. It looks like you're having a hard time right now, and that is precisely why this is the perfect time for you to engage in this activity. Oliver, take a look at the figurines and get started while I chat with Penelope for a little bit, okay?" She had been standing between them, but stepped to the other side of Penelope and squatted down beside her.

Frustrated, Oliver snatched the piece of plastic that was closest to him. It was a purple tiger. *Tigers aren't purple*, he thought in irritation. The last time he had seen a tiger, it wasn't purple. It was orange with black stripes. It was last summer, when he and Maggie took Henry to Chicago and they went to the Lincoln Park Zoo.

Henry had just turned three. He was an active little guy, and he preferred the animals that were as lively as he was. Therefore, he wasn't overly impressed with the tigers. They just sat in the shade. His favorite animals were the monkeys. He took great delight in their antics. When they reached the money exhibit, he wanted out of his stroller. They let him out and got a bigger kick out of him than they did the monkeys. He giggled and jumped up and down as he watched the little ones play. One of them scrambled up the fence right in front of them, leaped over to a rope and grabbed it with its tail. It hung upside down and swayed back and forth, watching Henry watch him. Henry waved at it enthusiastically and shouted, "Hi, muh-key!" The monkey then swung itself over to a platform, jumped down, and scrambled away. "Again! Again!" Henry took off around the cage after it. He tripped over a crack in the sidewalk and sprawled forward, skinning his knee in the process. He sat up and howled. Oliver and Maggie hurried to him.

The blood on Oliver's little boy's knees gushed everywhere, until it covered not only his knees, but his entire legs and up his torso. Henry cried in pain, and then he called, "Daddy! Daddy! Help, Daddy! Where are you?"

His heart pounded furiously. The room spun. He felt sick. He threw the tiger down and bolted out the door. He couldn't really see where he was going, and he collided hard with someone. It scared him and intensified his pounding heart, his dizzy head, and his nauseous gut.

Matt rushed across the room to help. "Whoa! Oliver, what's going on?" Matt grabbed ahold of him to steady him.

"I need my bathroom unlocked. I'm going to be sick!"

"Let's go." They hurried to his room, Matt unlocked the bathroom door, and Oliver rushed in. Because his stomach was empty, only bile came up. Then he dry heaved uncontrollably. It hurt, and it served him right. Matt grabbed Oliver's container of water and offered it to him. He rejected it and remained as he was, doubled over and heaving. Matt refused to go away, though, and he ordered Oliver to drink. Still, Oliver refused. Matt summoned another tech. Ted, the tech Oliver had met in the dining room of Side A on his first night at Airhaven, responded. Together, Matt and Ted helped Oliver straighten up but remained in the bathroom. Oliver shook with pain and exhaustion and fear and regret. Once again, Matt handed him the water and commanded him to drink. Oliver pushed it away.

"Oliver, that isn't helping you. Stop that nonsense and take a drink of water." Ted's voice was stern.

Oliver didn't seem to hear him. "Henry! No! I'm here! Please!"

"Who is Henry?" Ted inquired, his voice still firm. "Whoever he is, if he were standing here watching you, I'm sure he would also tell you to drink this water."

Oliver pulled out of their grasp and leaned over as the dry heaves resumed.

Matt shook his head. "Ted, no. Be quiet. I just want you to help me stabilize him. Let's straighten him back up." To Oliver, he said, "Okay, Ted and I are going to help you stand up."

The two techs held onto Oliver's arms and pulled him upright. Everything spun, and he wavered.

Matt and Ted each grasped him more firmly, and Matt said, "We're going to walk over to your bed so you can sit down."

Once they helped him sit, Matt returned for the water and held it in front of Oliver. "I'm putting the straw to your mouth, and you're going to take a few sips." Oliver complied. "Good. A few more."

Eventually, Oliver drank it all. He still felt nauseous and dizzy. He knew where he was, but he still heard Henry's cries reverberate loudly in his head. He put his hands over his ears, bent forward, and rocked. "I'm sorry, I'm sorry, I'm sorry." The words came in breathless pants as he repeated this mantra over and over again.

"That makes absolutely no sense. You need to explain that. Why are you sorry?" Ted demanded.

"Ted, I've got it from here. Thanks for helping me get him out of the bathroom and steady him."

"He doesn't look very steady to me. Are you sure you've got him?"

"I'm sure. Thanks."

"Well, holler again if you need me."

After he left, Matt muttered, "I won't be needing your 'help,' Ted." To Oliver, he said, "Ted's gone now. Let's talk. You were calling for Henry. Tell me about that."

Oliver removed his hands from his ears and hugged his torso. He remained bent forward, rocking. "The tiger in art. It reminded me of the time Maggie and I took Henry to the zoo. He was excited. He ran, but he tripped and fell. He scraped his knees. As I was remembering it, he asked me where I was. I wasn't there for them when they needed me!" He couldn't continue.

Matt rubbed his back. "This is a pretty strong reaction. Is this the first time that in your mind you heard him ask you where you were?"

Oliver shook his head. Then he nodded, and then he shook his head again. "No. Yes. No. I mean, whenever I start to remember detailed moments from the past, it always happens, but it's always Maggie who asks. This time, it was Henry. And his little voice was so pleading and he sounded so betrayed and lost and scared and…" He choked and gagged, but, because nothing came up, he remained doubled over at the edge of the bed rather than dashing to the bathroom.

"Here. Sit up." Matt gently pulled Oliver to an upright position. "Take it easy. I need you to breathe with me, slowly and deeply. Yes, like that. You've got it. You're getting good at this! Now, let's try again," he said after Oliver was under control. "You were telling me what happens when you remember moments with Maggie and Henry."

"It's so painful, yet I like remembering them. But every time I think of them, Maggie—and now Henry, too, I guess—ends up asking me where I was and why I wasn't there. I know I don't deserve to want this, but I really, really wish that I could remember without the reminder that I failed them. I know that sounds selfish. Oh, God! I am so selfish! Who am I to ask for a peaceful memory?" He pressed his hands hard into his eyes.

"That is absolutely not selfish. It is very normal. We all want to be able to remember things without being tormented. It sounds like everything is jumbled up inside of you right now and your memories are overlapping and interfering with each other. But now that you've opened up and you're participating in the groups, you are going to find that you can sort things out."

"I don't want to sort things out. I want to die. I don't want to live without Maggie and Henry."

"I hear you. I hear that living is very, very difficult. I also heard, just now, that you want to remember good times with your family without the memory turning and twisting on you. Is that right?"

Oliver nodded.

"Let's focus on doing something about your memories. I think that that journal of yours could be a useful tool. Journaling helps us get things out of our heads so we can sort through what we're dealing with. Didn't you and Penelope decide that you would each journal and share some of the things you put down on paper? Sharing can be a powerful experience. I really like the idea of you and Penelope doing that."

"Penelope! Matt, she was talking to me, but then the group started. Camille made us stop, but I wanted to keep listening to her. But Camille told me to do the activity. That's when I saw that tiger and got caught up in a memory and freaked out, and I abandoned her. Oh, God! Why am I so self-centered? Why do I keep forsaking people? The world will be better off without me, Matt, please!"

"Take it easy. Back up and think about the situation. You said that Camille started the group and made you and Penelope stop talking. You didn't have a choice. You didn't abandon her."

Oliver wrapped his arms across his stomach and bent forward again. "I got sick and ran out of the room, leaving her alone."

"It happened after you were told to focus on the activity. You couldn't have done anything differently."

"I want to go find her." He sat up straight and ran his fingers though his hair.

"First, you need to calm back down." Matt glanced at the clock. "This is perfect. The group will be done in five minutes. We'll sit together until then, and then you can go meet up with Penelope when she comes out, okay?"

"I hate myself."

"Well, I don't hate you, and I bet Penelope doesn't, either. We'll find out in a few minutes."

They sat in silence. Oliver heard the incessant ticking of the clock. He hated that damn clock. Every tick was a reminder that he was living another second and that Maggie and Henry had been gone for another second. And another. And another. He threw his hands over his ears again and hunched over in pain.

"Hey. What's that about?" Matt looked at him, concern etched into his brow.

"Uh, I need to get out of here. Can we wait in the day area?"

"You got it. Let's go."

Matt led the way to Oliver and Penelope's regular table. Oliver settled into a chair and, agitated, stared at the group room door, waiting for Penelope to exit.

CHAPTER 19

THE INSTANT THE DOOR TO THE GROUP ROOM OPENED, OLIVER SPRANG FROM his chair and rushed to meet Penelope. He didn't have to wait, as she was the first one to leave the room. "Penelope! How are you doing? Was the group okay for you? I am so, so sorry I left. I didn't mean to go away. I picked up this tiger, and…the zoo.…Maggie and I took Henry.…He fell, and he called to me and I got sick and had to leave…I'm sorry I left—"

"Oliver, slow down. It's okay. Please stop apologizing."

"But I really am sorry. I understand if you hate me."

"What? Why would I hate you? You're my friend now."

Matt had sauntered up and stood listening to them. At this last statement from Penelope, he spoke up. "Two to one, man. I told you she doesn't hate you."

"Of course I don't. I tried to follow you out because I was worried about you, but Camille made me stay. I didn't do the assignment though. I did something else instead. I made something for you in your journal. I thought of something that you might find helpful." She held up his notebook and a box of crayons, but didn't give them to him. She dropped her arm back down to her side. "I want to show you, but it took a lot out of me to make it, and I really need a cigarette now. It's break time. Do you want to come out?"

Oliver didn't know what to say or do. He didn't want to desert her yet again, but he wasn't ready to go outside into the courtyard. He had looked down on it from a window once, and it looked park-like. It even had a playground for the children who were part of the youth program here. He didn't want to abandon her, but he knew he couldn't handle being out there. Not in a park. A park.

Suddenly, a thought struck him: parks were dangerous, and what if something happened to her out there? He should go out to keep her safe. But he wasn't ready to go outside into the courtyard. He didn't know what to do. He shifted from foot to foot and ran his fingers through his hair.

Matt stepped in. "I think she was just making a casual offer. She goes out all the time, and I bet she doesn't mind that you need to stay inside, do you, Penelope?"

"Of course not."

"Maybe you should stay in too. It's dangerous out there. I don't want you to get hurt."

"I really need a cigarette. But you can stay here. I won't be gone long."

"No! I'll go with you then. I won't let anything happen to you. It will be okay. It really will. It will be okay. I'll keep you safe out there. I promise, okay?"

"Oliver, look at me," Matt directed. He waited for Oliver to comply then informed him, "It is a securely protected courtyard. It is very safe. No one from the outside can get in. There will be two techs out there with everyone; in fact, I'll be one of them. Do you trust me?" After Oliver nodded, Matt said, "Good. Penelope is going to go out for a break right now, and she will be fine, like she always is. You are not ready to go out there. I want you to sit at your table and breathe. When Penelope comes back, you two can have lunch together and she can show you what she made for you. Okay?"

"Okay. I'm sorry for making such a big deal about it."

"You're impossible. Now go sit down and wait for Penelope."

Oliver shuffled back to the table and slouched down. The minutes dragged on, and it felt like she had been gone a very long time. He began to worry. What if something had happened down there? Matt had said it was safe, but nothing was completely safe. Oliver hurried to the workstation to inquire about her, but just as he arrived, the elevator opened and delivered the group that had gone outside. His entire body sagged with relief; he hadn't realized he had been holding so much tension. He wanted to throw his arms around her, but he was afraid that that would be weird. Plus, the thought of hugging a woman other than Maggie, even if it was only in friendship, hurt.

"Oliver, what's that expression? Are you okay?"

"Yeah. I'm just glad you got back safely." He noticed his journal in her hands. "Can I see what you made for me?"

"Oh! Yes. I'm starving. Let's get our lunch then I'll show you while I eat and you drink."

Once they were seated back at their table, Penelope placed his journal in front of her. Before she opened it she explained, "My psychiatrist, Dr. Daniels, suggested that I keep a journal. I get confused really easily, especially when I don't take my medication. Even when I do, it still happens but not as intensely. The pills don't completely get rid of the other things, but they help make room for my own thoughts. I have a lot of ideas that come and go through my mind, and they all feel very real." She lowered her voice to a whisper. "Actually, to be honest with you, I think that they *are* all real. Very real. There are things that humans just don't understand. Other beings share our planet. Plants and animals and rocks are more alive than most people realize. They talk to us. The human condition would be so much better if we would listen. Ghosts know that already, and they interact with us. Take Eleanor Roosevelt. She's still around. If we tune our chakras to a broader range of frequencies, we can channel different life-forms and learn things from people like Mrs. Roosevelt, or from the other beings, or even from the plants, animals, and rocks. You know why there are different kinds of rocks? It's because each rock is a different race. That's why there are so many colors, too. We can also see the colors more brightly and in new ways if we open ourselves up to them. The colors are alive, too. They're not just there for us to look at. They are living, independent life forms. Our chakras are meant to receive other beings, but most humans plug up their chakras with pollution. Does that make sense?" She focused on Oliver's face. "Oh God, it doesn't make sense at all to you, does it? I never make any sense to anyone. See what William has to put up with? Imagine what it would be like for him to have to live with me forever. Oh, poor William." She put her head down on Oliver's journal, which was still in front of her.

Oliver wasn't quite sure what to say, but he believed that saying nothing would be far worse than whatever he did say. "You could help me understand, Penelope. I bet you could help William understand too. He loves you, and because of that, I bet he likes to just be with you and hear what's on your mind. Maggie was a lawyer, and I didn't understand the details of the law like she did, but I loved to hear her talk about it anyway. William probably feels the same way about you."

She kept her head down. "That's way different. That's not the same thing at all."

"Why not?"

"Because Maggie was normal. I'm mentally ill."

"And that means you're not worth listening to? To me, that's the thing that doesn't make any sense."

She kept her head down but turned her face so she could see him. "Really? You think I'm worth listening to?"

"Absolutely. In fact, I'd really like to hear about what you put in my notebook. I certainly can't put anything in it. I'm happy that you could, and I'd like to see it."

She sat up. "That's right. I almost forgot about that. I get going on these crazy tangents and lose sight of things. Do you really want to see it after listening to me go on and on like that?"

"Yes, I do. Very much. I need help, Penelope, and I'm touched that you put something in my notebook to help me."

She gave him a very small smile. "You just helped me. Let's see if this helps you." She patted the notebook but didn't open it. "Like I said, Dr. Daniels is teaching me that writing things down or drawing them out can help me back up and look at things in new ways. He says it can help me understand stuff. Some things can never be understood, like why I am schizophrenic, or why your family was killed."

At that, a lump formed in Oliver's throat; his emotions always ran so close to the surface and the slightest things easily revved them up. He ignored the lump and kept listening.

"But he says that putting my thoughts and feelings down can help me sort things out. I got to thinking that it might be good for you, too. You're dealing with a lot, and I bet it's hard for you to know where to start. Knowing where to start when I journal is difficult for me, too. So I thought really hard about what might be useful to you. I had to struggle because Mrs. Roosevelt was jealous that I was making something for you. She kept taking my ideas away and trying to impose her own, but I didn't want her ideas. I just kept concentrating on what I wanted to do, and she went away, and eventually I could do it."

"That's great! Are you proud of yourself?"

"No."

"Why not? It's pretty amazing that you were able to break out of Mrs. Roosevelt's control."

"Should I be proud of myself?"

"Yes. Absolutely."

"Okay. If you say so." She became quiet and appeared lost in thought. "Actually, I have never been able to take charge and stand up to her before. I guess I did do a good thing. Anyway, let me show you your notebook." She opened the cover. On the first page were his scribble, his star, and his crescent moon. She turned the page to reveal a large circle, intricately colored with the colors of the rainbow plus black, white, and brown. The image looked like a beautiful stained-glass window; however, rather than each color being distinctly separated from the others throughout the image, the colors blended together in places. The result was a striking combination of distinct, bright patterns and soft, blended lines. Underneath the image was a key, like a legend on a map, to indicate what each of the colors represented.

"Penelope! That is beautiful! Is this what you had to wrestle with Mrs. Roosevelt for?"

"This is part of it, yes."

"You are extremely creative. I'm really impressed."

"Thank you, Oliver," she said unemotionally. "Now I'm going to tell you what the colors mean. The drawing is my own creation, but the meaning behind it did not come from me. There are beings called Kerffies. They are microscopic but very complex. Even more complex than humans. They are so tiny, actually, because they are so advanced. They originated outside of our galaxy, and over millions of years, they evolved to their tiny size because they learned how to exist very efficiently. They're not wasteful like humans, and they don't need lots of stuff to exist and be comfortable. Humans are so imprudent; our bodies need lots of food and water, it takes a lot of material to cover us, it takes lots of stuff to make some people happy. We could learn a lot from the Kerffies if only we would listen. They left their home planet millennia ago to explore the universe, and they have civilizations on many, many planets, including Earth."

"Why are they here?" Oliver asked.

"Why is anybody here?"

They were both silent in response to that question. After several moments, Oliver said quietly, "Well, I don't know why I'm here. I don't want to be here. I don't want to be anywhere. I want to die,

Penelope." He held her gaze briefly before looking down. He picked at his fingernails.

"I know what you mean. I'd rather be dead than a worthless nothing."

He looked up sharply. "You are not a worthless nothing!"

"Yes, Oliver, I am."

"You are not," he said adamantly. "Take this, for example." He held up his notebook. "Look at what you created. It's amazing. And it's pretty complicated, too. It's neat. In fact, I think it's going to be helpful. Will you keep explaining it to me? You were telling me about the Kerffies. I didn't mean to get you off track. Will you tell me more?"

"Okay. As I was saying, they live here on Earth. Most humans just don't see them. Well, that's not completely accurate. People can see them, but they don't realize what they're seeing. Look! You can see some now. Come with me for a second. Let's move quietly so we don't disturb them. They are very peaceful, and we should be respectful and be in harmony with them."

She rose and tiptoed to the window. Her walk was exaggerated; she lifted her knees high as she walked and stepped lightly on the balls of her feet. Oliver did the same; to hell with the onlookers, he thought. She stopped a few feet away from a patch of sunlight that streamed through the window. "See the little specks floating around?"

"Are those Kerffies?"

"Oliver, I said that Kerffies are microscopic. Do you know what microscopic means?" She managed to ask that question without sounding the least bit condescending.

He smiled. "Yes, I do. In my job, I worked with microscopes on a daily basis to study tiny particles in water."

"Oh. Then you should know that these particles are too big to be the individual Kerffies, but you were close. These are Kerffie cities. Thousands of Kerffies live in each of these."

"Wow. I've seen these particles before, but I had no idea what they were. I always thought that they were just dust motes." Oliver was unsure where to take this conversation. He certainly didn't want to correct her or make her feel foolish, but he didn't know if indulging her beliefs was good for her, either. He did know one thing: retreating from her and her beliefs would be a horrible thing to do. Too many people did just that. Whether people shunned her because they were judging her negatively or because they didn't know how to respond, they were hurtful. As a friend, Oliver refused to be hurtful. He decided to steer the conversation back to his notebook. "The Kerffies taught you the meaning of the colors?"

"Not just me. They teach others who are open to them. I think a lot of Eastern philosophies are based on Kerffie knowledge and ideas. The Kerffies are just in the process of teaching me. Their language and their ideas are extremely complicated. My understanding of it is very rudimentary because I only know the basics. But I know enough to teach you in order to help you. Let's go back and I'll show you."

When they were once again seated, Penelope resumed her explanation of her creation. She ran her hand along the edge of the circle she had drawn and said, "This represents the orb of emotion you have inside of you. We all have an orb of emotion." She placed a hand on her stomach and moved it in a circle. "It's located behind the bellybutton, and it radiates up and down the spine and through little fibers to every cell."

Copying Penelope, Oliver put his own hand to his stomach and held it there while he listened.

"Each emotion is represented by a color. I've written down the meanings for you so you can remember them. You can always look back on them as you journal when you want to represent feelings. As you can see, red represents fear, orange stands for calm, yellow is disgust, green is acceptance, blue is love or friendship, indigo is anger, and purple is hate."

She had been looking at her drawing, but she looked up at him when she said, "I was surprised to learn about purple. It's kind of ironic when you think about it, isn't it? I mean, purple is often an important religious color, at least in Christian religions; I'm not sure about others. Churches say they promote peace and love, but in practice, they are sometimes about hating others who believe different things."

"I agree. And I'm pretty sure that if there is a God, he hates me with a passion. Maybe purple is appropriate for religions," Oliver said quietly. He averted his gaze.

"Are you okay? Do you want to stop looking at your notebook?" He shook his head.

"No, you're not okay or no, you don't want to stop?"

"Both," he admitted. "I'd really like to hear more, if you don't mind."

Immediately, she resumed her explanation. "So those are the colors of the rainbow. There are also black, white, and brown. Oddly enough, black represents happiness. People have no idea what they mean when they wear black to funerals."

"Oh. I wore black to…" He trailed off. He couldn't bring himself to say "their funeral."

"It's okay that you did that. You didn't know. I'm sorry I mentioned funerals. I didn't mean to upset you."

"That's okay." His heart thumped in his chest, and his limbs felt strange and weak. He needed to get his mind off of the idea of funerals. "What about white and brown?"

"Oh, yeah. White represents sadness. You know, because when we feel sad we often feel hollow. At least I do, anyway."

"Me too. And life without Maggie and Henry is very hollow. And empty. And sad." His voice had risen in pitch as his throat closed around his words.

"I think we should stop. You look like you are going to cry. I really didn't mean to upset you."

"No, please. I want to hear this. It's just that I've never actually talked about emotions before. I always think about the event, but never my specific feelings. I mean, I know I feel miserable, but thinking about the individual emotions is different. It takes me to a different level already, and all I'm doing is listening to you label them."

"That's why Dr. Daniels told me to journal. He said that sorting things out helps bring new levels of awareness, which is a good thing. Did I really do something that might help you?"

"I think I might be beyond help, but this is definitely not more hurtful than anything else is. I like it. Really."

"Maybe you're not beyond help. Maybe you just haven't had the help you need."

"I don't deserve it, Penelope."

"Yes, you do. You have been nothing but nice to me, and for that alone, you deserve good things."

Oliver opened his mouth to speak, but Penelope said, "If what you are about to say is an argument against what I just said, I don't want to hear it. I'm going to continue now. The last color I've included here is brown. Brown means desire, and it could be good desire or bad desire depending on the situation. There are many, many more colors, of course. These are just the basic ones. Like I said, their language and their ideas are intricate. You can see in my drawing how even the basics are complicated. They blend together in unique ways to create what the Kerffies call compound emotions. Let me give you just one example. See how here yellow and blue blend softly together?" She pointed to an area of her drawing. "That's disgust and love blending together. It seems like an odd combination, but think about it: sometimes we are disgusted by something that happens to someone we love, because we don't want to see them hurt. Or we are disgusted by something someone does, but it doesn't change the fact that we love them. It's fitting here that yellow and blue make green. Remember that green means acceptance? And we accept the people we love despite the fact that sometimes we are disgusted by something they do. All the colors dance with each other this way. Then, of course, there are colors like chartreuse or periwinkle. Some of them are colors in their own right that represent finer aspects of emotion, and others are subtle blends of a bunch of other colors. Feelings aren't simple."

Her description made his head spin. "That's for sure."

"I have more to show you, but do you have questions about the colors first?"

"I don't know. I definitely want to see what else you put in my notebook for me."

"Okay." She turned the page. She had filled the entire page, margin to margin—top to bottom and side to side—with lines and shapes in an elaborate geometric drawing. Nothing was colored in.

"Wow! This is amazing, too. I've never seen anything quite like it. You have a lot of talent."

"Mrs. Roosevelt doesn't think so. She likes her own work better."

"Well, I like your work."

"Thank you. That means a lot to me." Her tone was neutral and expressionless, but Oliver knew better than to think she didn't feel anything. There was no way she could have made that detailed drawing on the last page if she didn't experience emotion.

"Anyway," she continued, "first I need to tell you that I used black to create the shapes and that the insides of the shapes are white. That is just a coincidence. Here, the colors don't have a meaning. They are just a vehicle to create something else." She studied the drawing for a moment. "Actually, now that I think about it, maybe the colors here aren't a coincidence. The Kerffies are teaching me to find deeper meanings in all things. I think that maybe the colors are significant here after all. I chose black to make these shapes and lines. Black means happiness, and I was happy because I was making something for you, and also, I want you to be happy. They are white inside right now, not just because of the white paper, but because you and I are both very sad right now."

Her eyes met his. "Maybe we can fill in the emptiness with different colors. But I digress."

Her gaze returned to the journal and she continued to teach Oliver. "Like colors, shapes have meanings. I have learned the simplest of them, and I wrote them down for you. Shapes represent aspects of character. Lines mean truthfulness. All shapes are made from lines, so all shapes are true. Circles are caring, squares mean courage, triangles stand for respect, rectangles are fairness, and octagons are gratitude, which is neat because octagons are kind of circular; caring and gratitude often go hand in hand."

She watched Oliver flip through his notebook and study the pages. She had filled in more than half of it with various shapes. The early pages each had only one shape repeated in different sizes and positions; the later pages held combinations of shapes, some separate, some overlapping. "You might be wondering what you are supposed to do with all of this. I will give you a suggestion. I left you blank pages so you can create your own combinations of shapes and colors, but to help you get started, I made you pages to work with. You can fill these in over time. You can draw pictures inside them or write words. You can sort out your feelings and even your memories. With the circles, for example, you can think about all of the ways you are a caring person. You can think about ways you cared about Maggie and Henry and ways you care about others now. By doing that, maybe you'll stop hating yourself so much."

Oliver doubted that very much, but he wasn't about to crush Penelope by saying so. He realized that this counted as being caring. It wasn't enough though to ease his self-loathing. He tuned back in to Penelope. She was talking about adding colors. "...and because emotions superimpose themselves on everything, even our character traits, you can color these in when you want to. For example, I think you were very afraid that day when you arrived at the park and couldn't find Maggie and Henry. You cared about them and wanted them to be safe. You can indicate that in the circles using pictures or words and then color them in using red and brown.

"Dr. Daniels tells me that I need to face my schizophrenia head on in order to come to terms with it and be able to live with it. I think that goes for you, too. You need to face it head on in order to be able to deal with it. Doing that is very hard though. I hope this will help you face things and sort them out."

Oliver was speechless. He was completely overwhelmed. Her direct mention of his feelings in the park and the fact that he needed to face what happened left him feeling raw. He was also very touched by the fact that she had thought so hard about him and had made such an effort to create something she thought would help him. No one had done anything like that for him before. He experienced an odd mix of grief and warmth and guilt. He looked into her eyes. The tears that brimmed in his eyes made her appear blurry, but he could see the tenderness in her expression.

"Oliver?" Penelope touched his arm.

He blinked hard. He knew he should say something, but what could he possibly say? He had an idea. He turned to a blank page in his notebook. He reached for the box of crayons on the table and slowly slid out a blue crayon. He drew an octagon on his paper. His hand shook and he made the lines all wobbly, but it was still recognizable as an octagon. Inside the octagon he drew a stick figure with a ponytail and labeled it "Penelope." He drew a line under the octagon.

Tears formed in Penelope's eyes too, and now they rolled freely down her cheeks. She grabbed his hand and whispered, "Life sucks sometimes. I'm telling the truth too when I say right back to you that I am also grateful for your friendship."

CHAPTER 20

A T THE END OF THE AFTERNOON, OLIVER AND PENELOPE ONCE AGAIN SAT AT their table. Oliver clutched his notebook. "I wish I would have had a chance to use it this afternoon. I hope you know I really like it. I would much rather have used this in art group than have done that damn group painting activity. And then I was going to journal while you were in the exercise room; I didn't mean to fall asleep while you were down there. I'm sorry I haven't used this yet."

"Stop apologizing." She studied him. "You seem really tired."

"I'm exhausted."

"I am, too, and I hate it. My medication makes me so tired and groggy and just plain out of it. I don't like that feeling. William is on his way here now, and I don't have the energy I should have for him."

"I bet he understands."

"Understanding is one thing. Enjoying it and having to live with a lifeless lump is another thing altogether."

"Are you looking forward to seeing him tonight?"

"I don't want him to have to put up with me."

"That's not what I asked. How do you feel about him?"

"I love him with all of my heart, Oliver. That's why I can't do this to him."

"Listen to me. Love is the most important thing in the world. William seems to love you very much, and you just said that you love him with all of your heart. I know what that feeling is like, and I know what it's like when it's gone." The painful lump was back, and his voice cracked. He swallowed and pushed on, "Seriously, stay in his life. Focus on the love you have, and you can build everything else in your lives around that." Not wanting to break down and cause Penelope to focus on him rather than on her love for William, he fell silent.

He watched her. She seemed to be contemplating his words. "I'm confused, Oliver. I really don't want to be without him, but it feels selfish to make him live his life with a schizophrenic, medicated lump of a weirdo."

"That's an interesting label of yourself. I've never heard William call you that, but I have heard him say that he wants to be with you. You should listen to him."

"I just don't know."

"So don't do anything. Just hold onto him right now. I'd give anything to hold onto Maggie and Henry again. I miss them so very much. Please, please hold onto William." He fell silent again. A few moments later, he nudged Penelope and nodded toward the workstation. William stood at the desk as a tech looked through an insulated cooler and paper shopping bag.

"What should I do?"

"Do you love him?"

"I just told you that I do."

"Then go over there."

"I haven't made up my mind yet about whether I should set him free, and I don't want to mislead him."

"Ignore your mind right now. What does your heart want to do?"

In response, Penelope left the table and approached William. He stepped toward her as she approached, and she threw her arms around him. Oliver pulled the tattered and worn picture from his pocket, gently touched his wife and son, and whispered, "I want to do that to you. I'm so sorry that you can never, ever be hugged by anyone again." He continued to hold the picture in one hand while he wiped his eyes with his other. Lost in his desire to once again hold Maggie and Henry, he didn't notice William and Penelope approach. He jumped slightly when William touched his shoulder. He refocused on his surroundings.

"Whoops. I didn't mean to startle you."

"It's fine. You just surprised me a little, that's all." He pondered that; it seemed like he was becoming much less jumpy. He wiped his eyes again and invited William and Penelope to sit.

"You okay?" William asked him.

Oliver shrugged. "No, but don't worry; I'm not going to put you through a repeat of yesterday." The small jolt had been enough to pull him out of his intense longing and allow him to converse normally.

"Hey, I'm not worried about that, and you shouldn't be either." William gestured toward the picture Oliver still held. "That's such a great picture. I thought that maybe you might want to protect it so it doesn't get completely destroyed." He reached into his bag and produced clear, plastic laminating sheets. "I also brought you a frame, but the people at the desk confiscated it. It didn't even have glass, but they said that the frame itself was on your list of prohibited items." He shook his head. "Man, they're strict around here. I'm used to it though, so I brought these things, too, just in case. I didn't know what you could and couldn't have, so I played it safe and brought both."

Oliver was touched. "Thanks. I hate that this picture is so beat-up, and I really don't want it to get totally wrecked." He took the sheets from William and attempted to cover his picture. When he couldn't even peel the backing off the sheets, Penelope took them and did it for him. She went to the desk, had them trim the edges down, and then presented it to Oliver.

"Thanks, guys. This is nice. I wish I had thought of it a long time ago." He closed his eyes and sighed. "God, I couldn't even protect their picture, could I?"

"Oliver."

Oliver shook his head. "Sorry. It's okay. I just hate myself." He gave them a weak smile. Wanting to shift the focus away from himself, he said to William, "It looks like you brought dinner again."

"Oh yeah! I did." He looked at Penelope. "But first, I brought some things for you, too, sweetie." He pulled out a stuffed animal, a soft, fuzzy white cat. "Johixilan misses you, and I know how you feel about him."

"This is adorable! Thank you." She leaned close and pecked him on the cheek.

"And I bought you a book." Once again he reached into the bag. Solemnly, he handed it to her and explained, "It's Eleanor Roosevelt's autobiography. I was thinking that maybe we could read it together. You can start on it here if you want to, but I'd like to read it with you when you come home." He reached for her hand and held it as he said, "Penelope, I am not bothered by the fact that you hear her. You keep insisting that I must be embarrassed by it and ashamed of you. That's not true at all. I do hate that she seems to be so mean to you. I thought that if we learned more about her, maybe we could use what we know to at least change how she treats you." When Penelope said nothing, William asked, "Do you want to try it?"

"It sounds like a good idea," Oliver commented. "What did you say to me earlier today? That your doctor told you that you need to face this head on? This sounds like a perfect way to do that."

Penelope looked at Oliver but remained quiet. Her brows were knitted in apparent deep thought.

Oliver said, "You created my notebook and told me that I have to face what happened. I wasn't lying when I said that I liked it, but the truth is that facing it is painful and I don't know if I can do it. Maybe you could show me how. Watching you take charge of yourself might inspire me to do the same. If you agree to read this and learn from it, I'll agree to make an effort to really use my journal." Oliver dreaded the idea of having to do this, but this wasn't about him; it was about Penelope and William and their relationship. He wouldn't let more lives be ruined because of his selfishness.

Penelope looked from Oliver to William and back to Oliver before speaking. "Oliver," she began, "Would my reading this really help you?"

"Yes, it would."

She turned to William. "And do you really want to do this with me?"

"Absolutely."

"Because I care about both of you, I will try it. Thank you for thinking of this, William. It really does mean a lot to me that you're not shying away from me." She put the book down. Still holding the cat, she hugged him. He hugged back.

"William, I can't breathe."

He let go and sat back. "Sorry. I'm just so happy that you are willing to try this and that you didn't push me away." He looked at Oliver. "I think I have you to thank for a lot of that. Maybe this will help show my appreciation." He reached into the cooler for bowls, plates, and silverware. Next, he pulled out the food. "This is a chilled fruit soup," he informed them as he removed the lid of the pot, "and these are chicken and black bean sandwiches." He placed three foil pouches beside the pot. "Oliver, I don't know if you want a sandwich. I made you one, just in case, but you don't have to eat it. Well, you don't have to eat the soup, either, of course. I tried to think of something that you might like and find reasonably easy to eat."

"Thanks. I really appreciate this." Slowly, he filled about half his bowl of soup but didn't touch a sandwich.

They ate in comfortable silence for a time. As she finished eating, Penelope said, "Dr. Daniels wants to send me home later this week."

"What?" William and Oliver said in unison.

"He said he likes how all this new medication is working. He said that over the next months, both my symptoms of schizophrenia and depression will continue to get even better, but that it would be silly for me to stay here for months. He will have me come to appointments, but I don't need to be in the hospital. He wants me to stay a few more days and maybe go home on Thursday."

"You didn't tell me that," Oliver said quietly. This was great news for Penelope, and he knew he should be happy for her. Inexplicably, though, he wasn't. His heart pounded and he was filled with dread. He was disgusted with himself. His reaction made no sense. Penelope was just a fellow patient; it's not like they had a long history together. Why did this feel like a loss? He wanted to support these people, so he kept his mouth shut.

William, on the other hand, was ecstatic. He didn't even wait for Penelope to respond to Oliver's comment. "That's wonderful! I'm so happy!" He grabbed her hand then leaned over and kissed her head. When Penelope looked away, he questioned, "Aren't you glad? Don't you want to come home?"

"And face the outside world? And make you deal with me every single day? What kind of life are we going to have, William?" Penelope said in irritation. Then, meekly, the irritation gone, she said, "I'm scared. I hate this. But I really do love you."

William put his arm around her and pulled her close. He kissed her head, and then he picked up her hand and kissed that too before holding it tight. "I know you're scared and that you hate this. Let's just take it slowly, okay? I'm so glad you're coming home. The apartment is so empty and lonely. I just want you home again."

Silence descended upon them. It was Oliver who broke it. "Both of you remember that, okay? Please? Think of how empty and lonely you are without each other. What you're going through must suck, but don't make it worse than it already is. Loneliness and emptiness are unbearable. Penelope, I know what William means by an empty house. It's awful. Neither of you deserves to live like that.

It's miserable, and I hate it. I'm lonely and I'm empty and I want Maggie and Henry back." He put his head in his hands. Trying what he had been taught, he took several deep breaths then, head still in his hands, he muttered, "I'm sorry. I really didn't want this to be about me. The talk of loneliness just got the best of me."

"You don't have to feel completely lonely any more. You have us. We're friends now, remember?"

Oliver didn't look up, but he nodded and said, "Thanks, Penelope."

"She's right," William said. After a brief silence, he exclaimed, "Oh yeah, I just remembered something. I think you have someone in your life besides us, too."

Oliver sat back. "What do you mean?"

"I came across something last night. I was thinking about you, and I remembered something you said the other night. You said that no one knew or cared where you were."

"They don't."

"That's not completely true." William reached into the cooler and fished out a folded sheet of paper. He unfolded it and passed it to Oliver. "Seems like your sister cares very much about where you are."

Oliver stared at the page William had printed. His forehead creased as he took in the photo of himself and the paragraph his sister had written. Slowly, he picked it up and studied it.

He read the paragraph several times before gently placing the page back onto the table and looking at William and Penelope. "Oh," was all he could manage. He leaned forward again and, elbows on the table, put his head back into his hands.

Penelope's eyes widened as she read the paper Oliver had put on the table. "You disappeared? How? Were...were you kidnapped?"

Oliver shook his head. His voice was quiet but steady. "No. I left." He sighed. "I just couldn't take it anymore. Everywhere I went was a constant reminder of them. The little store where we would go for ice cream, the court house, Maggie's law firm, the grocery store, the sidewalks where we pushed Henry in the stroller and where he learned to pedal his trike. And of course, Algonquin Park. And our home…" He trailed off and sighed again. "I couldn't take the people anymore, either. Some people pitied me. I know they meant well, really, I do, but I couldn't handle them constantly asking how I was holding up or expressing their sorrow or telling me that I should stop blaming myself. Other people hated me, like Maggie's parents and their friends and some of Maggie's partners. As you know, they had a really good reason. After what I did, I don't deserve understanding, so I don't blame them for hating me. I thought it would be better for everyone if I left, so they could move on with their lives without me there as a constant reminder." He sighed again, but kept talking. "I couldn't even handle my job anymore. I was a biologist with the Great Lakes Water Quality Research Consortium. We were analyzing climate change and the long term health of Lake Michigan. It was so hard to concentrate, and I kept making big mistakes and screwing up everyone else's work. Plus, I just couldn't care anymore about things that used to be so important to me. I mean, who the hell cares about the condition of the lake when the people you love aren't around to enjoy the lake with you?" He swallowed hard and heaved another sigh as he sat back and looked at Penelope and William.

"I took off on the one-month anniversary." He remembered it vividly as he told them about that day.

After yet another sleepless night filled with nightmares, tossing and turning, and treks to and from Henry's room, he had showered before sunrise, dressed in the special outfit Maggie had bought for him—the one like the one Henry was buried in and would be wearing for all of eternity—and went to his boss's house. He was thoroughly startled when his boss swung the door open and exclaimed, "Good God, it's not even six in the morning!"

"Oh, yeah, I, uh, I'm really sorry to bother you, Stanley. It's just, uh—"

"Oliver! You look like hell. Step inside. What's going on?"

"No, I can't stay. I just wanted to tell you in person that I need to resign. I don't want to come in today and deal with it, so I hope you don't mind my coming here."

"Of course I don't mind. I meant it when I told you that you could call me or come over any time. But I do mind that you're resigning. Sorry, but I'm not accepting your resignation."

"Stanley, I can't do it anymore." He willed himself to stay steady.

"Look. It's only been a month. Be patient with yourself."

"How in the hell am I supposed to do that?"

Stanley considered him. "You know, I think you really could use some time to figure that out. You haven't had a break. You didn't even take any time off after the funeral."

"That's because being home is too hard. Work gave me some place to be for part of the day. But I can't escape it, Stanley. Even work doesn't take my mind off of them. And I don't want to take my mind off of them. Ever. But it's not fair to you or to the rest of the team for me to keep coming in day after day and spacing out, making mistakes, halting our progress, and just generally being a detriment. I need to quit."

"I told you that I'm not accepting your resignation." He stared at him. "But I do think that you need some time off. You're taking an extended leave of absence starting now."

"Stanley—"

"A leave of absence, Oliver. Take some time to mourn and to make sense of the world."

"The world doesn't make sense anymore, and it never will." Oliver was on the brink of tears, but he summoned the will to keep them at bay and carry on with the conversation.

"It sure as hell doesn't make sense. I'll never understand why good people have to suffer like this and why innocent lives are cut short. I'm not saying you'll find answers like that, but taking some time off will help you get your bearings again. Take all the time you need. I'm leaving this absence open-ended, and we're going to *continue to cover your benefits while you're gone so you don't have to worry about insurance and crap like that."*

"I don't give a damn about insurance benefits. I won't be needing them."

"What does that mean?"

"Uh, nothing. It's just that I don't want to trouble you."

Stanley put his hand on his shoulder. "It's no trouble. Starting immediately, you are on an extended leave, and you can return whenever you're ready. No sooner than that. And your benefits are covered the entire time. It's part of the perks that come with being one of our senior research directors. And it's coming from a caring friend."

"Thanks, Stanley." Stanley became fuzzy and seemed to melt with his surroundings as Oliver's eyes filled.

"For Christ's sake, stop standing in the doorway. Come in and sit down. Kimberly'll be wandering downstairs in a few minutes to start some coffee. Stay here a while. Have you really talked to anyone about this? Maybe talking it out would help."

"No, I can't, but thanks for the offer." Oliver extended his hand.

Stanley took it firmly in his and cupped his other hand around Oliver's. "Take care of yourself. And don't be a stranger. Come lean on us, okay?"

"Sure. Thanks, Stanley."

Oliver turned and walked away, never looking back. He walked straight to the grocery store—no florist was open at this hour—bought all of their flowers and a squishy stuffed monkey, and went to the cemetery. He shuffled to their gravesites and instantly dropped to his knees, spilling his armful of gifts onto the ground. "Hi, baby. Hi, little man. How are you feeling today? It's been a month. Are you tired of being in there? I'm tired of having you in there." He was wracked with sobs and, for a long time, couldn't speak. Finally, through tears, he said, "I brought you guys something. Here, let me help you with it." Weeping still, he took a long time displaying the flowers on Maggie's grave. He leaned the monkey against Henry's tombstone, but it looked lonely, so he borrowed some flowers from Maggie's grave and arranged them around it. He said, "I think your mom wants to share with you. Remember how much you loved the monkeys, little man? They were so lively, just like you. But now you're lying still, so this one is, too." He laid his arms on Henry's tombstone, put his head down, and cried harder.

"What are you doing here?" An angry voice from behind him scared him. He leaped to his feet.

Out of breath, he said, "Nancy. Mick. I needed to visit. I know it's not my time of day, but—"

"We had an agreement, Oliver, and you're breaking it. Get out of here."

"Nancy, please, I'm so sorry. I miss them, too."

"Sorry doesn't even begin to cut it. You should have been there with them a month ago, but you weren't. It's too late now. You let them down, and look what happened." Nancy gestured toward the graves. "Now when we want to see our daughter and grandson, we have to come here to do it. Get out of my sight, you son of a bitch!"

Oliver appealed to his father-in-law. "Mick, I'm sorry. I just need to stay here today. I won't talk to you. Please."

Mick's response was curt, "You heard Nancy. You're not supposed to be here. Your time begins at four o'clock. You can come back then."

Oliver sagged. He knew he could neither plead with them nor argue to change their minds so he could stay. Their hatred was completely justified. In fact, they were easier on him than he was on himself. Disheartened, he left Maggie and Henry to be with her parents.

He wandered aimlessly for over an hour before finding himself in church. He found Father Flannery in the sanctuary. "Excuse me, Father. I need to make a confession."

"Oliver! It's good to see you; it's been too long. How are you doing?"

"How I'm doing isn't important. Can we go to the confessional, please?"

"Of course." When they settled into the closet-like room, Father Flannery began making the sign of the cross, solemnly stating, "In the name of the Father—"

"Stop," Oliver interrupted. "I just want to get to the point."

The priest seemed taken aback. "Interrupting the Trinitarian formula could be considered by some a sin itself to confess."

"Fine. I confess that I interrupted." He paused and considered that. "That means nothing to me, you know. Not anymore. I, uh, I guess I don't even know why I came then. I'm sorry to have wasted your time." Oliver stood to leave.

"Please don't go. Something brought you here. What is it? I'm not here to judge; you may speak what's on your mind."

Slowly, he knelt back down. "Remember that this is an official confession, which means you are bound to confidentiality."

"Go on..."

"I'm going to commit a murder today. I'm taking my own life. I can't do this anymore. I want to go be with Maggie and Henry, Father."

"Hmm. You are correct that that is indeed murder, a very serious sin. Your life belongs to God, and you have no right to decide to end it. He put you here, and He intends for you to stay until He calls you home."

"No! My life does not belong to God! If it does, why doesn't he care more about me? Why did he take away my reasons for living?"

"That's only for Him to know, my son. Maggie and Henry belong to Him too. We all do. Only God can decide when we can come home to Him."

"Maggie's and Henry's home is here!"

"No. You are quite mistaken. Their home is in heaven. God loved them and called them home. It isn't—"

"Don't give me that load of crap!" Oliver's frustration rang loudly in the small confessional. "That's the dumbest thing I've ever heard. Their home is here, on Earth, with me. They were good souls and the world deserves to have them here." His voice faltered and he paused

to compose himself. When he spoke again, he spoke quietly. "I need them, I..." He broke down and couldn't continue.

Father Flannery laid his hand on Oliver's head and began to pray.

Oliver jerked back. "Stop that! I don't want your prayers! The only thing I want is to be with my wife and my son, and that's precisely where I'm going. I felt the need to confess, but now I don't know why. Thank you for your time."

He opened the door and stepped out, but he stopped when the priest said, "Please consider this carefully before you do anything drastic: You were drawn here today for a reason. You began with a confession of murder, and you were absolutely correct. As I said, our lives belong to God and we have no right to end them at our will. By killing yourself, you are risking eternal damnation."

"So what? I'm living in hell now. I'm already damned."

"You said you want to go be with Maggie and Henry. They are in heaven, waiting for you, but in killing yourself, you risk eternal separation from them. I can pray for your soul. Others can pray for your soul. But the ultimate decision lies with God. There is no guarantee that He will forgive you and allow you into heaven with your family. If you wait for death to come in God's time, you will be reunited then with your loved ones."

Neither man said another word. After standing frozen to his spot for many long seconds, Oliver quietly walked out of the church, head down in sad confusion.

"I didn't know what to do after that," he continued telling his story to William and Penelope, who sat listening with rapt attention. "I took care of a little more business, and then I just walked out of town. I didn't take my car because I didn't want anything traceable. I didn't want to be found. I just walked and eventually ended up in Chicago. I didn't have anywhere to go, and after some really rough and terrifying nights on the street, nights where I saw drug use and violence and was constantly reminded of the scene in the park and often ended up cowering behind dumpsters and puking violently,

I discovered a homeless shelter. It took two months of wrestling with myself, with what happened to Maggie and Henry, and with the priest's words before I ultimately decided what to do. I came to the conclusion that if there is a God, and I don't know if there is, he already hates me, so killing myself couldn't possibly make anything any worse. And I can't live without Maggie and Henry; I tried, and I just can't do it. So, on the four-month anniversary, I went to the roof of a building with the intention of ending my life. But I screwed it up and ended up here."

Penelope left William's side and went to Oliver's. She wrapped her arms around him and said, "I'm glad you screwed up and came here." She squeezed him hard, and then returned to her chair beside William.

"I'm glad, too." William added. "And I bet Frannie would be glad if she knew."

Oliver shrugged. "Did you contact her?"

"I started to but changed my mind. I wanted to talk to you first."

"Thanks. I don't want to see her."

"Why not?"

Oliver sighed. "I just don't want to face anybody from my past anymore. It's hard enough as it is. But seeing her will make it all worse. She has a family. I don't. I don't want to deal with the pain of that constant reminder."

"Don't you remember it constantly anyway?" Penelope asked him.

"Well, yes, but...I don't know. I can't explain it. I just don't want anything to do with my former life ever again. It's not the same without Maggie and Henry, and I don't want to try to live that life without them."

"I think you should let me contact her. You could use support. You'll always have us, and now you can have her, too."

"No. I don't deserve it. Who am I to ask for support?"

"If not for yourself, then for your sister. Imagine what she's been going through. She's also experiencing a loss, you know, and one without closure. She must be worrying about you every single day, wondering where you are and if you're even alive."

Oliver considered that. He put his head in his hands yet again. "Why, why, am I always so selfish?"

Penelope tried to reassure him, "You're hurting, Oliver. You are trying to deal with a horrible tragedy. You weren't trying to hurt your sister, just like you weren't trying to hurt your wife and son."

"But the truth is that I did hurt them."

"No. That's not the truth." Penelope traced a line up and down his arm with her finger. "The truth is that a druggie hurt everyone. You didn't do it. A user did. Do you feel the line I'm making? If I were telling a lie, I wouldn't be able to make this straight line. You can't make a line of truth while telling a lie. Here's another truth. You should let William contact your sister to let her know that you're here."

Oliver looked at Penelope then at William. William nodded his agreement. With a deep sigh, Oliver consented. "Okay. But only for Frannie's sake, so she can stop worrying."

CHAPTER 21

"You look pretty agitated over here. What's going on with you?" When Oliver didn't answer, Matt sat and gestured toward the notebook in front of Oliver. "Whatchya working on?"

It was Tuesday afternoon, and Oliver was sitting in the day area while Penelope was down in the exercise room. He had tried to lie down in his room, but he was all worked up and he couldn't hold still. Even the clock seemed unsettled; its ticking sounded louder than usual, impossible as that seemed. So he had come to the day area and was now sitting at his table. His left leg bounced up and down frantically, and he squeezed the stress ball over and over again in his left hand. His left elbow held his notebook in place while, with his right hand, he methodically made large Xs with a broken red crayon—he had squeezed too hard and it snapped in half—over the top of rows and rows of little squares. He had promised Penelope he would use his journal, but thus far, other than the picture he had drawn for her yesterday, he had been unable to create anything new. Instead, he used the pages she prepared for him.

When Matt sat down, Oliver put down the crayon and squeezed the ball with the fingers of both hands. He continued to bounce his leg. "This is just my journal. Penelope put stuff in it for me. It's actually helpful."

"What do the Xs mean?"

"They're red Xs. They're red because I'm afraid, and I'm crossing out the boxes because squares mean courage, but I'm nothing but a coward."

When Matt raised his eyebrows, Oliver gave him a crooked half-smile. "Penelope told me about her interpretations of shapes and colors."

Matt grinned. "Penelope has some interesting thoughts, doesn't she?"

"Yeah. I can't come up with decent thoughts of my own, so I figured I might as well try hers."

"It looks and sounds like you've got some thoughts of your own going right now."

"What do you mean?"

"Well, for one thing, I've never seen you so jittery like this. And I heard you mention fear and refer to yourself as a coward. I know those thoughts didn't come from Penelope. So what's going on right now?"

Oliver rapidly tossed the ball back and forth from hand to hand. He felt weird, like there was this great pressure inside of him making everything feel like it would explode. He sighed as he searched for words to communicate with Matt. When he tried to put words to what he was experiencing, it sounded ridiculous. But it didn't *feel* ridiculous. "I don't know," he finally managed to say. "I'm just being stupid. I'm making too big a deal out of it. Just never mind."

As he suspected, Matt wouldn't be dismissed. "Too big a deal out of what? Does this have anything to do with the phone call you received from William earlier? I don't know what it was about, but I noticed that you've been anxious since that call."

Oliver dropped the ball onto the table and ran his fingers through his hair. He kept his hands on his head and clutched his hair as he leaned back in his chair. "William went online and found a website my sister made because she was worried about me and wanted to find me. He and Penelope talked me into letting him contact her. He did, and she responded right away. She's coming here tonight, Matt. William is meeting her and bringing her with him when he comes." He was still bouncing his leg rapidly, and he tightened his grip on his hair.

"You don't want to see her."

"No, I don't! I mean, I don't want to hurt her, and I'd kind of like to see her, but no. Kind of. No. Just no."

"Take it easy."

"Don't even think about telling me to breathe."

"I'm telling you to breathe, and you're going to do it."

Once Oliver complied and calmed down a bit, Matt prodded, "I'm guessing this has to do with the fear and cowardice you mentioned."

Oliver furrowed his brows, squeezed his eyes shut, and nodded. After another sigh, he opened his eyes and tried to explain. "I'm afraid to see her. I hadn't thought about her being worried. Big shock there, huh? You know by now what a selfish bastard I am. But I didn't mean to be hurtful. I've just been out of my mind with grief and I didn't think about anyone else."

"Do you think she's going to be angry?"

"It would serve me right. But Frannie being Frannie, she probably won't be. She has every right to be, though. I'm worthless and no good and I really, really don't deserve to be alive. I curse myself for being a coward on the ledge last week. I should have just jumped without hesitation. But no, I was afraid. Not of getting hurt; I was actually hoping that I would feel the impact before I died. I mean, Maggie and Henry died a painful death, and that's what I deserve, too. But I hesitated, because I was afraid I wouldn't be reunited with them. I want to be with them, but what if by killing myself, I would be kept away from them for all of eternity? Or what if there is nothing after death? That's okay with me because even nothing would be better than living, but that would mean they aren't in heaven, they're just gone, and that thought is awful. I stood on that ledge, afraid for what has happened to their souls, and afraid I would never be with them again, and by the time I summoned the courage to just say to hell with it and jump, people had inflated a landing pad, and I lived. Why was I such a coward?" He crossed his arms on the table and thumped his head down onto them.

Matt's silence prompted him to continue. He sat up. "And I'm afraid of seeing Frannie because I have no idea what to say to her. I know I hurt her by running away, and I feel bad, but I don't know how to make it better. Plus I'm afraid of seeing her, because she's part of my past life, the one where I was happy, but I can't have that life anymore and I don't want to be reminded of that fact. I'm afraid that seeing her will make everything even worse, even though it's not really possible for things to get any worse."

He sighed and ran his fingers through his hair. "I know I'm not making any sense. I can't explain it, but I just feel...I don't know." He stopped talking and looked at Matt.

"You are making perfect sense. All these feelings are normal human emotions and normal responses to loss and trauma, so first, cut yourself some slack and ease up on the harsh labels. In your own words, you're out of your mind with grief. You are not now, nor have you ever, set out to purposely hurt anyone."

"But I did hurt people, with tragic consequences."

"People have been hurt, including you. But did you ever act with the intent of harm?"

"No, of course not, but—"

"Stop. No buts. We're leaving it at that for now. You need to keep reminding yourself of that simple fact. Nothing you have done was planned by you to cause harm. Give me your notebook."

"Why?"

"Because I'm going to write that in there." Oliver made no move to hand it to him, so Matt reached across the table for it and wrote the sentence inside the cover. He said it out loud as he wrote it, "Nothing…you…have…done…was…planned…by…you…to…cause…harm.

"There. Read that over and over and over, about a million times per day. Now, your sister will be here soon. What's the first thing you're going to say to her?"

Oliver put his head in his hands. "I don't know," he groaned. "Probably just 'hi,' or 'thanks for coming,' or something lame like that."

"That's not lame. Either one of those would be ideal. You'll say hi, she'll say something, you'll say something back, and the conversation will just happen. William and Penelope will be around, and they'll add to the conversation. Starting the conversation is now one less thing you have to be afraid of."

Oliver thought about that. "I suppose you're right."

"Damn right I'm right. Take it one step at a time. Start with greeting her, and the rest will just happen."

Oliver focused on that advice for the rest of the afternoon. Knowing it was okay to say something simple and let others take the lead with the conversation helped, but he was still nervous and unsettled. Because he couldn't sit still, he and Penelope walked around the perimeter of the day area. He tried to follow her conversation, but he couldn't focus.

"Oliver, are you even listening?"

"Yes." He sighed and looked at her. "Not really. I'm trying. I'm sorry, Penelope. I enjoy listening to you. I just can't concentrate. They're going to be here any minute and…" He stopped in his tracks. William was at the front desk, and Frannie was at his side. Oliver's stomach lurched, and his heart pummeled his chest. He realized at that moment how much he had missed her, and he instantly regretted having left without the courtesy of telling her goodbye. He debated whether to go to her, stay where he was, or retreat in shame to his room. Before he decided what to do, she turned and scanned the room.

"Ollie!" She dashed across the room and didn't slow as she neared him. She threw her arms around him and hugged him with such force he nearly fell backwards. He caught his balance and returned her hug with equal force. The hug felt familiar, like family and safety and love, and he ached inside. He ached because this wasn't his wife. He ached because it was his sister, whom he cared about and was sorry he had hurt. He ached because it was a comfort he hadn't allowed himself since the day his wife and son were ripped violently from his life. He ached with appreciation for his friendship with William and Penelope. He ached with love lost and love found and with loneliness and reunion. He wanted to pull away and look at her, greet her like he had practiced in his mind all evening, but he found that he could neither speak nor let go. He simply held her and let himself be held, and he didn't even care when the tears let go.

After what felt like a long time, Frannie pulled back and wiped her own tears away from her eyes with the tips of her fingers. "Like Lucy always said to Linus, 'I oughtta slug you!'" She looked at him from head to toe. "But you look too pathetic for me to do that to you. Oh, God, I was so worried about you! I'd ask if you're okay, but it's pretty obvious that you're not."

"I'm so, so sorry, Frannie. I didn't mean to make you worry. I just couldn't take it anymore."

She ran her hand along the side of his face then pulled him close again. "Oh, Ollie!"

Eventually, someone else squeezed Oliver's shoulder. "Hey. Soup's on," William said. "Do you two want to join Penelope and me?"

Oliver nodded. William squeezed his shoulder again. Frannie looped her arm through his and rubbed his arm as they walked to the table. He felt the same prick of guilt as when Penelope had held his hand and put her head against his arm. He wanted to reject this solace, but he couldn't.

Penelope was spooning William's soup of the night into bowls when the three reached the table. She looked up and froze momentarily, and then dropped the spoon on the table with a loud clang. She tucked her hair behind her ear and picked up the spoon but didn't continue dishing up.

Frannie extended her hand. "Hi! I'm Oliver's sister, Frannie. You must be Penelope."

Still holding the spoon, Penelope turned and walked to her room.

"Penelope!" William followed her, but she shut the door on him. He knocked. "Penelope, please come out."

Oliver watched as William tried to appeal to Penelope through her door. "Frannie, I'll be right back." When he reached Penelope's door, he called, "It's Oliver. Why'd you leave? I feel white without you there."

Penelope cracked her door open and peered out. "Mrs. Roosevelt took my words away and told me to leave," she whispered.

"I'd like you to come out. Will you listen to me like you listen to her?" William asked gently.

"I think I should stay here. I might not be able to talk, and I'll embarrass myself and you."

"You're talking now," Oliver pointed out.

"I'm whispering. Shhh. I don't want Mrs. Roosevelt to find out. She doesn't like me talking in times like this, and she is forcing me to stay here. She put up an invisible force field, and I can't get out."

"Would you be able to find the strength to break through it to help me?" Oliver asked. "I'm drowning in my own emotions out here, and I really, really need the help of my new friend."

"William is there. He's very supportive. He makes me feel good, and I'm sure he can help you too."

Oliver looked at William and slapped him lightly on the back. "How about that? You make her feel good." To Penelope, he said, "I'm glad that William is here, but I really need you tonight too. Please, Penelope?"

"I don't know how to get out. And besides, I feel stupid. Frannie will hate me."

"My sister is nice. She won't hate you. Can you throw something at the force field to get out?"

"Hmm. Will you hand me your green stress ball? Objects can pass through the field this way, but I can't get out. It's a one-way field. But maybe I could throw the ball at it and break it. The ball is round for caring. I think my caring about you is stronger than Mrs. Roosevelt's desire to keep me in here. Plus the ball is green, and I do accept that you and William want me to come out. Let's try it." When Oliver handed her the ball, she pushed her door open, stood back, and threw the ball as hard as she could through the opening. It sailed across the day area and whacked the wall on the other side.

"Did you hear that noise? That was the force field shattering. I can get out now. Thank you for the idea, Oliver. Mrs. Roosevelt, I am going out now because I need to help, just like you liked to help others. You want me to be like you, don't you?" She stood still and cocked her head as if listening for something. Her eyes widened as she stood there, and she looked at William. "That worked. She agreed. I've been reading parts of the book you brought me, and I remembered something I used to know. The reason I've always admired Mrs. Roosevelt is because of how much she worked to help humankind. You were right, William. I can use this book to work with her, and maybe she'll treat me differently. Thank you for helping me." She kissed him on the cheek. She turned to Oliver and kissed his cheek too. "You are also helping me. Thank you."

Leaving William and Oliver at her door, she crossed the room to retrieve Oliver's stress ball, and then returned to the table where Frannie sat waiting. A bit stunned, Oliver and William still stood by her room. She called to them, "What's the matter? Are you stuck? If I can break through a force field, certainly you can find the strength to walk across the room."

William looked at Oliver and chuckled. "Well, then." He threw his arm around Oliver's shoulders. "Thanks for your help. Come on; let's go talk to your sister."

CHAPTER 22

FRANNIE EMBRACED OLIVER AGAIN BEFORE HE SAT DOWN BESIDE HER. "I'm going to keep doing that, you know." She still held him, but she leaned back to look him in the eye. "I have missed you so much, and I've been worried sick. Ollie, I was afraid you were dead. I know that everything was so incredibly painful, but why did you leave without telling me? And why in the hell did you go to the police station and give them a statement declaring that you were simply leaving town so that a missing person's report couldn't be filed? You must have known that I would be worried. Why didn't you at least keep in touch with me?"

"I'm sorry Frannie. I'm so sorry. I am. I'm sorry." She pulled him close again as he repeated, "I'm sorry," over and over again.

"Ollie. Oliver, it's okay. I'm not angry. I was just worried." When he wouldn't stop apologizing, she said, "You're not just sorry for this, are you? Oh, Oliver, you weren't the one who killed them."

"He feels like he is, even though we're trying to make him realize that he's not. And you should probably get used to it, because he apologizes for everything all the time."

The sound of Penelope's voice helped pull Oliver back to the moment. He let go of Frannie and stepped back. Feeling rather weak, he sat down. "We should be eating. Frannie, William is an outstanding chef who has been gracing Penelope and me with his meals. I'm sorry I kept you all from eating."

"See?" Penelope said. "He apologizes for everything." Before Oliver could comment, she asked, "Do you usually go by Ollie? I'm sorry I've been calling you Oliver if you go by Ollie instead."

"No!" he said emphatically. "Sorry. I didn't mean it that way. It's just that it's a childhood name; I haven't been called Ollie since I was a kid." He looked at Frannie. "You're not going to start calling me that, are you?"

"Don't worry; I won't. I was just so emotional when I saw you standing there. You looked so vulnerable, and for some reason it felt like we were kids again." She took his hand. "God, it's good to see you."

He nodded. "It's good to see you, too. Frannie, I truly am sorry."

"Oliver, stop that. I know you are, but there's nothing to be sorry for."

Oliver groaned and put his head in his hands.

Frannie rubbed his back. "William filled me in a little bit about what you've been up to. He said you've been here about a week, and before that you were in a homeless shelter. A homeless shelter. You poor thing! That must have been awful. I want to hear about it, but I also want to know how you got from there to here."

He sat up straight and looked at William. "You didn't tell her?"

William shook his head. "She was upset enough. I figured all the details could come later."

"Tell me what? What details? Oliver, what are you guys talking about?"

"Frannie." Oliver heaved a deep sigh and looked down at his bowl. He absentmindedly swirled his spoon through the uneaten soup. Quietly, he told her the story of his life in the shelter and the pain and suffering that led him to leap from the edge of an eighteen-story building. When he finished, Frannie was in tears.

"I want you to come home, Ollie," she whispered. "Let me take you home. You've suffered enough. Stop running from it and come lean on me to get you through this."

Misty-eyed, Oliver averted his gaze. "I don't know if I can handle going back there. It's not that I don't want to be with you, and I do want to see David and the kids, but I don't think I can handle it there." He closed his eyes and took a few slow, deep breaths to keep himself in control. "And my home," he whispered. "On one hand, I long to see my house. I want to see their pictures and their things and to smell their smells, but on the other hand, I don't think I can handle it. I doubt I could make it through a single night in that bed without Maggie. I just can't, Frannie."

"Then we'll take it slowly. You need to be with family, big brother. You won't be alone. You'll have us. I don't think you should stay at home; you'll stay with me. We'd love to have you. The kids miss their uncle. You can stay with us and we'll help you work your way into other things."

Oliver shook his head. "I couldn't ask you to take me in. You have a busy life and your own family to care for. You don't need to take on this. In case you haven't noticed, I'm a mess. No way."

Frannie put one arm around him and laid her other hand on his arm. "Oliver. We're family. We've always been there for each other. Why would things be different now? After Mom and Dad died, what did you do? You took a full year off college, more than that actually, because you came home the night they died and didn't finish the semester you were in, plus you stayed with me the whole next school year. You stopped your life to come help me. I was a junior in high school, Oliver, and very alone. What would I have done without you? You were there for me when I needed you. Let me be here for you now. Please."

By now, tears ran down Frannie's cheeks again. Oliver pulled her toward him, and they took comfort in each other as they remembered the past. When he opened his eyes and saw William and Penelope, he felt bad for leaving them out. He explained to them, "Our parents were killed in a car accident. They had gone into Milwaukee for a symphony concert one February. Thankfully, Frannie had homework and stayed home. When they drove home, it was late at night, and the roads were icy. They lost control on a curve, and, well, they were both killed instantly."

"That's awful. I'm so sorry," William said quietly.

Penelope spoke quietly, too. "That must have been so sad for both of you. God, Oliver, you really can't get a break, can you? First your parents, and then your wife and son. I can't imagine how hard that would be."

Oliver bit his cheeks and looked away. He felt the all-too-familiar pressure behind his eyes, and he pushed back at it with his thumb and fingers. He would not cry, yet again, in front of people.

Frannie said tenderly, "Ollie, come home with me."

Oliver couldn't yet let up on the pressure against his eyes. Unable to get words past the boulder in his throat, he just shook his head.

Penelope made an appeal for Frannie's case. "It's really good that you had each other back then and that you still have each other now. Oliver, listen to Frannie. Go stay with her. You keep telling me to keep William in my life. Well, what's good for the goose is good for the gander. You need to keep your sister in your life. If it's okay for me to live with William, it's okay for you to live with Frannie for a bit."

"I agree with these two." William took his turn at convincing Oliver. "It's a smart idea. A hospital is no place to be. You should be in a familiar place with people you know and care about. Lean on your sister for a while as you get used to being in Fairmont. Let your family help you go home again."

Everyone fell silent. Oliver felt them all watching him. It made him uneasy. He tested the pressure behind his eyes by relaxing his fingers slightly. When nothing leaked out, he slowly lowered his hand. He sighed deeply and addressed Penelope and William. "Do you know the home Maggie, Henry and I lived in is the house Frannie and I grew up in? Mom and Dad fully owned it, and they had a will. They left it to us, so we were able to stay there after they died. Neither of us really wanted to sell it, so we kept it and rented it out once we were both in college. When Maggie and I decided to move back to Fairmont—she's from there, too, but we went to different high schools and colleges and didn't meet until graduate school—she fell in love with the place. We bought Frannie's half from her, and that's where Maggie and I built our life. Henry's room was the room I had as a child." His voice had grown quieter as he spoke, and by the time he finished it was a barely audible whisper. He sighed a long, uneven sigh. "I'd like to see it again, but I really don't think I'm ready."

"Then don't yet. There's no rush. Stay with me, and let me go with you when you are ready."

Oliver looked at William, and then at Penelope. "Well, I, uh, I kind of don't want to, uh...I feel like a grade-schooler, but what I'm trying to say is that I would hate to lose your friendship. I know that I haven't known you very long and that I'm just some guy in a behavioral health center, but, well..." He sighed and ran his hand through his hair. "I'm sorry. I sound really stupid. Never mind."

Penelope reached for Oliver's hand. "You're not stupid. Do you have any idea how much that means to me? Oliver, I'm a freak I—"

William stopped her emphatically. "You're not a freak. Don't talk about yourself that way."

"You're wrong, William. I am a freak. People shun me and can't get away from me fast enough when they see me." She turned back to Oliver and continued to reassure him, "You, though, treat me with respect and kindness. Some people can be really mean because of who I am, but—"

Irritated, William interjected, "Then they are the ones with the problem, Penelope, not you. I—"

"William! Please stop interrupting me and let me finish. This isn't about me, it's about Oliver." William exhaled loudly in frustration but said nothing further. Penelope turned her attention back to Oliver. "William knew me before and still sees the old me, but you only know this me. Yet you still want to be friends. I need your friendship, and I plan to keep it while you are staying with your sister. I'm strange and I feel like I'm not smart like I used to be, but I do know how to use a computer and a phone."

William spoke again, but the exasperation had disappeared from his voice. "You're not a freak, and you're not stupid and strange, sweetie. I really wish you wouldn't talk about yourself that way. I will say, though, that I, too, appreciate you, Oliver. Go home with Frannie. We'll still be in touch. And we can visit each other, you know. We're just over an hour away."

Oliver nodded. "Okay. But how do I get out of here?"

"Are you being forced to be here?" Frannie asked.

"I don't know. I was brought here even though I didn't want to come, but I'm pretty sure I can leave. I wasn't ordered by the court or anything."

"Talk to your doctor tomorrow," William advised.

"What time does he see you? I'll come talk to him with you," Frannie offered.

"It's a she. Dr. Willis. She's usually here a little after eight and sees me any time between then and about nine-fifteen when she leaves again."

"I can give you a ride here in the morning to make sure you're here on time," William said. "Penelope, Frannie's going to stay at our place while she's in Chicago. Is that okay?"

"Oliver's sister is welcome in our home any time," Penelope said. "I'm not even going to check with Mrs. Roosevelt about it. I think it's fine, and she'll just have to deal with it."

William leaned over and kissed her cheek.

"Thank you guys. I really appreciate it. It's settled, Oliver. I'm coming tomorrow morning, and we'll talk to Dr. Willis about your coming home."

ɔ⅃

"I don't think that's a good idea," Dr. Willis said firmly. It was Wednesday morning, and she was meeting with Oliver and Frannie in Oliver's room. "Oliver, you are far from ready to leave here at all, much less return to the lion's den."

"My being here doesn't change the past, nor is it helping me feel any less miserable. I'm going to be sad wherever I am, so what difference does it make if I'm here or at home?"

"What you are experiencing goes far beyond being sad, and I think you know that. You are correct that being here at Airhaven doesn't change your feelings instantly, but that doesn't mean that being here isn't helpful. Here, you are surrounded by trained staff who provide twenty-four-hour support."

Frannie interjected, "He will be staying with me, Dr. Willis. I will be there for him whenever he needs me."

"Who will be with him when you are at work?"

"I don't work outside the home; I have devoted myself fulltime to parenting. I will always be home with Oliver."

"And you will have children to care for as well."

"Yes, just like you have other patients here."

"Plus a full staff. He needs to remain here."

"I disagree. He needs to be with family. I can provide the care he needs."

"Hello? Am I a stray puppy you're trying to find a place for or something? I'm a grown man who doesn't need babysitting. You make it sound like I'm incapable of caring for myself."

Dr. Willis gave him a stern look. "Mr. Graham, your idea of caring for yourself was to take a dive off the roof of an eighteen-story building. We haven't even released you from suicide precautions yet. Your bathroom and closet remain locked, and the items you have access to are restricted. When you leave here, you will have unlimited access to anything you might decide to use to hurt yourself."

"But—"

Dr. Willis held up a finger and interrupted Frannie. "I haven't finished. You said that we make it sound like you are incapable of caring for yourself. Currently, you are not caring for yourself well; just getting you to eat is a challenge." She looked at Frannie. "Are you going to be able to get him to eat?" She continued without waiting for an answer. "And what about your nightmares?"

"Yes, I am plagued by nightmares, but they are far less intense than they were. I don't wake up drenched in cold sweat and screaming anymore. The images aren't so vivid; it's more about the feelings now. Also, I'm much less jumpy. I'll keep taking the medication you prescribed, so I'll stay less jumpy. I believe I can handle being released from the hospital."

"The medication is indeed part of what is helping your nightmares and your heightened startle response. However, that is only part of it. You are in a muted, safe environment here. You are protected from triggers. Your memories plague you and have occasionally prompted flashbacks. What's going to happen when you are back in the location where you experienced the traumatic loss of your family?"

"Dr. Willis, I am officially stating that I would like to leave. I honestly don't believe that I will be any more miserable with my sister than I am here at Airhaven. I appreciate your concern, but I am legally able to make my own decisions, and I would like to be discharged."

"I disagree wholeheartedly with your decision; however, you are correct in that you have the legal power to decide whether to stay or go. You will need to sign a release stating that you are leaving despite medical advice to the contrary, and the two of you must work with me to develop a written safety plan because Oliver, you are still considered suicidal."

"Okay," Oliver said.

"That's fine, Dr. Willis. I just want him home with me. I know him, and I can help him through this."

"I understand your desire to help your brother. Do keep in mind, though, that if it's too difficult for either of you, it is okay to return here."

"Thank you, Dr. Willis. Thank you, too, for what you have been doing for him. It's not that I don't think you've been helpful; it's just that he needs to be with family. What time can he leave?"

"He can leave some time tomorrow. Today, we need to work on that safety plan, and we need to work on transitioning him out. Oliver, I want you to have a day to consider your decision too, and make sure it is what you want to do. Process this during groups today, and talk to people about it if you want to. You seem to have developed a good rapport with Matt; perhaps let him give you some pointers about how to handle things when you're out of here."

"Can I be with him here today?" Frannie asked.

"No. We restrict visitors to evenings and weekends for the well-being of our patients. You can certainly come back tonight. You may stay a while longer, though, because I'd like to begin creating his safety plan."

With that, Oliver began to prepare to leave Airhaven.

CHAPTER 23

"WHAT'S GOING TO HAPPEN, OLIVER?" ON THURSDAY AFTER LUNCH, Oliver and Penelope sat together in the day area. They hadn't gone to the second art group; they were waiting for William and Frannie to arrive to take them home. "I don't know if I can do this."

"You can. You're doing really well. And remember what Dr. Daniels told you; the medication will keep working better and better."

"But also make me feel sicker and sicker. It's bad without it and bad with it. William is going to be sorry."

"You're wrong. William won't be sorry."

William and Frannie had arrived and approached as Oliver said this. He slid his arms around Penelope's waist from behind her and pulled her against him. "I took today and tomorrow off, and you'll see just how not-sorry I am."

Oliver couldn't bear to see William cuddle her, so he turned his attention to Frannie. "Hey. Are you sure you want me to come stay with you? Dr. Willis told me again this morning that if I changed my mind, I could stay here."

"I want you to come home."

Matt approached with the final discharge papers. After Penelope and Oliver each signed theirs, Penelope said, "Well, I guess this is it. Good-bye, Oliver. Will you call us tonight? Or we could call you, because we have Frannie's number."

Suddenly, the reality hit Oliver. His heart raced, and his heart beat loudly in his head. His chest constricted, and it felt as though he couldn't get enough air. His head spun, as though the floor were tilting. He muttered, "Yes, of course I'll call. Excuse me for a second. I need to check my room one more time to make sure I have everything." He took off across the day area, made it to his room, and shut his door behind him. He leaned against the door briefly, trying to gulp air, and then he pushed off and paced around the room with his hands clasped behind his head in an attempt to breathe. He felt sick and rushed into the now-unlocked bathroom. Nothing happened, but he remained there anyway, ignoring the knock at his door.

Matt entered. "Breathe with me," he instructed and led Oliver through the familiar breathing exercise. As Oliver began to breathe normally, Matt asked, "Do you feel like you need lorazepam?"

Oliver shook his head. "No. I'm okay. I'm sorry about that. I don't know what got into me back there."

"That was just a little panic attack, a normal part of PTSD, even when you're not experiencing a flashback. You're anxious about leaving, aren't you?"

"I guess. I don't really know."

"Are you sure you want to leave now?"

Oliver shrugged. "With Penelope leaving, I don't have a reason to stay, and I don't want to hurt Frannie. I've put her through enough. I do want to go. But I feel all, uh, I don't know. I just have this huge knot inside. It's crazy. It's not like William and Penelope died or something, so why do I feel like I'm losing them? And I'm glad to be with my sister, so why do I feel a sense of dread?"

"It's very normal to feel that way. You're extra sensitive to any sense of loss right now. The best thing to do is to keep in touch with them. And you're going back to where everything happened. Of course you're nervous. Don't beat yourself up over feeling this way."

Oliver just nodded.

"Want me to go tell Frannie that I want you to stick around a little longer?"

Oliver shook his head. "No. It's okay. I'm fine. Let's go."

"Okay. Listen to me, though. You might have more panic attacks. You know how to breathe through them. You're also leaving with a prescription for lorazepam. Take it when you need it. Be sure to take all your medications regularly like you've been doing here; the exact instructions are on your discharge sheet. Use that journal of yours, and keep your safety plan on you. It has instructions for what to do if you're feeling out of control, and it has the phone numbers you need: William, Penelope, and Airhaven's emergency line. Use them any time, Oliver. Understand?"

"Yes. You and Dr. Willis have both been through this with me already."

"Well, it's important. I do believe you're capable of getting through this, you know." Matt looked Oliver in the eye. "And I sincerely believe that you deserve to get through it too."

"Thanks. Thank you for everything, Matt."

"Of course." Matt slapped his shoulder lightly. "Ready?"

"Yeah. Let's go."

Back in the day area, William, Penelope, and Frannie were waiting for him. Frannie stepped toward him and hugged him. "Are you okay?"

He nodded.

"I'm glad. It's time for you to come home where you belong." She let go of him. "God, I am so glad you are coming home."

"Penelope, that's how I feel about you, too, you know," William said.

"I know. I just hope that this is the right thing for you. I really have missed you, William, and I do like to be with you. Even though

I'm worried, I'm glad, too. Plus it's nice to get out of hospital clothes."

Oliver hadn't had much to say during the conversation. Feeling increasingly overwhelmed at the idea of returning home, he hadn't been able to talk. At the mention of clothes, though, he was able to contribute. "You can say that again. I was so relieved to have my clothes back, and it feels really good to be able to wear them again." When he had been given permission to change just before lunch, he had grabbed his items from his unlocked closet and buried his face in them in relief and reunion. As good as it had been to have his special outfit back though, it hadn't taken long for him to realize that this was as close as he would ever come to holding Maggie. That awareness had caused him to go instantly weak from head to toe, and he stumbled onto the bed and curled himself around the bundle that he wished were Maggie. As he had lain there, he registered the sound of the infernal clock. It accentuated his misery. He had realized suddenly that he wouldn't have to listen to it anymore because he would soon be leaving. And that meant that he could actually wear his clothes again. Why the hell was he just holding them, when he could finally put them on? At that thought, he had stood and practically ripped off his hospital attire. He couldn't get Maggie's outfit on fast enough. Once it was on, he closed his eyes and reveled in the feel of what his wife had picked out for him. What was the outfit like for Henry now, he had wondered then. Could Henry feel his? Or not? The momentary happiness had drained from his entire being. He had returned to the day area with a bizarre mix of relief and grief to join Penelope for lunch.

He still felt that odd mix as he discussed clothing with his sister and friends. He focused on how nice it was to be out of the hospital garb and into his own precious clothes.

Frannie commented on them. "What on Earth have you been through, Oliver? Look at you. I've never seen clothes so ragged and tattered and wrinkled in my life. As soon as we get home, let's get you something decent."

More desperate than angry, he declared, "No! These are special, and I'm not wearing anything else. It's too bad that they've gotten worn out, but I'm wearing them anyway. I keep them clean, Frannie. I wash them regularly, so it's not like they'll be offensive to you. Do you think I would disrespect Maggie by being dirty? As long as I'm clean, what's it to you what I wear?"

"Whoa, settle down! I didn't mean to upset you. I assumed you would want to change into something different, but if you don't, that's fine. I'm not going to argue with you. I just want you home, Ollie; I don't care what you wear. I want to help you, not stress you out."

Oliver felt awful; he hadn't meant to react so strongly. "I'm sorry. It's just that they made me take these off here and it's so nice to finally have them back. I don't want to change clothes." He ran his hand through his hair as he tried to explain himself. "I'm really sorry for getting upset just now."

Frannie hugged him again. "Oh, Oliver. If that's your idea of being upset, then the world would be a much better place if that is what upset truly meant. It's okay. I'm here for you. I want to work with you, not against you. Let's get you out of this hospital."

Once in the parking lot, Oliver and Frannie said their good-byes to Penelope and William. William shook Oliver's hand, and then pulled him in for a brief man hug. "Thanks, man," he said.

"For what?" Oliver asked.

"For a lot of things."

Oliver was a bit confused, but he didn't question further. He turned to Penelope and said, "I'm, uh, I'm going to miss you, and William, too. Remember how much you and William love each other. Nothing else is as important as that." They hugged each other for a long time.

When William touched Penelope's shoulders and gently tugged her toward him, she said to Oliver, "I'll talk to you tonight." She turned to William, then, and said, "I'm not so sure about this, you know."

"I know. And I also know that everything is going to work out. It's going to be okay. Just give it a chance." With one last good-bye to Oliver and Frannie, William led Penelope to his car.

As Oliver watched them drive away, he thought of the people driving away from the cemetery as he had stood all alone beside the fresh graves. He thought of Maggie and Henry being removed from his life. He thought of his parents driving away from home that night and never returning. He didn't feel well physically or emotionally, and he wanted to lie down right there in the parking lot and cry himself to death. Someone touched his arm and said his name. He looked in the direction of the voice and saw his sister beside him with a look of caring and concern. He knew he had put her through hell by running away, and he felt bad for doing so. If he gave into his emotions right now, she would only worry more. He didn't want to make her suffer, so with tremendous difficulty, he pushed his thoughts and feelings aside. "We've got some catching up to do," he said to her. "Let's head home, and as we drive, I'd like to hear about what you and your family have been up to."

They drove in silence as Frannie navigated out of the city. Once they were on the interstate and headed north, she glanced at Oliver. "How're you doing?"

He shrugged. "I'd rather talk about you right now. Other than worried because of me, how've you been?"

She turned her attention back to the road. "I've been fine." Oliver noticed her tighten her grip on the steering wheel.

"Come on, Frannie. I know you. Saying you're fine means you're not fine. What's up?"

"Oliver, I'm fine. Really."

"Frannie."

"Look. It's not a big deal. You need to concentrate on getting better; I don't want you focusing on me."

"Alright, now I know there's something going on. Out with it."

She sighed. "David and I are having some issues," she said flatly. "I discovered recently that he had an affair last summer."

"While you were pregnant with Ellen?!"

"Yes."

"What a bastard!"

She sighed again. "I found out a few weeks ago at his company picnic. Someone from his office said something to me because she thought I knew about it. Apparently the whole goddamn town knew about it, other than me, of course."

"Oh, Frannie. I'm so sorry. That's awful. I always thought you and David were close and had a great marriage."

"So did I."

"Does he know that you know?"

"Yes. I confronted him the night I found out. He was really upset, and he cried and apologized and swore that it was just a brief thing and the biggest mistake of his life, and he begged me for forgiveness."

"Can you forgive him?"

"That's the thing. I'm trying. I really am. I don't want to be one of those women who holds a grudge and becomes bitter. We've had a good relationship, and I don't want to ruin it, but I just can't get over the fact that he was screwing another woman while I was pregnant with his third child, a child he wanted. I want to move forward, but it's hard not to think of that. I thought we had it so good, and now this...I don't know what to do, Oliver. I want to make it work. I want our closeness back, and I don't want the kids to have to grow up in a broken home, bouncing between parents, but I can't get over it. It hurts. How could he have done this to us?" She kept one hand on the steering wheel and wiped her face with the other.

Oliver put his arm around her and rubbed her shoulder. "Oh, Frannie. That really sucks. I'm so sorry. What can I do to help? Can I punch David's lights out when I see him tonight?"

She chuckled. "Yeah, right. Like you would do that. You wouldn't hurt a fly." She smiled at him nostalgically. "Remember how, when we were kids, every time someone would find a bug in the house you would gently take it outside and put it on a plant?"

He responded with a small, sad smile. "Yeah. But this is different. I would punch David in the face for hurting you."

"You're a good brother. But I don't want you to do that. In fact, please don't say anything at all to him. I don't even want him to know I told you. We're trying to work through this. I just needed to tell somebody about it."

"You can tell me anything any time. I mean that. And if you don't want me to say anything to him about it, I promise, I won't."

"Thanks, Oliver."

They drove in silence for several miles until Frannie asked him what the hospital had been like. He filled her in about the various groups and people there, and he told her about Penelope and her struggles with schizophrenia and how it had completely turned her life upside down.

Before he realized it, they were approaching Fairmont. Its buildings were visible in the distance. His heart raced, his head pounded, and everything spun. When they passed the sign that read, "Fairmont next five exits," he exclaimed, "Frannie, pull over!"

"Why?"

"I'm going to be sick!"

She jerked her minivan to the shoulder of I-94 and screeched to a stop. Oliver opened the door and leaned out. Painful dry heaves again, but nothing other than that, thanks to his inability to swallow even his liquid lunch. He leaned back in his seat and closed his eyes, willing the lightheadedness and nausea to pass. "Sorry about that," he said.

"Don't apologize for feeling sick. Are you going to be okay? Do you want me to drive to the next exit and pull off so you can get out and walk around?"

He shook his head. "No. I'm okay. Seeing Fairmont and the exit signs freaked me out, I guess." He sighed. "I don't know if I can do this, Frannie." He pressed his hands into his eyes. His breathing accelerated, so he intentionally took deep, deliberate breaths. He lowered his arms and folded them across his abdomen. Still leaning back against the seat, he turned his head and looked at his sister. "Sorry for making you stop. You can keep going now; I feel a little better again."

She put her arm around him. "Are you sure? Oliver, maybe I did the wrong thing in making you come home with me. What if Dr. Willis was right and you aren't ready to handle this? I don't want to cause you any more pain."

He turned his head the other way and looked out the window. Fairmont was out there, and Maggie and Henry weren't in it. He had run away from that fact but had continued to feel their absence just as keenly as when he had been home. The truth was that no matter where he was or what he did, the world caused him tremendous pain. Well, it really wasn't fair to blame the entire world; his own selfish insistence on training that day rather than being there for his family—in a place that he himself had suggested—was what caused him pain. Moping around the streets of Chicago or in the rooms of Airhaven wouldn't change a thing. Maggie and Henry were dead and they were never, ever coming back no matter where he was or what he did. There was absolutely no escaping that fact, so he might just as well let Frannie take him back to Fairmont. Besides, he felt incredibly guilty for making Frannie worry about him and for not being there when she needed him. Why was it that the only thing he seemed to be good at was being absent when he was needed the most?

"You're not the one causing me pain. I'm ready now. We can get going again." As she pulled back onto the interstate, he asked, "By the way, how did you react so quickly when I told you to pull over?"

"With a six-year-old, a four-year-old, and an eight-month-old, I'm an expert at handling things like that quickly. You know how kids are; a parent gets used to reacting instantly." She grinned and looked at him. Her smile faded. "Oh, God, Oliver, I'm sorry."

"It's okay." Her comment made him realize something he hadn't thought of before: he would have to see her kids. The realization made him feel sick again, but he didn't ask her to pull over this time. He just rode along in silence, dreading the moment she would pull into her driveway.

Unfortunately, the moment came too quickly. Frannie rolled into her driveway, put the van in park, and turned off the ignition. Oliver looked out his window at the freshly mowed green grass, the large pots of red geraniums, and the green-and-yellow John Deere tricycle parked on the sidewalk beside the sparkly pink bicycle with training wheels. Maggie had always had flowers, too: pots with various flowers in their front yard and a beautiful flower garden in the back yard. And Henry had had a trike, too, but his had been red. He used to pretend that it was his fire truck. Last summer, Henry had made watering the landscaping really fun.

"Whee-ooo! Whee-ooo! Whee-ooo!" At the top of his lungs, Henry made siren noises as he scooted around on his trike. Oliver and Maggie were in the yard, pruning bushes and watering trees.

"Don't you want to try to pedal, Henry? Scooting like that is a lot harder, you know."

"No, Daddy! This is faster. I have to get to the fire!"

Maggie nudged him. "Leave him alone, darling. He's not ready to pedal yet. He just turned three, after all. Wait until next summer. He'll be such an expert pedaler that you'll wish he were still scooting."

"You're probably right. But that just looks so awkward."

"It looks like he's doing fine to me." They watched him scoot around the driveway making his siren noises. Suddenly, he stopped and jumped off the trike. He ran to the hose that was delivering water to a big maple tree and picked it up. To his dismay, the water merely trickled out of it. He cupped his hands around his mouth and shouted, "We need more water, men! That means you, Daddy! Turn it up!"

Oliver laughed. "Where does he get these things?"

"He's got a great imagination. Probably from all the books we read him."

"More water, Daddy! Hurry!"

"You heard the fire chief. You'd better go assist."

Oliver went to the spigot and turned it up. On his way to go help his son put out the fire, Maggie called over to him. "Oliver?"

"Yes, honey?"

"Where were you?"

Oliver bolted upright so hard, his seatbelt locked and forced him backward. He jerked against it. "I'm here!" It remained locked. "No!" He struggled to get free. "I'm here!"

"Oliver!" Someone else called his name. "Take it easy. What's the matter?"

He continued to thrash and struggle. He needed to get to them! Why was he stuck? He couldn't breathe.

"Ollie! Ollie, calm down! It's okay."

Someone touched his face with both hands, and it scared him so much he jumped. The seatbelt was already locked tight, and it wouldn't give. As he searched for a way out, he heard his name again, "Ollie!" That was his childhood name. "Ollie, it's okay!" There it was again, the childhood name. What was up with that? Wait. Was that Frannie's voice? He focused on her face and returned to reality. He looked around and saw his sister's house and the yard and the bikes that triggered his memory. He couldn't get to Maggie and Henry to help them, and he couldn't go play fireman with Henry. He swallowed hard and closed his eyes. He tried to breathe through it like Matt had taught him, but the lump in his throat made it difficult.

Frannie had come to his side of the van and had opened his door. "Hey," she said softly, "What was that about? Are you okay? What can I do to help, Oliver?"

He looked at his sister through brimming eyes. "I'm sorry. I was just remembering last summer, and the memory got a little messed up, that's all. No biggie."

She knitted her brows. "Do you want to talk about it?"

"No. Thanks, though. Sorry about reacting that way." He still breathed heavily. He tried his breathing exercises. He needed his lorazepam, but he didn't want to trouble Frannie.

"You don't have to be sorry. Are you ready to go in, or do you want to stay here a little longer?"

He was not at all ready to go in; after all, if he couldn't handle seeing some flowers and toys, how in the hell could he face his nieces and the nephew who was almost the same age as Henry? But sitting here certainly wasn't doing him any good, and the longer he sat out here, the more explaining he would have to do to David. Frannie had told him that David had been working from home for the last few days so she could go retrieve Oliver in Chicago, and if he could see them in the driveway now, he was probably wondering why they weren't coming in. He sighed and replied, "It's okay. Let's go in."

Frannie went in first, and Oliver followed close behind. At the sound of the closing door, her family emerged from the kitchen. "Mommy! You're home!" Lacey, the oldest of Frannie's three children, raced to her and threw her arms around her. She hugged her mother only briefly before turning to Oliver and hugging him. "Hi, Uncle Oliver. We missed you! Where were you?"

The question felt like a blow. He couldn't find his voice. He stood there dumbly and fought for control.

"Don't ask personal questions, Lacey," David chastised. He stepped forward, Ellen in his arms. He balanced her on his left arm, extended his right arm to Oliver, and shook his hand. "Welcome back, Oliver. It's good to see you." Oliver barely returned the handshake, but David didn't seem to notice, as the baby had pitched forward upon seeing her mother. He yanked his hand away from Oliver's to catch her. "Whoa, little girl." He tossed her up into the air, eliciting a streak of giggles, and blew on her stomach before handing her off to Frannie.

Suddenly, Oliver felt as though he were watching the scene from far away. It was surreal. Time seemed suspended, and he felt removed from it all. He was aware of every rapid beat of his heart, cognizant of the individual beads of sweat that had formed on his forehead and on his palms. He felt himself shake David's hand limply, but the movement seemed like it were happening in slow motion, and almost as though someone else were doing it. Oddly, he could see the scene taking place, like he was looking down from above and seeing someone else. He was aware that it was indeed himself, though, because he recognized the way he looked. The noises of kids and adults talking and the baby squealing sounded echoy and tinny. His entire body felt strange, as though he were floating.

A small force slammed into his legs and he crashed back to normal awareness. He looked down to discover that his nephew had literally thrown himself at him. The boy looked up at Oliver. "Hi, Uncle Oliver! Did you bring Henry with you? I want to play with Henry!"

Lacey rushed over and elbowed her brother. "David Jonathon Hammond the Third, you were not supposed to mention Cousin Henry! We told you that!" She looked at Oliver and apologized, "Please forgive him. He is too young to understand. He doesn't get it." She glared at her brother and elbowed him again.

"Ouch!" he cried.

Frannie and David both reacted and stepped in, but Oliver ignored them. He knelt down to his nephew's level and said quietly, "It's okay. Don't feel bad. I'm a grownup, and I don't get it either."

The little boy looked his uncle in the eye and said, "I'm happy you're here. I missed you. I wish Henry and Aunt Maggie were here, too. They were fun. Hey. You're crying!" He turned to his father then and said, "See? Big boys do too cry!"

"Yeah, they do. I don't know why I told you they don't. Come on, Davie. We need to go work on the pizza we're making."

"Oh yeah! C'mon, Lacey! I'm doing the cheese, remember? Don't touch the cheese!"

Lacey and Davie ran out of the room to finish what they had been doing. Before joining them, David said to Oliver, "I'm really sorry about that. I want you to know how glad I am that someone found the website and contacted Frannie. And Frannie said you're going to stay with us. You are more than welcome here; that guest bedroom downstairs is all yours for as long as you need it."

"Thanks," was all Oliver was capable of saying.

As David returned to the kitchen, Frannie tended to Oliver. She helped him back up and then she hugged him tight and let the minutes pass by before saying, "You're homecoming wasn't supposed to happen like that. I'm so, so sorry. Here, come sit down."

"Actually, I'd like to go downstairs and freshen up a bit, and I kind of need to lie down for a little bit if that's okay."

"Of course it is. I'll take you down."

"No. Stay up here with your family. They haven't seen you in a couple days. I know where the guest bedroom is." Unable to stand any of it any longer, he headed down the stairs and threw himself on the bed. He pulled the picture out of his shirt pocket and stared at it until he could no longer keep his eyes open. Still holding it tightly in his hands, he fell asleep.

CHAPTER 24

"**O**liver?" He heard Frannie call his name, but he remained curled up on the bed with his eyes closed. She approached his side and touched his shoulder. "Ollie?" He opened his eyes. The room was dark and he could just make out her outline. She held something in her hand. "Hey. I'm sorry to wake you up. You've been sleeping soundly for hours, and I hate to bother you, but Penelope's on the phone for you. She says it's urgent. Do you want to take the call, or should I tell her you'll call her tomorrow?"

He sat up and rubbed his eyes. While it was true that he had been sleeping, he had not experienced uninterrupted sound slumber—nightmares had punctuated his sleep—but he didn't feel like talking about it, so he didn't correct Frannie about the nature of his rest. Instead, he just took the phone from her. She left him to talk to Penelope privately.

"Hey, Penelope. How're you doing?"

"Terrible. This is a disaster. I can't do this, Oliver. It was horrible, so I just left. I remembered that you went to a shelter when you left your home, but I don't know what it was called. I'm trying to find it, but it's dark out and I don't know exactly where I am. I can't figure it out because darkness hides the true nature of the shapes and the colors. Mrs. Roosevelt is mad at me for getting lost, but she won't let me call William. I don't know if I want to call him anyway because I'm trying to do him a favor, but I'm scared." The lack of emotion in her tone didn't match the content of her words, and if Oliver hadn't come to know her so well, he wouldn't have understood how serious she was.

Oliver stood up and turned on the lights so he could fully wake up and concentrate on Penelope. "It's going to be okay. I'm glad you called me. First, we need to get you off the streets. How far away from home are you?"

"I don't know."

"How long have you been walking around looking for the shelter?"

"I don't know. What time is it? I didn't pay attention to the time on my phone when I called you."

He glanced at the clock on the bedside table. Ten-thirty. Really? When Frannie had said he had been sleeping for hours, he didn't think she meant more than six. He wondered if the kids had been disappointed that he didn't eat their homemade pizza with them, and he felt bad.

"Oliver, what time is it?"

Now he felt bad that his mind had wandered. Why was concentrating such a problem? "I'm sorry, Penelope. It's ten-thirty. What time did you leave home?"

"Six-fifteen."

She had been wandering aimlessly through the city of Chicago for over four hours, looking for something that she didn't even know the name of, much less the location? And now it was dark. Was she even in a safe area of the city? Oliver remembered his early, unsheltered nights, and he shuddered. "Okay. That means you left more than four hours ago. Have you been walking the entire time?"

"Yes. My feet hurt. My legs do, too."

Four hours of walking could have taken her pretty far. Even if William were out looking, finding her would be nearly impossible, especially if she had gotten a head start. Oliver remembered how panicked he had been when he couldn't find Maggie and Henry and figured that William must be frantic right now. "Have you talked to William at all since then?"

"No. He's called me a lot, but Mrs. Roosevelt won't let me answer. She says that it's mean to lead him on by talking to him. The last four times he's called, I've tried to answer it, but she has held my arms down so I can't get at my phone. I could feel her grip on my wrists, and I felt the pressure of her strength holding my arms against my sides. I tried to get free, but I'm tired and hungry, so I'm too weak."

"What's going on right now? You were able to call me. How did you do it?"

"I told her that I needed to check on you. When she didn't want me to, I reminded her that she used to travel all around the country and all around the world to check on people to make sure they were okay, so I should at least call you. I read about that in the book William brought me. She didn't want to let me call you at first, but I really wanted to talk to you because I'm lost and scared. I yelled at her. She yelled back. We had a fight right here on the busy street. People looked at me strangely, but I didn't care because I needed her to let me call you. I'm glad I kept at it, because she went away. She's gone right now and that's why I was able to call you."

Oliver pictured Penelope, exhausted, afraid, and alone, standing somewhere in Chicago yelling at someone no one else could see. He remembered the looks she received in the hospital and the way patients steered clear of her, and he could about imagine how people near her reacted as she stood there, struggling with something within her. He knew that no one had come to her aid, for it was Penelope herself calling him, rather than someone calling on her behalf, and she hadn't said that she was with someone now. What the hell was wrong with people? There was no time to think about that though; he needed to get her back safely to William.

"I'm really glad that you found the strength and the courage to overcome her and to call me. Where are you right now?"

"I told you I don't know. I'm lost and it's dark so I can't interpret the shapes and colors. There are no Kerffies around for me to ask, either. They're recharging in the stratosphere. If it were light, that would be different."

"Go to the nearest corner and tell me the street signs."

"Okay." There was silence on the line after that, and Oliver hoped that she was just walking to a corner. The silence continued. What was taking her so long? Finally she said, "Melrose and Greenview. How do I get to your shelter from here? Am I close?"

Oliver exhaled. He didn't know until then that he had been holding his breath. "I don't know because I'm not familiar enough with Chicago."

"Well, how did you find it in the first place?"

"Some street outreach people approached me and told me about it. They took me there with them, but I don't know where I was at the time. I have no idea what's around you right now because I really don't know the city. But it doesn't matter because you're not going to the shelter."

"Oliver, where am I going to go then? I don't want to go back to Airhaven, and I wouldn't know how to get there, either. And now you're telling me that you can't help me get to your shelter. What am I going to do? I'm tired and hungry and I don't feel well. Part of the reason I don't feel well is the medication's side effects, and part of the reason is because I missed my last doses of everything. My medication is at home. I'm all alone; I don't even have Mrs. Roosevelt with me because she left when I yelled at her. I'm scared, Oliver."

"I was scared when I was alone there too, so I understand. Listen to me: you aren't completely alone. You have William, and I bet he is trying to find you right now. I don't know what happened tonight, but I bet William didn't want you to leave, and I bet he just wants to find you."

"I don't know. I really, really miss him right now, but…"

"No 'buts.' You miss him, and I will bet anything that he misses you. Now here's what we're going to do: I'm going to call him for you, and I'm going to tell him where you are so he can come get you. That means I have to hang up the phone, but I'm going to call you right back after I talk to William so you have someone to talk to while you wait for him to pick you up. You need to stay right where you are because if you leave, William won't be able to find you as easily. I'm going to hang up and call William. Do you promise to stay there?"

"Yes. Please call me back quickly. I need to hear your voice. You make me feel better."

Oliver felt an inexplicable warmth wash over him. "Thanks. You know what? You make me feel better, too. You ease my despair a little bit, Penelope. I really want to help you get home. Will you stay put, please, so I can get William to come get you?" His voice faltered ever so slightly as images flashed through his mind of what could happen to her all alone in the dark, somewhere within the city. He was overcome by an intense desire to get there to help her, but he was over an hour away. Once again, he wouldn't be able to get to someone he cared about. He started to sweat, and his heart thumped forcefully as his chest constricted in what felt like a heart attack. A wave of nausea and lightheadedness forced him to sit down on the edge of the bed. No! This couldn't happen; there wasn't time. He used deep breaths to calm himself and focused on what he could do, rather than on what he could not do. "Hang on, Penelope. It'll be okay. I'll call you right back."

"I'll wait here like you said, Oliver."

He hung up, yanked his safety plan out of his back pocket, found William's number, and dialed faster than he had ever dialed a phone before. Agitated, he paced while it rang. He ran his hand through his hair. Finally, after what seemed like dozens of rings, William picked up.

"This is a Wisconsin number; please tell me it's you, Oliver. Penelope is gone, and I can't get ahold of her."

"Yes, it's me." The tense worry in his voice equally matched William's. "Why did it take so long for you to answer? Penelope called me. You need to get to her right away before something happens to her."

"Oh thank God! Where is she? Hey, what do you mean what took me so long? I answered on the second ring."

"You did? Oh. Sorry. It just felt...Never mind. You need to go to her." He related the conversation he had had with Penelope, and then told him, "She's in Algonquin Park. You've got to get to her before something bad happens."

"Where?"

"Algonquin Park. It's dangerous. Hurry!"

"No, Oliver, she can't be in Algonquin Park. That's in Fairmont. She's in Chicago. Calm down and think about what she told you. I need to know where she is so I can go get her and keep her safe."

Oliver was confused. He couldn't think. He squeezed his hair with his free hand and closed his eyes. Words were overpowered by pictures that all came at once and flooded his mind: fights on the dangerous streets of inner city Chicago, a crazed, drugged-up man shouting and threatening and shooting a gun, Maggie screaming, Henry crying, the two falling together in pain, blood flowing everywhere, Penelope standing alone, mocked and laughed at, the same drugged man turning on her and chasing her, shooting her, making her fall to the ground, bleeding, a car accident, blood gushing out from under the car, blood-covered bodies stuck inside. He panted hard in a panicked attempt to breathe. He couldn't move. Sweat stung his eyes. He heard someone call his name, but it wasn't Maggie or Henry or Penelope. It was a man, and he recognized the voice. Where was it coming from? He heard it again, right in his ear. He became aware once again that he was holding a phone, and someone was talking to him through it. William!

"Oliver! I can hear you breathing, and I know you're still there. Listen to me, please. I need to know where Penelope is. You can help her by telling me where she is."

That's right; Penelope needed help, but she was okay right now. He had just talked to her. What had she said about where she was? He closed his eyes, took slow deep breaths, and replayed the conversation in his mind.

"Think, Oliver! Where is she?"

"The corner of Melrose and Greenview!" he blurted into the phone. "That's right. I had her walk to a corner and tell me what the street signs said. She said Melrose and Greenview. William, I promise that's right. I'm so sorry I was out of it for a second. You've got to get to her. She's going to stay right there until you come."

"Good Lord, that's clear across town! I'm on my way right now. Oliver, thank you. I don't want to be rude, but I'm going to hang up. I need to call her. I hope she answers this time."

"No! That's dangerous. Don't drive through Chicago while talking on the phone, especially when you're all worked up. You could get into an accident and die. I told her I would call her back and talk to her until you arrive."

"Yeah, I guess I just need to focus on getting to her. But no one's going to die. It's all going to be alright. I'll drive, and you talk to Penelope. Tell her I'm on my way but it will take a while for me to get all the way over there. I'm heading out now. And will you tell her I love her?"

"Of course."

The moment they hung up, Oliver called Penelope back. She answered on the first ring. He was so relieved to hear her voice that he thought he might cry. He needed to stay calm for her though, so he didn't. After relaying William's messages, he said, "Now tell me about today. What happened that was so terrible?"

"Well, the afternoon started out nice. We went home, and I got to see our cat. William and I sat and talked and read about Eleanor Roosevelt together. He told me I was beautiful and that he loves me, and he wanted to have sex, but I think I'm getting fat and I didn't want him to see me naked. He told me that I'm not getting fat at all, but I know I am because of the medication. I've gained several pounds already and I've just started this new stuff. He wanted to prove to me that I'm still attractive, and he kissed me. One thing led to another and we went to the bedroom and had sex. I was worried that I'm not as good in bed anymore because I just don't feel as passionate, but William said it was really good. I hope he meant it." She paused, and when Oliver said nothing, she said, "Oh. I'm sorry. I probably shouldn't have talked about that, should I have? I hope that I didn't make you uncomfortable. It's just that you are such a good friend. I feel like I haven't had a friend to really talk to for nearly two years when I was first diagnosed with schizophrenia. I feel like I can talk to you about anything, Oliver, and you won't judge me. I'm comfortable with you. I'm sorry if I said something wrong. I wish I could take it back."

Truthfully, Oliver had been incredibly uncomfortable. He felt as if he were somehow violating their privacy, even though he hadn't asked about their sex life. Shamefully, this conversation also reminded him how he missed Maggie in every way imaginable. However, Penelope's admission just now instantly changed his perspective. He realized that he, too, felt a closeness in their friendship. He told her as much.

"Oh, I am so happy about that. Thank you." She immediately continued with her story. "So after we got dressed again, we decided to go for a walk. That was nice, too. It was when we came back home that the trouble happened. William and I have a new neighbor who moved in down the hall while I was in the hospital. Her name is Mariska. She saw us in the elevator, and she invited us into her apartment. William has already met her, and that's fine. But as we stepped inside, do you know what she said to me?"

"What did she say?" What callous thing had this woman said? Why were people so insensitive and clueless?

"She said that she's heard a lot about me from William."

That was it? He waited for more, but when she said nothing further, he asked, "What's wrong with that?"

"Everything is wrong with that. I have schizophrenia. I'm mentally ill, and she knows it. She said she has been looking forward to my coming home from the hospital so she could meet me."

"Penelope, that doesn't sound bad at all."

"Her apartment is painted in reds and yellows, Oliver."

"So?"

"Red and yellow. Fear and disgust. She said she had been looking forward to meeting me, but everything around her said the opposite. Walls are straight lines, remember, and straight lines mean the truth. The truth is that she's afraid of me and disgusted by my mental illness. I tried to ignore the colors, but it's hard to ignore colors. Then Mrs. Roosevelt started talking to me, telling me that I was an embarrassment to William. She sometimes brings other people with her to help her make her point. I don't know who they are, just that there are a lot of them; Mrs. Roosevelt is a very popular person. They all started talking at once and I couldn't understand a thing they said. I just heard all of these voices shouting in my head, and I was scared and confused and upset. The three of us were sitting down in the living room at that point, and William and Mariska were talking but I couldn't say anything because Mrs. Roosevelt had taken my words, and she and the others were using them to play keep-away from me. I wanted to talk, but I couldn't. I just sat there like a moron and the voices all roared in my head and I knew that I was being embarrassing. I struggled really hard to find words, and I managed to tell William that I need to get something for a headache and that I'd be right back. I knew if I just ran out of there he would follow me and I wouldn't be able to get away. I was able to convince him to stay. As soon as I left Mariska's apartment, I went right to the elevator and left. Oh, Oliver, why do I have to be schizophrenic? I hate it so much."

She fell silent. He could hear her sniff repeatedly, and he knew she was crying. "Penelope, I can only imagine how hard it would be, and I think it sucks that you're going through this. But are you sure Mariska really was afraid of you and disgusted by you, or was Mrs. Roosevelt trying to convince you of that?"

"I told you about the walls."

"But maybe Mariska doesn't know. I didn't understand about the colors and shapes before you taught me about the Kerffies. It might just be a coincidence."

She sniffed again. "I didn't think about that. Do you think it might be so?"

"I do, Penelope, and that's the truth."

"Oliver, I don't know what or who to believe. I'm so confused all of the time."

"Do you think you could try just listening to people's words and keeping them separate from the other things you hear? Go only by people's words and see what happens."

"Maybe."

"Why don't you try it? You can tell me how it goes, okay?"

"Okay. Oliver, William is here. I see him. Here he comes."

There was silence on the phone, and Oliver imagined they were hugging. He could almost sense through the phone William's happiness at finding her safe. He sighed and hung up, flopping down on the bed and putting a pillow over his head to block out the blinding light above him. When the phone rang, he jumped. He flew to his feet, sending the pillow flying. Oh no, was he going to start being so edgy again? Heart racing, he answered.

"Why did you hang up?" Penelope asked.

"Well, William is there and you don't need me anymore. I figured you two wanted to get going rather than standing on a street corner at almost midnight talking to me."

"Well, I'd like to tell you goodnight first. So goodnight. Thank you so much for everything, Oliver. You really rescued me tonight. Thank you for helping me. I don't know what would have happened without you."

"Any time, Penelope. I mean that."

"I'll talk to you tomorrow. Don't hang up. William wants to talk to you."

"Hey, Oliver. Do you have any idea how grateful I am for you? I was worried sick about Penelope. Thank you for your help tonight."

"Of course. You don't have to thank me."

"You need to know that you saved her tonight."

Oliver nodded. He was glad that he had been able to help. Why hadn't he been able to help Maggie and Henry when they needed him?

"Oliver? You okay?"

No. "Yeah. Go take Penelope home. She's tired and hungry and her feet hurt."

"I've got her in the car already. We're on our way home now. I'm so glad she's okay. Thanks again, man. I'll talk to you tomorrow."

After they had hung up, Oliver stood there, numb, for several minutes. He spotted his picture on the bed and reached for it. "I wish you had been able to come home with me and that you were okay," he whispered. Keeping the picture in his hand, he went to the dresser where his paper bag from Airhaven was sitting beside a water bottle. Frannie must have put them there when he was napping. He opened it and removed the contents, the collection of his medication. Among the pills for depression, anxiety, sleep, and nightmares, there was nothing for a broken heart. He took all the things he was supposed to take—not for himself, but because he had promised both Penelope and his sister that he would take everything the doctor had prescribed to help him. He thought about heading upstairs to see if Frannie was awake, but he didn't have the energy. Instead, he went back to bed to try to get some sleep between the nightmares.

CHAPTER 25

GRADUALLY, OLIVER BECAME AWARE OF A STRANGE NOISE. IT WAS KIND OF A vroom-vroom sound. He opened his eyes. He was groggy and his vision was blurred, but he could make out someone small sitting on his bed. A child, playing with something. Henry! It had all been just a horrific nightmare, and his family was okay after all!

"Henry!" Overjoyed, he lurched toward the little boy and threw his arms around him. He scrambled to his knees and, despite the head rush from the sudden motion, he tossed the little boy into the air, caught him, placed him back down on the bed, and tickled him. With his eyes closed, Oliver kissed his head.

Squeals and giggles erupted from the child. "Uncle Oliver, I'm not Henry! I'm Davie!"

Instantly, Oliver's jubilation gave way to anguish. He rolled onto his back and covered his face with his arms. He wanted to scream at the kid that no, he was not Davie, he was Henry and everything was okay again. But that would have been ridiculous, and it would have scared his little nephew to pieces. Instead, he muttered, "Of course you are Davie. Sorry about that."

Davie plopped himself on top of Oliver, legs straddling his chest. Little fingers pried his arms off his face. "What did you say?"

Oliver studied Davie. He looked so different from Henry. Davie had hair so light it was almost white, and it was ramrod straight. It was cut short so it looked neat. Henry's had been dark and flippy and a bit unruly because it was a little on the long side. Davie's pale blue eyes were a sharp contrast to Henry's dark brown ones. But they both looked like active little boys. Davie's face was streaked with what looked like dirt and Cheetos. Henry had usually been a mess too, for he was quite agile and skilled at dodging washcloths.

"I didn't understand you. What did you say?" Davie repeated his question.

"Uh, I said sorry. Of course I know you're Davie. I was just confused for a second, that's all."

Davie stared at him. Soon Davie looked around the room as though searching for something. He looked back at Oliver, and then he wriggled out of his shirt.

"What are you doing?" Oliver asked.

Saying nothing, Davie wadded it up and put it in Oliver's face. He wiped it clumsily back and forth across Oliver's eyes. "When I don't have something to wipe my face, I use my shirt. I'm wiping your tears off for you because I want you to be happy again." He kept wiping Oliver's face the way he would wipe a spill off the floor with a large towel. It kind of hurt, but it was such a sweet gesture that Oliver couldn't bring himself to ask him to stop. It was something Henry would have done, because he'd had such a kind heart. "Uncle Oliver! I can't keep up with your eyes."

"Sorry, Davie."

"That's okay." Davie stopped wiping and slid down off Oliver's chest, leaving the shirt on Oliver's face. Oliver pressed his hands into the shirt. He heard Davie leave the room, and he wondered if he should follow. He remained where he was, though, because he was in no condition to make an appearance upstairs.

It wasn't long before Davie returned to the room, climbed up onto the bed, and, once again, pried Oliver's arms up. Davie left the shirt where it was and pressed something soft into one of Oliver's hands.

Then he moved Oliver's arms back down over the top of the shirt. Next, he felt Davie cuddle up against him. He curled himself right up to Oliver's side. One of his small hands reached up to Oliver's hair, and he played with his shaggy curls with his fingers. Oliver lifted the shirt slightly and peered through the space. Everything was blurry, so he dabbed his eyes with the shirt and tried again. Davie's head rested on Oliver's shoulder. One arm was close against his little body, and tucked into it was a ragged-looking stuffed dog. Oliver lifted the shirt further off his eyes and peered at his own hand. The soft thing that Davie had placed in it was another stuffed dog. It was equally ragged. Davie's eyes had been closed, but he must have felt Oliver lift up the shirt, for he opened them and gazed at Oliver. "I'm not supposed to mention it to you," he whispered, "but I'm sad, too. Henry was my bestest favorite friend." Davie closed his eyes again. Oliver felt his shoulder getting wet.

Oliver put one arm around Davie and pulled him even closer. "It's okay to mention it to me, Davie. I'm sorry Henry is gone." With the stuffed dog in his hand, he pressed down hard on the shirt. He pressed so hard he saw bursts of white light, but it wasn't hard enough to stop the tears. A sob escaped, and Davie let go of the stuffed animal and put his hand across Oliver's stomach. Oliver sat up and scooped up Davie, letting him fold into him and rest his head on his shoulder. Davie wrapped his arms around Oliver's neck and ran the fingers of both hands through his hair. Oliver held Davie tight and rocked him.

He wished with all of his heart that he could hold Henry like this again. At the funeral home, when he had reached into the tiny casket and hugged him, Henry had stayed stiff and cold and lifeless. Oliver had been instantly sorry that he had done that, because he didn't want that to be his last memory of holding his son. Thankfully, he did still remember the soft, warm hugs that Henry had always lavished upon him.

They stayed like that for a long time, long after both of them stopped crying. On one hand, this tore at Oliver's soul; on the other, it was actually nice. Comforting a child felt good, and he was touched to the core by Davie's attempt to comfort him. Seeing Davie was so hard, but he was a sweet little boy, and his nephew, and he was clearly grieving too. As difficult as it was to be here, as long as he was here, he wanted to help Davie deal with his loss.

After more time passed, Davie started to wiggle. Oliver loosened his grip, and Davie leaned back and looked at him. "Want to come upstairs with me, or do you need to sleep today too?"

"What do you mean, 'today too'?"

"You slept all day yesterday, Uncle Oliver. You've been sleeping down here since you got here on Thursday, and today is…today is… What day is after Thursday?"

"Friday."

"And what day is after Friday?"

What day is after Friday? What was he talking about? Just how long had he been down here? "Saturday?"

"That's it! Today is Saturday." Davie nodded his head in satisfaction.

Oliver put his hands under Davie's arms and lifted him into the air. The boy shrieked in delight. "Hey, are you teasing me?" Oliver's arms felt weak and shaky, so he brought him back down.

"No. I'm serious. It…is…Sat…ur…day." Davie spaced out the syllables in emphasis.

Oliver thought hard. He vaguely remembered Frannie waking him and handing him pills and a drink of water. She had done that more than once. She must have been giving him his medication. Had he had any nightmares? He thought harder and recalled some bad dreams that caused him to toss and turn, but not fully wake up. After three months of sleeping on a cot in a homeless shelter and more than a week in a hard hospital bed, sleeping among chaos and noise and a ticking clock, sleeping only intermittently between horrifying nightmares, apparently his mind and body had welcomed a comfortable bed in a familiar, safe place.

"Wow. I've been sleeping a long time then, huh?"

"Yes. And Lacey and I have been waiting for you."

"Well, then, what are we doing sitting down here on the bed? Should we go upstairs?"

"Yeah! Let's go!"

"Hold on. I need to brush my teeth and freshen up a bit first. Will you wait here for me?"

"Okay."

When Oliver returned from the bathroom, he found Davie playing with toy cars on the bed. The two stuffed dogs were lined up, side by side, and they had cars stacked on their backs. "The cars are racing, and the winners get to sit up here." Davie patted the animals as he talked. "Are you ready? Can we go up now?"

"Let's go."

Davie stood, jumped on the bed, and then took a flying leap into Oliver's arms. While he looked drastically different than Henry, he sure acted a lot like him. For his nephew's sake, Oliver shoved away the pain that the thought caused, and with Davie on his hip, he headed upstairs.

Voices reached them as they neared the top of the stairs. Frannie and David were talking in the kitchen.

"Shhh!" Davie put his finger to his lips and whispered, "I'm supposed to be in my room taking my afternoon nap."

"Davie!"

"I tried to stay in my room, but I was lonely. I wanted to be with you. Are you mad at me?"

Oliver held him tighter. "Never in a million years would I be mad at you for coming to see me." In response, Davie planted a wet kiss on his cheek. Oliver kissed him back. On the inside, he crumbled. On the outside, he stayed intact. He removed the focus from the feel of his nephew in his arms and placed the focus on the conversation coming from the kitchen. The kitchen was around the corner from the partially closed door at the top of the stairs, so he couldn't quite make out the exact words, but he could tell from the intensity of their tones that Frannie and David were arguing.

He wanted to hear what they were saying, but he didn't want their son to hear it.

"Okay big guy, here's the plan," Oliver whispered. "We don't want you to get in trouble, do we?" Davie shook his head vigorously back and forth. "So here's what we're going to do. Do you know where Lacey is?"

"She's probably in the back yard."

"Perfect. Listen up. We're not going to lie to your mom and dad and make them think you've been in your room, but I can talk to them first and let them know that I was glad you came down, okay?"

Davie looked Oliver in the eye with a very solemn expression. He nodded.

"Right now, I want you to tiptoe quietly through the living room and go out the front door. Then head to the backyard and play with your sister. I'll explain things to them before we all come outside. Sound like a plan?"

Davie saluted him, and then slid down out of Oliver's arms. With exaggerated tiptoeing steps, he moved through the living room and slipped quietly out the front door. Oliver went to the top of the stairs and concentrated on the conversation in the kitchen.

"...and how many times can I say I'm sorry before you start believing me?"

"I believe you that you're sorry."

"Then what's the problem?"

"You need to give me time to stop hurting, David. I feel embarrassed and betrayed, and I keep trying to figure out what was so bad about me that drove you to another woman."

"Frannie, it was just an impulsive fling. There is nothing about you that drove me away."

"I find that hard to believe. What was it, then? Huh? What, David? What was so fucking alluring about her?"

"Honestly, Frannie. It was nothing. And it was stupid and I didn't like it and I just want us to go back to the way we were."

"It's going to take time."

"We've been trying to work through this for a month already, and it feels like we've gotten nowhere." David sounded highly frustrated.

Frannie sounded equally frustrated. "You can't expect this to just wash down the drain with the dirty dishwater or laundry or bath water." She paused. "Maybe that's part of the problem. We're too wrapped up in all of our chores and tasks and work and to-do lists. I think the only way we can work through this is to spend time together, just the two of us. We need to go out on dates, away from everything, and try to rebuild what we used to have."

"If that's what it'll take, then fine. Let's go on dates together. I love you, Frannie, and I want us to be okay again."

"Let's start tonight."

"Tonight? That'd be great, but it's Saturday afternoon. How are we going to get a sitter on such short notice?"

"Yeah, you're right. Wait. We have a babysitter. Oliver can stay with the kids." Frannie's voice brightened.

Oliver's heart pounded. He didn't know if he was ready to take care of kids, especially these kids, children who had been an integral part of his life with Maggie and Henry.

David snorted. "Oliver? Frannie, you've got to be kidding."

A little shock ran through Oliver. What the hell was that supposed to mean?

"What the hell is that supposed to mean?" Frannie asked David, her tone now defensive.

"Come on. Really? You think your brother can take care of our kids?"

"Yes. I do. He's done it before. He's great with them, and they adore him."

"No way. That was before Maggie and Henry were killed. For God's sake, he's been gone for three months. He just up and took off because he couldn't handle anything. We had no idea where he was until some guy he met in a mental ward contacted you. You had to drag him back here, but he's clearly not ready to be back. He most definitely is in no shape to care for our kids. He walked through the door two days ago, went down to the basement after Davie made him cry, and has been sleeping down there ever since. You think he is capable of babysitting? And besides, he wasn't there for his own family. What makes you think he'll be there for ours?"

"David! How could you say that? What happened in the park was absolutely not his fault!"

"No, of course it wasn't. I didn't mean that it was. I take that part back. It's not about that at all; it's about his condition right now. I don't know if it's good for the kids, or for him, to ask him to babysit…"

Oliver stopped listening. He felt sick. Weak from lack of food and the blow from David's words, his legs could no longer support him. He sank down and sat on the step. He put his hands to his head in an attempt to counteract the throbbing and to push all of David's words away. They wouldn't go away, though; instead, they intensified and echoed in his mind. David was right; it was most definitely his fault, and he was no longer trustworthy. He was no good to anyone anymore. Goddamn landing pad. Maggie was gone. Henry was gone. He couldn't be trusted to help Frannie and her kids. Penelope was off with William in Chicago, and he had nothing to offer them. His work as an environmental scientist was over; despite what Stanley had told him, he knew he couldn't go back. He couldn't be trusted to concentrate and do his job correctly. Everything good in his life was gone. What reason did he have to live? He shot to his feet and, blinded by the head rush that accompanied the swift action, hurried back down the stairs so quickly that he slid to the bottom. He grabbed hold of the handrail to steady himself and paused only briefly to recover his balance. He dashed into his room. Maybe Dr. Willis had been right and the medication could help him after all. It would help him do what he wanted to do. He'd swallow all of it at once and be done with all of this.

As he reached for the first bottle, he caught a glimpse of the bed in the mirror. On it were the stuffed dogs and pile of toy cars. The sight stopped Oliver in his tracks. If he took all of these and lay down on the bed and died, what would that do to Davie? Davie had just attempted to comfort him, and he had also shared that he missed his best friend. How much would it scar him to have his uncle die shortly afterward, in that very bed, beside the stuffed animals he had brought in for consolation? His head drooped. Gently, he placed the bottle back on the dresser. He still wanted to die—he just couldn't live his life any longer—but now wasn't the time. He couldn't do that to Davie. And Frannie. What would it do to her to find her brother's body in her guest bed? Besides, when he had rocked Davie just a short time ago, he had promised himself that as long as he was here, he would help him.

David was an ass. He had betrayed Frannie and the kids, and he had just said some awful things about Oliver. He had promised Frannie that he wouldn't say anything to her bastard husband, so, for her sake, he wouldn't confront him. What he could do for Frannie and the kids, though, was to put aside his own misery and take care of them. He sighed. Who was he kidding? He couldn't put aside his misery. He continued to stare at Davie's treasures on the bed. Fine. He'd do this despite his misery.

He turned and marched up the stairs. Davie and Frannie were still in the kitchen. He had no idea what they were talking about now because he hadn't taken the time to pause and listen. He didn't care, anyway. He barged in and interrupted. "Look, just a little while ago I was on my way upstairs, and I heard you say that you don't trust me with your kids. You have every right to think that, but I'm telling you that I love those kids and I wouldn't let anything happen to them. I'm not going to leave when I'm supposed to be watching them, and I'm not going to break down or go downstairs and sleep or anything like that. So go on your date, and I'll babysit them, and I'll do a damn good job with them because they're my nieces and nephew. I can be trusted." He ran his hand through his hair and kept his hand on his head. When he realized that might make him look unstable, he folded his arms across his chest and leaned against the counter in an attempt to look nonchalant.

Frannie rushed to his side. "Oh my God, Ollie. I know you can be trusted. I would put my children in your care any time. Did you hear that part of the conversation?" Frannie glared at David.

"No. I went back downstairs for a minute. But I'm here now," he was quick to point out. "I'm fine, and I want you to go out tonight. I'm sorry I slept so long, David, but I really haven't slept well since April twenty-first, and I guess it finally caught up with me. But I'm not going to fall asleep while I'm caring for your kids. I wouldn't do that."

David exhaled noisily and stepped toward Oliver and Frannie. He slapped Oliver on the shoulder awkwardly. "I know you wouldn't. I'm really sorry I said that."

"You seem to be sorry for a lot of things lately, David." Frannie glared at him again.

"Frannie, don't be mad at him." Oliver didn't want to be responsible for any further strain on their marriage. He had ruined two lives already—well, "ruined" was putting it mildly; "ended" was more accurate—and he didn't want to be responsible for causing anyone any more pain. "He was just being a good dad and caring about his kids. I don't mind staying with the kids tonight if you two would like to go out. I'll take good care of them for you, I promise."

"David?" Frannie's tone bordered on challenging.

David took his wife in his arms. "I would enjoy getting away for a while with you, and I would love it if your brother would watch the kids." Seeing them embrace, knowing they were going on a date, intensified Oliver's ache for Maggie. He felt lightheaded, and his knees threatened to give out. He braced himself on the counter. Both David and Frannie looked at him

"Oliver! Are you feeling okay? Yes, we can trust you, but maybe this would be too hard on you." Frannie sounded worried.

"I told you, I'm fine. I just feel a little weak, that's all. I haven't eaten since I had half of an Ensure for breakfast on Thursday."

"Why didn't you say something? Sit down, and I'll make you something to eat." Frannie rummaged through cupboards and the refrigerator. "We have leftover lasagna, or I could make you hot dogs or a grilled cheese sandwich."

Oliver gagged involuntarily at the mention of food. "Uh, actually, I'll just take an Ensure and head outside with Lacey and Davey." He stood and went to the fridge. Grabbing his drink, he headed for the back door.

"We'll go out with you. Lacey's out there, but Davie is taking a nap. Ellen, too. They should both wake up pretty soon, though."

"Actually, Davie's outside." He gave them an abbreviated version of Davie's time downstairs. "He and I did just fine," he stated as he finished the story. "And the kids and I'll do fine tonight. I promise." To indicate that the discussion was closed, he brushed past them and joined the kids in the backyard.

◌ℛ

Six hours later, he was back in bed in his sister's guest room. He stared at the phone in his hand momentarily before pulling out his safety plan to look up Penelope's number. Frannie had told him that both Penelope and William had called him multiple times while he slept, and that she'd had some interesting conversations with Penelope. Oliver was glad that Frannie had taken the time to talk to Penelope. She had called again while he was babysitting, but he only talked with her briefly. As promised, he was calling her back now.

"Hey there, Miss Penelope. How are you? Sorry I haven't talked to you. I guess I kind of crashed from exhaustion. And want to know something stupid? I'm wiped out again. I think I could sleep for at least another two days." He didn't add that he'd like to go to sleep and never wake up.

"Stop apologizing, Oliver. I don't know how I'm doing, to be honest with you. How was babysitting?"

"Fine. Tell me about you."

"No. I want you to tell me how it was for you tonight first."

He sighed. What could he possibly say? That every single second was torture? That hearing their laughter reminded him that Henry could never again laugh? That seeing Frannie and David go off on a date together, even though he knew the circumstances behind it, hurt deeply because he would never, ever again have a special date with Maggie? That he managed to fake it and pretend to have fun playing Barbies-Go-to-the-Monster-Truck-Races (a combined game to appease both Lacey and Davie) but even though he was only pretending he still felt that he was betraying Maggie and Henry by moving on? That holding baby Ellen reminded him of the joy he and Maggie had felt at the successful birth of Henry? That he had to repeatedly lie to the kids and tell them that his eyes were watery because of allergies? He didn't know how to answer Penelope, so he remained silent.

"Oliver, you're hurting, aren't you?"

"Yes, Penelope, I am," he admitted quietly into the phone. "What should I do?"

"Think of our friendship and how important you are to me."

He didn't tell her that might not be enough. "Speaking of that, you haven't told me yet how you're doing."

"I'm nervous. Tomorrow William and I are spending the afternoon with friends."

"That sounds nice."

"It's not nice. We were friends when I was normal. It's awkward now."

"You're still you, Penelope."

"You sound like William."

"Well, listen to him, and to me. I think you are caring and kind and gentle. You are intelligent and creative and imaginative. I enjoy being around you, and I know that William does, too. I bet these friends of yours just might feel the same."

"I don't know. But maybe you're right. I'll give it a try tomorrow. Can I call you if I need to?"

"You can call me any time you want to. I'm so sorry I slept so long before."

"Don't be sorry. I'm tired, too. This medication makes me feel bad. I'm going to go to bed now if that's okay."

"Of course it is. And despite the fact that I slept for two days, I'm exhausted all over again. Let's get some sleep so we can at least try to make it through the day tomorrow."

After they hung up, Oliver curled up around the dog Davie had given him to sleep with. He flipped back onto his back, pulled the picture of Maggie and Henry out of his pocket, kissed it, and tucked it into the collar around the dog's neck. He curled back around it and tried to think of how he had helped Frannie and the kids tonight, and about how Penelope had said his friendship was important to her. He just couldn't come to internalize those things though, because they were trumped by the self-hatred that came from the knowledge that it was all his fault that Maggie and Henry were gone.

CHAPTER 26

Late Sunday morning, William looked in the bedroom mirror and adjusted his baseball cap, and then assessed how it looked with his White Sox jersey. He turned to Penelope, who was sitting cross-legged on their bed watching him. "What do you think? Too much?"

Nimbly, she unfolded her legs and swung them off the side of the bed. She rose effortlessly and walked toward him. She looked him up and down. She took the hat off his head, leaned in, and kissed him on the lips, replaced the hat and adjusted it, and stepped back. "No. Not too much. You look really sexy."

For a moment he stood there and stared at her, wide-eyed and speechless. His eyes became slightly misty, and he stepped toward her and put his arms tenderly around her. "Penelope," he whispered. "You haven't done something like that in a long time. Do you have any idea how much that means to me? How happy that makes me feel?"

She hugged him back and nuzzled his neck. Goose bumps formed on his skin, and his entire body responded to the feel of her pressing closely against him. She rubbed her hands up and down his back. "I do love you William. I really do. I just want to do what's best for you, because I care about you so damn much."

He moved his head so he could look her in the eye. "What's best for me is to be with you forever. I don't want to live my life without you, Penelope. Look at Oliver and how much pain he is in without his wife and son. I realize that this is different, but I know that's how I would feel without you."

"I've been thinking about him too. He keeps telling me to focus on the love that you and I share, and to treasure it and not let it go. I'd like to honor him and the love he had with his family. And he is so sad and lonely. I don't want either of us to have to suffer that way. William, I do love you. I don't see how you can love me anymore, I really don't. I am just not loveable, plain and simple. But I told Oliver that I would try to listen to your words when I am confused by the difference in what you say and what my mind tells me. Your words say that you love me, and that's what I'm trying to pay attention to." Still holding him close, she looked down at the floor. "It's hard though." Her voice was barely audible. "Even as I sat on the bed watching you, Mrs. Roosevelt said things to me. She told me I should take off my own baseball hat and stop pretending to be normal. She reminded me that baseball caps are half circles, and by wearing one, I'm indicating that I only care about you half way." She looked back into his eyes. "That's not true, William. I care about you all the way."

"I care about you all the way too." He kissed her ever so softly then stopped to ask, "Would it be okay for me to show you how much? It would involve us taking off our White Sox gear."

She unbuttoned his jersey. "Please show me. And I will show you. I'll show you that I care and that I am trying to listen to you."

✸

Over an hour later, they walked hand in hand as they approached Rod and Paula's apartment. Rod answered the door. "Where the hell have you been? I thought we would be there by now. The game starts soon; we might miss the beginning."

"Hello, Rod. So good to see you, too. We're doing fine today, thanks for asking," William responded cheerily.

Paula pushed her husband out of the way and addressed William. "Never mind him. Like it really matters if we miss a few pitches. It's not like there won't be about a thousand more to see during the game. And we'll see the bat swing over and over ad nauseam too, so it's not a big deal."

Do you see how Paula ignores you, Penelope? She doesn't have the time of day for you. It's William that she likes. You're a nothing. Penelope's heart sank as she heard Eleanor Roosevelt sneer.

Paula turned to Penelope and hugged her. "Penelope! It's so good to see you. How are you feeling?"

She just had to ask about how you're feeling, didn't she? She didn't ask William how he's feeling. Do you know why she didn't ask him? Because she knows he's feeling fine. It's you who isn't fine, Penelope, and Paula knows it.

It was hard to formulate a response with Mrs. Roosevelt butting in. Penelope wasn't sure what to say; Paula had said it was good to see her, but Mrs. Roosevelt had pointed out, correctly, that she had asked how Penelope was, implying that there was something wrong with her. Penelope was confused. Oliver had told her to focus on the content of people's words. She would try it. She hoped she would have a chance to listen to them.

As she stood there trying to formulate an appropriate response to Paula, not to Eleanor Roosevelt, she noticed Paula's gaze shift from her to William and back again. "Penelope?" Paula asked. "Is everything okay?"

"Yes, everything is fine. It's good to see you, too. Should we get going to the game?" Penelope looked at the three people standing with her. She saw Rod and Paula exchange glances, and she wasn't quite sure what to make of it. She looked at William.

He grinned broadly at her and kissed her cheek. "Absolutely we should get going. Great idea, sweetheart." Still holding her hand, he led her down the sidewalk, without talking further with Rod and Paula.

For Penelope, the entire car ride was incredibly distressing. It began with awkward silence. She felt better for a while when William took one hand off the steering wheel and reached over and took her hand. He rubbed his thumb soothingly across her skin, and it reminded her of how much she loved him. It was difficult to stay focused on that feeling though, with Rod and Paula talking to them from the back seat and Mrs. Roosevelt commenting on the conversation from time to time.

Things got worse as they entered U.S. Cellular Field and settled in to watch the game. By then, Mrs. Roosevelt had become interested in the things Penelope's companions had to say and attempted to participate in the conversation. Every time Penelope tried to say something, Mrs. Roosevelt interrupted. At first, Mrs. Roosevelt acted so naturally that Penelope wondered if the others actually knew she was there. Once, when Mrs. Roosevelt asked what was happening on the pitcher's mound when a bunch of players and coaches gathered there, Rod explained that the pitcher had just allowed three hits in a row, which had caused a run to be scored, threatening the White Sox's narrow lead, and that if he were the manager, he'd yank the pitcher's ass out of the game so fast his head would spin, causing great discomfort to the pitcher, given that his head was up his own ass. To Penelope's surprise, Mrs. Roosevelt laughed hysterically. The way Rod and Paula looked at her though, made Penelope wonder if it was Mrs. Roosevelt who had laughed, or if it had been her. She didn't think she had laughed, because she really didn't think Rod's comment was all that funny, but she was confused and didn't know.

Then, Mrs. Roosevelt wanted others to join the fun, so she summoned whomever it was she summoned when she called on others. As usual, Penelope found it overwhelming to hear numerous voices in her head all talking at once. She could rarely sort out what they were all saying. This time, while she couldn't really pick out individual sentences, she could tell that they were all watching the game and cheering and shouting and commenting. Mrs. Roosevelt got lost in the shuffle, and Penelope no longer heard her. There was a loud roar, and she threw her hands over her ears in an attempt to get it to stop. She felt an arm around her shoulder. Oh no! Were they going to start touching her now too, poking her and tickling her? She struggled to get it the arm off. It squeezed tighter, and she felt herself being pulled to the side.

Rattled, she looked in the direction she was moving in and saw William. He was saying something. What was she supposed to do during these times? Oh yeah, focus on his words and listen to what he was saying. She couldn't hear him, so she stepped closer. He put both of his arms around her and said, "The crowd went pretty wild, didn't they? I guess I did, too; sorry if I shouted in your ear. But did you see that? Konerko hit a grand slam!"

So the noise had been outside her head? It wasn't some weird, disembodied voices, but the actual fans at the game? She needed to block out everything in order to check out what was going on in her mind. William touch always helped center her, so she stepped closer to him and rested her forehead on his chest. His arms moved up and down her back, and she concentrated hard on the feel of his hands and on the way his chest felt on her forehead. She closed her eyes and listened. She heard voices, but they were coming from around her on the outside and were those of the baseball fans. She heard someone shout various food and drink items; that was likely one of the vendors who roamed the stadium selling things to people who didn't want to make the effort to actually get up and walk to the concession stand. She heard a loud crack and understood it to be a player's bat connecting with the ball. She did not, however, hear a peep from Mrs. Roosevelt, nor did she feel her presence. The others were gone too. Had they even been there in the first place, or had all of those sounds simply been the noisy stadium? She was puzzled and upset. Why did even a simple baseball game have to be a problem?

William kissed her head, and she looked at him. "You doing okay?" he asked.

"I don't know. Thanks for holding me just now. It helped."

He held her tighter. "Would something to eat or drink help too?"

She realized she was hungry. "Actually, yeah."

"What would you like? I'll go get us something."

"Surprise me."

"Will do. I'll be right back."

Rod saw William start to leave and said, "Hey wait. I'll go with you." He stepped over Paula, who was sitting down, and brushed past Penelope. As the two men went to find food, Penelope sat down beside Paula. With Eleanor Roosevelt out of the way, Penelope could talk. Not wanting to discuss herself, or her recent stay at Airhaven, she asked Paula about her job. As Paula talked, Penelope realized how far removed she was becoming from her old life. Paula discussed career-related triumphs and complaints, but Penelope had no such stories of her own to share anymore. She had left her job a long time ago. She missed working, and Paula's stories only served to remind her of her losses. Afraid she would cry if she continued to listen, she turned her attention to the game and pretended that it was the most interesting thing in the world to her. She began to comment on the players and the action and hoped she was making at least a little bit of sense.

Paula looked at her quizzically. "Since when are you so into baseball? You and I always used to make fun of the guys for their obsession with it. They come here to watch the game; we come here to socialize."

"Oh, well, it's actually really interesting. William's been getting me up to speed, and I guess I'm hooked." She turned back to the game. The crowd was booing something, so she booed, too. "Can you believe that?" she said to Paula, gesturing toward the field and pretending to be incredulous about whatever it was that had just happened. Then she turned her full attention back to the game and hoped that William would hurry back. She felt increasingly anxious. She didn't want to listen to Paula's work stories any more. She would have changed the subject, but she couldn't think of anything to talk about. She thought about making comments about the game, but she really had nothing to say other than obvious things like "Oh, that guy in the outfield caught the ball." What kind of conversation would that be? What was taking William so long anyway?

ॐ

William stood in a long line at the concession stand. Like Penelope, he tried to keep the focus of the conversation on baseball, but Rod wouldn't cooperate. "Knock it off, Vaile," Rod said.

"Knock what off?"

"Quit changing the subject back to baseball. Seriously, how are you doing with all of this?"

"With all of what?" William knew exactly what Rod was talking about, but he wanted to play dumb to avoid having to discuss his personal life.

"Come on, don't play games. How are things at home, you know, with the way Penelope is now?"

"Don't start, Rod."

"You don't have to get defensive; I'm not trying to 'start' anything. I'm just being a concerned friend, that's all. I want to know how you're doing. This can't be easy, man."

William let out an exasperated sigh. "Okay, fine. You're obviously talking about Penelope, but I really don't see why you won't let this go. She's home from the hospital, her medication is working better and better, and she's fine. We're both fine. You are reading way too much into this."

Rod let out a small laugh. "You're kidding, right? Who's the one with the delusions now?"

To keep from punching Rod, William folded his hands tightly across his chest. "What?" he asked coldly.

"Look at her, William. I mean really pay attention. You're trying so hard to see the old Penelope that you aren't seeing how she truly is now. You need to open your eyes. She's mentally ill. Sure, she's got a bunch of pills to help her function, but that's all they do. They help her function. They can't take away her schizophrenia. They just cover it up, but if you ask me, they do a lousy job of it. Think of how she's been today. She hardly talks anymore, and when she does, it doesn't seem to make a whole lot of sense. It's—"

"Damn it, Rod—"

Rod held up his hand. "Shut up and let me finish. You always do this. I try to say something helpful, and you get all pissed off and won't listen. This is for your own good, and even if it's not what you want to hear, you need to hear it anyway. It's really noble and all that you want to stick by Penelope, although I'll admit I don't understand your obsession with it. You've said that you don't give up on people, but you're taking it too far. You need to be realistic about who she really is and come to terms with the fact that you're never going to have the life you thought you would have with her. You can stick with her without ruining your own life in the process. Be her friend, but not her husband. It's possible to do that, you know, and it wouldn't be that hard; you've said yourself that she keeps wanting to call things off. It's time for you to listen to her. Do her a favor, and yourself one, too. Call off the marriage, William. Be Penelope's friend if you feel some moral obligation to do so, but keep it at that.

"And it's not like you'd be alone, you know." William's stunned silence afforded Rod the opportunity to rush on. "That new neighbor of yours was all over you at the event we catered last Saturday. I watched her after she left your side and returned to her picnic. She looks lively and fun, and she's not too shabby to look at, either. She clearly has a thing for you. I bet she's pretty hot in bed, too.

How's Penelope these days? Is she as lifeless during sex as she is when she's away from the sheets?"

William was beyond seething, and at that last comment from Rod, he snapped. Impulsively, he hauled back and punched him in the face. Rod's hands flew to his nose briefly before he responded in kind. Rod was bigger and in one blow sent William sprawling across the ground. Instantly, William sprang to his feet and charged at Rod, throwing his arms around his waist and tackling him to the ground. He landed one more strike before Rod knocked him off with a strong punch to the gut. William fell off Rod. As he reset himself, Rod struck him twice across the face. William shook it off and stood up. Just as he was about to lunge at Rod again, someone grabbed him from behind and pulled him away from Rod. Someone else grabbed Rod and pulled him back, too. William struggled briefly against the restraint before rationality set in. Breathing heavily, slightly bent forward in pain, his face covered in blood, he relaxed his muscles. Whoever was holding him back still did not release his grip. "It's okay," he panted. "You can let go; I'm not going to do anything." He gestured toward Rod with his blood-covered chin. "This asshole isn't worth it." To Rod, he said, "You really aren't worth it. You are self-centered and narrow-minded. You're the one to be pitied, not Penelope. And the one I feel sorry for is Paula." He shrugged free and walked away. He made it only a few feet before security stopped him. "Don't worry," he told them. "You don't have to bother to kick me out because I'm leaving. I'm going to go get my fiancée." He looked angrily at Rod as he said this. "And then we're going. You might want to kick that guy out though—" again he looked toward Rod, "—simply because he's a fucking asshole."

Followed by two security guards, William stomped to get Penelope. She sat stiffly beside Paula. Neither woman was talking. Penelope seemed focused on the game. William's heart melted. She looked absolutely adorable with her hair pulled back into a pony-tail and stuck through the opening in the back of her baseball cap. When he looked at her, he didn't see a schizophrenic; he simply saw the woman he loved, a wonderful human being. He scrambled down the rest of the stadium stairs and slid into his seat. It was an aisle seat, so he didn't have to crawl over a bunch of people to get to Penelope. He slid his arm around her and planted a kiss on her cheek. "It doesn't look like Paula is being very much fun," he said quietly. "Come on, let's go home."

Penelope looked at him and gasped. "Oh my God, William! What happened?"

Paula looked in their direction. "What happened to you? Where's Rod?"

"He might still be talking to security. You'd better get your things together, because you'll probably have to leave. He's up by the concession stand, but frankly, if I were you, I wouldn't go near him."

"What?" Paula exclaimed, her tone upset.

"Nothing. Penelope, we have to leave. Is that okay?"

"Yes, it's okay. Let's get you home. I want to take care of you and hear what happened. But don't we have to wait for Rod and Paula, to give them a ride?"

"Nope." William led her up the stairs and out of the stadium.

☙

Later that evening, Penelope brought William another ice pack. He was relaxed on the couch, slouched in the corner, with his head against the back of it and his legs stretched out in front of him. She set it gingerly over his eye and positioned it lengthwise so it extended down over his swollen and split lip. Lowering herself back onto the couch and snuggling into him once again, she pressed play on the remote control to resume their movie. Promptly, she paused it again. She sat up. "I still don't understand why you won't tell me what happened between you and Rod. I'm not an idiot, and I know it had to do with me. What was it?"

William lifted the ice pack off his face. "Sweetie, I told you it's not important. Rod's a moron. There's nothing to talk about."

"He's your best friend. You got in a fight because of me, and you won't even tell me exactly what it was about."

"You're my best friend, and you have been since the moment we met. I've told you that a thousand times over the last few years. I care about you, not Rod." William took the remote out of her hand and pushed play.

She took the remote back and paused the movie again. "No! It had to do with me, and I want to know about it."

William sighed. "It's not important. He just thinks we shouldn't get married, but he's wrong. He won't listen to me when I talk, so I tried to knock some understanding into him. Nothing more." He grabbed the remote and pushed play.

See the misery you cause? Mrs. Roosevelt, who had been blissfully absent since the stadium, was back. *Look at him. Look what happened to him because of you. You selfish bitch! He is giving up everything because of you, and now here he sits, cut and bruised and probably in pain, all because of you. Get out of his life, Penelope. Go away. Go away, go away, go away! Even Rod knows you shouldn't get married. You don't need William, anyway, because you have me. Let's go back to Kentucky together. Look at him. I said look at him! He's miserable, and you do it to him. He will be miserable as long as you are with him.*

Penelope burst into tears. William tried to pull her toward him to comfort her, but she remained stiff. She felt Mrs. Roosevelt sit down on the other side of her and try to pull her in her direction. Just then, her phone rang. She tried to reach into her pocket for it, but with both William and Mrs. Roosevelt pulling at her, it was difficult. She elbowed Mrs. Roosevelt so hard she cried out and left. With Mrs. Roosevelt gone, she could pull her phone out of her pocket. It was still ringing, and she saw it was Frannie's mobile number. Oliver couldn't have picked a better time to call. Still in tears, she answered the phone. "Is this you, Oliver? I'm so glad you called. Oliver? Are you there? Oliver! What's wrong?"

CHAPTER 27

IN HIS NIGHTMARE, OLIVER SLIPPED AND FELL. THE SIDEWALK TURNED TO A river of blood, and it threatened to drown him. No! He had to get to them. Frantically, he struggled against the strong current that held him down. Despite his full adrenaline-powered efforts, he couldn't break free. He thrashed harder. Damn it! No! They needed him. Someone help! He screamed. His eyes flew open and darted about. He didn't see Maggie and Henry. Where were they? Where was he? He needed to get to them. He flailed around more, but he was stuck. He was drenched in sweat. Or was it blood? Was it their blood? His hair was soaked in their blood, matted to his head, and large drops of blood rolled down his face and neck and back. He cried out loudly for help because he couldn't move his arms or legs and he needed to get to them. His heart pounded. He willed his arms and legs to move as quickly as his heart was beating, but they wouldn't take him to Maggie and Henry. Again he screamed for help.

Two people burst through a door and rushed to him. A door? What the hell? What was a door doing in the park? Never mind that; he didn't have time to think about it. "I can't move!" he yelled,

"Help me! They need me! I have to get to them before it's too late! Please!"

"Oliver!" A woman's voice called to him. It wasn't Maggie's.

"Where's Maggie?"

"Oliver! Settle down. You had a nightmare. Look at me. It's Frannie, your sister. Take deep breaths and calm down."

He tried to move again but remained where he was. "I'm stuck, and I need to get to them!"

"You're tangled up in the blankets. Stop struggling, and we'll get you out. David, help him get loose." Frannie rushed to the dresser, scanned his discharge instructions for the name of the stuff he was to take as needed for panic, and found the bottle labeled "lorazepam." She quickly read the directions, removed a single tablet, and then stuck it in Oliver's mouth. When he spit it out, she shoved it back in and held her hand there to keep it in. "Oliver, you need this to calm down, and I'm going to make sure it stays in your mouth."

The hand over his mouth made him feel even more trapped, and he tried to jump up. Because David hadn't successfully untangled the blankets, he went nowhere. "Why are you blocking me from helping Maggie and Henry?" he shouted. With Frannie's hand on his mouth, though, it came out garbled.

"You had a nightmare. You're in bed at our house, and no one other than you needs help right now." Oliver heard the man's voice. Was that David? What was he doing here? He heard him speak again, "Listen to me. You are completely tangled in these blankets, and I think that's what's freaking you out. Hold still so I can unwrap you."

Oliver looked around in an attempt to make sense of what they were saying. Frannie hovered over him, and David yanked on sheets and blankets. He saw furniture and walls, but no emergency personnel, flashing lights, sky, sidewalks, or grass. He slowly registered the fact that he'd had a nightmare, but his breathing and heart rate hadn't yet caught up to what his mind was beginning to understand. The lorazepam hit his bloodstream though, and his heart rate slowed and his breathing to regulated. His muscles relaxed, and he stopped fighting David's attempts to free him. Frannie removed her hand. He looked from Frannie to David and back again before closing his eyes and leaning his head back against the headboard. He sighed deeply.

"What day is it? Did I sleep through more days?" His voice was hoarse but steady.

He jumped slightly when someone touched the top of his head, but as Frannie stroked his hair, he relaxed again. "No, you didn't sleep through more days. You've been sleeping for about sixteen hours, though. It's Sunday, and it's about one in the afternoon." She continued to caress his hair rhythmically. He kept his eyes closed. David had removed the blankets, and he felt much less constricted.

"Oh. Sorry. I didn't mean to sleep so long. This bed is too comfortable, I think. Sorry about being so loud and making you come down here. Did the kids hear me? I hope I didn't scare them."

"They're fine," David said. "We just finished lunch and they're back outside playing. We were just cleaning up when we heard you yell for help."

"Oh. Good. I'm glad they didn't hear me. They're probably wondering if I'm ever going to get out of bed. I'm sorry I've been a terrible uncle." He opened his eyes, and his gaze met Frannie's. She gasped slightly, and her expression grew tender. Oliver thought she might cry.

She took his hand. "Oh, Ollie. I've never seen you, or anyone else for that matter, look so miserable. You're going through a hell of an ordeal, so give yourself a break, okay? You haven't been a terrible uncle. You're a terrific uncle, and they're lucky to have you. I love how you get right down on their level and really play with them."

When Oliver didn't respond, David added, "She's right. They had fun with you last night. Lacey and Davie were full of stories this morning."

Oliver could only sigh in response; playing with the kids last night had been devastating and had left him too numb to talk about it, even now. "I'm getting up now. I'm going to shower and stuff, and then I'll be up to see the kids."

"Your clothes are drenched. Would you like something of David's to wear today?"

"No!" Oliver shook his head vigorously. When he saw the looks of surprise on their faces, he said, "I mean, no thanks. These will dry pretty quickly. I'm sorry for reacting that way; I do appreciate the offer."

"Oh, Ollie, it's okay." Frannie hugged him. "Do you need anything right now?"

Yes, he did. He needed Maggie and Henry back. "No, I'm fine. Go ahead and go back upstairs. I just need to get ready quickly, and then I'll join you."

After he shooed Frannie and David away, he went to the dresser and looked at the lineup of pharmaceuticals. One by one, he opened the bottles and removed what he needed. He studied the colorful assortment in the palm of his hand. They looked like candy, but they weren't. They were stupid little things that were piss poor replacements for his family. Angrily, he threw them at the mirror, sending them bouncing and flying in various directions. He caught a glimpse of himself in the mirror. Unable to stand the sight of the bastard that stared back at him, he went to the bathroom to prepare for the day. He avoided looking in the bathroom mirror.

A short while later, he trudged up the stairs and joined Frannie and her family in the backyard. He stepped quietly through the patio doors; no one noticed him at first. He stood beside the house and took in the scene. Ellen lay on a blanket in the shade, and Lacey colored beside her. Davie played in the sandbox. The sandbox. Maggie and Henry had been playing in park's sandbox when…. His knees went weak, and he thought he might faint. He leaned back against the house for support. No, he couldn't give in to this. He had already been a problem today. For Frannie's sake, he had to pretend that he was okay. He took a deep breath and continued to look around the backyard.

Frannie and David sat in chairs, David reading a book, and Frannie talking with the children. Oliver sighed. If Maggie and Henry were alive, it was highly likely they would be here too. It wasn't unusual for the two families to get together on a Saturday or Sunday. Today, though, it was Oliver alone who stood in Frannie's yard, taking in the scene. A new wave of weariness washed over him. He was about to return to bed when Davie spotted him.

"Uncle Oliver!" Davie shouted. He scrambled out of the sandbox and, covered in grains of sand, ran to Oliver and jumped into his arms.

Oliver caught him. "Hey, Davie! What are you up to over in the sandbox?"

"Lacey and I are playing hide-and-seek with my cars. It's my turn to hide them in the sand. Do you want to play with us?"

By then, Lacey had run over to Oliver, too, and she hugged him. "Davie is burying four cars. We can each find two. Come on!" She tugged at him.

Frannie stepped in. "Whoa, you two. Oliver just got out here. Why don't you give him a chance to sit down for a little bit first?"

"No, it's okay. I've been lying around in bed for sixteen hours. I don't need to sit down and rest." He looked down at his niece and nephew. "Let's go play."

He searched with Lacey. Guilt instantly stabbed at him, as it had last night. He used to do things like this with his son. How could he just go on with life, moving on to different kids as if Henry didn't matter? Of course Henry mattered! Henry would have loved playing this game with his cousins. But Henry couldn't play this game with his cousins. Like the cars, Henry was buried in the ground.

Oh, God! Oliver squeezed his eyes shut and fought the wave of nausea that overcame him. He suddenly realized that he had been back in Fairmont for several days, and he hadn't even gone to see Maggie and Henry. What kind of a husband and father was he? He put his shovel down and sat back. "Hey you guys, I just remembered something. I need to go do something, but I'll be back to play later, okay?"

"No!" Lacey and Davie said together.

"What? Oliver, where do you need to go? Whatever it is, can't it wait? I don't think you're ready to venture out alone," Frannie sounded worried.

Oliver stood. "I'm fine," he told her. "I just need to go make a visit." He gave Frannie a pointed look. He didn't want to say aloud that he was going to the cemetery for fear that he might upset the kids, especially Davie.

Frannie's eyes widened, indicating she knew exactly what he meant. "Let me come with you."

"No. I need to go alone. And besides, I might swing by my boss's house while I'm out." The part about going to see Stanley was a blatant lie, but he wanted Frannie to back off. If she thought he was going to talk about work, she would think he was okay enough to go out on his own.

"I don't know," she replied. "David, do you think this is a good idea?"

David looked at Oliver and appeared to be studying him. "I don't know, but he's a grown man, Frannie. Let the guy go see his boss."

"Fine, but I don't like it. Here." She handed him her phone. "Take this, and call us if you want us to come get you."

He took it. "Okay. But I'm fine, really. I might end up talking to Stanley for quite a while, so don't worry when I'm not back quickly."

"Do you want to take my van, or David's car?"

"No. I'll walk. Remember that, too. It's going to take longer because I'm walking, but that doesn't mean anything is wrong. Don't worry if I'm not back right away."

"Why do you keep saying that?"

Oliver hugged her. "Because you're a mother and I know you worry. But don't, okay?" He gave Davie and Lacey a hug too. He bent and tickled Ellen before walking out of the yard.

As he had on the day he left town, he stopped and bought flowers and a stuffed animal before going to the cemetery. This time, though, he bought a dog in honor of Henry's bestest favorite friend, Davie. He walked down alleys and side streets to get to the cemetery. He didn't want to run into anyone he knew and have to explain where he had been for over three months. Fairmont was large enough that the chances of that happening were slim, but it was still a possibility—a possibility he did not want to happen.

He felt strange as he traipsed through town, and as he walked, he again experienced the scary sensation of watching himself from a distance, similar to what had happened to him when he stepped into Frannie's house on Thursday afternoon. Everything, including his body, seemed to move with exaggerated slowness. He felt strange and numb. He wanted to touch something to see what it felt like, and he watched himself reach out in slow motion and touch a tree. He watched his hand rub slowly up and down the trunk. He felt it, so he knew it was actually himself who touched it, but it felt incredibly far removed from him. As he walked, he saw from above things that reminded him of Algonquin Park, and flashes of images from that day drifted through his mind. Usually when he saw the images, he was in the middle of a nightmare or a flashback, and they felt real. This time though, he knew they weren't real, because they just came and went, and when they flashed through his mind, they were distorted, like items in a painting by the surrealist Salvador Dali. But even though he knew they were only memories, he was still highly stressed and disturbed and frightened—which was precisely why he had begun avoiding the outdoors soon after finding the shelter in Chicago. Again, though, right now, his reaction was strange. On one hand, he felt as though he were being crushed to the core, and he wanted to cry. Yet, on the other hand, he was just plain numb, and his eyes remained dry.

He felt himself shuffle through the cemetery, and he watched himself approach the gravesite. The dissociation came to an abrupt stop when he saw Maggie's parents. He rushed to a nearby cluster of arborvitae and hid. His head throbbed to the rhythm of his pounding heart. Damn it. What was he supposed to do now? He just wanted to see his wife and son. He didn't need this. He looked at his wrist, a habit from the past, but he wasn't wearing his watch. Somebody had beaten him up and stolen it when he was on the streets in Chicago. Then he remembered Frannie's cell phone, and he took it from his pocket. The background was a picture of her kids. Oliver's heart caught in his throat. He glanced at the time and quickly shoved the phone back into his pocket. It was three-fifty. Technically, according to the agreement he had made with Mick and Nancy, their visiting time would be over in ten minutes. He remained crouched and waited. He expected them to leave at four o'clock.

Four o'clock arrived, but Maggie's parents made no move to depart. Initially, Oliver was irritated. They were infringing on his time. But, of course, they didn't know he was there. He had been gone for months, and in his absence, they didn't have a visitation schedule. He sighed. He didn't want to hide in the trees; he wanted to see Maggie and Henry. He could see their headstones, and he was struck by an overwhelming desire to be close to them. Unable to stand it any longer, he emerged from the bushes and approached their graves.

He opened his mouth to inform his in-laws of his presence, but no sound came out. He was nervous, and the emotion took over. His palms sweat, his heart rate increased, again, and he couldn't speak. He walked up tentatively and stood dumbly to the side of Maggie's grave, arms dangling at his sides, flowers in one hand and stuffed dog in the other. He remained behind Mick and Nancy.

Instantly, he forgot about them. When he saw the words "Margaret Graham" etched in large letters across the tombstone and read the dates of her life, tears sprang to his eyes. Everything spun, and he felt sick. A small choking noise escaped his constricted throat. Both Nancy and Mick turned sharply toward him.

"You!" Mick bellowed. "What the hell are you doing here?"

"Uh—"

Nancy marched up to him and slapped him across the face before he had a chance to answer. "Why are you here? You took off months ago." She looked him up and down and said coldly, "How typical of you. Maggie called me that morning, you know. She was excited that you suggested a picnic. You suggested it, Oliver. It was your idea. Imagine my shock when she then informed me that you wouldn't accompany them to the park because you had to get your precious workout in first. Oh, she defended you. She thought it was just fine." She gave a sarcastic snort. "Her love for you was so blind. In her mind, you could do no wrong. She was so misguided. It was her fatal flaw. You abandoned your family on the day they died, just so you could train for that damn triathlon, and then after they died, you completely up and left. You don't deserve to be here."

"I—"

"I'm not finished," Nancy interrupted him, her tone frigid. "I'm sorry to see that you've returned, Oliver. Like I said, you don't deserve to be here. I'm sure Maggie and Henry are looking down and are aware that you are here. How do you think that makes them feel? You weren't there when they needed you, and I'm sure they are disgusted to see you here now."

Oliver went weak all over. He agreed with everything she was saying, and he was powerless to interrupt her.

"To be honest, we actually thought you were dead. We figured maybe you did the world a favor and committed suicide. Who else has to die while you're alive? You are nothing but bad luck. People close to you seem to die, Oliver; your parents, and our daughter and our grandson. You probably cursed them when you named our poor grandbaby after your dead father. I want you to leave, and I don't want to see you again. Go crawl off somewhere and kill yourself."

"Nancy!" Mick exclaimed loudly. "You've gone too far! I hate Oliver for not being there to protect Maggie and Henry, but you can't blame him for the deaths of his parents, and to tell him to kill himself..."

Oliver barely heard Mick's words. His blood rushed through his ears with a loud roar before it drained rapidly from his head. Stars spun around his head. He hit hard ground, and everything went black.

℘

Gradually, he became aware of a sharp pain. His shoulder throbbed. His head ached terribly too. What had happened? He opened his eyes. Maggie's tombstone. He closed his eyes again quickly. The memory of his encounter with Mick and Nancy rushed back. He opened his eyes again and searched for them. They were nowhere in sight; they must have left after he fainted. He sighed deeply and a sharp pain shot through his abdomen. Had one of them kicked him? He had no idea and, frankly, didn't care. With another sigh, he worked himself into a sitting position and massaged his shoulder. He must have landed on it wrong when he fainted. Nancy's words had really hit home. They replayed now in his head, over and over again, and he breathed heavily in response. He put his hands to his head to try to stop the words, but it didn't work. He closed his eyes and tried to breathe slowly and deeply, the way Matt had taught him. Doing so helped calm his body. His emotions, however, were another story. He struggled to his feet and stood between the grave of his wife and the grave of his son. He stood only briefly before his legs gave out and he dropped to his knees. He reached back for the flowers and dog he had dropped, and he placed them tenderly against the headstones.

He wanted to talk to Maggie and Henry, to tell them how sorry he was and how much he missed them. He tried, but he couldn't speak. Alone in the cemetery, he fell apart. He cried until he was all out of tears. To be sure, the pain and despair were still there, but his weak and dehydrated body could form no more tears.

He knelt and stared at the graves of his beloved wife and son for a long time, long past the time when his entire body screamed in agony for him to stand up. Sitting there, he made a decision. He kissed each grave before standing and walking away. He strolled down a different path and paid a visit to his mom and dad. Seeing them this time was more difficult than it had been since their funeral. He knelt in front of them and ran his hands along their joint headstone. "I'm sorry, Mom and Dad," he whispered, "I bet if I hadn't been born, you'd still be here, wouldn't you?" The only answer was the wind whooshing through the trees. With a sigh, he rose to his feet. His movements were slow and laborious because his pain was so great that his heart and soul could no longer contain it. It spilled over and seeped into every cell of his body.

He left the cemetery. Again taking side streets and alleys, he slogged to his home, the place where he had grown up, the place where he had made a happy life with Maggie, the place where his baby had been born.

The mere sight of his home from the street caused such deep agony he felt it throughout his entire being. He stopped moving and stood in the street, leaden. He paused only briefly. With a sigh, he continued on his mission. He climbed the stairs to the porch, found the hidden key, still in the same place after all these months, and entered. With a turn of the door knob, sights and smells overpowered him. He stood in the entryway and waited for the tears to dry up again. He was still dehydrated, and it didn't take long; he was surprised he had any at all. With a single-minded focus, he shuffled up to the attic.

He knew exactly what he was looking for, and he knew exactly where it was. He found the large safe and unlocked it. He closed his eyes for a moment when he saw the contents. Memories flooded back, but he pushed them aside. With a sigh, he opened his eyes again and reached for the box he sought. Slowly, reverently, he opened the lid. Inside, in perfect condition, were the pistols his father had carried. The bullets were there, too, just as he knew they would be. He and Frannie had packed everything away after their parents died. Oliver had wanted to keep his dad's police stuff, and now he was glad that he had had the foresight to do so. He resisted the temptation to look at his dad's badge and uniform, to touch them, to scoop them up and hug them tightly. He shut the safe, walked back to the stairs, pulled the string to shut off the light, and shuffled all the way back down to the first floor.

With purpose, he went to the kitchen, the last place he had seen his family alive. He positioned himself on the floor where they had all played build and destroy with Henry's blocks. He pulled his picture of Maggie and Henry from his pocket and stared at it. Then, with trembling hands, he loaded the gun. He rested his head against the kitchen island and brought the gun to his mouth. He was about to pull the trigger when he spotted something under the pedestal stand of the dining table. It was one of Henry's crayons. It reminded him of Penelope. The crayon was even blue, for love. He realized as he sat there that he had actually grown to love her, in a platonic sort of way, of course. She had William, and he had Maggie. No, he didn't have Maggie, not anymore, anyway. He had lowered the gun when he spotted the crayon, but at that thought he once again brought it to the roof of his mouth. He couldn't tear his eyes away from the crayon though.

He shook his head. Never mind that; he was on his way to Maggie and Henry. He took one last look at their beautiful, happy faces. Then he noticed the laminate covering the picture. It had been really nice of William and Penelope to protect the picture for him.

Now his splattering blood wouldn't ruin it. He pictured Penelope working so carefully to cover the photo nicely for him. Penelope.

He wondered how she was doing. Didn't he at least owe her a good-bye? He sighed. Carefully, he placed the gun beside him on the floor and shifted so he could take Frannie's cell phone out of his pocket. He pressed the button to wake it up so he could make a call. Lacey, Davie, and Ellen grinned at him. "Sorry, guys," he whispered. "I really do love you, but I just can't do this anymore."

He didn't want to look at them, so he activated the phone and dialed Penelope's number.

It rang several times before she answered. "Is this you, Oliver? I'm so glad you called."

His heart skipped a beat at the sound of her voice. He realized he didn't know what to say.

"Oliver? Are you there?"

Still, he said nothing. To his surprise, a sob escaped from deep within. He had been operating with such a driven purpose, he hadn't been aware of the large lump that had formed inside him until it burst. Another sob slipped out before he could stop it, but he was determined not to let any more out. He bit his cheeks and remained silent.

"Oliver! What's wrong?" Penelope asked.

CHAPTER 28

Aʟʟ ᴏꜰ Pᴇɴᴇʟᴏᴘᴇ'ꜱ ᴡᴏʀʀɪᴇꜱ ᴠᴀɴɪꜱʜᴇᴅ ᴡʜᴇɴ ꜱʜᴇ ʜᴇᴀʀᴅ ᴛʜᴇ ɢᴜᴛ-ᴡʀᴇɴᴄʜɪɴɢ sound of Oliver in despair. Out of the corner of her eye, she saw Mrs. Roosevelt approaching her. She was rubbing her gut where Penelope had elbowed her. Penelope turned toward her and screamed, "Go away!" To her astonishment, Mrs. Roosevelt turned around and disappeared.

"Oh, I...I'm sorry to have bothered you, Penelope. I just...I just wanted to say...good-bye." Oliver's voice was rough and unsteady.

Penelope felt her eyes widen. "What? No! I wasn't talking to you. I was shouting at Mrs. Roosevelt because I want her to leave me alone. Wait. What do you mean, Oliver? What do you mean you wanted to say good-bye?"

William quickly sat up straight, sending the ice pack to the floor and causing his head to explode in pain. He blinked a few times to clear his vision then he asked Penelope, "What's going on? What's he saying?"

Penelope ignored him and focused on Oliver. "Oliver, answer me. What do you mean?"

Oliver remained on his kitchen floor with his head back against the island. He was distraught beyond all ability to think and converse. He just wanted to get this over with and be done with it all. Part of him knew that he wanted closure with Penelope though, but he didn't know how to go about it. He heard the distress in her voice when she said again, "What do you mean? Why aren't you answering me? Are you still there?"

That odd, scary feeling came over him again, the one where he felt removed from himself and could see himself from above. The Oliver from above told the Oliver on the floor to answer his friend. Laboriously, his mind formulated the words and relayed them slowly to his vocal cords and from there to his mouth. "Yeah, I'm still here."

"Good. What are you doing?"

"I'm sitting on my kitchen floor with my dad's police gun. I tried, Penelope, I really did. But I can't do this. How can I just go on living when I killed the two people I lived for?" Floating above himself, he felt numb and detached. He watched his hand stroke the gun. He could feel it, too. It was cool and smooth, but the handle was bumpy. He was aware that he was detached enough to analyze the feel of the gun. It was weird.

"Oh my God, Oliver, you are not going to shoot yourself!" Penelope turned to William. "He called me to say good-bye. We need to stop him! What are we going to do?"

William was already putting on his shoes. "Get his address and tell him we're on our way. Tell him it's going to take about an hour. Keep him on the phone; don't let him hang up."

"Oliver, William and I are on our way to see you, but we need your address."

"No."

"William, he won't give it to me."

"Tell him I'm going to call his sister. I have her home number on the copy of his safety plan."

Penelope relayed the message.

No! Frannie couldn't come here and see him like this. He didn't want her to be the one to find his body. Reluctantly, he gave Penelope the address, and she relayed it to William who hastily scribbled it on a piece of paper. "Got it," William said. "Give me the phone for a minute." When Penelope handed him the phone, he said, "Hey, Oliver. You've gotta promise me something, man. We're on our way to you right now. Promise me that you're not going to do anything until we get there, okay?" At the sound of silence on the line, William instructed firmly, "Don't do anything. I mean it. For Penelope's sake, don't do anything. Let her see you. We kind of had a bad day, and she needs to talk to you about it, so don't pull the damn trigger."

"Oh. Okay," Oliver answered meekly.

"Promise me, Oliver."

"I promise." His voice cracked as the words forced their way around the lump in his throat.

"Good. Now we're in the car and I need to drive, so I'm handing the phone back to Penelope. She's going to keep you company, just like you did for her the other night. Do you remember that? Remember how helpful you were the other night? Remember how you were there for us and saved her? We'll get there as soon as we can." He handed the phone back to Penelope and said, "Just keep talking to him, and try to get him to talk."

"Here I am again, Oliver. William is hurrying. Can you tell me what happened?"

"Well, uh…" Oliver trailed off as he recalled the events of the days since he returned to his hometown. He thought of Frannie's kids, especially Davie, of the cemetery, of Mick and Nancy, and he also thought of how alone he felt. He swallowed hard and sniffed. "It's not that I don't want to tell you; it's just that I can't…I can't…" He paused and struggled for composure. "Penelope, if I talk about it, I don't think I'll be able to keep from using this gun. Will you just talk to me?"

"Of course I will. It's going to be okay, Oliver. We're on our way, and I'm going to talk to you while we drive. Please don't use the gun because I really, really need to see my friend."

Oliver watched himself nod. He told himself to answer her, and he managed to croak out, "Okay."

"What would you like me to talk about, Oliver?"

"Will you tell me more about the Kerffies?"

"Really? You actually want to hear about them?"

"Yes. And I bet William will want to listen, too." As his final gift to Penelope and William, he wanted to encourage her to include William and let him be fully part of who she was. He wanted to help her stop pushing him away. He would like to leave the world knowing that he had done one good thing for someone he cared about.

He heard her tell William, "He wants me to tell him about the Kerffies, and he says you would want to hear about them, too." He didn't hear William's response, but he almost smiled when he heard Penelope say, "Wow. I didn't know that you wanted to hear about what I know. I think that the stuff I'm about to tell you is the truth, but I'm confused about what's real and what's not. It's embarrassing, and I don't want to make you hate me. Thank you, William, for wanting to listen to me. Thank you, too, Oliver. That makes me feel happy." And without further prompting, she slowly began to tell William and Oliver what she knew about the extra-terrestrial, miniscule beings that inhabited the planet. She talked about who they were and where they came from and what they believed, and she talked a lot about how they sent her messages and communicated with her. She shared that she felt privileged that they had chosen not just Eleanor Roosevelt but her too to talk to, and how she was honored to receive special messages and teachings in books, newspapers, signs, songs, billboards, television, and movies. She described how words and letters would rearrange themselves just for her and float in front of her eyes like images in a three-dimensional movie. She also admitted how scary it was to be the recipient of these special messages.

Hearing her talk calmed Oliver, and at some point, the strange floating sensation stopped and he no longer watched himself sit on the floor. He felt more deeply connected to Penelope than ever before. He was honored that she felt comfortable enough with him to share the inner workings of her mind. He was glad, too, that she had William in her life, because she most certainly deserved love. He wondered what William was thinking as he listened. He was fairly certain that William felt a connection to her too, but he wanted to die knowing with certainty that their love was strong enough to keep them together. He continued to sit on the floor with his legs outstretched.

The picture of Maggie and Henry lay on his knees, and his dad's gun rested comfortably in his hands on his lap. He rubbed the gun with his fingertips and listened to Penelope. He was relaxed and unaware of the passing time; he was almost lulled to sleep, but he bolted to full alertness when he heard her voice coming not just from the phone but from inside his house.

His exaggerated startle reflex sent his heart pounding and his breathing became more rapid. He pulled his knees up tight against his chest, and he gripped the gun firmly and placed it against his head. He was so intent on killing himself that the motion had been a reflex.

William and Penelope rushed to his side. "Oliver, no! You promised!" Penelope wailed.

Oliver gasped for breath. He wanted desperately to pull the trigger, but he remembered that William had said that Penelope needed to tell him about her day. Plus, he didn't yet have the confirmation he wanted that the two of them would stay together forever. He put his hand down, but he held the gun firmly against his chest so no one could take it from him. "Sorry. You just scared me, that's all." He looked from one to the other. "It's good to see you one last time. Penelope, I loved hearing about the Kerffies. You really helped me calm down. William, did you like to hear her, too?" he urged.

The two of them kneeled side by side on the floor next to Oliver. William put his arm around Penelope and rubbed her shoulder. "Yes, I did. Very much so. Thanks for that idea, Oliver. I'd like you to stick around so you can give us more of your good suggestions."

Oliver shook his head. "I can't." He told them then about how hard it was to be around Davie, Lacey, and Ellen, and he talked about his encounter with Mick and Nancy at the cemetery. "I simply don't have a reason to live anymore," he concluded quietly.

Penelope stood and walked around the island. Oliver heard her rummage through a couple drawers. She returned and calmly sat back down, folding her legs gracefully underneath her. With deliberate determination, she raised a knife to her throat.

"Penelope!" Oliver shouted.

"What the hell are you doing?" William yelled at the same time

"You're right, Oliver. Life sucks. Like you, I don't have a reason to live."

Instantly in tears and thoroughly alarmed, William pleaded, "What about me? Aren't I reason enough to live?"

It was Penelope's turn to relate the events of the day. She concluded by saying, "Rod was right. You shouldn't ruin your life by marrying me. If I go away, you'll be free to live better."

"I never said that he said you're ruining my life!"

"No, you didn't. But why else would you have punched him? If he didn't say it in those exact words, he said something close enough to that to make you get into a fight about it. No matter how he worded it, Rod was right in saying that you shouldn't marry me. But as long as I'm alive, I know that that's what you'll try to do. With me gone, you could find someone else. Maybe even our new neighbor, Mariska."

"Damn it, I don't want Mariska! I want you. I love you so much! Penelope, put the goddamn knife down. Please!"

Penelope tightened her grip and pushed it against her skin, pricking it and causing a small amount of blood to pool on the blade.

"Penelope! Stop!" William was frantic.

Oliver was just as frantic. "Oh my God, Penelope, no! I'm sorry. I'm sorry! Nancy was right; I am a curse on everyone! As soon as I'm gone, you'll be able to live, but I want you to promise me first that you're going to stick around and live with the man who loves you. Promise me, Penelope, so I can shoot this gun and bring peace to all of us.”

William stood and paced the room. He ran his hand through his hair. “This is a fucking disaster. Both of you knock it off! Help me out here, okay? I don’t want either of you to die, but I don’t know what to do to make you stop!”

“Penelope, look at William,” Oliver implored. “You’re freaking him out, and you’re freaking me out, too. You said you don’t have a reason to live, but that’s not true. You have love, Penelope. And love really is the only thing to live for. Trust me, I know.”

“Killing myself will be my act of love to William.”

“No!” William cried.

“Listen to me, Penelope. That’s not how you show him you love him. Show him by marrying him and living your life with him.”

“I’m not the person he fell in love with.”

Oliver spoke slowly and deliberately in a quiet, gentle tone. “You developed schizophrenia, and I know from talking to you that it’s scary and frustrating and it has brought a lot of changes to your life. But it’s not who you are, Penelope. It is merely something you have to deal with. Your mind plays some pretty nasty tricks on you sometimes, but that doesn’t mean that you are unlovable. Saying that you’re worthless and that you’re ruining William’s life just because your mind thinks differently than it used to absolutely does not make sense.”

Penelope seemed to ponder what Oliver had just told her. “I hadn’t thought about it like that before,” she said quietly, “I see what you’re saying, but it doesn’t change the fact that I hate being this way.”

“It’s okay to feel frustrated for having to deal with this illness, but don’t hate yourself because of it. This illness is only a tiny part of you.”

“Other people don’t see it that way.”

“Like who?”

“Like friends we used to have. Like Rod and Paula.”

"You know what? Then maybe it's time for some new friends. Does William agree with Rod and Paula?" She shook her head but said nothing. Oliver pressed on. "And what about me, Penelope? I didn't know you before. You had schizophrenia when I met you, and I wasn't repulsed. Quite the opposite, actually. I like you a lot. I find you unique and delightful and honestly quite helpful. I don't think you have any idea how much I care about you. And what about my sister? Frannie likes you a lot; she even told me so. And this new neighbor of yours? It seemed to me that she wasn't judging you, either. Maybe it's time to let go of the past and embrace your new self and your new friends. Let your love for William and his love for you be what rules your life."

Softly, William added, "Remember the book, sweetheart? Eleanor Roosevelt herself said, 'No one can make you feel inferior without your consent.' Please don't let close-minded people make you feel bad about yourself. Like Oliver said, pay attention to the people that care about you."

Penelope looked from one man to the other then dropped her gaze. She muttered, "I'm confused. I hear what you're saying, I really do. And it makes sense, and I want to believe that what you're saying is possible, but I don't see how I'm supposed to let go of the past and embrace this new me, especially when I really do feel inferior. I had a career that made me happy; I loved working in advertising, but I had to quit my job because of my bizarre thoughts and behaviors. Sure, the medication I was on at first was somewhat helpful, but it made me feel sick. I'm afraid my new stuff will be like that, too. I can't function in the world without medication, but I can't feel healthy and good with it, either. I just want to have a career again, but I don't see how that's possible." She sighed.

Avoiding William's eyes, she continued to address Oliver. "And what about where William and I are making our lives? I've always loved Chicago, but now it's just big and scary and overwhelming to me. Not only that, but I'm not connected to people in Chicago anymore. You listed off a few people that are new friends to me. I don't know Mariska very well at all, so she doesn't count. You're a good friend, and Frannie is, too, but you guys live in Fairmont, Wisconsin, not Chicago. I'm starting to hate Chicago, but I don't know what to do. Mrs. Roosevelt wants me to take her to Kentucky, but I don't want to go there, either. Where can I go, then? Plus William is in Chicago. How can I do what you're saying, Oliver, and marry him and love him and embrace a new life, when I can't function anymore in the city I once cherished?" By the time she finished, her face was wet with tears. They rolled onto the fist that gripped the knife and onto the blade itself. With her free right hand, she wiped her face. She continued to hold the knife to her throat with her left hand.

"So don't stay in Chicago, Penelope. Sometimes embracing a new life means getting a completely fresh start." Oliver was struck with an idea. "Hey, you could come to Fairmont. You already have connections here, and it's still pretty close to Chicago, so you could visit there if you wanted to."

William, who had been standing stiffly in tense attention to the conversation, jumped on the idea. Practically diving to the floor, he chimed in, "That's a fantastic idea! Penelope, what do you say? We could get away from bastards like Rod and Paula and get a fresh start."

"What about your career, William?" Penelope asked, still skeptical. She hadn't lowered the knife. "You are a chef at a five-star restaurant in downtown Chicago, and you were just promoted to sous-chef. It's what you've always wanted. You love your job. I'm not going to be responsible for you giving up your dreams!"

"My dream is to be with you. I love *you*, Penelope. A job is a job. Honestly, I'm growing tired of the place. I don't like the people I work with, and I'm finding that as sous chef, I'm further away from truly preparing the food. I don't like that. I've been disappointed by it, actually. Things change. You know what I'd really like to do? I'd like to own my own restaurant and be able to develop my own dishes and menus, and prepare food more intimately on a smaller scale. We could move to Fairmont, and I could do just that. And you could help me, sweetie. You said you miss working. You could help me develop and market our new restaurant as you get back on your feet again, and then, if you want to, down the road you could do something different. If you started out by helping me, it would be good for both of us." William grew more excited the more he spoke. He almost forgot that Oliver and Penelope each held weapons they wanted to use against themselves. "I'm totally serious about this, Penelope. I think this would be good for us. Listen to what Oliver and I are telling you."

"We don't have a place to live." It was the only argument against this outrageous plan that she could think of.

Oliver spoke very quietly and offered, "You could live here, in this house. You could rent it from me, or maybe even buy it. This house is full of special memories and love, and I don't want just anyone living here. It would mean so much to me to have good friends live here. To get married and live happily here."

"Well, this all certainly sounds crazy." Penelope looked at William, who stared at her with a hopeful, expectant, expression. "But I guess I'm supposed to be embracing my new life, aren't I, and so crazy is definitely fitting." She slowly lowered her hand and rested it in her lap. She looked down at the knife, with its small spot of dried blood. No one moved. No one spoke. Finally, Penelope reached up over Oliver's head and laid the knife gently on the counter. She sat back and looked at William. They locked eyes briefly before Penelope threw her arms around him. "I love you so much, William. Oliver is right; that's all that matters. After talking about this new plan, for the first time in almost two years, I feel hopeful. For once I don't feel like my life is over. I still hate this so much, but maybe we can make it work."

William wrapped his arms around Penelope and pulled her toward him. He held her tight and croaked, "Thank you." Oliver watched with mixed feelings. His heart ached with pain and loneliness, but he felt happy that he had helped Penelope and William remain together. Knowing, too, that they would stay in his home gave him a sense of peace.

Penelope continued to embrace William, but she turned to Oliver and thanked him. "Your friendship means a lot to me, you know. I'm glad I'm going to be living in the same town as you."

"No, Penelope, you won't be. You will have Frannie here, though, and I think you two are going to be great friends."

"What? Where are you going to go?"

He raised the gun to his head. "I don't know where I'm going to end up. I can only hope that it will be with Maggie and Henry." His carefully controlled voice cracked. "I can't do this anymore. I just wanted to stick around long enough to help you and William be okay again."

"No! Stop! What was all that you were saying to me about love and friendship?"

"I—"

"No! I don't want to hear what you were going to say! It's your turn to listen now. You were so right; love is important. I am so, so sorry that Maggie and Henry are gone, but you aren't completely without love. I love you, Oliver. I love you as a dear friend. I thought you cared about me, too."

"I do, it's just—"

"Then how can you do this?" she beseeched. "I need you, Oliver. I finally have a close friend—other than William, of course— who understands me and accepts me. Yes, Frannie will be a friend, too, but she can't replace you. I care about you a lot, Oliver, and you said earlier that you care about me more than I even realize. You also said that killing myself is not a good way to show William that I love him. Well, the same goes for you. I need you. You keep saying that you weren't there for your family when they needed you. You're totally wrong that their deaths were your fault, and you need help coming to understand that. I'm not saying that their murders were your fault, but I am saying that if you want a chance to be there for somebody, be here for me now."

Oliver's eyes filled with tears. He swallowed hard. He couldn't speak, and now he was the one who was confused. He didn't know what made sense, and he didn't know what to do. He continued to hold the gun to his head. It suddenly felt extremely heavy, so he gripped it tighter to keep from dropping it.

William broke the silence that filled the room. "You know, I need you too. I need someone who knows the town to help me get started here. And Penelope's not the only one who could use a new friend who isn't judgmental, you know. And I don't think Penelope and I are the only ones who need you. Your sister loves you. She already lost her parents. Do you want her to lose her only brother now, too? You talked about your nieces and your nephew. Uncles are important, man. I had a pretty rough home life growing up; I'll tell you the story sometime, but that's not important right now. I only mentioned it because it was my uncle who helped me through it. The only person I had to turn to when I was a kid was my Uncle Jack. If it weren't for him, I don't know how I would have turned out, or even if I would have survived. Don't underestimate the power of your love and influence on those kids."

Oliver thought, then, about how Frannie and David might divorce. If that happened, the kids would need a good uncle. And he wasn't sure what to make of Penelope's declaration that he had a chance to be there for her. His chest filled with a warm sensation at the thought of being there for Penelope—and William and Frannie and Davie and Lacey and Ellen. Yet no amount of good behavior on his part would change the fact that he hadn't been there for Maggie and Henry, and nothing would bring them back. What Penelope and William were saying did make some sense though. Oliver squeezed his eyes shut as he grappled with the information.

Penelope took advantage of his apparent uncertainty to tell him, "Oliver, I know you are hurting. Whether or not you are ready to believe it, you are very important to a lot of people, including me. I need your friendship. It must be so difficult to imagine living without Maggie and Henry, and I'm so, so sorry that you are going through this. But stay here, and let us help you. It's not about finding a cure for your broken heart or about forgetting them or about making your pain completely disappear. It's about learning to live despite the pain and finding new reasons to live and to keep Maggie and Henry alive in your memories. You can't bring them back, Oliver, but you can honor them with your own life."

Quietly, almost pleadingly, he asked, "What, exactly, do you suggest I do right now? I can't be here in Fairmont. It hurts too much. I am completely and totally devastated. What you are telling me makes a little sense, but I just don't know how to go on."

William placed his hand on Oliver's shoulder. "I think you need to go back to Airhaven for a while," he informed him kindly. "I don't think you were ready to come back yet. You can go back with us tonight. I'll call Frannie and let her know, and I've got Airhaven's emergency number. I'll call them and tell them we're coming. Remember how Matt said you could request to speak to him directly if you needed anything, that you could do that any time of day and the phone personnel would contact him? I'll do that, and I'll have him meet us there later tonight. I know he'll do it. While you're there, we'll visit you every day. I'm going to put in my notice at work tomorrow, and you can help us make our plans to move here. When you're ready, we can all make the move together. We'd love to rent your home from you, and when you come back you can be here or at Frannie's or both. But first, let's get you back to Airhaven for a little bit longer, okay?"

The arm that held the gun was going numb, so Oliver rested it on his knee, sliding it across his forehead in the process. He brought his other arm to his knees, too, and used that hand to steady the gun. He moved it absentmindedly back and forth across a small part of his forehead as if gently scratching an itch. The metal felt cool and smooth and offered the promise of relief. He shut his eyes again and thought long and hard about what Penelope and William had just said. He was such a selfish bastard; how could he abandon everyone? He didn't want to be responsible for causing even more pain. He truly cared about Penelope and William and Frannie and her kids. Maybe he did have a reason to live after all, but he just didn't know how. Perhaps William was right and he needed to get more help.

He let his hands drop between his knees. He heard the gun thump against the floor just before he heard William and Penelope each exhale loudly. With slow and deliberate motion, muscles cramped from sitting so long on the floor and his body weak from emotional upheaval and lack of nutrition, he stood. He placed his gun on the island beside Penelope's knife. Forlorn, bereft, and completely spent, he looked at Penelope and William, who now stood beside him. He trembled. It began in his chin and worked its way down into his shoulders and into his abdomen. By the time the tremble reached his legs, it had turned into uncontrollable shaking. Penelope stepped forward. She reached for him and pulled his head gently down to her shoulder, and then she wrapped her arms tightly around him. "We're going to get through this together, my friend," she whispered to him.

William let out a long breath. He grabbed the knife and the gun and stuffed them in a cupboard, out of sight. Then, as Oliver and Penelope continued to take comfort in each other, he made the necessary phone calls.

CHAPTER 29

OLIVER SAT IN HIS LIVING ROOM WITH WILLIAM AND PENELOPE, WAITING FOR Frannie to arrive. She had become hysterical when William told her what had happened, and she had insisted on seeing him before he left for Airhaven. At Oliver's request, she was also bringing his journal so he could use it at Airhaven, as well as the stuffed dog Davie had given him in his attempt to comfort him. He sat quietly, for he was incapable of speech. He looked down at his hands, and his heart swelled with fondness as he saw Penelope's hand intertwined with his. He looked at her, and then he looked over at William. He wanted to tell them a story. He closed his eyes and sighed, and then in a gravelly, weary voice, he began.

"You guys are going to like it here. I remember the first time Maggie saw this house."

"Oh, Oliver, this is charming! I love it!"

"It is kind of charming, isn't it? It's an old house, built in the twenties by a wealthy family before the Great Depression hit. It's got character. There are a lot of nooks and crannies. I had a blast making secret forts and hiding places when I was a kid."

"That's adorable! I can just picture a little Oliver running around here living in an imaginary world, making forts."

They continued to explore the house, and Maggie absolutely fell in love with it. "Oliver, how would you feel about us living here? I can picture us here, honey. I love this place already. And when we have kids, they'll have as much fun as you did exploring the nooks and crannies and wreaking havoc by building forts all over the place."

His heart soared. He had such fond memories of growing up here, and he wanted nothing more than to build a family here with Maggie. What a way to honor his mom and dad too. It would probably please Frannie, as well, for while she didn't want to live here, she didn't like the idea of selling it to an outsider either.

"Margaret Graham, I think you're absolutely brilliant."

"I want to grow old with you, Oliver, and I can't think of a better, happier place to do it. When we're in our nineties, with great-grand-children making forts in these nooks and crannies, think of all the stories we're going to be able to tell them."

"Maggie, I love you so much." He pulled her close and kissed her passionately.

"Oliver?" She pulled back briefly from their kiss.

"Hmmm?"

"I love you, too."

About the Author

Tanya J. Peterson holds a Bachelor of Science in secondary education, Master of Science in counseling, and is a Nationally Certified Counselor. She has been a teacher and a counselor in various settings, including a traditional high school and an alternative school for homeless and runaway adolescents, and she has volunteered her services in both schools and communities. She draws on her life experience as well as her education to write stories about the emotional aspect of the human condition. She has published *Losing Elizabeth*, a young adult novel about an abusive relationship, *Challenge!*, a short story about a person who finds the confidence to overcome criticism and achieve a goal, and a book review of Linley and Joseph's *Positive Therapy: A Meta-Theory for Positive Psychological Practice* that appeared in *Counseling Today*, the national publication of the American Counseling Association. She lives in the Pacific Northwest with her husband and two children.

Tanya writes about mental health on her website's blog. Visit her at www.tanyajpeterson.com.

ACKNOWLEDGMENTS

I'd like to extend a sincere and heartfelt THANK YOU to some very deserving people:

Heather Sharfeddin, I am so grateful for your mentorship. You have amazing talent—I so enjoy your novels—and I'm truly honored that you helped me. I appreciate your feedback and insight, and I value our discussions. Your early encouragement kept me going when I doubted myself.

I'm proud to be a member of the Oregon Writers Colony. What a great group of people! It's wonderful to belong to a nurturing group of fellow writers. Thanks for all of the many things you offer (workshops, programs, events, and the Colonyhouse, to name a few).

Everyone at Inkwater Press, you deserve a shout-out. You are all magnificent! Sean Jones, thanks for spending so much time talking with me at Wordstock in Portland. I was thrilled when you invited me to send you my manuscript for consideration; I'm so glad I did. Linda Franklin, thank you for bestowing upon me your literary skills. From your literary critique to your help with my title (the most difficult part of an entire novel), your expertise has been invaluable to me. Emily Dueker, I am awed by your talented design skills. This book looks fantastic because of you. Thank you also for creating my website. Your artistic eye and technical know-how are things I cannot possibly do without. John Williams, working with you is a delight. You have a wealth of good ideas and connections and information, and without you I would go nowhere. To everyone at Inkwater Press, even those of you with whom I don't work directly, I extend my gratitude. Your services are indispensable. Thanks for accepting me as one of your authors, and thanks for continuing to put up with all of my lengthy e-mails. I'd like to promise you that my e-mails will become more succinct, but they probably won't.